BOOKS BY TIM MCBAIN & L.T. VARGUS
Casting Shadows Everywhere
Fade to Black (Awake in the Dark #1)
Bled White (Awake in the Dark #2)
Red on the Inside (Awake in the Dark #3)
Back in Black (Awake in the Dark #4)
The Scattered and the Dead Series

The Scattered and the Dead

THE SCATTERED AND THE DEAD

BOOK 1

TIM MCBAIN & L.T. VARGUS

The Scattered and the Dead

It all started in Florida.
Of course.
Fucking Florida.

Rex

Panama City, Florida
68 days before

Rex ripped the IV needle out of his wrist, machines tattling on him with shrill whoops and cries. He didn't give a shit. He wasn't going to die in some hospital room by himself. Hermetically sealed in a plastic shrouded death box even though there were thousands of "Ebola-like" cases in Florida alone, the number growing by the minute? No thanks.

He rose from the bed, his legs wobbling beneath him for a second. His vision swam along the edges, so he put a palm on the mattress to steady himself. He closed his eyes, took a few deep breaths. It seemed to get better.

Still, wobbling legs and dodgy vision comprised the least of his problems. His head felt like a swollen watermelon about to burst. It hurt like nothing else he'd felt in his life.

He was 43. He knew pain. This was un-fuckin-real.

Throw in the periodic projectile vomiting of thick, red blood, and you've got the makings of a serious problem. It was almost comical to have a doctor weigh in on this. Pretty straightforward diagnosis, he thought: You're fucked.

He knew he didn't have long, had known so for a while. In some ways, his fever rising to the point that his consciousness faded out into madness had been a mercy, had protected him from the worst of the suffering as he disconnected from reality.

But for the moment, at least, the fever had died down some, and his thoughts were clear. He had a last meal in mind, a final resting place. It'd involve hard work, but his life had been full of that. It might as well end on a familiar note.

He prodded at the plastic sheeting cordoning off his bed from the rest of room, fingers searching for a flap or a slit or some opening to get to his things in the wardrobe. This wasn't a normal isolation room. Those were long full by the time he was admitted. Hospital workers employed plastic sheets here to convert this normal room into a quarantine one. He figured this was for the better anyhow as it increased the odds that his keys were still around. If he could find a way to get to the other side of this damn plastic anyway.

The only opening went toward the door of the room, the opposite direction of where he needed to go, but he guessed it would work well enough. He turned himself sideways, trying to make his barrel chest as svelte as he could. He sidled between the plastic and the wall, found the wardrobe, opened it. His hand fished around in the dark. There. His shorts, and in his pocket, the keys.

After a moment's hesitation, he slid the shorts on, but he didn't bother with the t-shirt, leaving the hospital robe to adorn his upper body. Fashion matters little to the dying, but he didn't like the idea of pressing his bare ass into the leather seat of his truck.

Hot leather pressed up against his sweaty taint? Fuck that noise.

He kept moving between the plastic and the wall, reaching the window and sliding it open. Here was the perk of being on the ground floor. He could pop out, cross a bed of petunias and some grass and be in the parking lot without passing a single nurse. The thought made him smile. If they knew, they would surely try to detain him under the guise of preventing the spread of the disease. What a joke that was. The world was already fucked. You weren't going to unfuck it by keeping him in a room with shower curtains for wallpaper. It didn't take Dr. Oz to diagnose that shit.

He dangled his legs out the window, lost his balance a little on the edge and tumbled down into the reddish mulch surrounding the flowers, his hands and knees jamming down into the wood chips. His head felt like swollen tectonic plates were crashing into each other just under the surface, threatening to rupture the shell of cranium surrounding them.

Everything went black and silent, and reality filtered down to only the pain. It just about knocked him out.

Un-fuckin-real.

Once the hurt passed, though, he chuckled. His hands retracted from the mulch, and he stood and brushed away the red bits clinging to his shins. The sunlight made him squint his eyes, but the heat and humidity wrapped themselves around him like a toasty blanket. He'd lived in Florida his whole life. This sticky, hot-as-balls air felt like coming home after all of that time in the air-conditioned plastic nightmare.

He staggered over the grass and into the parking area, his legs tottering under him, shaky and weak. No damn clue where his truck was, but he didn't mind looking around a bit. Being upright and ambulatory felt good as hell. The blacktop scorched his feet, but it didn't bother him. He'd walked over the hot sand on the beach since he was knee high.

After wandering up and down the rows, he spotted the truck and closed on it. If walking around felt good, opening the door and sitting down felt better. He was winded already, his head had that swelly feeling, and the world was just faintly blurry along the edges. Still, he made it.

Inside, the truck was stifling. This was beyond a toasty blanket. He liked the heat, but the sun beat down on the windshield all day. This was dog-killing hot. He started it up and put the air conditioning on.

And suddenly the victory of his escape seemed much smaller. His life would still end the same way: He would die alone, unable to visit his family for fear of infecting them, unable to walk more than a couple hundred feet without getting the brain bloat headaches or whatever the shit that was all about.

It wasn't supposed to go down like this. He'd planned for this, had a fallout shelter stocked to the brim with food and water and weapons. He had two bug-out vehicles. He had caches of supplies in strategic locations. He was a prepper, an intelligent and thorough one.

Unfortunately, the disease cared not. It killed without prejudice, whether you feared and respected it or doubted and ignored it.

He was supposed to make doomsday his bitch, and instead he was going to be among the first to go.

He reached into the glove box and pulled out a can of Skoal. It felt empty, but he was relieved to find a little left in there. He packed a wad into his lip, felt the nicotine tingle through the membrane and into his system. He leaned back and reveled in one of the few pleasures he could still enjoy.

The final meal would come soon enough, but for now he would close his eyes and feel the tobacco in his lip and feel the stimulant enter his bloodstream and feel the temperature inside the truck return to something reasonable.

His thoughts drifted to his family. Maybe he would triumph over doomsday yet. Not by himself but by his kin.

His children were tough kids. His oldest, Ryan, got dared to go down a 25 foot ladder face first when he was twelve. Rex came out of the house just in time to witness the disaster. Ryan fell, of course, banging his head on every rung on the way down. When the battered kid finally hit the bottom and stopped, he laughed. Everyone was frozen, mouths agape, certain that they'd just watched a 12 year old break his neck six or seven separate times, and the kid fucking laughed about it.

His younger boy, Dylan, was a hell of a football player, too. Not the fastest kid, but one of those head-hunting safeties that just about decapitated any receiver that dared to go over the middle. If he were a step and a half faster, he might even be SEC material, but the coaches told him to expect to start hearing from the smaller schools as soon as his junior highlight reel got around.

His daughter, Mia, was the toughest of the lot. She was the bully of the family. Rex didn't know if it was a middle child thing, but she had a temper to her and had beaten up both of her brothers more than once, along with what seemed like half the kids at school. Personality-wise, she was the one that took after him the most.

Those kids waded through some hard shit already. Like when their mother died of stomach cancer a few years back.

He was proud of the way they handled it. Not one of them bottled the pain up, they let it out, they lashed out, and in time they found ways to deal with it. They didn't get over it. Rex didn't think you got over shit like that, nor were you supposed to. But they found their own ways to deal.

They'd be without their mom and dad now, but if they hunkered down and survived the first wave of this thing, those kids would be all right. He had no doubt of that. He wouldn't be leaving them high and dry. They had a mountain of food and guns and ammo thanks to his diligence.

Rex sat up and opened his eyes. He felt better. He plucked an empty Dew can from the cup holder and spit tobacco juice into it. Except what came out of his mouth was bright red and a little too thick. Almost gummy.

Shit.

He glanced into the rearview mirror to find red tears draining from his eyes. The scarlet rivers pouring down his face seemed to be gaining momentum.

Shit.

He looked away from his reflection. This was it. This was how it ended. He wouldn't get to eat that final burger after all.

He coughed and red spattered onto his fist. He felt the liquid churning in his gut, more of the same ready to come out the other end, he knew. As the flow increased to a gush, the blood filled his vision, turning it red then black.

He leaned his head back onto the head rest again, closed his eyes and felt the wet warmth of life spilling out of him. The fear crept over him now, made his torso quiver, made his breathing ragged. He hadn't been scared this way often in his life, but he was now. It reminded him of being a little boy, home alone in the dark.

And yet, he would die in his truck, not surrounded by his family but thinking of them. He could think of worse ways to go.

Baghead

Rural Oklahoma
9 years, 126 days after

Lightning lit the sky above the city. Thunderless. Silent. Flashes of white light that showed the toppled buildings, the crater pocked ground, the streets turned holes filled with rubble. Mangled steel girders splayed through shards of concrete like fingers poking up from the sand.

He'd been here before. Many times.

In his dreams, he walked among the wreckage of the dead cities, where the wind blew endlessly and no living soul stirred apart from his own. His feet trod upon the ash, upon the blackened remnants of civilization. His fingers gripped the serrated edges of asphalt to climb the heaps of them. He touched the decay, felt the pieces crumble in his hands. The snapped off buildings stood around him like he paced in a mouth full of broken teeth.

Every night he walked through memories, some real and some which never were. He walked through images of destruction, some recalled, some invented.

And he wondered what lit them. He knew that these bolts from the heavens lit the sky here, flashed their light upon the dead cities, where the buildings once stood, where the people once swarmed. But what lit these pictures in his head when he slept? What lit the pathways of our brains, burned inside of us all? He looked into the sky, into the stars, the same sky and the same stars mankind had looked into always, and he wondered. What spark, what flare, what stars or current or energy glowed inside of us to make us all go? And what for?

He woke, disoriented, flaps of canvas obscuring most of his vision. He sat up, hands scrabbling over his head to pull the slack out of the bag so the eye holes lined up correctly. It slid against his forehead with a slight tickle, and the canvas climbed out of his field of vision like a rising curtain unveiling a stage. There.

Sunlight glinted through the windshield onto the dashboard in front of him. The empty bottle rested between his feet. Of course. He was in the car he slept in, a rusted out Ford Focus with four flat tires. He didn't think of it as home, but in some ways it was. For now, anyway. The bottle, he figured, had a hand in his confusion. He didn't drink often.

He sat back, his chest holding inflated and rigid another moment before it sagged and let out a long slow breath.

He unzipped the zipper in the canvas bag that ran along his chin and felt his jaw. Beard hair shrouded the knobs and growths there, though he could feel the vague shapes of them as his fingers riffled through his beard. The hair was getting long. Bushy. He'd need to trim it soon. He didn't like when it got so big that it puffed into the canvas and got caught in the zipper when he ate. He zipped it back up.

He let his neck go half limp, his chin drooping until it almost touched his chest, and his eyes crawled over the floor. Mud caked the carpet where he'd tracked it in a couple of nights ago when it rained. Flattened cigarette butts accompanied the mud, though those weren't his. They predated his residence here.

He lifted his head, letting it lean back on the headrest, feeling the canvas scrunch and wrinkle around his neck. His mind remained fogged with sleep, but he knew he was supposed to do something today. He was meeting someone about something. Something important.

His eyes fell upon the card resting on the dash, tracing over the ominous design printed on it. He could appreciate the aesthetics of the thing even if it was meant to threaten his life.

That's what he was supposed to remember. The Hand of Death.

Mitch

Bethel Park, Pennsylvania
43 days before

When Mitch got home from work, his wife called him out into the kitchen and told him that he would need to kill her.

"Finally," he said, opening the fridge. "Thought you'd never ask."

The fridge light flickered over leftover meatloaf and mashed potatoes. A bunch of almost empty condiment bottles. Nothing looked good.

She didn't laugh at his joke. She didn't say anything. The only sound was the tick-tock of the grandfather clock in the hall.

He retracted his head from the fridge to find a grave expression on her face. She hadn't been kidding. He blinked. Twice. Three times. He tried to say, "What the hell are you talking about?" but his chest got all tight. Constricted. He couldn't make a sound.

"I'm sick," she said.

She didn't elaborate. She didn't need to. He knew what she meant. Everybody knew about the shit going down in Florida. Mitch guessed it finally made its way here. They said over and over again on the news that it was being contained, that it would never reach the Northeast. But in their hearts, Mitch thought, everyone knew it would.

It would spread over the surface of the globe like the piss

puddles creeping ever outward over the blacktop when he and his friends used to urinate behind the school as kids.

Nobody spoke for a long moment. The pair of compact fluorescent bulbs buzzed in the light fixture above them, trying and failing to keep the awkward silence at bay. And in the quiet this suddenly felt real, Mitch realized. Life itself felt real, all the way real, for the first time in a long while.

Moments like these hadn't come around often for Mitch; moments that shook him out of the half awake state in which he plowed through much of his life; moments that made him open his eyes and see reality in a flash of searing light, all the painful truths illuminated all at once. He saw his life with brutal clarity in this instant: He dragged through days at work and spent the evenings motionless in front of the TV, his brain more or less hibernating. During the weekends he helped it stay asleep by chugging Coors Light while various football games flickered across the plasma screen in the living room. His wife and kids shuffled in and out of the room periodically to share these moments with him in some sense, but it was like none of them were all the way there. None of them were all the way engaged in life, all the way connected to each other. They were just kind of half there.

Or here, he supposed. This was not some theoretical "there" in his imagination. It was here – a concrete world where real live human beings breathed and laughed and dreamed, blood thrumming through their veins.

And got sick. They got sick, too. Sickness unto death sometimes.

And sometimes something worse than death.

Janice blinked, and the motion brought him back to the

kitchen. It occurred to him that she'd been talking when the sound of the real world faded in with her mid-sentence.

"-maybe 8 to 12 hours," she said. "Maybe less."

The world got swimmy along the edges. His knees buckled below, but he caught himself.

He braved another look at her face. Her voice sounded detached. Cold. Distant. Like she was toughing her way through. She looked so soft, though. Her expression betrayed the sound of her.

There'd always been something hard in Janice, some toughness that Mitch never possessed. She was the hard-nosed one. When their older son, Kevin, got bullied in first grade and the school wouldn't do anything about it, she went down to the office where her temper exploded like a hydrogen bomb. The principal went all bug-eyed. The bully got a one week suspension within minutes. It was the same woman sitting there in front of Mitch now, but the toughness had been plucked from her being.

He didn't say anything. He kneeled down, opened the cabinet under the sink, pulled the half gallon bottle of Black Velvet free, removed the lid and pressed it to his lips. The whiskey burned all the way down in a way that made him feel a little alive even still.

The kitchen was small. Cramped. Janice often complained about the lack of counter space. With the tension in the room, it felt claustrophobic. For Mitch, at least.

He thought he'd buy her something nicer someday. One of those ridiculously huge kitchens that they cook in on Food Network. Granite counters that stretched out into the horizon. The stove top would be set in an island in the middle of the room with a big griddle built into it.

But no. None of that was real. This would be her final kitchen after all. Cramped and shitty.

He sat in the chair across from her, put the bottle on the table between them. He tried to piece together the bits of what she'd said, make some sense out of them. He felt like there was a big piece he had lost in the shock.

"What were you saying?" he said, his lips juicy and tingling from the booze. "I'm sorry. I can't concentrate."

She eyed the bottle a moment before answering. He thought she was about to take a slug, but she didn't.

"I'm sick," she said again.

As though to provide evidence on this point she sneezed and two strings of snot rocketed out of her nostrils and hung from her tilted head. It reminded Mitch of the ropes of saliva dangling from the corners of a basset hound's mouth, except the shade and opacity of butternut squash soup. Her hand reached out for the box of kleenex, but she couldn't quite reach. He pushed the box to her hand and took another big gulp of Black Velvet as she gathered the mucus.

"Good thing it's not airborne," she said, and a couple of snorts of laughter came out of her nose, sniffles accompanying them.

Only Janice could laugh in this moment. He wanted to be mad about it, but he couldn't.

"If it's not airborne, how did you get it?" he said.

She leaned forward and peeled the cuff of her jeans up toward the knee. It took Mitch a second to realize what he was seeing. An oval shaped crater of angry red pocked her ankle like a chunk had been torn from her leg, and rivulets of black snaked out from the wound in all directions. They looked like wisps of smoke trailing about her lower leg, the longest almost reaching her knee.

"What the fuck?" he said.

"I got bit," she said, letting the leg of her pants fall back down.

"Bit?" he said. "Bit as in the past tense of bite?"

She hesitated a second, nodded.

"Yesterday afternoon. In the break room."

"And you didn't mention that? A human being broke your flesh with their teeth, ripped free a chunk of ankle meat, and you didn't see that as noteworthy enough to bring up at dinner last night?"

"Quiet now," she said. "The kids will hear."

A little bit of that hardness crept back into her face as she scolded him. It made him feel the slightest touch better, like some part of him still believed she couldn't actually die. She was too tough for that.

"What the hell happened?" he said, his voice hushed but somehow still intense.

She took a deep breath and the words came trickling from her lips.

"I told you about the rumors at work. About Carlos being sick."

He nodded, his jaw clenching and unclenching involuntarily.

"I guess they were true after all," she said. "He came in looking like warmed-over death. Looked sick as hell, all pale and sweaty, but he said he wasn't bleeding or anything. Not like they described the people bleeding on TV. He said it was just the flu was all, and he didn't have the sick days left to stay home. Couldn't argue with that, though I planned to keep my distance."

Her index finger traced along a divot in the tabletop while she talked.

"He went to his cubicle and got working, but not for long. He looked out of it, kept resting his head on the desk. Eventually he shuffled into the break room. Never came back out."

Her fingernail now scratched at the flaw in the wood, a scrape-thump at a steady rhythm that seem to lay a slow drumbeat under her story.

"A good 15 or 20 minutes went by, so I went to check on him. When I stepped through the doorway, he was sprawled on the floor, face down, lips mashed into the carpet. Motionless. I mean full-on, not-breathing motionless. I froze for a moment in shock. It was so still. When I got a hold of myself, I took a step forward, and he lunged. He was gums deep in my ankle before I could react. He was like a wild animal. It wasn't Carlos, you know? The look in his eyes. He was gone. It was someone else. Something else. Anyway, I guess I screamed and people came to help me. I don't remember it very well, but I remember they got him trapped in the break room, and I took off. Never looked back."

She looked far away.

"Wait. When was this?" Mitch said.

"Like I said, it was yesterday afternoon," she said.

Mitch thought a second, reaching through the fog of shock to recall the night before.

"So we all sat around here last night eating meatloaf with

you knowing this," he said. "Jesus, Janice. Why didn't you tell me?"

Her shoulders twitched in a half-hearted shrug.

"I was scared," she said. "You saw all of the stuff on TV. About Florida and all. I guess I thought maybe it'd go away. Like if I kept it quiet, it didn't have to be real. I didn't know what to do. I didn't want you panicking. The boys panicking. And what difference would it have made? Can't you see how it wouldn't change anything? Knowing or not knowing? Nothing can change it."

He sat quiet a moment, his mind feeling along the edges of this impossible idea: his wife sat here in front of him, breathing, talking, alive and normal like any other day. And this time tomorrow she wouldn't be.

"24 to 36 hours," she said. "That's how long it takes from bite to death. A few cases have been reported making it a little longer, but based on the way my wounds look, I won't make it through the night."

"What if you're wrong?" he said. "I could call the sitter and take you to the emergency room, get a doctor to look you up and down. Maybe you just need some antibiotics to clear up that infected stuff swirling off of the wound. That's all."

"Antibiotics won't do shit," she said. "You've seen the stuff on TV? Well, that's the edited version. That's what the government wants you to see. The internet has the real shit. A bunch of photos of bites that look just like mine, yeah? All those people die. And they don't just die. They come back. I will turn like they did. Like Carlos."

Mitch realized he was holding his breath and made himself inhale. Then he took a big drink of booze.

19

"I don't want that," she said. "I want to die in my own home, on my terms. We'll do it in the basement, I figure."

"You know I can't do that," he said.

"You have to," she said. "I can't do it myself."

It took him a second to catch her meaning. For her, suicide meant an eternity in hell.

"Think about it from my perspective, Jan," he said. "If I do it, I'll wonder forever if maybe I was wrong. Maybe you could've pulled through or something."

She pressed her lips together, and wrinkles surrounded her mouth. This expression always surfaced when something wasn't to her liking.

"Fine. You're right," she said. "I know what we can do."

Mitch plugged the tip of the bottle into his face and drank long and deep.

"After this, you have to get out of here, out away from the city. Pack up everything you can and find a place away from everything. A place fit for living without electricity and all. A place with a well with a hand pump and a fire place or wood burning stove or something like that. A chimney, you know? My parents' cabin on the lake would work, maybe. I can't remember if it has a hand pump."

"I think it does."

"No matter how all of this plays out, you have to take care of those boys," she said. "Because I can't help them anymore."

Tears welled in her eyes. He watched her face shrivel as she fought to hold them back, her bottom lip shimmying like it always did when she tried to avoid crying. Mitch could tell it wasn't going to work, though. Not this time. He moved close to hug her.

Baghead

Rural Oklahoma
9 years, 126 days after

He followed the dirt trail across the field, the grass reaching dewy blades out to smear their wet against the ankles of his pants at every opportunity. Clouds of dust kicked up with each step so it looked like his tattered shoes were smoking, and his head stayed angled toward the ground like it always did, eyes peeking through eye holes to watch the earth slide by below. The strip of dirt cut a diagonal way toward the village, a gash through the weeds where feet had pounded the life out of the plants.

He didn't mind walking. He'd done it plenty. For where he was headed next, he would need a car, he knew, though, and he would need gas. You had to know somebody to make that happen. You had to talk to people. And so he would.

He thought about dead mice as he walked, the decapitated ones that littered the ground outside of his car. The gray cat always left them there. After he'd eaten the heads, of course. Sometimes the cat even managed to get one into the car, climbing through the hole in the rear windshield that served as his cat door with a carcass pinned between his teeth. He wondered if his cat would still be around, still sleep in the car with him, by the time he got back here. If he ever did.

When he didn't dream of the dead cities, he dreamed of

21

women. Nothing sexual, at least not usually. Just variations of the same dream over and over. He'd be staying in a cabin somewhere with a girl, and she'd get to asking about his hood. And in the dreams, he could peel the fabric from his head to find his old face underneath. Clear, clean flesh restored, filling him with an almost religious feeling, like something one would feel upon witnessing the resurrection of a dead child. He'd stare in the mirror, tilting his head to look upon himself at every angle, overwhelmed with relief, overwhelmed with the sense of his self made whole once more.

And when her fingers reached out to brush along his jaw, he felt the smooth skin of all of femininity. But that's what always woke him up, what made him realize that this was a dream, that it couldn't possibly be real.

Reality wasn't feeling whole, he knew too well. It was the other kind of hole. It was a hole you never stopped falling into.

The bar was mostly empty this early. Light flickered behind the frosted glass of the sconces along the walls, the flame trying and failing to fight off the gloom in here that persisted even in broad daylight. Day or night, it felt like walking into the shade of a thick patch of woods to enter this space. Dark and dank.

He stopped a couple of paces inside the door, glanced around the room, examining things in silhouette, waiting for his eyes to adjust. He saw the shape of the bartender standing over the bar, the flickering light reflecting off of the glossy wood countertop before him.

He saw a figure a couple of feet to his left that he first

thought to be a man and now believed to be a coat rack draped with a couple of jackets. He moved into the room, striding down two steps and weaving around a couple of tables on his way to the bar.

The bartender didn't look up. He never looked up, at least not at the bagged head that stood in front of him now. Lots of people were like that. They didn't like looking at his baghead, at his one messed up eye visible through the hole. He thought it looked insect-like in some way, the bad eye.

"Guy in the corner was looking for you," the bartender said. He flicked his head to the left, eyelids fluttering, though he never looked up.

Baghead turned and headed that way. Color and contrast began to repopulate his vision, rising up to replace the shaded tones. The tables and chairs came fully into focus to his immediate left and right. Looking beyond them, a man sat in the corner, heavy stubble shrouding his jaw, shaggy hair hanging in his eyes. The man stared straight at Baghead as he approached, a half smile curling the corners of his mouth. He brought a cigarette to his lips, the smoke spiraling through the candlelight over his head.

As the gap between them whittled down to arm's length, the man spoke.

"I'm going to go out on a limb and guess that you're the guy I'm supposed to meet here. The one who signs his letters 'Baghead.'"

Mitch

Bethel Park, Pennsylvania
43 days before

Mitch got the kids fed and put them to bed early. He thought shock must have fully set in by now. He didn't panic. Instead he watched the world through a lens adjusted to a soft focus, just on the edge of getting blurry. He stared off into emptiness, nodding periodically while his younger son, Matt, described the plot of an episode of Sponge Bob. He supposed the whiskey helped keep things that way, helped keep reality at arm's length.

Janice slept on the couch through this process, and she still slept there afterward while he watched TV from the recliner next to her. She hadn't wanted to sleep, had fought it, but he coaxed her into relaxing for a few minutes, and she passed out. She needed it. Even if she was right and she didn't have a lot of time, she needed it.

He flipped through the channels. Most every station spouted grisly details about people shitting and coughing up blood until they croaked all across the southeastern United States. CDC people rehashed the same talking points as always: blah blah ebola-like symptoms mixed with flu-like symptoms, blah blah reasonably contained, blah blah no cause for panic, blah blah wash your hands. That was his favorite. Wash your hands. Like if you start hacking out your insides, just spritz a little water on your hands. Should clear things right up.

Janice's shoulders jerked, and she moaned faintly in her sleep. As his eyes swiveled to her, his mind lurched back to that moment when he walked into the kitchen and she dumped all of this on him. He still couldn't quite grasp it. The concept was too big. His brain couldn't digest it all at once. Not only would his wife be dead in a few hours, he would need to kill her.

What the hell? Kill her? But then... Maybe that would be better than bleeding out through the eyes, ears, nose and rectum. That was how they described bleeding out the ass on the news. "Rectal bleeding." Or maybe it was better than...

Christ on a crutch.

He didn't want to think about it, so he stopped. He clenched the tip of the bottle between his teeth and tipped it back for a long guzzle. The whiskey was almost gone now, but there was an old bottle of rum under the sink as well, a few beers in the fridge.

His gaze fell back to the TV where a government official spoke directly into the camera, assuring everyone this wouldn't spread to the rest of the country.

Right. It's all sunshine and cookies from now until the end of time. Definitely no rectal bleeding for the lot of us.

Mitch turned the volume down and watched the images flicker on the screen in total silence. The end of the world was happening, and he was watching it on network television. As reality TV goes, this wasn't very entertaining. He'd rate it a 3 out of 10 on IMDB so far.

Janice's ribcage expanded and contracted on the couch in slow motion. She was all the way out. He wondered if she'd be mad that he let her sleep. Maybe it would be best to wake her up before long here.

He remembered how things used to be, when they first met. Before life became a blur of kids and work and asses parked on the couch all evening every evening, they'd been happy. Life had been exciting and strange. Every experience was new.

They went to film festivals and concerts. They were still young enough to seek out connections to art and culture in earnest. As adults, movies and music felt more like commodities than anything human or honest that meant much to anyone. But when they were young, they were on fire to figure out the world around them. They wanted to connect to it however they could, to connect to each other however they could.

He remembered that after a film festival in Chicago, they wound up parking behind an abandoned barbecue place and fucking in the back seat of the car. He was 23. They had been together for a year and a half. Thinking back on it now, it felt like those were two different people than the ones in this room.

Now? Now he was watching TV. Even though his wife had something like 10 hours to live, he was watching TV. But then what else was he supposed to? He thought maybe that was how life worked. You went through it with a feeling like you should be doing something important, but you could never quite figure out what that was, so you watched TV instead.

He rose from the recliner and placed a hand on her shoulder. He thought perhaps mere contact would wake her, but it didn't, so he gave her upper arm a shake. Her eyelids fluttered and opened, and her head jerked upright.

"You let me sleep," she said. Her voice sounded thick and tired, though she didn't sound as angry as he expected.

"I figured you could use the rest," he said.

"How long has it been?" she said. "You know what? It doesn't matter."

She hesitated for a long moment, craning her neck to look around as though something interesting was happening on the ceiling.

"It's time," she said.

Mitch mopped the back of his wrist over his lips, eying the empty bottle on the end table a few paces away.

"Already?" he said.

"It's time."

Baghead

Rural Oklahoma
9 years, 126 days after

"Wait until you see my car, Bags," Delfino said as they circled out behind the bar. "It's a piece of art. A big old tank, man. Older than you or me, but it runs like a dream. A wet dream at that. Heh."

Again dust kicked up with every step they took, the land out here a mix of sand and gravel with the periodic weed sprouting out. The car he slept in sat near the river, where there was at least a little green around. Out this way, it was pretty barren. Pretty brown.

They rounded the stucco corner of the building, moving into the dirt lot out back. Delfino didn't need to point out which car he meant. There was only one vehicle parked here, a boxy 1970's beast of a sedan. It looked less like a piece of art and more like a piece of shit, he thought. Windshield cracked down the middle and spattered with pebble wounds, fenders all rusted out. Two creases gouged the passenger side from front to back where it looked like the car had dragged along a fire hydrant or something. He couldn't tell if it was off white or just dirty. The thing was possibly worse looking than the Ford Focus he'd been sleeping in, though the tires weren't flat, at least.

"This is the classic," Delfino said, tapping the hood. "1973 Oldsmobile Delta 88. Hop on in."

Bags opened the door, and it sank a little as he pulled it toward himself, pulling half out of the hinges.

"What's with the door?" he said.

"Don't sweat that. You've just gotta, like, lift it as you pull it closed."

"Right."

He sat and managed the lift-and-pull maneuver. An odor struck his nostrils right away, strange and familiar, a particular old car smell he hadn't experienced in a long time. A blend of must and stale smoke and the faintest hint of old fries and Werther's Originals. Cigarette burns pocked the upholstery everywhere, jagged little circles in the cream.

Delfino started the car. Where Bags might have anticipated choked sounds and stuttering growls, the engine provided only a smooth purr. Didn't sound too bad, at least.

"Listen to that shit. That's the trick, see?" Delfino said. "Looks like ass. Runs like hell yass. I doubt anybody will ever try to steal it, but it gets me around just the same."

Bags nodded, looked out at the dusty landscape around them.

"So what does this thing get, like 12 miles to the gallon?"

"Funny. Nah, I've worked on this fucker, man. Put some serious hours into retooling that shit. Mileage is a helluva lot better than that. Believe me."

"Seriously, though. Will this thing actually get us there?"

"Oh, hell yeah. I've made the run seven times in this old bastard."

"The full run?"

"Absolutely, my man. I shit you not."

Bags searched the man's face, found no signs of deceit,

only manic enthusiasm. He nodded.

"Well, it's not like I have any other options."

"Shit, man. That's exactly what I tell every girl I'm with."

Delfino hissed a laugh between his teeth, amused by his own joke. He took a tin out of the breast pocket of his shirt and pulled a hand-rolled cigarette from it, resting it between his lips.

"Before we settle up," he said, the cigarette bobbing with every syllable. "I want you to know that I've read one of your books. Good as hell, man. You're a real good writer."

"I don't write much of it, you know. Just the introduction for some of the books, really. They're letters and excerpts from diaries I've found out there. I pick the best and weave them together."

"Right, well, you know what I mean. You put it all together in a way that tells a bigger story, man. It makes it, uh, greater than the sum of its parts and shit."

Delfino put the car into gear, and it lurched forward. The sound of the tires grinding the gravel into the dirt reminded Bags of the sound of popcorn popping in the microwave, though he wasn't sure if he was remembering the sound correctly.

"Which one did you read?"

"Postcards from an Empty World, Volume 3. Good shit. I want to read the rest, but I'm a slow ass reader, man. Never been big on the written word, you know? Too quiet for me. I'm more of a talker."

Baghead nodded.

"Well, it might be tough to come across Volume 1 at this point. We printed it on a hand crank printing press in someone's basement in Virginia. It got messed up, and the title got left off the thing. It just said 'Decker' really big on the front page. No other title or author name or anything."

"Decker?"

"Yeah. That was the guy's name. The one who wrote the letter in the book."

"Well, I guess now I know what to look for."

The sound below changed as they moved off of the dirt and onto the asphalt, the popcorn sound cutting off. Now the rubber of the tires hummed.

"You know what the best thing about reading that book was? It made me remember how it really was. How things used to be and how things changed. All those little things you forget about through the years. All the shit we've lost, you know? Things we used to do or see or think about every day that are gone for good. Some of that is irreplaceable. That's how these things go."

They fell quiet for a second before Delfino went on.

"Like I had this gigantic porn collection, yeah? Gone. All of it. Lost it in a fire. See, I was old school. It was all about the magazines for me, and I had a ton. I'm telling you, it would've stood taller than me had I stacked them up in one pile. That's a lot of jerk material, right? Enough to capture my dumb imagination for a lifetime. Now? Now my mind just lusts after images it can't have. It's fucking painful."

The Delta 88 reached an intersection, and Delfino took a right. He pulled a Zippo out of the same pocket the tin came out of, but he didn't light the cigarette dangling from his lips just yet.

"Some people are pretty squeamish about these things.

They don't want to talk about it. But what the hell? I'm an idiot animal with a sex drive. Why would I pretend to be anything else?"

Bags didn't know what to say, so he said nothing.

"Some people get into like one kind of porn, right? Like a fetish, I guess. Not me. I was an all-around porn fan. A jack of all smut, you could say. Black girls. White girls. Asian girls. Latinas. Sweet, sweet Latinas. Big boobs. Small boobs. I mean, yeah, OK, I went through a serious anal phase for a while there, but generally speaking-"

Baghead interrupted.

"Look, you don't need to tell me all of the particulars."

Delfino smiled. He finally lit the cigarette and took a big puff. When he exhaled, the cloud blew into the windshield and parted, smoke rolling in all directions.

"Right. You're right about that. Anyway, yeah, we should talk about the money."

"The amount I mentioned in the note. I'll pay half now, which is what I have on me, and half when we get there."

"Well… I don't usually work on spec that way, but I'll trust you. Only because that was a good ass book, though."

He scratched his chin.

"It's about an hour's ride to the place I'm staying. We'll need to gear up before we hit the road."

Travis

Hillsboro, Michigan
44 days after

The grocery shelves looked skeletal. All the meat had been picked off the bones like some unidentifiable carcass lying belly up in the jungle. Certain items remained here and there – the dishwashing detergent was largely untouched, for example. The parts you couldn't eat were intact. But the edible items, the most useful items, had all been scavenged.

Travis already knew that, though. He'd kept an eye on this place, watched the people come and go over the past 40 days, sometimes exiting with just a couple of items on hand, sometimes taking multiple truckloads of stuff. He'd heard gunshots and screams and terrible sounds that reminded him of a pack of jackals laughing from within the building. During quiet moments, usually in the middle of the night, he'd crept in to gather some things for himself. In time, he'd amassed plenty. Anyway, he wasn't here for groceries now.

His eyes traced a smear of blood trailing off toward the produce section. He wasn't headed that way, so he'd never see where it led. Probably for the better, he thought.

He fingered the serrated edge of the key and smiled. The whole walk here, he'd barely been able to keep his hands off the jagged part of the metal. It felt like a magical item tingling in his pocket. A talisman that would unlock the door to a kind of happiness the hero could take back home.

It hadn't been easy to acquire, the key, but he had it finally, and he was here. He walked into the gloom in the back half of the store, crossing the line into the area that the sunlight from the front windows could not touch. The dark closed in on him all at once, made him feel surrounded, enveloped, like walking into dense jungle foliage. His eyes strained. He could only really discern vague shapes in front of him now, the color palette around him going black, blacker, blackest.

He slowed down, one hand flailing around in front of him to prevent any collisions. He had a lighter, but he didn't want to use it. Not yet. His eyes adjusted over the next minute or so, and he could finally see a little bit.

As he crossed a wide aisle and moved into the electronics department, he saw the first body. Technically, he smelled it before he saw it. He thought it had been rotting beef from the meat department, but as he advanced, it smelled more and more like ripe roadkill. The odor kept growing.

He stopped when he saw it. He flicked the lighter, held it up. To make sure. He had seen plenty of death, the bodies bloated along the sides of the street and congealed into car upholstery in traffic jams gone permanently still, but this was the first child. A little boy with platinum blond hair lay face down in front of the glass case where the video game consoles used to be locked. A puddle of blood surrounded him, soaked into his white t-shirt. Flies circled near the back of the head, swooping down to land on the face concealed by hair. He was glad he couldn't see it. It was hard to tell, but Travis figured he might be eight or nine.

The positioning of the body made it seem like the kid died

trying to steal an Xbox or Playstation or something, which wouldn't make much sense since there was no way to play them. And yet, the shelves were empty. Someone had looted the consoles and the games anyway.

Lifting the lighter higher let the light drift farther down the aisle, and he saw a dead man leaned up against some video game accessories. Maybe he was the boy's father. The corpse's head hung down, chin resting on his sternum so shadows shrouded his face. Red stained his shirt which was torn in some places. In the half light, it was hard to decide if the holes resulted from bullets or a blade. Travis didn't care to get any closer.

He released the lighter button, that claustrophobic jungle feeling coming over him again as the dark returned. He brought his drink to his mouth and sucked on the straw. The citrus and liquor odors overwhelmed that of death, made it disappear all at once. He closed his eyes and drank. Warm. Other than that, it was a fine Long Island iced tea, he thought. He'd only ever had one or two before all of this, but he wanted to try his hand at it.

He juiced the lemons and limes himself, made a simple syrup on a fire in the backyard. The fruit was at least a month old by then, but even though the rinds were hard and dried out, there was still a surprising amount of juice inside.

No ice, though. Had to mix it up warm.

Today was a liquor day. He had a rotation.

He moved on, and the door took shape in front of him, less than 20 feet off now. It looked a little dinged up along the edges, but it remained intact. Nobody could bust through.

That's where the key came in.

He took another warm drink. The alcohol taste made him pucker up. Wouldn't have happened if it was cold. In a way, he couldn't wait until the winter, when he could pack the bottles of booze into the snow to keep them chilled.

Then again, he was about to make the booze days a little more boring anyway.

He pushed the key into the hole, twisted it until the deadbolt moved out of the way with a snap, turned the knob, crossed the threshold into the backroom of the pharmacy. The level of excitement he felt bordered on sexual. This room was darker still, almost pitch black. He pulled his lighter out, his thumb grinding the flint wheel around until the spark caught the butane.

By flickering flame light, he pulled open a few drawers to check. Pills, pills, pills. Yes. Everything was still here. It was all his.

He plopped two duffle bags on the floor and went to work filling them up.

Back at home, he stood in the kitchen, mixed himself another drink. More Long Island iced tea. The drink of the day. Wait. Great Lakes iced tea?

No. That was lame.

It was getting dark now. He looked out the window into the yard, his vision doubling for a split second as he watched the dusk give way to night. The wood fence that separated the yard from the alley turned a muted purple like the whole thing was bruised. The two mounds of dirt in front of it were the only things that had gone fully black. His eyes flicked away from them right away.

He reached into his pocket, touched it. Now it was a blister pack of pills he couldn't keep his hands off of, his finger running along the foil, along the bubbled domes of plastic. So many pills. He kept this pack of pills close, a symbol of all of the others he'd stashed away with the booze and the weed and the mountain of cigarette cartons. He locked all of them in the bedroom, in his parents' bedroom. Not like they were using it anymore.

He was finally starting a family of his own, maybe: alcohol and nicotine and oxycodone and the rest. His kids. He loved all of his children, but he had a favorite. The new addition. The pills. So much pain would be killed. So much anxiety would be Xanaxed and Valiumed and Klonopined away into nothing, into bliss, into painlessness without end.

He had to wait. Tomorrow. Tomorrow would be a pill day. He had a rotation.

He chugged down the rest of his drink and took a step forward on the ceramic tile, his legs going a little wobbly underneath him. He smiled. This was all he wanted. He felt numb, and tomorrow he would feel number still. That was the game plan. From now until oblivion.

He walked into the living room and sat down, pulled a pack of Parliaments from his pocket. Cigarettes had been his first stop, before food even, and he had a ton: Marlboros, Camels, Winstons, Pall Malls, Newports, Basics, Kents, and on and on. Brands he'd never even heard of. He had counted the cartons up, but he couldn't remember the number now. 226 or something like that. A lot. If he smoked a pack a day, he had enough for over six years. He kind of figured he'd cut back to half a pack a day toward the end to stretch them out for another year or two.

He knew he was all the way drunk, because he couldn't read the writing on the back of the blister pack of pills when he held it up in the candlelight. Not a single letter was discernible, no matter how much he squinted or tilted his head. It was all just blurry lines that ran together and wouldn't quite hold still. He used to be able to feel when he was really drunk, some change in his thinking or sense of awareness. Now he wasn't sure until he tried to read. He didn't know what that meant, and he didn't care.

He remembered the cigarette in his hand just then, lit it, rested the filter in his lips, watched the smoldering tube of tobacco hover at the bottom of his vision. He exhaled smoke, and it fluttered through the area of illumination above the candle on the end table.

He hit the tobacco shop the day the power went out. He was proud of that. Not proud to be a thief, proud that he was smart enough to know that this was the end of how everything was, perceptive enough to realize that manufactured supplies were scarce and everyone would be fighting for themselves. He put a brick through the front window and had his pick, all alone in the building. It was like a dream.

Within days groups of raiders would form, riding from town to town to work at organized looting, but he beat them to it, at least here in Hillsboro. He was set for years based on nothing more than his intellect. Maybe intellect was the wrong word. He was a community college dropout after all. Maybe it was more like street smarts or instincts or something like that.

The day after the tobacco shop, he made it to the liquor store. He wasn't alone this time. Some local drunks had pried open the back door and were working on clearing the place out. Even so, he hauled a lot of product home, making several trips with a Radio Flyer wagon from the neighbor's abandoned garage — case after case of Jim Beam black label, Smirnoff, Jose Cuervo, Dekuyper Triple Sec — cheap, but he liked it.

He got some beer, too, but it was a bit useless to him warm. Liquor he could tolerate at room temp, especially in a cocktail. Warm beer made his throat close up. He couldn't get it down. Yet another reason to look forward to the days getting shorter and colder.

There was an irony in hoping for winter, though. When he thought of the booze and pills and to some degree the weed, he thought of them as ways to feel warm inside. So he wanted it to get cold outside to better help him feel warm inside.

He liked that.

He thought about it when he ate. He wished he could never stop eating, never end the comfort he got from putting delicious food into his face. He wanted that feeling forever.

He thought that's all anybody really wanted in life, to feel warm inside. They deluded themselves into looking at the thing sideways, always glancing at it out of the corner of their eye so they didn't have to see it straight on. They'd accept it so long as it was somehow indirect. Call it abusing Xanax, they don't want it. Call it anti-anxiety medication, and it's OK to take Xanax every day.

No matter what anyone else thought, though, he knew

that was all he wanted. The words came to him often these days:

Just help me feel warm inside.

He drank and smoked and ate things to get that feeling inside and keep it for a while, and it worked. It worked just fine.

But the body wasn't designed to be loaded up with these substances all of the time. He knew that. That's why he had the rotation. He wasn't a doctor, but he could apply a little common sense. Liquor does one type of damage, weed does another, and pills do another. So you rotate them and spread each type of damage out. One day a week, he abstained altogether. Sunday. Sunday was the worst.

But yeah. Moderation. Everything in moderation.

The cigarette was burned down to the butt. Damn. He stubbed it out in the ash tray. They always went faster when he was drunk like this. He wanted to light another one, felt the itch of the pack in his pocket, but he had to wait.

It'd been his plan all along to get into the pharmacy, of course, but as others had obviously learned that was not as easy as it might seem. The room was well secured.

Ah, but Travis had an advantage over the biker types passing through to loot the place. He knew the pharmacist, knew where he lived. Don Grigsby lived on Ash Avenue in a large brick house with a white picket fence running around an in-ground pool in the back. Much nicer than Travis's house.

When he'd checked the place, it had been empty, though. No Grigsby. No keys to the pharmacy that he could find. The only cool thing he found was a hunting rifle and ammo to add to his growing armory. He noted that the pharmacist's mini

Cooper was not in the garage.

For 17 days after that, he spent a few hours per evening patrolling the town on his bike in search of the car. He finally found it a couple of miles outside of town. Apparently Grigbsy was trying to get out. He had another gun, a 9mm, on his decaying person, and $66,000 cash in a brown paper bag on the floor on the passenger side. Travis figured that to be useless, but he took it anyway. Grigsby also had the key. That was all Travis really cared about.

He leaned over to blow out the candle and then resettled in the recliner in the dark. The acrid smell of the extinguished candle filled his nostrils, and he pictured the smoke pirouetting off of the end of the blackened wick.

He leaned his head back and closed his eyes. He knew all of this was pathetic in a way. He knew it was no life. Staying drunk or high all day? No life at all.

But he also knew that if people knew the things he'd seen, nobody would judge him. If they knew, nobody would blame him for his hasty retreat from reality.

Nine days after the EMPs hit, he'd ridden out by the highway and sat in the grass. He drank whiskey sours out of a pair of huge mason jars he'd prepared for the journey while he watched military people haul off dead bodies in dump trucks. A second group of soldiers came six days later and burned a bunch more corpses in a big ditch just past the grocery store. It smelled like Korean barbecue, like some kind of sweet and sour beef dish with a good char on it. He almost vomited at first, but he got used to it.

He thought they must think that burning the bodies

would help quell the spread of the disease. Didn't make much sense to him, but what did he know?

The military didn't come anymore after the fire, though the dead continued to gather here and there throughout town, collapsing face down in gutters, bloating on their porches and patios, and many still sat in their cars from all of the accidents and traffic jams. Hell, Travis thought, probably the soldiers died before they could make it back. Handling diseased bodies can't be great for one's longevity.

Now he rode his bike around the empty town. Wind blowing leaves provided the only sound and movement. All else was still. He tried to keep the words at bay, but they came to him anyway:

Deathly still.

Hillsboro had been empty for a while now. Weeks. The bodies had become part of the scenery, like mannequins at the mall spread all over and set up in death poses. He didn't notice them much. In his experience, they mostly kept to themselves. Supposedly, there were reports of zombies on the East coast, but that was hard to believe.

Then again, all of this was pretty hard to believe. He never would have thought that the masses of humanity could be diminished so greatly within a week or two. Was this extinction? He looked out over the empty landscape that stretched as far as he could see. Close enough, he thought.

Mitch

Bethel Park, Pennsylvania
42 days before

Mitch sat on a green and white striped canvas chair, one of the fold out varieties generally used for the patio or camping. He wasn't outdoors, though. He was in the basement.

Across from him, Janice sat on a dining chair partially wedged between the washer and dryer. Her hands were tied together behind her back, with each hand individually lashed to the back of the chair as well. Similarly, her ankles were bound to the wooden legs of her seat. He had been thorough at her insistence. This was how she wanted it.

Her eyes were closed. He was pretty sure she wasn't asleep at the moment, though she had been in and out.

He had one job now, a basement night-watchman-type position. His duty would be to stay awake, to patrol the basement for any signs of his wife dying and/or resurrecting from the dead. Pretty straightforward.

He tipped his head back to finish another can of Red Bull and set the empty on the concrete floor next to the other drained cans and bottles. The hollow sound of the aluminum tube touching down caught her attention, and she opened her eyes.

Her cheeks looked puffier now, he thought, and her mouth puckered into the faintest frown perpetually as though she couldn't quite clear her palate of some sour note. He thought she might speak, but instead her eyelids fluttered a couple of times and closed again.

His eyes tingled with that wide open energy drink feeling, almost like an electrical current buzzed along the edges of his retinas, and yet he was pretty drunk. He felt the drunk more in his respiration. It felt slow and easy and more pleasant to breathe somehow. It reminded him of times years ago, he and his future wife huddling on stoops with other drunks after the bars closed. Once everyone was drunk enough, the night quieted down, and he somehow felt more alive, just sitting and breathing and looking out into the dark. No matter the time of year, when it got late enough, the night got that chill to it, the air got thicker. Janice often leaned up against his shoulder. He liked those moments when reality filtered down to something simple like that. When there was no need to talk, no need to look very far ahead. They could just be together and breathe and feel alive.

He wasn't looking too far ahead now, either. Maybe that's the magic of alcohol. It dulls your senses, lowers your inhibitions, and diminishes your motor skills, sure, but maybe what it does best is root you in the immediate moment. It blocks out the anxiety that obsesses over tomorrow and lets you live in today.

Anyway, he thought it might be impossible to look ahead all that far in his current scenario, the version of the near future laid out by his wife. His brain couldn't make that leap, couldn't picture her being the mostly normal woman in front of him one second and some kind of mindless monster the next. Couldn't picture her body gone still, never to stir again.

Or worse than that, even, that it *would* stir again and not be her anymore.

The word occurred to him then: Unthinkable. That's what these ideas were. He tried to conjure these images, tried to consider these possibilities. He couldn't.

The unthinkable.

She slept now, he was pretty sure, her chest rising and falling and her eyes moving beneath her eyelids, swiveling and flicking. He wondered what she might be dreaming, what someone might dream when they're convinced that death is closing in on them.

As they had moved down here and set things up, he believed her. As he went through with tying and taping her into the chair, he trusted her read on things, her prognosis regarding her condition. But that had been hours ago. Doubt crept in, slow and small at first, but it blossomed in the silence after their conversation trailed off. By the time she nodded off a little over half an hour later, he was more sure than not that this was ludicrous. They'd walk out of here together tomorrow morning like tonight never happened, go get her those antibiotics and be done with it.

But maybe that wasn't right, either. He could only really trust things as they were, this state of anticipation in the basement, this underground concrete chamber that seemed stuck between worlds in some way, this time and place where his wife seemed to hover somewhere between life and death.

At least their basement was on the dry side as far as basements went. It wasn't all mildewy and dank. Though dusty and cool and smelling faintly of kitty litter, it ultimately wasn't unpleasant to sit down here.

He fished a beer out of the cooler at his feet and twisted the cap off of the bottle. It tasted more bitter than usual, and he felt the corners of his mouth curl down in an involuntary frown. He considered the notion that the brew had somehow gone skunky, which seemed odd. He'd just bought it a couple of days ago. Then he remembered the Red Bull. It was some kind of shock to the taste buds to go back and forth between the sweet of the energy drink and the bitter of the beer. His tongue couldn't get used to it.

A nauseous feeling came over him, a bloaty feeling in the gut. It wasn't caused by the beverages, he knew. It was the reality of this scenario creeping in again, the fear taking hold.

He looked over his wife, her hair hanging down in her face as her chin drooped toward her chest in slumber. Her features looked intelligent. Alert. She always smirked when she slept, like she was perpetually making sarcastic remarks in her dreams. He thought that to be fairly likely, knowing her. She looked older than when they'd met but not by much. She'd certainly aged better than he had, a notion he verified by glancing down at his beer belly.

He watched the rise and fall of her chest, saw the faintest pulse ripple in the flesh of her neck over and over. It reminded him of a pebble disturbing the surface of a pond.

And then the flood of questions overtook his thoughts again: Would that pulse really cease tonight? Could any of this be real? Could a person just end like this? Not just a person. The one he wanted to spend forever with. The person he always thought would be around.

He guzzled down half the beer to try to kill the brain cells where the negativity wriggled. He didn't figure it'd work, but what the hell?

It didn't seem right. None of it. What sense could there be in the world working this way? The people we love weren't supposed to die. It didn't make sense.

He adjusted in his chair, trying to ease some of the strain on his lower back, and his shoe scuffed on the concrete. The sound must have woke her as her head floated back to an upright position, and her lips jerked. After a second she opened her eyes.

"What time is it?" she said, her voice sounding a little hoarse.

He glanced at his wrist.

"2:56 am," he said.

A little later than he'd figured, though he didn't voice that thought aloud. He felt tense about the time since she was so sure about the window of hours during which she'd turn. Anyway, hearing her speak made his panic die down, made his imagination veer back toward believing predictions of her imminent death to be crazy talk. Here she was in front of him, breathing and blinking and licking her lips. How could that just end?

"You getting tired?" she said.

"Nah. Not really," he said.

"Good," she said. "You can't fall asleep."

"I know," he said. He sounded a little more defensive than he meant to, so he smiled to try to cover it.

The quiet settled over the room again, but she didn't close her eyes this time. She looked around, took a deep breath and let it out slowly.

"Maybe it's better this way," she said.

"What do you mean?" he said.

"I mean the waiting," she said. "Waiting for it to happen. Waiting to die. It seems crazy, but it's a lot less dramatic this way. I mean, it's actually pretty boring when you think about it. Isn't it dull? Sitting down here in the basement?"

He pawed at the stubble sprouting along his jaw line.

"Yeah," he said, because he didn't know what the hell else to say.

"I mean, let's face it. We're not passionate people. We're not one of those passionate couples, you know?" she said. "Maybe we were for a little while. I don't think so, though. There was no button ripping. No romantic getaways. No shivering torsos. We were too busy working and changing diapers and paying bills and making peanut butter and jelly sandwiches for the kids and doing loads of laundry."

She nodded toward her purse on the dryer behind him.

"Can you light me a cigarette?" she said.

She had quit smoking over 10 years ago, but… he guessed cancer was no longer such a threat.

He pulled the soft pack of Winston Lights out of the purse, shook one loose, lit it. He took a puff. Terrible. He'd never picked up the habit. He walked over to her and put the cigarette in her lips soundlessly. She hit the cigarette and went on talking:

"I wonder if those passionate couples even exist, really? I mean, can it really exist over the long haul? Doesn't that kind of romance require novelty which can't sustain itself very long by default? A flame can't burn bright forever. It either slows down or burns itself out."

Mitch said nothing. He peeled a corner of the soggy label

away from his beer bottle.

"I got a little sidetracked. The waiting. It fits us is what I'm saying," she said. "It's what we did, mostly. It's a fitting end."

He examined the lines in her face, looked for malice in the set of her brow and eyelids, but he couldn't decide what to make of her expression. Was she trying to hurt him? Was she expressing bitterness about the life they'd made together, lashing out with the intent to injure by summing up their existence as a boring one? Or was this less angry and more of a cold, detached look at how she really felt, how things really were?

"You know you're going to be fine," he said. "Need some antibiotics for that leg, but the rest of this talk... I don't know, Janice. Let's not get ahead of ourselves. Let's wait and see."

She smiled a little, but it wasn't that mean smile she sometimes got when she wanted to rub his nose in something. This smile was a little sad.

"I'm sorry," she said. "I don't think that speech came off how I wanted."

He thought she would go on, but instead she gazed out into the room, her eyes slowly going unfocused so she looked like one of those creepy porcelain dolls lined up on the beds in the guest bedroom at his grandma's house when he was a kid. Hideous things. They didn't look like inanimate objects to him. They looked dead.

He peeled the label the rest of the way off of the bottle and let the sopping sheet of paper flop onto the floor. He thought back on her words, tried to think of how else she might have meant them. Nothing came to him. In some way, he thought she was saying that they were together physically but not emotionally, at least not all of the way. She didn't need him. He knew that, and he knew it was true, that it had been true for a long time.

But the inverse wasn't true. He did need her. Left on his own, his life itself seemed meaningless, an exercise in cruelty and humiliation and defeat.

For the first time, their relationship reminded him of the way she had always described her parents' relationship: The hard-nosed lady with the meek husband, a nice guy but one that no one could fully respect. As her mother was dying, Janice joked, "Mom can't die. Who will tell dad what to do?"

Of course, her dad had surprised everyone and remarried seven months later, but that was beside the point.

Mitch tipped his chin back to finish off the beer and went to work on another Red Bull. He watched her stare break off into a series of blinks as she seemed to come back from some place far away.

If it were just the two of them, he would surely kill himself after she was gone. But it wasn't just the two of them. He would have to find a way. For the boys.

"Remember when we watched that house for the Gundersons?" she said.

"Yeah. The house out in the woods?"

She nodded.

"Yeah," he said. "I remember."

He remembered it well. One summer, just before they got married, they'd watched a house for some rich friends of her parents. He remembered grilling burgers on their screened-in second story deck that overlooked dense woods, a green thicket that stretched out as far as you could see. He remembered watching their HD projector cast movies onto a 90-some-inch screen, messing around in their sauna and hot tub. You couldn't see any of the neighbors' homes from the yard, not through the tangle of greenery, anyway. It felt so relaxing to head out there after work and feel apart from all of the people, alone with his girl. They lived the good life for six weeks while the Gundersons cruised the Mediterranean or something like that.

"I dreamed that we were back there," she said. "When I was sleeping just now, I mean. I dreamed that we were sitting on the deck, and you had something cooking on the grill. I watched wisps of smoke spill out from around the edges of the lid, smelled the charred smell. We didn't say anything. We just looked out into the woods, and it was peaceful."

Mitch stroked his thumb over the can in his hand. It traced a line into the sweat coating the aluminum.

"That was fun," he said. "At that house, you know. We had a good time there."

He wanted to tell her that he had dreamed of that place, too. Not recently, but he had dreamed of it off and on through the years. In some ways maybe that was the high point of their time together, of his life. Six weeks that left a high water mark they'd never touch again. He wanted to tell her that in his dreams, he could still feel what it felt like to be young with her, when they felt all the way together, and it felt like anything was possible. He wanted to tell her, but he thought better of it.

The words describing his dreams percolated up to his tongue, but he held them back.

"We had fun there, didn't we?" he said.

"We did."

He wondered if the Gunderson home was really as great as it felt in his memories. Was the hot tub really so wonderful? Was that massive screen that special? Or was being young with a life of endless possibilities in front of them what they really missed? And even then, was it really like that, or was nostalgia flattering reality, making all of the colors look brighter, all of the images clearer and more pure.

The conversation trailed away to a shared moment of thoughtful silence and from there degraded into nothing. In time she fell asleep again. He watched her eyelids now, closed with a dark undertone radiating purple hues from beneath the flesh. The hot water heater rumbled a while behind him and then kicked off.

And alone in the silence he grew angry with himself. How had he gotten so soft? So unable to express himself, unable to even feel his own emotions all the way, numbing them always with TV and beers and detachment. How had he let life rush past like this? He remained sedentary as the fruit withered on the vine, as the time dried out and blew away in the wind.

One of the fluorescent bulbs began flickering above him, an uneven crackle accompanying the strobe effect. He didn't find it unpleasant, though. It was more like a little white noise that broke up the starkness of the quiet. Janice didn't seem to mind, either. She didn't wake anyhow.

Disease.

Death.

Shit. How do you prepare for this? How do you brace yourself? You can't, can you? He knew it couldn't be all the way real until it happened, knew that he couldn't anticipate the depth or scale of the thing, but he understood one thing: This was going to hurt so bad.

If it was real, anyway. It could all be fake after all, couldn't it? She could be wrong. She could be.

These concerns and doubts circled in his head in an endless loop as his eyes drooped closed, and his head nestled into the chair, and he drifted into unconsciousness.

Travis

Hillsboro, Michigan
45 days after

Travis sat on the gliding swing on the front porch, rocking in silence. He was so high on oxycontin that he periodically jizzed a little bit in his boxer shorts. Not a full load of ejaculate, just a little squirt, like pre-come. He was aware of each and every spurt, intensely so, but gave no thought to changing his shorts or pants. The swing kept right on going, and the air tingled and swirled outside of him, around him, a living, spiraling thing he could breathe in. The world was bright and blurred and a little bit farther away than usual. His core was so warm, but the tip his nose was icy cold.

As the swing moved, the blue sky rose and fell in his field of vision. The houses across the street lurched up and down like boats on an angry sea.

The street was dead, as it had been for many days. Most everyone was gone in one way or another. Today, he didn't see anyone until Sean stopped by in the afternoon. With all of the people dying and fleeing for the government camps, Sean was the only person left in the neighborhood that Travis knew. He'd been three grades ahead of Travis in school. One of those achiever types. While Travis looked for ways to spend the school day with a buzz, Sean got good grades and lettered in multiple sports. Between that and the age gap, they'd never been friends or anything, but now here they were with no one else.

Sean climbed the front steps and stood on the porch. It was September, a little chilly, but he was still wearing those Adidas sandals he always wore. Travis found this amusing but didn't say anything.

"What up?" Sean said.

"Swingin'," Travis said, still gliding back and forth. "How's it going?"

"I'm good. You seen them raiders around?"

"Not in a couple of weeks. I think they got all they wanted and moved on to rape and pillage larger towns."

He tried to look at Sean while he talked to him, but he had a hard time focusing. The blur of all things smeared right up onto his neighbor's face, the whole world smudged and clouded like butter on the sides of a glass bowl.

They fell silent a moment, Sean turning to look out in the direction that Travis and the swing faced. The vacant house across the street wasn't all that interesting, but they looked at it anyway.

"You haul anything good lately?" Travis said.

"Mm... Snagged about ten more propane tanks at that Shell station outside of town," he said. "Busted the lock off of the cage by the air compressor."

"Nice."

"So my grill has plenty of fuel. Wish we had meat to cook," he said. "We gotta go fishing or something, man. I need the protein."

Travis smiled, nodded. Sean squinted at him.

"Bro, are you fucked up?" Sean said.

Travis tried to hold back a chuckle, but he couldn't.

"Nah, man," he said.

Sean tilted his head as if mulling this over.

"Your eyes look funny is all," he said.

Travis chuckled again. *I'm full of pills, idiot.* He laughed a little harder. Yes, liquor was fine, and he liked marijuana OK, but the pills pulled heaven down inside of his brain and held it there for a while. Euphoria. Bliss. He felt untouchable.

And he closed his eyes and drifted into the blackness behind his eyelids for a moment, the warm feeling swelling up to take his consciousness for a few seconds, pulling him under. And images of blood smeared on black and white ceramic tile came to him with violent intensity like they were being burned into his imagination. He heard whimpering so shrill and pathetic.

His head bobbed back up, shaking off the nightmare. He was scared for a second, but then he felt the warmth, felt heaven inside of him once more.

Sean just stared at him.

"I'm sorry. Did you say something?" Travis said.

"No. I didn't say anything."

He turned to face the street, and the two of them watched the empty neighborhood again. Eventually, Sean said goodbye and wandered off, but Travis stayed out there for a long time. The swing lurched back and forth, and he smiled, and a little more jizz spurted onto the semen already crusted to his boxer shorts.

In the evening, Travis felt itchy. A mess of tingles piled on his skin and crawled all over each other like snakes. He sat in the living room, candlelight flickering on the walls around him again. He rubbed another oxy in a wet paper towel, his fingers and thumb shifting the soggy paper back and forth over the tiny pill. This process removed the time release coating that ensured the medication would be doled out slowly over a period of 24 hours. Instead, eating this uncoated tablet would deliver the full dose at once. Crushing and snorting it would put all of it in his bloodstream within seconds.

Decisions, decisions.

This wasn't part of the plan. He was supposed to follow a strict regimen of rationing, and it certainly didn't involve snorting. Discipline. Following the rules. That's how the rotation worked. But maybe his sense of dosage was wrong. All of this pill stuff was new. He would need to dial things in, right?

The coating removed, he set the pill aside and lit a cigarette. Camel Lights today. His favorite. Smoke swirled off of the end of the cig, and his thoughts swirled as well. He felt guilty. He was already breaking the regimen on day one? That didn't bode well. He was set for a long time, a few years. Running out of pills and booze any faster than necessary would be a nightmare. And from the more dramatic angle, he had enough intoxicants on hand to kill himself many times over if he were reckless. He didn't figure this to be a real risk. He wasn't gluttonous that way, but it wasn't impossible if he started sliding down that slippery slope.

Without thinking, he picked up the remote off of the end table and tried to turn on the TV. It didn't work, so he pressed the button a few times. Oh. Right. A single laugh puffed from his nostrils, and he tossed the remote. It tumbled end over end, glanced off of the wall and landed somewhere behind the couch. Perfect place for it, he thought.

Damn. He missed TV, though. He missed the internet. He missed being around girls. He hadn't had a girlfriend in a while. Too busy working and getting high to keep up with all of the other stuff. Still, he missed the fleeting interactions he'd had with them of late. He missed the smell of them. Seemingly few of the local females had survived, and those who had lived hadn't stayed around. He wasn't certain when he'd last seen a living woman. It had been days. He hit the Camel, let the smoke billow about in his lungs a moment before he exhaled. He missed his parents, too.

And the images came to him again, the memories. He tried to stop them, but he couldn't.

He peeked around the corner into the kitchen, crouched, afraid. Red puddled out across the black and white tiles. His dad was already dead, crumpled in the corner in a loose fetal position, throat slit by the looks of it, though it was hard to tell for certain with all of the blood.

The man's hands gripped his mother's throat in the center of the room. He straddled her, his knees pinning her arms to the floor. Her eyes looked wide, wild, almost comical if not for the circumstances. The man smirked, somewhere between disinterested and mildly amused. He lifted her then, and bashed her head into the floor. The others in his group looked on, their faces similarly blank, like this wasn't a real human skull being cracked on the ceramic tile like an egg on the side of a frying pan, like it wasn't really happening, just something on TV, some rerun they'd seen countless times before.

But Travis couldn't stay for the end of this episode. He

turned and ran, gliding through the hallway and the living room, fleeing through the front door, feet pounding down the steps, onto the sidewalk, into the street. He ran a long time. It wasn't until he stopped that he realized that he was crying.

With the candle out, he sat in the dark in the living room. The cherry on the tip of his cigarette provided just enough light to see its red glow. All else was black. And quiet.

He squirmed in his seat, the chair squeaking under him, and he thought about the room around him that he couldn't quite see. Living room. It seemed a strange term all of the sudden. Living room, the room you mostly lived in, he guessed. But was he living here? Not really. He was slowly killing himself in the living room with drugs and drink. Dying in the living room. It might take years, but that's all it was.

He stood and walked out to the porch, dragging his fingertips along the wall to feel his way. The air was cool out here and thick and wet. He felt the cold humidity grip his torso like a soggy hug, though it felt somewhat far away thanks to the numbing flame of narcotics burning inside of him.

Around him, the black night stretched out forever. Total silence and nothingness stood in front of him. No moon or stars lit up the sky. Just gloom. He couldn't even see the house across the street.

He brushed the back of his hand at his mouth and felt the vomit crusted to his chin. Whoops. Forgot to clean that up, apparently. He licked his fingers and tried to scrub at the barf.

He'd puked in the backyard after snorting that last oxy. That happened to him often, though. Whether he ate it or snorted it, oxycontin usually made him throw up, a weird watery vomit. Clear, mostly. And then as soon as he puked, he could feel the euphoria kick in, and nothing like puking really mattered quite so much anymore. He guessed that was why he forgot to wipe off his chin.

With the crust removed to his satisfaction, he felt around for the swing, found it, sat on it, and rocked in slow motion. Cold air tingled against his arms in a pleasant way, though his nose felt like a pointy piece of ice.

He thought of his parents again, this time remembering the process of dragging them out into the back yard to bury them. He'd cried the whole time. Inconsolable, shaking sobs like a baby. Then he cleaned up the puddle of blood where his dad bled out, the smear of red where his mom struggled. He mopped and scrubbed the tiles until the light ones went from red to pink to white again.

The power was still on then. People were sick and dying everywhere, and order was breaking down, but there was hope that things might get back to normal. It almost seemed funny to think back on it now.

He rocked the swing harder, and the cold dug its fingers deep into the meat of his arms. He flicked his cigarette butt out into the yard. That used to piss his dad off like nothing else, but it didn't matter anymore. He was gone. Everyone was gone.

Diseases came and killed some, and people came and killed some, and the others all left once the power went out. And when his family needed him most, when life and death teetered on the line and they needed his help, he ran. He ran and ran and ran until he puked chili into the bushes outside of the post office, his lungs on fire, his throat on fire, his mouth on fire. He bent at the waist for a long time trying to get his breath back, a string of saliva dangling from his bottom lip, a pile of half-chewed beans in the dirt at his feet.

He'd run away. He'd always run away. The first time he got punched, he was outside of a gas station where kids bought Coke and junk food after school. He'd mouthed off to a kid with zits all over his face and the back of his neck. Couldn't even remember what he said to him, but he was sure he was just busting balls. Nothing too mean. Running his mouth was all he ever did when he was in high school, all any of them did, but he was harmless, so nothing ever came of it, usually.

Anyway, this kid didn't like it. He didn't say anything in retaliation. He walked up and punched Travis, a right hook that went a little wide of the mark and got him in the ear. It didn't hurt that bad, but Travis ran home crying. He was 14. Too old for that response, he knew, but so it went. The other kids made fun of him later, of course. He didn't care. He was a coward. He knew that well enough without anyone pointing it out.

He slowed the swing down so he could light another cigarette. The burst of flame from the lighter made the world seem bright and warm for a split second. It hurt his eyes a little, and a pink splotch hovered in his vision where the fire had burned. He sat back, rested his shoulders against the swing, and breathed smoke while the oval of pink danced across the black nothing.

Mitch

Bethel Park, Pennsylvania
42 days before

They walked on the beach in his dream, bare feet sinking into that wet sand right at the water's edge. The wind blew so hard it felt like it might knock them down. It was cold as hell, too. The chill enveloped him, snaked icy tendrils deep into the core of his body, but he somehow found it more exhilarating than miserable. He stretched his arms out to the sides, and his jacket billowed and flapped behind him.

Mitch looked at Janice, but she did not look back at him. They walked together, but it somehow felt more like she was passing by. She stared into space, her face expressionless like one of those dead porcelain dolls again.

Dead. That seemed important. Mitch thought about it, tried to make sense of it. He looked down at the water while he thought, watched the wet lap at the sand.

A thud emitted somewhere nearby. It sounded like it came from straight ahead, but there was nothing there but sand, so he stopped walking and swiveled his head around. He saw nothing. Just beach that stretched out forever, and water that went farther still. The sound didn't fit this place, either. It sounded like something solid landing on asphalt or concrete. Things landing in the sand would make a muffled noise, and things landing in the water would mostly sploosh, he thought.

What the hell?

He couldn't puzzle it out, but he knew now that something here didn't make sense. He jogged a few paces to catch up with Janice. They walked on a while, and there were no more sounds but the wind and the waves.

Still, he couldn't shake that paranoia, that tingling feeling that he should know more about what's going on, that he was missing something obvious.

As soon as the scraping started, he knew the beach must be a dream. He recognized the noise. It was the distinct sound of something dragged over cement. Something heavy. Maybe something on a sidewalk or a driveway. He pictured someone pushing an upright piano over the sidewalk in front of their house. The scrape sounded warbly and far away, though, almost like it was wet. In Mitch's experience, that's the way the real world sounded when you heard it from within a dream.

He turned to Janice.

"I'm dreaming," he said.

She said nothing. She didn't look at him, just walked into the wind with that same dead look in her eye.

"I need to wake up," he said.

The wind blew harder now, and sand whipped at his face, the grit getting in his eyes after a second. He leaned over and rubbed at his eyelids with the heels of his hands. He knew you weren't supposed to do that, that you could scratch your cornea, but he couldn't help it. He needed to wake up.

He couldn't remember how that worked. Did he have to do something to make the waking up process start? What if he couldn't remember? Would he be stuck asleep forever?

The panic welled in him, and he inhaled sharply and opened his eyes.

He jerked awake to find himself staring into flickering bulbs, bursts of light and dark jittering up and down two glass tubes about five feet in front of his face. Reality occurred to him one piece at a time, his brain processing things in short, blunt statements:

He knew these lights. The wood above them. He was in the basement. He was staring at the basement ceiling. He fell asleep down here. He wasn't supposed to do that. He dreamed something. Something important, maybe.

And then wood scraped over the concrete. No longer muffled by swaths of slumber, the sound seemed harsh and dry.

And close.

His heart beat faster. He leaned forward, his vision tilting away from the ceiling as his head left the hammock-like indentation it had pressed into the canvas head rest. Pain shot through the muscles in his neck, which felt stiff. He must have pinched a nerve or something, too, as he felt the pain twinge all the way into the crook of his jaw. He rubbed the rubbery ball of muscle on one side of his neck, felt the tenderness there. It'd be sore as hell for the next few days.

Motion caught his eye as the scrape erupted again. His pupils traced the movement, though it took a full second to process what he was seeing.

Janice.

Not good.

His wife had flopped the chair to the floor and was now wriggling on the ground, torso hunched into a capital letter C, shoulders twitching and writhing in small circles without discernible purpose. He tried to get a read on her state of mortality, but her hair swung into her face to cover all but the tip of her nose.

One of her hands stretched forward, apparently only loosely bound at this point. It was only a few feet from his ankles. The outstretched hand flopped about on the concrete, seeming to contort in odd ways, perhaps lacking the normal level of articulation, but he wasn't sure. The curled fingers clawed at the ground, found purchase, and the chair inched forward as she pulled, the cement grinding at the wood, the hunched figure sliding toward him.

"Janice," he said, his voice just louder than a whisper.

The hand retracted, the arm coiling against the chest, and she stopped moving. It reminded him of a rabbit hunching down and freezing in the back yard once it realized a human being was present. He watched her for a long moment, trying to decide whether or not she was breathing based on the movements of her torso. He wasn't certain.

"Janice?" he said again.

Nothing. No movement.

He scratched his chin, leaned forward in his chair. Should he take a closer look?

The hand reached out again. As it looped away from the body, he realized the finger tips were bloodied up pretty good. She must have been working at scooting toward him for a long while as he slept. Again the hand arched and flopped like a dying fish before the fingers tensed up to grip the floor. Again the chair lurched forward in slow motion.

No. This can't be real.

He knew what was happening, but he somehow kept any sense of panic at bay. For now, at least. Apart from a vague sense of nausea in his gut and an elevated heart rate, he found himself calm. To an alarming degree. His thoughts seemed clear. Was he in shock? Still half asleep? He couldn't say.

He knew this was one of those in-between moments life sometimes presented. This chair straddled the line between the way things used to be and what they would become for the rest of his time on the Earth. For right now, he could sit here in between the past and future versions of the world and watch her moving about on the floor, not quite 100% certain whether his wife was living or dead. It still felt like she was here with him, still a conscious being that existed on the same plane that he did, even if the circumstantial evidence suggested otherwise. He knew she must no longer be herself, but it didn't feel real. As soon as he rose from this seat, that would change. It would become real, and his life itself would very drastically change. He was pretty sure how this chapter would end, too.

Death would do them part. Again.

After one more drawn out scoot, he couldn't sit still anymore. He stood. He would need to verify her state, and he would need to *take care of it*.

He took a step toward the stooped figure, still trying to get a look at its face to be sure. He had to be sure. The hair still covered her eyes, however, hundreds of thousands of strands of brown strung across her visage with a few white thrown in.

He stepped again, going diagonally to the left instead of straight at the thing, still hoping to get an angle that made things clear. His neck spasmed. It killed. He leaned his head back and rolled it from side to side a few times, his lips and nose wrinkled up.

When it moved again, he didn't hear it. He felt it.

The hand grabbed his ankle, the steely grip somehow more insectile than human. He kicked a couple of times, trying to shake his leg loose, but the thing was latched on. He leaned back instead, trying to pry it free. And finally a touch of panic bubbled to the surface as the notion that he might not be able to pry himself loose took shape in his mind. It wasn't even the idea of the thing biting him or hurting him at all. Just the irrational fear of being stuck, powerless, helpless.

He yanked hard, a quick backward stroke, and got loose. It reminded him of plucking a tick from the back of his neck, one that came away with a wad of skin in its mouth. The arm flailed at him a couple more times and retracted back to the coiled position at its chest.

The nightmare feeling didn't retreat now that he was free. He realized this as he brought a trembling hand to his forehead and found it sopping with sweat. He pressed the heel of his hand into the moisture. It felt more like grease than sweat. French fry grease stuck to his face. His hand slid down into his eye socket, so he pressed on his eyeball instead. Pink splotches filled half of his field of vision, the shapes shifting as the pressure from his hand increased.

Fear surrounded him, submerged him in a feeling like defeat, like shoving his face underwater and holding him there. Laughing while he struggled.

No more dicking around. He had to know. For sure.

He moved in a semi-circle around the body, light on his feet, nearly soundless, until he stood at the back of the chair.

He didn't hesitate. He leaned down, grabbed a handful of hair and flung it out of her eyes, jumping back immediately. The arm struck, but it fell short, like a cobra trying to strike something too quick for it.

And then his vision shifted to the face. The whites of her eyes had gone blood red. Her complexion looked like melting butter pecan ice cream, like all of her skin would drip away before long. Streaks of smoky black trailed across the yellow, similar to those around her wound.

And it was real.

He felt his jaw clench and his eyes snap shut. He couldn't move. He couldn't breathe. He thought he might vomit or pass out or explode into a red spray or all of the above.

No.

No, no, no.

It was all real. Janice was gone. Forever.

A thing writhed in her body. A thing that wasn't her at all. How?

How could the world work this way? How could it just erase someone? Take them away from here, and put something else in their place. A wretched thing. A dead thing.

He realized he was crying, or something like it, when spit hissed out between his teeth. Hot breath heaved in and out of his mouth, stuck open in a silent scream.

Death.

Death.

The feelings pulled him down into a black place, into some kind of primal heat where his thoughts became murky, more like flashes of emotion than words or images. But one part of him stayed apart, detached. It observed the rest of him, and it noted that he wasn't sad, exactly. He wasn't pitiful and inward and some neutered weakling the way he thought he was.

He was hatred. He was fire. He wanted to detonate and take the rest of the world with him. He wanted to watch it all blacken and turn to ash.

She was gone. This couldn't be real, but it was.

Baghead

Rural Oklahoma
9 years, 126 days after

The lightning lit the sky again. The black dream replayed. Another variation.

He climbed a staircase in an empty apartment building. Craters blemished the walls where moisture had gotten in and worn drywall away. What was left looked mushy and gray like some combination of oatmeal and brains.

He walked the halls where much of the ceiling bulged down toward him like a fat belly, looking poised to cave in. Still, he moved along, going door to door in search of letters and diaries. That's all he desired. Memories and dreams and ideas written down and lost or left behind. He found them, and he kept them. All of the people gone and forgotten and scattered about, in a way he found them. He collected them and cared for them. That was his life. Collecting the scattered and the dead.

Even in sleep he searched for them, stalking through buildings both remembered and imagined. Looking for a thousand little stories that told the bigger story better than any other way he knew.

He sifted through papers on a desk. Fast food cups and bills and insurance documents. Nothing good. So he moved on, onto the next room with holes blasted into the walls like someone took a shotgun to it at close range, to the next where browned bloodstains crusted the carpet around two shriveled bodies.

Sometimes he dreamed the old way, when he looked like a normal man, when his face was still his own. Sometimes he dreamed the new way, when the hood covered him. Sometimes, like now, this switched mid dream, which was jarring somehow. Upsetting.

Shadows surrounded him now, dark shapes flitting over the canvas bag on his head. His thoughts jumbled, confusion about how he got here, where he'd go next. An endless hallway sprawled before him, though, and he meant to check behind every door. He knew that much.

Mitch

Bethel Park, Pennsylvania
42 days before

Upstairs, he got the kids up and around to get ready for school. In a daze, he directed them to brush their teeth and then hovered in the kitchen as they ate their cereal. The boys were quiet, mostly. They usually were when they just woke up.

He paced slowly over the linoleum while spoons dinged against cereal bowls and Frosted Flakes crunched and milk slurped. He watched the circle of light reflect on the floor, watched the lit-up spot seem to move as he walked like it was also pacing, also jittery, also had a lot on its mind.

While he worked his way through the phases of the morning, his mind remained on the being in his basement tied to a chair. It occurred to him that he hadn't once considered how he would proceed with this problem, that he and Janice never got into what specific steps he would take. They didn't own a gun. What would he do, then? Would he stab the thing that used to be his wife? Bludgeon it?

He tried to picture it, some lead pipe bashing his wife's head in, her skull all caved in with red seeping out of the cracks.

Christ on a crutch.

He shuffled out by the front door, got the boys into their jackets. He tried to smooth Kevin's hair down a little with his hand, but the cowlick bounced back up.

"Where's mom?" the boy said.

"She had to visit grandma and grandpa," he said.

The ease with which the lie formed on his lips surprised him. He sounded so normal.

"Are they OK?"

"They're fine," he said. "Why do you ask that?"

"Oh," the boy said. "Just you said she 'had to' visit them. Sounded like something bad happened."

"No," he said. "Nothing bad."

He gave them lunch money and sent them out to wait for the bus. It seemed crazy to be sending them away considering the circumstances. It made him feel sick to watch them walk out the door and down the front steps, turning onto the sidewalk and moving toward the corner. It made his stomach churn in turbo speed like it was trying to eat itself, but he needed them out of the house for a bit anyway. He probably wouldn't be sending them back to school tomorrow, but for today it was necessary. He promised Janice the kids wouldn't see her this way. So they wouldn't.

Once the kids were gone, he poured himself a huge coffee, dumped a ton of sugar and cream into it and sat down at the kitchen table. The coffee was a little too hot to chug, so he blew steam off of the top of it between sips.

A quiet fell over the house, a calm. He found his thoughts growing clearer. He wasn't sure if that was due to the caffeine or the silence. Maybe a bit of both. His chair faced the window, so he looked through it, looking at the neighbor's yard without actually seeing it while his mind tumbled rocks around.

So how would he actually do this? He needed to brain the thing downstairs, so he would need to select a weapon. He figured that had to be step one. His eyes swung to the counter, danced over the block with all of the knife handles sticking out of it. He supposed he could make it work, but a butcher knife would be kind of a brutal way to do it. Close range. Violent in a way that required a lot of aggression. Messy, too. There must be better options.

Red movement caught his eye out the window and made his vision come back into focus. A cardinal landed on the neighbor's fence, twitched its tail a few times and flew on.

Damn it. If only they had a gun. He had considered buying one, a few times pretty seriously. When the house two doors down got burglarized four years back, he wanted to get a handgun or possibly even a shotgun he could rack in the dead of the night to scare intruders away. He looked into the pricing and everything. Janice didn't believe in it, though. She said she'd feel like Ted Nugent or something. She said she didn't want to give in to the culture of fear, didn't want to live a life of paranoia.

Sure would be handy right now. Christ. Could he really bash his wife's brains in? Bury an ax in her forehead?

He picked the mug up, sipped, the coffee tingling all the way down. Should he go buy a gun now? He turned his head to look at the basement door.

No. No, he couldn't leave with her down there. It felt like she was exposed somehow. Alone.

He saw it again in his mind, the toppled chair, the scrawny frame, the tip of the nose poking out of the hair, the arm folding up to tuck against the chest.

It reminded him of when they found Mitzi dead in the driveway. The cat sprawled on her back on the line where the cement and grass met, one front paw partially extended above her, the arm locked in that position with rigor mortis. Her eyes were open but blank. He touched her to make sure: cold and stiff. It was such a shock. Janice burst into tears. Inconsolable. They stood around for a moment, and then they went right back into the house out of instinct, maybe to try to process it.

Once they were inside, though, he didn't feel right. They couldn't leave her out there in the open. It wasn't right. He paced around and looked out the window every two seconds, nausea building in his gut. He only made it a few minutes before he went out to gather her up and bury her.

He felt that sickness times 1,000 right now. It wasn't a cat. It was Janice. And she was worse than dead. She was wiggling around without her say so. It was a violation.

He remembered her as she was before all of this, a montage of images playing in his head with the saturation turned way up so the colors were brighter than real life.

Yellow sun shined on her face, reflected off of her hair, shadows framing her jaw on the opposite side in grays and blacks. Her jaw was distinct, feminine, striking, attractive. It made her look sophisticated somehow, intelligent, clever. When she smiled, it transformed, her chin becoming more prominent, emitting some wave of happiness into the air, making her seem a little more approachable than the sophisticated version of herself. She was smiling when they first met.

Even as she pulled on a shirt and her face was draped in t-shirt fabric, he could recognize her by her jaw alone when the fabric pulled taut enough to reveal its shape. He couldn't believe it had just happened that way by chance and biology and genetics. Someone must have sculpted it, must have painstakingly selected the lines and forms for it to turn out with such striking character. It was the only way.

That image faded, and blue water lapped at her shins, her skin pale and smooth as always like cream. She waded out into the water, the sky gray and cloudy above them, the wind roaring all around them.

Then she stood in the kitchen with her back to him, her neck angled so her head rested beneath her shoulders as she worked to prepare a meal. As she moved to the cutting board, strands of hair shook loose from the rest, spilling from the back of her head to hang down on each side of her face. He saw her arms move, heard the knife thump out a rhythm against the wood as she chopped up some ingredient he couldn't quite see.

He smelled her smell now, heard the rise and fall of her voice, felt the smooth and cool of her skin against his.

There were no words for the weight these memories piled on his shoulders and chest, no words to capture the sense of great fortune and misfortune he felt all at once, a mix of the best and worst luck—the best in knowing her at all, the worst in having her torn away in one swift motion, a gaping void left in her place, a negative somehow, like a black hole threatening to collapse all nearby reality.

He sat there in the kitchen, shoulders hunched, elbows resting on the corner of the table. Alone in the quiet. The weight of it stacked up on him until it became hard to breathe. He choked on the emptiness, the wind catching in his throat for no good reason. His face got all hot. He wanted a drink, but he couldn't now. Not for a long while perhaps. He had to keep it together. For the boys.

Yes. He rubbed his eyes, willing himself to focus on the here and now. He patted a hand on the tabletop just to feel something solid, took the last sip of coffee, lukewarm now.

Weapon. He needed a weapon. At some point they had inherited an ax, but the handle snapped years ago, and he never got around to replacing it or repairing it. Still, he could probably still use the half-handled ax like a hatchet. With the reduced leverage of the short handle, he might have to hack at it a few times to finish the job, an opportunity he didn't relish.

The other option was a sledgehammer that had been in their shed when they moved in, abandoned by the previous owners. It had hardly moved in seven and a half years. That would probably cut down on the time necessary to do the deed, pare it down to a single stroke of the hammer. On the other hand, it was heavy to the point of diminishing its mobility, making it a lot more awkward to administer than the ax, especially if the thing was moving at all.

So the same basic question remained: Chop it or bludgeon it? How could he decide something like that? How could anyone?

He fished a hand into his pocket, fingers riffling through keys until he found what he was looking for. A quarter. Fortune would decide. Heads for ax, tails for hammer.

He flicked his thumb and the coin tumbled in the air, paused a moment at the apex of its arc and spiraled down. It slapped the table, bounced three times and then gyrated a while before it finally settled down enough that he could see the face of it.

Tails.

So it was decided.

He stood, his knees creaking, his mouth dry. He moved to the back door. An odd awareness of his surroundings came over him, like he would remember this moment, this walk out to the shed, forever. The way the morning sunlight slanted into the windows, looking bright but not quite all the way warm yet. The sound of his footsteps, the clap of the impact followed by the floorboards faintly squealing from somewhere below. The cool of the door knob against the palm of his hand.

He pushed the screen door and passed through the doorway, the chilly air surrounding him now. He inhaled, and the cold shocked the flesh inside his nostrils, stinging. He opened his mouth, and his gasp and ensuing breath coiled into swirls of steam in the air in front of him. Too damn cold, especially for May.

He shuffled toward the shed. His feet crunched on the grass. The sun sat just above the treeline in the distance, the ball of light unable to muster enough warmth to keep the chill at bay.

His fingers undid the latch and he gave the shed door three tugs before it screeched and came unstuck from the frame. He stepped into the building. It took his eyes a second to adjust to the the lack of light. Once they did, he could make out the handle protruding from the pile of things in the rear left corner. The hammer was where it was supposed to be. He picked his way past a lawnmower and snowblower, and he shifted a few boxes out of the way. There. He gripped the handle, lifted it, felt the heft of it in his mitts.

He tried to imagine the swing. He could muster a sense of how it would feel in his hands, the strain in his arms reaching the pinnacle of the swing and then the power of the downward stroke as gravity chipped in to hurry its descent. He couldn't picture it, though, couldn't picture her as the object of his aggression... or the thing that used to be her. In his mind, he could only imagine a pumpkin on the other end. A jack-o'-lantern bursting into a mushy orange spray.

He stood there for a long moment with the head of the hammer hovering at ankle height. His heart hammered in his chest, and he could feel the throb of the blood in his ears. He felt a tingle in his eyelids, an almost electric sting along the perimeter of his vision that made it seem like he needed to turn the brightness of reality down. His mind was blank. Empty.

Finally, he shook his head, turned and walked back over the grass through the back door and into the kitchen. He carried the hammer in front of him, holding it out in an awkward dangle like something he was loathe to touch or maybe a little bit frightened of.

He opened the basement door and flipped the light switch. The fluorescent bulbs flared and brightened. He listened for a moment. Silence. That was good... right? Somehow the quiet made him uneasy, though, and the overwhelming urge to close the basement door and deal with this later buzzed up and down his limbs.

He brought the sledgehammer up and let the head lean over his shoulder like a baseball player waiting in the on-deck circle. That'd be easier to manage during his descent. Again, he listened. Still nothing.

Screw it. Enough pussyfooting, already.

He started down the stairs, scowling and shaking his head a little for the first few steps. His disgust with himself faded as he got closer, though. He needed to focus.

He moved with care now, each step revealing a little more of the basement floor below. Two steps shy of the bottom, the chair came into focus. Part of the chair, anyway. It had come apart. The back and seat were still connected, but the front legs were gone. More importantly, the seat was empty. She was... He corrected himself. *It* was gone.

A scraping gasp made the hair on the back of his neck prick up. Then he realized that it came from his own mouth. Shit.

The main chamber of the basement stood empty in front of him. Motionless and silent aside from the flicker of the fluorescent bulb over the canvas chair he'd sat in the night before. The rest of the basement remained out of his view, though. He'd need to take a sharp turn upon hitting the floor to get a look.

Sweat greased his palms and sluiced over his forehead, soaking his brow. His heart beat like a kick drum about to cave in, every thump throttling his ribcage.

Again, the impulse to run up the stairs came over him. He could feel it like a fiery itch in his legs that he could only scratch by turning about and sprinting.

But no. Enough of this. No more fear. He had the hammer. Just two more steps and he could see what he was up against.

His foot lifted off of the step in slow motion, heel then toe. The wood sighed as his weight shifted, and he froze in that position for a couple of seconds, like a flamingo with one leg up. Nothing happened, so his motion resumed, the foot sinking down to the next step, twisting a little as it settled in without sound. Now the other heel and toe lifted, hip rotating forward, foot nestling down on the next step.

One step to go. This was it. He closed his eyes, sucked in a long, deep breath, and before he could exhale, he felt icy fingers grab his hand. He opened his eyes, tried to free his hand to be able to use both arms to bring the hammer down. Her grip held, though, and he only succeeded in pulling her closer. Wrenching against her hold again, he lost his balance and crashed backward onto the stairs, the hammer falling away and landing beneath him.

Now her torso lurched forward, her head bobbed. He tried to scramble backward, elbows and hands pistoning, scrabbling along the hard edges of the stairs, but it was too late. Her face got close. The lips brushed just shy of his wrist. Her hair swung down, concealing his hand from view, and then he felt the cold teeth pierce his flesh.

Travis

Hillsboro, Michigan
46 days after

Sean sat on the swing next to him. They rocked and watched the daylight hitting the street swell and wane over and over as clouds passed in front of the sun. The day drained from yellow to gray and back before them.

All he wanted was for Sean to leave, which he realized held some irony. They were the last two people in town, the population whittled from 6,600 to two, and he just wanted to be rid of the guy.

"Saw raiders at the supermarket again last night," Sean said. "Took a look after they moved on. Looks like they finally got into the pharmacy over there. Too bad. I was hoping to stockpile some antibiotics, you know?"

"Yeah, that sucks."

Sean tilted his head at Travis, squinting.

"Did you happen to get any?" he said. "Antibiotics, I mean?"

"Me? Nah."

The squint intensified for a second and let up. Sean looked out toward the street.

"Damn raiders. They'll tear you a new one," he said. He said that a lot. He seemed to either not quite grasp the meaning of this idiom or love it so much that he tried to shoehorn it into every vaguely applicable situation. Travis found both possibilities equally amusing.

He took a drink and Sean followed suit, both lifting jars to their faces, tipping them. They drank sun tea. Lukewarm.

It was a booze day, but Travis didn't want to drink in front of his uninvited guest, didn't want to tip off the mountain of booze and pills and cigarettes he was sitting on. He didn't know if this was out of pure greed or a sense that something like that could come between them. There were no laws out here now. If you wanted something enough, you could take it or even kill for it without much chance of consequences. Travis had something he knew people would kill for. A lot of it. He doubted Sean would be the person to do so, but still...

"You think you'll ever leave here?" Sean said.

"I don't know. You?"

"Think I might have to eventually," he said. "I've got enough to get through this fall and winter, but even if I got a kick ass garden going next spring, I don't know if I could build up enough food for another Michigan winter, you know what I'm sayin'? I mean, sure we could go door to door to scavenge more canned goods, maybe even a lot, but a lot has been looted, and at some point those will run out, too. It just seems smart to go south sooner than later, you know?"

"Yeah, maybe. I guess I'm not worried about it yet."

"Hell, you don't worry about much, do you?"

Travis shrugged.

"That's cool, though," Sean said. "I wish I didn't worry so much. You'd think keeping busy most of the day would prevent anxiety, but it sure doesn't. I can tell you that."

He wondered what Sean even did all day. Dudley Do-

Right-ing must get exhausting, right?

Just leave so I can drink, dickface.

"Hey, though, here's another reason to get out of here," Sean said. "Girls. There are no girls here, man. Not one. The end of the world is a frickin' sausage party, at least in this town."

"That's true."

"I mean, we've got a lot on our plates at the moment, but that's going to become a problem," Sean said. "I haven't gone this long without getting laid since middle school, man."

Christ, what a douche, Travis thought. And a liar. Sean was one of those guys that had no idea how to talk to girls. He endlessly described things that happened in video games or professional wrestling matches to them. They might even be interested in him, but he'd squander it by being horribly, horribly dull or even outright annoying. There was no way he'd been with many girls.

Not that Travis had acquired a lot of sexual experience, either. He'd had sex with three girls. Two of them he'd known throughout school and had long term relationships with. The third was a black girl he met at a party who was inexplicably really into him. She seemed ashamed the next day. Maybe they all were to varying degrees, but the party girl made no attempt to conceal it. He also might have gotten a blowjob from a stripper at Isaac's bachelor party. He didn't remember it very well, but someone made a vague joke about it one time, and when he thought about it, it seemed like a thing that possibly happened somewhere in the drunken blur.

"Seems like you're doing better, though," Sean said. "Those first few days were rough, you know? I kind of thought...”

Travis avoided eye contact as Sean trailed off. He stared straight down at the planks of wood under Sean's sandals, noting the green shade the wood was taking on as the weather wore it down and stained it, wondering if he should try to slap a coat of that waterseal stuff on there to protect it while he still could.

“Look, I kind of thought you weren't going to make it is all,” Sean said. “Maybe I'm full of shit, but it just seemed like you were going this way.”

All Travis wanted to do was look away, but he couldn't. His vision panned along with the movement of Sean's hand as it rose to his head, shaped itself into a finger gun and fired into his open mouth. Sean rocked his head back, his eyes staring up at the chipped paint on the wood overhead, holding still in that head-blown-off position to complete the suicidal pantomime.

Go.

The fuck.

Away.

Travis didn't say anything. He looked at the house across the street, wished there were some way he could teleport there, some way he could will himself into being alone.

Sean popped up from his death pose, and Travis couldn't help but see his massive smile out of the corner of his eye. Sean laughed and wiggled his feet in a way that made his sandals slap against the porch a few times.

“Hey, I'm sorry. Come on, though,” Sean said. “That was funny as hell, and you know it.”

Erin

As her torso skimmed over the back of the couch, Erin wondered how her life had led to this, this belly flop onto a dead man's sofa. Even when she was Izzy's age, when most kids have a touch of daredevil to them, she wouldn't go down the playground slide face first.

Izzy stood on her tip-toes and poked her head through the open window, whispering.

"Hey, Erin."

"What?"

"Watch out for zombies."

Izzy's grin was punctuated by the missing teeth on her top jaw.

Erin squeezed her eyes shut. She'd told Izzy to quit with the zombie stuff. Which had been a mistake. Want an eight-year-old to never quit doing something? Ask them not to do it.

She rolled off the couch and onto the carpet, trying to channel her inner ninja. Quiet. Calm. Not scared shitless. She wiped her hands on her jeans before picking up her only weapon -- a hammer. A real ninja would probably have some kind of sweet sword. A katana, or whatever. Also real ninjas probably didn't get sweaty palms.

She took two steps, brushing past a recliner. She glanced

86

down and gasped.

Izzy thrust her head into the living room.

"What happened?"

Erin waggled the hammer at her, shooing her back out of the window.

"Nothing. Stay there."

The corpse lounged in the chair, stretched out like it was just getting settled in to watch the big game. The flesh was almost completely gone. What was left behind was just skin and bones. Literally.

Erin pushed out a quavering breath. Not the first body she'd seen. And it definitely wouldn't be the last.

She inched forward, hunched over in a defensive position, reaching a hallway with three doors. She paused after every step, trying to listen over the *kerthump-kerthump-kerthump* of her pulse. Flattening herself against the wall, she pressed her fingers against the first door. It was like being on the world's worst game show: *Johnny, tell us what's behind Door Number One!*

Brand new car or brain-eating monster?

She pushed the door open, hammer clutched in front of her, like that would protect her if a zombie came charging out, teeth bared, intent on taking a big old bite out of her noggin.

Now that she thought about it, she was less ninja and more like a squirrel running into the middle of the road and then stopping to face the car bearing down on it. Staring at the grill, probably thinking to itself, "Oh fuck."

Lucky for her, Door Number One was an empty bathroom.

She took another breath and moved on to Door Number Two. As this door swung open, she couldn't help but imagine the homeowner shotgun-blasting her in the face. But this room -- a bedroom -- was empty, too. Same for the office across the hall. Just like every other house they'd been through since they left the FEMA camp, this house was vacant.

Unless you counted the dead.

Back in the living room, she addressed the stiff on the Barcalounger.

The skin was a dark, mottled brown, dried out like leather. And yet so thin she could see through it in spots. She thought of the crispy brown shell left behind after a cicada molts. Maybe that's what happened to this guy. He didn't die. He just shed his old skin and left this behind.

The hair was gone, and so was the nose. The eyes were just empty sockets, but she could still clearly make out ears. The mouth gaped, showing off a set of perfectly straight teeth. Good genes or braces, Erin would never know.

It wore a red shirt and jean shorts, both stained from when the body released its juices. Like a Porterhouse on a hot grill.

She almost retched at the thought of meat in the presence of this stench. Meat was actually one of the few things she didn't miss from Before. Not that their diet was completely devoid of meat, she supposed. The cans of soup had those little gray gristle chunks floating amongst the noodles and broth the color of radioactive waste. Technically chicken.

In the beef stew, a darker shade of gray gristle chunks waded in a pool of gravy, mingling with mushy carrots and potatoes. Supposedly beef.

And then there were the Spaghettios, some of which had the nutritious addition of franks! She didn't even know what kind of meat those spongy pink tube slices were claiming to be. She probably didn't want to know.

It was all for the best anyway, because there wasn't any fresh meat. Unless she wanted to learn to hunt and butcher her own. And she did not, thank you.

She got another whiff of death. It wasn't really the time or the place to be thinking about food, really. And yet food was the whole point of her being there.

Before she headed to the kitchen, Erin grabbed an afghan from the back of the couch. The corpse's shirt said, "I'd Hit That," with a drawing of a golf ball on a tee. Add some sunglasses and a can of beer in a Palm Beach koozie, and it could pass as a bad Halloween prop. She tried her best to keep Izzy from seeing the bodies, fake-looking or not. The bonus here was that she also protected Izzy from seeing that stupid shirt.

She unfurled the blanket like a flag and draped it over the remains, then signaled that Izzy could come in. Izzy squatted on the windowsill and cannonballed onto the couch, plugging her nose because of the smell.

"Hey, Erin."

She started almost every sentence this way, demanding Erin's full attention before she'd actually start the conversation.

"What?"

"Do you think zombies poop?"

"What?"

"They have to, if you think about it," Izzy continued. "Otherwise they'd keep eating brains, and it would keep building up and building up, until eventually they just exploded."

Erin just shook her head. Crossing by the lumpy form under the blanket, she noticed one hand protruding from the edge, the bones looking more like a claw than anything human.

The thing that struck her over and over was how much they all looked the same. Sometimes the clothes tipped off the gender and maybe the age. Like in this case, she'd guess: male, 45 years old and up.

But for the most part, it didn't matter if they had been skinny or fat, black or white, Catholic or Muslim, gay or straight: they all looked the same once they were dead and rotted. It made all the crap that happened in the world -- politics and war and bigotry of any kind -- seem extra stupid and pointless. Now that the world had ended, most stuff from Before seemed stupid and pointless.

Even the little things. Like how she used to spend half an hour on her hair every morning. Washing, blow-drying, flat-ironing. All to get her already-straight-hair a little extra straight. Now she barely looked in the mirror in the mornings.

Or how her mom had a conniption fit if she got a C on her report card. Because all that Trigonometry was really coming in handy in the post-apocalypse. She could have done with a little less tangent and cosecant and a little more How to Build a Fire.

How to Forage for Food.

How to Kill a Zombie.

She whipped through the cabinets in the kitchen, finding a few ketchup packets and a box of strawberry-banana sugar-free Jell-o. She turned to the sack of bones on the recliner.

"Congratulations, sir. You've just won the Worst Food Stash Ever award. The prize is a box of sugar-free Jell-o, which I will accept on your behalf."

Plastic crinkled as she pulled a shopping bag from her pocket and shook it open. She plunked the so-called food into the bag, feeling like Charlie Brown with his trick-or-treat bag full of rocks.

She reminded herself that they didn't actually need the food. They had a pretty good cache back at the house. But it was mostly beans. And she hated beans.

As she passed the lounger, she noticed a box next to the chair. It was red and yellow and proclaimed, "26 Sticks Inside!"

It looked like she and Izzy would soon be snapping into roughly 26 Slim Jims. Hurray.

At least it wasn't more beans.

Her lips pressed together in a line as she read the description of the product: Mild Smoked Meat Snack. They weren't even allowed to call it beef jerky.

"I spoke too soon, sir. Obviously you were a man of impeccable taste."

She tucked the box into the shopping bag with the rest of the haul and made for the door. Now that would have been a useful class: How to Survive the Apocalypse with Nothing but a Box of Slim Jims.

Travis

Hillsboro, Michigan
47 days after

The bike juddered between his legs, his knees absorbing the shock and jolt of every rock he rode over. And then the tires moved back onto asphalt, the ride went back to being smooth, and he sat once more on the bike seat. There were cars piled up here and there on the road, places where he had to ride into the rocks to get around them.

It was Sunday. No booze. No weed. No pills. It was his off day. He had a rotation.

It was unseasonably warm. Some last gasp of summer or something, Travis thought. The sun was a ball of fire in the sky, pushing its heat down onto the back of his neck. He felt like a paper tray of chicken nuggets resting under those infrared lamps in the high school cafeteria. He had sweat through his t-shirt, and the moist fabric clung to his back. If he'd known it would be this hot today, he wouldn't have worn black.

Another group of cars cluttered the street, front ends bashed in and stuck together in some permanent four-way car-kiss. He veered off of the road again to get around them, droplets of sweat gliding down his back when the bumps shook them loose.

From what he and Sean could tell, the EMPs had knocked some of the newest models of cars out—the ones with the electronics and microchips and such—which, along with the general panic, led to a bunch of traffic jams and wrecks that day. He thought the burst of energy would render most every car useless like it did to computers, but apparently not. From what Sean had told him, and he'd apparently confirmed the validity, some of these could have the electronics reset merely by unplugging the battery for 30 seconds and plugging it back in. The ones from the late 90s and early 2000's could be salvaged in many cases, along with anything older. Anything newer than that had fried chips and motherboards, though. They were all junk. Either way, nobody was going to come along and clear all of the streets for him, so Travis stuck to his trusty bicycle for now.

He rode on. No destination in mind. Just a ride. A task. A movement. A stretching of the legs. A rapid beating of the heart. Fresh air pumped into the lungs. Something to pass the time, to fill the time, to kill the time. Something to do to feel human in an empty world.

He pedaled harder and felt the warmth in his gut, the fire in his legs, the perspiration pouring from his chest and back. An idea popped into his mind, a fully formed thought that seemed to take shape in his head all at once as though broadcast from somewhere outside of himself. He thought maybe his life wasn't so different in some weird way, some fundamental way. He pedaled hard with no place to go. Isn't that what he did before? Isn't that what he'd always done? He toiled without purpose. He spun in place, never went anywhere. He'd never found a passion, a sense of place, a guiding light. He just was.

He tried to remember his life, how it felt. He remembered

the events, working at the factory assembling showerheads, the occasional trip to the bar, the occasional night out with a string of girls he never really got to know.

He remembered having his own apartment for a year when he was 19. It was a total dump, a studio with barely enough room to take a deep breath, but it was his, and that was pretty great. Total freedom. Total independence. When his dad had a stroke and couldn't work, his parents asked him to move home to help out, though, so he did.

He remembered moving back in, toting boxes and boxes up the stairs to his old bedroom, hanging up the old posters to make it feel like his again. No more apartment, yeah, but no more bills. That much more money to throw around on narcotics and booze and gifts for those girls he never really got to know.

He remembered these things, yes, this sequence of events that comprised his life. He couldn't really remember how it felt, though. He couldn't remember what he thought about, what he desired, what he worked toward or dreamed of or hoped for. He could watch replays of scenes in his head like playing an old movie, but he couldn't find his way back inside there, inside of his old self.

He breasted a hill and coasted down the other side. Steep as hell. He ran the back of his hand across his forehead as the bike picked up speed, felt the sogginess of his eyebrows. His hand dislodged some of the sweat so it drained down the sides of his face. He tasted the salt of it in the corners of his mouth.

He moved through a rich neighborhood and locked eyes on a house enclosed by a big iron gate that he'd always been curious about. The fence was comprised of thick iron bars and looked out of place, even in an upscale neighborhood like this. He'd always been especially intrigued that the gate in front of the driveway was controlled by a little number pad that could be used to unlock it. It was like something on TV. In high school, he'd witnessed the owner leaning out of the driver's side window of his Lexus to punch in the code, watched the gate roll out of the way automatically, his mind blown.

He always thought the gate attracted attention more than anything else, though. He could easily climb the thing. And anybody looking at it couldn't help but wonder what the owner was trying to protect with this lavish setup. What was he hiding? What would possess him to spend thousands of dollars to have this thing installed? It was basically begging for burglary.

And there were no laws left now. Almost no people at all. His bike ride achieved a destination after all. He'd get a look inside the gate.

His bike overturned in the driveway, he put his hands on the iron bars. He let his eyes scan across the yard, skimming past the two-car garage and basketball hoop to gaze upon the yellow siding of the main building. In most respects, the house itself was nothing special. It looked the same as the other homes in this subdivision, none of which apparently necessed an elaborate gating system. It was a tri-level built in the 1970's that he estimated to be about 1,800 square feet, assuming the basement was finished. It was possibly even modular, though he wasn't certain about that. The one across the street looked like an awfully similar house in a different color, an eggplant or plum shade rather than the light yellow of this house.

He slid his hands off the vertical bars, hopped up to grab the horizontal bar and pulled himself up. His arms shook a little as they hefted his weight, but he didn't find it too difficult. He rested his chest on the cross bar, adjusted his hands to inch his belly up onto the beam, then swung one leg up and over followed by the other, his body doing a 180 in the process. Faced the other way, his abdominals once again rested on the bar. He took a breath and eased himself to the ground.

He took a couple of deep breaths and brushed the dust off the front of his shirt. Yeah. That was too easy. So easy, in fact, that it was almost a disappointment. He felt a little twinge of doubt, some sense that maybe there was nothing interesting in the house after all, but it faded. There must be something here. There must be. Still, if they wanted to keep people out, Travis thought, they probably should have made the fence taller than six feet.

He walked to the house. The wind kicked up, and he realized how sweaty he was as the air swirled over the back of his t-shirt. All of the places where sweat adhered the fabric to his skin went cold, and the wet became bothersome. He shimmied his shoulder blades to try to get the soggy shirt to release from his back, but it didn't work. He picked at it with his thumb and index finger, pinching and pulling the fabric away from his flesh. It snapped back right away, of course, but he thought maybe it felt a little better afterward, at least.

His feet trod over the asphalt, which gave off a considerable amount of heat. He didn't realize how much until he stepped onto the grass and felt the cool there. It was a big relief, a sudden freedom from a smothering force he was only vaguely aware of in the first place. It was strange, though, to wade through this knee high grass. It suddenly didn't feel like he was really outside of someone's house. Looking upon the waving stalks gone to seed from a distance was one thing. He'd gotten used to that. Walking through the tall stuff, feeling the cool of it brush against his calves, was another. He'd push-mowed the lawn at home for something to do when he was drunk, but all of the other yards were well overgrown now. He guessed they would be from now on.

He padded over to the big front window, cupped his hands around his eyes to try to see inside. Dirt smudged the glass, though, and the glare from the sun was pretty bad. He couldn't see much, just sun lit spots on white walls and the vague shape of a rounded doorway leading into the next room. He couldn't even see these things exactly, just some hazy sense of them.

He took a step back and looked up and down the house again. The front door was a few feet to his right. He would try it, and he'd circle around back to try whatever doors were back there, too, but he figured there was a pretty good chance he'd need to break a window to actually get inside.

He moved to the front door, turned the knob. Locked. Shocking. He crossed a bed of gravel, turned the corner and trudged through the tall grass once more. It seemed itchy now. He couldn't help but imagine ticks protruding from the tops of the plant life, disgusting little limbs extended, waiting for something with a beating heart to come along.

The back door popped open as soon as he turned the

knob. He wasn't expecting it and did a stutter step, almost falling into the damn place. He stood up straight, letting go of the knob. The screen door pressed against his back, though he wasn't sure if it was consoling him after the near mishap or trying to help push him down.

He stepped into the house, removing his arm from the screen door to let it close. It took a second for his eyes to adjust to the shaded interior, so the first thing he noticed was that the air felt different, somehow drier on his skin and in his throat as he breathed. He stood in a little back porch area, a four-foot square section of linoleum flooring covered with shoes and boots in various sizes. The basement steps descended in front of him, and the doorway to his left led into the kitchen.

He took the step up and passed the fridge to round the corner. His skin crawled right away as he crossed the threshold into the actual house. He squinted. It looked like a normal kitchen, a nice one even, but some part of him was certain that something was wrong. He stopped, eyes gliding over shiny black countertops, the pile of mail and magazines on the snack bar, the open jar of dry roasted peanuts next to that, as though someone would walk back into the room any minute to continue snacking.

A whiff of something like death hit his nostrils soon as he moved past the snack bar into the living room, but a muted version of it, something much smaller than the odor of the dead boy in the grocery store, he thought. He couldn't quite be sure what to make of it.

White leather furniture filled the living room. Travis might have found that amusing if he wasn't so nervous.

Diagonal bars of sunlight shined through the window pane, making meaningless patterns on the wood floor.

He pressed on, some determination welling in him to see what wonders and horrors this place must hold. He didn't know why this felt necessary, but it did. All part of him wanted was to run right back the way he came and never look at this house again, but all he could do was put one foot in front of the other, advancing whether he liked it or not.

The living room contained nothing of interest, and the same held true for the den or whatever this family might have called the room with the books and the recliner. The bedroom downstairs was similarly empty of intrigue as was the bathroom. That left the upstairs.

Unlike the wood floors stained dark throughout the downstairs, cream carpet covered the steps. Plush. His foot sank down into it and the wood beneath squeaked as he took the first step. He mounted the steps slowly, listened to his heart bang away in his chest. He no longer was sure if he was looking for some rich person's well-protected treasure or the rotten bodies of a dead family. Maybe it was both at once.

The third step from the top moaned as his weight settled on it, a throaty bark of a sound like a walrus begging for fish at Sea World. His hair pricked up again, and he paused, hand clutching the banister. For the first time he considered that someone living might still be here.

Or some*thing.*

He stood there for a long time, three steps from the top, his head swiveling back and forth, straining to listen for any tiny noise.

Nothing. Nothing but the sound of his beating heart.

He climbed the final stairs, feeling somehow vulnerable, almost naked, as he released his grip on the banister and moved into the open space of the hall at the top of the steps. His palms tingled. His chest spasmed breath in and out. His blood roared.

There were four doors up here, two to the left, one to the right, and one straight ahead. All of them were closed but the one at the end of the hall which was opened a crack. He figured the one to the right must be the master bedroom. He may as well start there.

His feet plodded in that direction, the carpet inching up to grip the soles of his shoes with each step before releasing them with some reluctance.

The smell hit as soon as the door squeaked out of the frame, a musty version of the roadkill smell at the grocery store. And then something charged at him, a dark blur, its movements familiar but not quite human.

He froze.

The dog hurled itself at him, tongue lolling out of its mouth. Its paws slapped at his knees as it pogoed straight up and down, its tail wagging with great gusto. It was part greyhound, he thought, based on the large rib cage to tiny waist ratio, a 20 pound blur of red fur that didn't hold still long enough to really get a good look at, though from the glimpses of its face he got, it looked like it was smiling.

"Hey dog," he said, brushing at its head.

It dropped its feet to the floor and pushed its head into his legs, smearing its eyes on his jeans. That's when he realized how emaciated it was. Every rib was visible. It was starving. He patted the side of its barrel chest.

With the moment of crazy fear gone, his senses faded back in, and the smell hit again. Death.

He finally let his gaze dance across the rest of the room. Dead bodies sprawled in all directions. Two lay on the bed, adults, judging from the size of them, though they were badly decomposing and torn up pretty good. Their heads seemed to have congealed bloody smears instead of human faces. Two children folded over each other in a pile of rotting limbs on the floor. From his angle, he could see that the legs had been partially eaten.

He scowled as he thought this over. If they were stuck in a closed room, how did they...

He looked down at the dog, its front legs still hopping off of the ground over and over, sometimes going into alternating stomps like it was playing piano. He couldn't see blood around its mouth, but he knew. He knew that it did what it had to do to live on for days after the people passed on. Claw marks gashed the door and the wood trim around it. It had tried to get out, too.

And then the smell was too much, and he was running away. Tears filled his eyes as he hurried outside. Not tears of sadness. Involuntary tears in response to the noxious fumes. He leaned over the tall grass, dry heaving a few times. He stayed in that hunched over position for a long time as the nausea faded. At some point he realized the dog was next to him, its tail wagging like mad.

He looked up to find the world unchanged, unmoved. Heat distortion shimmered above the blacktop. The air was still.

Erin

There was something different about this house. She could feel it.

Erin's shoes scuffed across the sidewalk as they made their way up to the front door. Golden fronds of overgrown grass reached over the path, brushing her knees as she passed.

A small white butterfly fluttered near her face, and she batted it away. If only she could get rid of the ones in her stomach that way.

What did Izzy call them again?

Her eyes drifted over to Izzy, brown curls bobbing up and down with each step. The kid lifted a dirty sleeve and swiped it across her face, wiping at her nose.

What the hell was she gonna do with this kid? The booger-smearing was the least of her concerns. She was sixteen. Not old enough to take care of some eight-year-old kid.

Bubbleguts. Instead of "butterflies in the stomach", Izzy called them bubbleguts.

Erin had bubbleguts.

But why now?

"Rub… barb," Izzy said. "What's Rub-Barb?"

Erin stopped at the base of the stairs leading up to the house. "Huh?"

Izzy pointed to a white sign just barely visible above the jungle of the lawn. Erin read the big black hand-painted letters, then laughed.

"Rhubarb."

Izzy repeated the word, overemphasizing the first syllable the way Erin had done.

"ROO-barb."

Izzy's head bobbed forward like a bird when she said it.

"You look like a chicken," Erin said.

She made wings with her arms and flapped them a few times, jerking her head forward and saying, "ROObarb, ROObarb."

Izzy swatted at her arm.

"That's how *you* said it!" She wrinkled her nose and wiped at it with the back of her hand. "So what is it?"

The wood of the stair rail was warm from the sun under Erin's hand. She gripped it as she made her way up the steps.

"It's a fruit," she said, then paused. "Actually, I guess it would really be considered a vegetable. It sort of looks like celery, except it's bright red. And it's really sour."

"Why would you eat that?"

"You have to add a lot of sugar to make it taste good. My grandma used to make these mini custard tarts with rhubarb on top."

A surge of saliva filled her mouth at the thought of the delicious little pastries. She could go for about ten of those right about now.

When she reached the door, she paused and looked back at Izzy.

"You've really never had rhubarb? Strawberry rhubarb

pie?"

Izzy's shoulders quirked into a shrug.

Erin placed a hand on the door knob. She gave it a twist, and it resisted.

Locked.

There was a stupid part of her brain that was glad it was locked. It hoped all the doors and windows were locked. Because, her brain said, then she wouldn't have to go in.

But they always found a way in.

A try at the sliding window at the back of the house was more fruitful. It was sort of surprising how many people took the time to lock their doors, only to leave a window unlatched.

She peeked inside and noted the washer, dryer, and utility sink. The door of the laundry room stood open, but she could only see the blank wall of the hallway beyond.

The metal frame squealed as she slid the window all the way open. A neon green bucket she found in the breezeway between the house and the garage made a perfect stool.

She perched on the bucket, one hand on either side of the window frame. Izzy stood behind her, hand glued to her forehead to shade her eyes from the sun.

"You know the drill, right? You wait here until I tell you it's clear-"

Izzy rolled her eyes and let her tongue loll out of her mouth.

Erin sighed.

"Fine, then you tell me the rest."

"Stay out of sight. Be quiet. Look both ways before crossing the street. Don't talk to strangers." Her voice took on a mocking tone as she progressed.

"Smart ass," Erin said, then hoisted herself through the window and into the house.

Izzy whispered from behind her.

"Language!"

Once Erin was inside, she just squatted there for a moment, letting her eyes adjust to the dimness. Listening for any sounds from inside the house.

She rose and took three silent steps to the door. At the threshold, she waited a beat and then darted her head out, glancing quickly to the left.

Before the hallway veered to the right and out of view, there was an open archway leading into a den.

Her head swung out again, this time to the right.

Two more doors. One open, which she liked. One closed, which she hated.

She cleared the den first, just stepping to the edge of the room and scanning it from left to right. So far, so good.

Next came the open door, which turned out to be a small bathroom with floral wallpaper that was certainly not of this century.

Now for the closed door, which upon further inspection wasn't all the way closed. It stood open just a crack, not enough to see in. Erin inched forward, stopping shy of the particle board and not quite pressing her ear to it. Not breathing. Just listening.

She heard nothing.

It didn't make her feel any better. That same nagging feeling was there, whispering doubts in her ear.

She counted to three and gave the door a little push. The

hinges let out a shriek loud enough to wake any of the dead that weren't already awake. Instinctively, she threw herself forward into a crouch, bracing herself.

Nothing happened.

She let out her breath and stood straight again.

A bar of sunlight shone through the crack between the curtains, illuminating a large four poster bed, dressing table, and a privacy screen with an Asian motif.

She sniffed the air.

That's what it was that kept bothering her. The smell. For once, it wasn't the reek of death. Which was… nice. But weird. Had she really become so desensitized to the grimness of it all that smelling something pleasant instead of something foul was setting off warning bells?

She breathed it in. God, it was so familiar.

This smell was something safe. Something that reminded her of childhood.

She stopped and closed her eyes. Inhaled. Let it percolate. If she tried to force the memory, it wouldn't come. She had to let it bob to the surface on its own.

She cleared her mind, letting the smell take over.

Pipe smoke? No, that was a sweeter smell.

Shag carpet under bare feet? Close. But that was a feeling, not a smell.

Light filtering through louvered windows in the morning. Again, not a smell.

But wait.

Shag carpet, pipe smoke, wood slats over the windows? Grandma and Grandpa's house.

Boom.

She took another breath, nodding.

Mothballs.

She couldn't believe she hadn't come up with it right away. It was obvious from the decor that this was an old lady's house.

She poked her nose into the closet and behind the privacy screen- better safe than sorry- before deeming the ground floor all clear. At the dressing table, she rifled through the jewelry, picking out the stuff that looked like it would be worth something. She stacked bracelets and watches onto her wrists and rings onto her fingers. Three necklaces were big enough that she could just loop them over her head. The rest she tucked into her pocket.

Back at the window, she helped Izzy climb in. Hoisting under her skinny kid arms, Erin lowered her to the ground.

"Stay here until I'm done checking upstairs."

One of the steps creaked as she put her weight on it. She paused, listening for anything stirring above, then continued up the stairway.

The upper level held two more bedrooms, another bathroom, plus the kitchen and living room. All empty.

She was just about to call out to Izzy when she got a whiff of something. And this time it wasn't mothballs.

She took a few steps, trying to pinpoint where the smell was coming from. A pocket door, just off the kitchen. She'd missed it before.

Looping a finger through the brass latch, she closed her eyes and said a little prayer.

The door groaned as she slid it aside, and she inhaled sharply.

"Holy shit."

Baghead

Rural Oklahoma
9 years, 126 days after

He woke, startled to feel the car seat vibrating below him, to hear its engine humming, the Focus moving somehow as he slept. He sat forward and pulled the top of the bag back so the holes lined up with his eyes, revealing Delfino in the driver's seat of the Delta 88 instead of the Focus.

Right. He leaned back in his seat, let his neck go limp so his skull flopped against the headrest. Jesus, it felt wrong to fall asleep so quickly in the presence of a stranger like that, especially with everything that was going on. He'd known this hired driver for less than an hour, and their journey hadn't even officially started yet. For all Bags knew, Delfino could be one of the five.

He looked out the window at the weed pocked sand all around them, watched the wind spiral up little clouds of dust and let them fall.

"Mind if I ask you something?" Delfino said.

"Go ahead."

"This is about the Hand of Death thing, right? You needing a ride and all, I mean."

Bags wheeled his head around, one hand scratching at his chest.

"Where'd you hear about that?"

"Hey, come on now. Assassins get sent out with

instructions to kill a man by holy order? People talk about that kind of thing. Damn, man. It's all over the place."

Bags looked away again, his head facing the window but his eyes not focusing so they only took in a sandy colored smear.

"Hand of Death is some serious shit. Why do you think Father wants you dead?"

"Because he doesn't like what's in my books."

"Not a fan?"

"He's threatened by them."

"Why would a bunch of letters from the old days threaten him?"

"You'd need to ask him that."

Delfino pulled out another cigarette, lit it.

"Ol' Father's kind of got it made, eh?" he said.

"What do you mean?"

"The People's Temple, you know? I'm sure you've heard the crazy stories. His thirteen wives. Living up in a mansion with generators, fucked out of his mind on pills most of the time, and yet thousands of people are willing to work and bleed and die for him if need be."

"Same as any other cult leader, I'd say."

Delfino puffed on his cigarette, smoke rolling out of his nostrils as he talked.

"I guess you're right. It's hard to remember some of that stuff. Here's my question, though. Why bother with the Hand of Death? If Father wants someone dead, why not just call it the death penalty and make it happen. Why make the extra rule about five assassins and the stipulation that if the accused survives all five attempts, it's God passing judgment the other way?"

"Well, I think people like that kind of thing. Father is an entertainer first and foremost. I think with a lot of this stuff he's just entertaining himself. Making life and death a game, you know? I don't know about the particular origin of the idea, though. I always assumed he saw it in a samurai movie or something."

"Have any of them come at you yet? The assassins, I mean."

"No."

"Damn. Five to go. Well, the first one is usually a puss, right? They save the mega badasses for the fourth and fifth slots."

"Sometimes. It seems pretty random other times. From what I hear, anyway."

Delfino took a puff off of his cig and ashed it on the floor.

"So here's the big question: If the People's Temple is out to kill you, why are you paying me a bunch of cash to drive you straight to them?"

Baghead shrugged his shoulders, and it wrinkled up the sides of his bag, so he smoothed them out with a few strokes.

Mitch

Shock drowned everything out. He held motionless, almost catatonic. His hands and knees rested on the kitchen floor. His head hung beneath his shoulders, neck craned toward his torso so his field of vision was filled with his heaving chest, his open mouth panting for breath like a dehydrated dog. He blinked a few times, eyelids fluttering, and let his gaze fall on his wrist. Blood streaked down from the wound, two rivulets of scarlet tracing down the back of his hand like red rain running down a window.

That was it. That little scratch on his arm, skin broken just enough to draw a little blood, that was how it would all end for him. He pictured Janice's ankle, black tendrils snaking away from the wound like smoke running beneath her skin. He knew the same would happen to him, that it wouldn't be long.

He closed his mouth, tried to breathe through his nostrils. At first his breath was ragged, a little panicked. His head went all light and tingly, but he focused and reigned it in. Deep breaths, in and out.

His arms shook a little. Physically, he went through the motions of panic, but in a crazy way, his mind was clearer now than ever. A meandering life suddenly had an end game, a purpose, even a ticking clock with a fairly precise deadline.

He had somewhere between 24 and 36 hours. His life was forfeit, yes, but a path to redemption remained open to him: he had to try to set his children up so they could make it, to give them whatever he had left to give. That was all the mattered now. It wasn't everything. It was the only thing.

For a guy about to die, he almost felt lucky. We all have an expiration date, but most people don't get to see it. Death sneaks up on them or the years get away from them. They miss their chance to correct their flaws, to make things right. He had that chance.

He leaned back, his hands peeling free from the linoleum with a sound like a cellophane wrapper being peeled open. He sat back in an upright position. His breathing was under control now.

He felt alive.

His mission was clear. That thing still roamed in the basement, however, his blood on its breath. He would need to take care of that first. Enough screwing around, though. No more old fashioned tools. He was going to handle this the Ted Nugent way: shoot it in the face.

The gun felt right in his fingers. They both did, but for now he was handling the Berretta M9. It was all black, had a classy look to it, he thought. Something about the Glock, on the other hand, made it look a little like a toy to him. But it didn't feel like a toy in his hand. It felt right, too. They both had a nice heft to them.

The light turned green, so he flopped the firearm back onto the passenger seat and drove. The guns clattered into each other as the car lurched forward, a little metallic sound that reminded him of a sound effect in one of those video games where you stalk from room to room, laying waste to every human being you come across. Maybe it was like the sound of reloading. He wasn't sure.

He drummed on the wheel at another stoplight, willing himself to keep his hands away from the metal in the seat next to him. The sun had raised itself higher than when he'd last looked upon it. It must be creeping up on noon already. Time flies when you're getting bit by a goddamn zombie, right?

Shopping for guns was an odd experience since he didn't know anything about them. On the ride over, he had planned to get a shotgun, had pictured himself wielding it in the basement, disintegrating the thing's face with a load of buckshot. But as he got within a few blocks of the pawn shop, it occurred to him that maybe the kids wouldn't be able to handle the recoil.

He was thinking handguns after that, but he didn't know where to start. The guy at the pawn shop told him these would be the easiest guns to get ammo for, no matter what might happen. He told him they were reliable, sturdy, durable. He told him he could use them to hammer nails all day, and they'd still shoot straight. That sounded good enough to him. The guy had a gun holstered at his side as he imparted these nuggets, so he must know something.

Another stoplight. It seemed like there were a ton of pedestrians out, all streaming in the opposite direction of his car. He watched the swells of humanity flowing on both sides of the street. It reminded him of disaster footage on TV, of flash flood water gushing down city streets, picking up cars and taking them along for the journey.

He wondered what the zombie was doing right now, what it was thinking. Did it even think? Did it have any notion that he'd be back? He pictured it in the basement, stumbling from one corner to the next, waiting for some sign of life to pounce upon.

I've got your sign of life right here, he thought, petting the gun. Then he realized that this didn't really make sense and laughed.

And then he remembered that he wouldn't actually have any signs of life for much longer... but there was no time to think about that now.

He took a left onto Vine Street and noticed smoke a few blocks in the distance, thick black clouds rolling into the sky. As he drove up on the source, he found an apartment building fully engulfed in flames, fire reaching out of the windows on most every floor. A group of people watched it from across the street, hands cupped around their eye sockets to shield them from the light. It had to have been burning for some time to get this big, but there were no police or firemen around. He knew things were starting to break down, but he didn't realize it was this bad.

He accelerated out of instinct. Just as he began to wonder why he was doing so, he watched a teenage kid throw a brick through the front window of a stereo shop. The glass spider webbed, white lines spreading out from the hole at the point of impact. It hesitated like that just long enough to remind him of a cartoon featuring breaking ice under some doomed character's feet, and then the whole thing collapsed. People streamed out of the door with arms full of amplifiers, tweeters, and subwoofers. Mitch realized it was already being looted before the window dropped, realized that all of the stores around him were under siege, that he'd driven into a riot.

Kids cradled stolen candy in their arms. Baseball bats and other blunt objects maimed the windshields and rearview mirrors of cars that had lost the parking spot lottery.

Goosebumps rippled over his forearms and thighs. Fear gurgled in his gut, lifting acid to the back of his throat so he could taste it. Under the fright, though, some animal part of him was exhilarated by the violence of it all. It made his eyes open wider, made his posture right itself, made his breath tingle in and out of his throat, made him feel more alive. That surprised him. Was that a weird response? He didn't know. It wasn't violence against people so far as he could see. It was violence against property. He wasn't in favor of it, of course, but there were worse things people could do.

Without thinking, he reached over and pulled one of the guns into his lap, kept his hand on it. He glanced down to confirm that it was the Beretta. Good. Maybe he had a favorite after all.

He sped through the next several blocks, endless mayhem unfolding along the sides of the street. He saw no more fire, but he did see more broken glass, more people toting flat screens and jewelry and one guy with an arm full of what looked like chicken patties from a fast food restaurant.

And then he saw the beating, saw the crowd circling, the rise and fall of a crowbar and a piece of pipe and hands and feet, all pummeling a figure on the ground of which he could only make out the limp legs wearing blue jeans, the motionless feet wearing what looked to be an expensive pair of Nikes.

Everything slowed down. Reality filtered down to just that image of weapons and fists raining down on a human being gone totally still. Bashing it. Bludgeoning it. Stomping it. The faces of the attackers looked indistinct. They seemed to tuck back into each other's shadows, to blur together. A bunch of brows furrowed into the same aggressive shape became the only detail he could discern.

The beating stretched on for a long time. Too long. Thinking back on it, he wouldn't be sure if he subconsciously slowed down the car to watch it or the sense of time slowing was solely due to his perception shifting into slow motion. Either way, it couldn't have been a very long time — just a few seconds, most likely -- but it seemed like several minutes went by.

And then the figure beneath the attackers was still no longer. The fallen man bucked his hips, his torso jerking partially upright. The attackers fanned out. They backpedaled a couple of steps in all directions, their movements so perfectly in unison that it either looked like they were performing a synchronized routine, or that they were somehow knocked back physically, like some force field suddenly repelled them.

Their victim looked like a dead man somehow sitting up, like a top quality special effects makeup. His forehead was dented, partially caved in. An exposed section of skull above his right eye looked like a cracked eggshell. Blood and bruises shrouded the rest of his face in reds and purples. His eyes looked in different directions. He bucked again, his body jerking in a way that seemed involuntary, and then he remained still, his expression blank, as the attackers circled him again, adjusting their grips on their various weapons and inching closer.

When the victim's head leaned back unnaturally and his arm looped out in a pathetic attempt at grabbing one of the attackers, Mitch released the gun to bring a hand to cover his mouth. The motion was somehow familiar, the rigid neck, the inarticulate movements of the fingers, the dim look about the face. It was like Janice, or whatever Janice had become, at least. This thing was back from the dead. Perhaps that's why they were beating on it in the first place.

One of the attackers stepped forward and swung the crowbar like a baseball bat, his legs and hips rotating into the swing with explosive force. The bar struck the eggshell skull, a solid connection knocking it to the side with a high-pitched sound like a tossed horseshoe colliding with the steel stake. A few pieces of chipped skull fell and skittered across the ground like Chiclets.

The zombie lurched, flailing arms cinching around an ankle before the crowbar guy had a chance to retreat. It brought its head forward, moving toward the captured leg, mouth open wide. The other men swelled around the attacker, tried to help him rip free of its grip. One guy kicked at the thing, but it didn't help.

Mitch watched through the screen of the passenger side window, suddenly acutely aware that he was one step removed from this scene. He found himself focusing on that eggshell forehead. He couldn't see the actual bite, couldn't see the teeth sink into the back of the man's calf. The leg shielded the face from his view. So he watched the broken skull bob just above the ankle, heard the man's scream hit a falsetto note, saw the others stumble backward, all of their aggressive expressions morphing into terrified ones.

And then it was all gone. Behind him. Shrinking in the rearview mirror. The car moved on. Time seemed to speed back up, and other flickering images of violence played out on the street side, though none were quite so dramatic.

Travis

Hillsboro, Michigan
48 days after

    Clouds blocked the sun and leached some of the color out of everything. He walked down the sidewalk in this muted version of the world, and the dog trotted along just behind him. It felt strange to have a companion now. He looked down, made eye contact with her and watched her tail beat faster. Some part of him couldn't believe she was still here.

    When they'd gotten back the night before, he'd taken a bowl of oatmeal out to the porch and fed her, gave her a little peanut butter for dessert. He didn't figure she'd want to be inside after all of that time trapped, so he didn't try to get her to do that. Instead he sat with her on the swing until it was dark and she'd been asleep a long while. He went to bed, expecting her to be gone when he woke, but the next morning she was sitting up on the swing.

    Now he needed dog food, and he knew where to look.

    The Caslers lived four houses down. Everyone in the neighborhood knew their dogs well enough, three big coon hounds that made noise at all hours. They barked and howled and stood on their hind legs to rattle the chain linked fence of their pen. About twice a week they made weird throaty noises that Travis thought sounded like a man turning into a werewolf.

    He'd watched them leave. It must have been five or six

days after he buried his parents, weeks ago now. The whole family had been there: The father with the tree trunk legs, perpetually sweating through polo shirts. The mother with big hair that Travis presumed hadn't changed a bit since her senior pictures circa 1991. The high school aged son, scrawny and pale. They packed most of their things into their SUV, much of it in those big Rubbermaid bins. A few boxes went into the trunk of the son's hatchback, and the last step was coaxing the three dogs into the back seat of the subcompact, which they accomplished with some difficulty.

Anyway, Travis didn't think there was any way they could have loaded all of the dog food they must have had on hand. Time to pillage that shit.

He cut through the yard toward the front door. He felt funny as soon as he set foot on their property, like someone would see him, and he'd somehow get in trouble. He hesitated, taking a little half step and pausing. Nothing happened of course.

He knocked on the front door, an empty gesture, he knew, and tried the handle. Locked, of course. Gauzy curtains covered all of the windows. He thought about circling the house to try the other doors, but some part of him wouldn't have it.

There was no point in pretending any of these formalities were necessary. He had watched all of the people die or leave, could still see many of their corpses bloating around town. This was just an empty building in an empty city in an empty world. He picked up a rock about the size of a softball from a decorative circle of stones surrounding a bird bath. He cupped it in his hand in front of him, hefting it up and down a few times to get a feel for its weight. Satisfied, he chucked it through the big front window.

The rock punched a hole in the glass and flew straight through, ruffling the gauzy curtain and disappearing. There was something very cannonball-like about all of it. The sound of the glass was percussive. It rang up and down the street like a giant bell. The dog flinched, and Travis couldn't help but swivel his head around, looking for some authority figure to pop up and yell at him.

Nothing happened, of course.

He threw another and another, big triangular shards of glass falling and shattering moments after the cannon balls knocked out their circular holes. The window frame was now the house's shocked mouth, open wide. The dog cowered behind his legs, back hunched, tail tucked.

"It's OK," he said. "No more rocks."

Her back straightened a little, though she still looked concerned.

He looked up at the house. A row of jagged glass fangs still hung from the top of the opening, but the bottom was clear. He boosted himself up to the sill and pulled himself inside head first, hands reaching into the shade to find the floor and secure his landing, managing to avoid the glass as much as possible.

He got his feet under him, squatting with rocks and broken bits sprinkled all over the dark wood floor below. The quiet in here seemed pronounced after all of that exploding glass. It made him uneasy. All he could imagine was taking a single step forward to have something pounce at him, attaching itself to his face with two rows of claws or a maw full of teeth before he even had time to flinch. He moved his foot a little, glass grinding into the wood. Nothing responded to the sound. Of course, he knew no one was here. Sean was the only person he'd seen on this block in weeks. Still, he couldn't quite shake that uneasy feeling.

He shuffled forward a few paces, out of the glass and rocks, still squatting on the floor. He found himself in a living room, a nice one with brown leather furniture that looked like it belonged in a shrink's office on TV. The space still felt lived in. A nest of pillows and two rumpled afghans coiled into a pile on the couch, like some place a creature would bed down. A nature magazine lay open on the coffee table, opened to an article about endangered jungle species. He could imagine someone emerging from the hallway any second to curl up in the blankets and resume reading, but another part of his brain knew they wouldn't, of course.

He looked to the front door, considered letting the dog in, but he thought it better to get in and out as fast as he could. He wasn't sure she'd be too keen on going inside any building so soon after nearly starving to death trapped in a room. Besides, she would wait for him out front, he figured.

He crouch-walked forward, still paranoid enough to be unwilling to stand upright, as though staying low somehow protected him. The air felt thicker as he moved away from the window. Heavy. Dank. A musty smell assailed him right away as he reached the kitchen door. It reminded him of rotting fruit and mold mixed with some sour smell like pickle juice.

Something small crunched when he took a step onto the gray and brown flecked ceramic tiles of the kitchen floor. He looked down. Nothing. Another step brought about another

123

tiny crunch, rocking his foot from heel to toe slowly revealed a series of miniature pops and cracks. What the hell?

Oh. There were no brown flecks on the gray tiles. Instead dead fruit flies covered the floor. They looked bigger than any he'd seen, almost the size of fat mosquitoes, and apparently they'd been here long enough to get crispy as hell. Sheesh. They must have made quite a swarm at their peak, he thought.

He stepped again, the moving air around him pushing fruit flies along like an invisible broom. Bowls of shriveled bananas sat on the counter. He pulled open a few cabinets and drawers to reveal cereal boxes, utensils, spices and a lot of empty spaces.

The pantry held what he wanted: a big tupperware bin of kibble, mostly full. He picked it up, finally standing. As he left the kitchen, he again imagined something leaping on him as he passed through the doorway, but he was fine.

Mitch

Bethel Park, Pennsylvania
42 days before

He watched himself in the bathroom mirror, watched his hand lift the gun to eye level, watched his finger slide to the trigger. He squinted, aimed for the reflection of his face, right between the eyes. He squeezed the trigger and nothing happened because of the safety, so he made a little gun noise by popping his lips, did a pretend recoil where he tipped the barrel up. He felt the need to do this, to run through some kind of mental repetition so that when he got down in the basement, got face to face with this dead thing, he'd know what to do. He'd have something, some kind of ingrained sense or maybe even muscle memory, to fall back on if he panicked.

He ran through it one more: ready, aim, pretend to fire. Satisfied, he lowered the gun and nodded. He looked like hell, purple under his eyes, puffiness to his cheeks. He considered peeling back his sleeve to get a look at his wound, but the image of Janice's ankle flashed in his head, the missing chunk, the smoky tendrils fouling her flesh. He shuddered. Not now. He couldn't look. He'd take care of this first.

He stepped out of the bathroom and paced back and forth in the hallway a few times, gun dangling at his side, fingers on the opposite hand brushing back and forth over his lips. The day was creeping into the afternoon now. The kids would be home from school soon, and then the real work would begin. He couldn't think of that now, though, couldn't look even an hour into the future. It was too overwhelming.

He still had that bile taste in the back of his throat, that film of acid his nervous belly had fluxed up into his mouth. The taste reminded him of cafeteria pizza when he was a school kid, that grease that sat in the pieces of pepperoni that contorted into cups as the edges cooked faster than the middle. Maybe it was the grease mixed with the cheap sauce.

All right. OK. No more bullshit. Time to do it.

He walked to the basement, opened the door. His hand moved toward the light switch and stopped. It was already on. Right. He'd never turned it off during his post-bite retreat.

OK, that was OK, he told himself, trying to will himself to not be upset. The truth was that he didn't like it, though. Didn't like the surprise. Didn't like feeling out of control before the encounter even started.

He hesitated there, his toes resting on the threshold. He looked down into the chamber below, watched the strobe effect of the fluorescent light flickering around on the floor. He saw no movement down there, heard nothing. Without thinking, he brought the grip of the gun to his forehead, used the rough part to scratch between his eyebrows, the metal cool on his skin.

He started down the steps, pressing forward with some urgency though he was light enough on his feet to remain near silent. His chest heaved, some instinctual pre-aggression deep-breathing thing kicking in, like a boxer sucking wind just before a match starts. He had to really concentrate to keep his respiration quiet.

His feet touched down on concrete, and his head swiveled to locate his target. His eyes flicked their way around the perimeter of the room, both hands on the gun with a twitchy thumb more than ready to flick the safety off.

Nothing.

What the hell?

Could it have gotten out? He tried to imagine it, shoulders hunched, shambling up the steps, hooked fingers somehow opening the door. Impossible. Right? It had to be impossible.

His chest started heaving again, faster this time, shallower. The word "hyperventilation" popped into his head. He stopped himself, forced a long, slow inhale upon his diaphragm, felt his chest get tighter and tighter as his ribcage expanded. Then he let it out all slow, felt the panic subside a touch. Then another deep breath, the expansion of his chest fixing his posture. He squinted as he exhaled, felt the tension ease a little bit more in his neck and shoulders.

OK. He made himself focus. He held his breath and let his eyes do one more rotation around the room, forcing them to take it slow this time.

There. He could see its arm sticking out from behind the folded up ping pong table. The dumbass thing had wedged itself up against the wall. He doubted this was out of some clever attempt to hide. It was just an idiot animal snuffling around at random, falling into motionless dazes like this for long stretches.

He took the barrel of the gun into his left hand so he could wipe the sopping palm of his right on his jeans. It was still moist, but it was better.

He took a deep breath, making no attempt to be quiet

127

now.

"All right, fucker," he said. "Come and get it."

The thing banged into the ping pong table a couple of times before it made it out into the open. It shuffled toward him, its head and shoulders leaned so far forward that it seemed to be falling and catching itself over and over with choppy steps, legs staggering to keep up with the thrust of forward momentum.

He raised his arm just like he did in the bathroom upstairs. He aimed, flipped the safety off and fired. The Berretta blazed and popped. The first shot missed, the bullet thwacking into the concrete wall, but he did it again right away, and the second one hit dead center in the forehead, spraying brains out of the back of the skull. The projectile mess hit the ping pong table with a wet slap, smearing red across it like someone had flung the contents of a full jar of slightly runny strawberry jam at it. The impact stood the body straight up for a split second, and then it bent at the knees and went down, folding up into something small on the ground.

His ears rang. His hands tingled. His head got light. A rush of euphoria came over him then, a feeling of accomplishment like none he'd ever felt. He couldn't fully embrace it, though. He couldn't quite celebrate, even for a second. Maybe he wasn't quite as useless as he'd always feared, but he was finding it out too late. His wife was gone, and he was heading for the same destination rapidly. No victory could erase those things.

He grit his teeth, the muscles in his jaw bunching and unbunching in rapid succession.

He still had something, though. He would help those

boys. He would make one thing right, as right as he could make it, anyway. But first he would eat lunch.

He figured this turkey sandwich wouldn't be his last meal, but it was close enough in a way. He had no reason to go light on the mayo now, no concerns about piling the meat as high as he could get it or controlling his portion of potato chips. He filled a small bowl with pickles. It was a delicious meal. It reminded him of being young. Before Janice, when he lived on his own, he ate sandwiches like this often, chugged Pepsi all day. It was a simpler time. There were less apocalypses going on.

Though the meal was satisfying on some gluttonous level, he found himself growing more and more restless as he ate. Sating his hunger finally left his mind able to wander to other things, to mull over his wife's death. His feelings on the subject seemed to be coming unblocked, to be welling up from beneath the surface, though they still seemed somewhat muted.

Instead of the anticipated sorrow or defeat, however, he found only the heat of rage crawling up to flush his face and make the blood vessels in his temples throb. He felt the sting of it in his eyes and in his teeth, in all of the muscles in his face gone taut.

Some part of him wanted to flip the table over, sweep the condiments and pickle jar off of the counter to send a rushing wave of pickle juice and mustard and broken glass over the linoleum. Then he could go through the rest of the house trashing it. Exploding vases, shattered mirrors, holes punched in drywall.

He felt duped. Like he could suddenly see through the cracks in reality and make out the lack of light underneath.

What was reality, really? Society had created this paradise of distraction, built on novelty and convenience and bright lights and loud noises. But it was all emptiness. Filling his life with TV, movies, video games, sports, treating those like the things that actually mattered. At some point, Mitch thought, it became hard to remember what was real, what was important.

What was it all a distraction from, though? Death, right? Death was something that happened on TV to the bad guys. It was a tragic ending of a Lifetime movie. It wasn't supposed to happen to him, to his wife, maybe even his kids. How could that be how things worked?

They sold him a better reality, made it seem like the paradise of novelty could be his forever if he played along, that he could connect to some painlessness, some eternal bliss at some unspecified future date. But it was a ponzi scheme. He did his part. He paid with his money and effort and time, giving his life for what? For nothing. For sitcoms and superhero movies and football and beer that tastes great and is less filling.

This was the long con. It kept him obedient and productive, made it so death could blindside him.

Christ on a crutch. Is that the best life can be? Distract yourself for as long as you can.

Just as he crunched down on his last bite of pickle, something creaked behind him. The front door opened and closed. He froze, his mouth stuck in a strange mid-chew. All he could picture was dead Janice stumbling through the doorway to head out on the town.

He turned back to look. No zombies. Instead, Kevin and Matt were taking their shoes off, hanging up their coats. Was it so late already? He glanced at his phone. 1:26 PM. The kids walked into the kitchen.

Kevin's long face resembled his mother, though he had red hair and paler skin than she did. Matt's round face showed that he still had some of that little kid chub to him, and his hair was so blond it sometimes looked white in the right light.

"School get out early?" Mitch said, his mouth still half full of pickle and turkey and bread.

They nodded.

"There's a riot," Matt said. He delivered this bit of news in a matter of fact way that seemed funny to Mitch. He was 8. He probably barely knew what a riot was.

"A riot, huh?" Mitch said, a smile curling on the corners of his mouth.

He wanted to get the kid to expound upon this notion, to get him to explain his idea of a riot. But then he pictured the rise and fall of the crowbar and the piece of pipe, the eggshell skull bobbing as the mouth closed in on the ankle, and it didn't seem as funny anymore.

He ruffled Matt's hair, which he knew the kid hated. The boy made a face, his top lip curling and protruding so that it almost touched his nose. He jerked away from his father and smoothed his blond hair back down with a rigid hand.

"You hear from Mom?" Kevin said, digging a root beer out of the fridge.

Mitch pictured the dead body in the basement. He'd

thrown a scrap of tarp over it, but it wasn't big enough to cover the whole thing. The feet stuck out at the bottom, one pink Chuck Taylor and one bare heel touching concrete, the ankles limp so the toes pointed out. Apparently the thing had lost a shoe stumbling around in zombie mode.

"No," he said. "I'll try to call your Grandpa again."

He scrolled to the number in his contact list, brought the phone to his ear. His heart felt like it was beating in the base of his neck. He was paranoid that the boys would try to go into the basement, though there was no reason for them to do so. All he could picture was one of them and then the other twisting that door knob while the phone rang and rang.

"No answer," he said. He set the phone on the table. This was his third attempt at calling. He'd hoped to convince the grandparents to take custody of the boys more or less, and he'd help all of them get set up at the cabin. The well with the hand pump, the wood burning stove and ample lumber supply. That was the place to be.

Kevin sipped at his root beer, lines creasing his forehead. He was the worrier of the two brothers.

"I'm sure everything is fine," Mitch said. "Don't worry about it. We'll head over there in a bit."

The room fell quiet. Kevin didn't seem convinced.

Jesus, should I just tell them? Don't I have to at some point?

"Hey, listen. I got you guys something," he said.

They stood in a line in the back yard, the sun shining down on them and clouds scuttling across a blue sky. When you looked up at that, Mitch thought, you had no sense that the world was in the process of being flushed down the crapper.

A line of bottles and cans formed a row on the picnic table at the back of the yard, awaiting execution.

"Cover your ears," Mitch said.

He watched to make sure they did as he said, and then he pointed the gun at the array of targets, settling his sights on a tomato soup can. He squinted one eye and fine-tuned his aim until he felt good, flicked off the safety, exhaled for a beat and squeezed the trigger. Wood and paint shavings splintered up from the top of the picnic table where the bullet grazed it. The two targets nearest the point of impact wobbled, but they didn't fall over much less take any damage.

The boys chuckled, Matt even throwing his head back in delight, blond hair whooshing back to cover his forehead when he righted himself. Mitch flicked the safety back on and handed the gun to Kevin.

"Swing and a miss," the boy said, taking the gun. His eyes glowed like it was Christmas when he gazed upon the firearm in his hand, like he'd just gotten something better than any video game console.

"Hey, I made contact. Could've been worse," Mitch said. "Practice makes perfect, right?"

Kevin rolled his eyes. He aimed the gun.

"The safety is there," Mitch said, pointing.

"Yeah, I get it," Kevin said, without breaking his concentration.

"OK," Mitch said.

Matt's head swung from the gun to the bottles and back. The palms of his hands smothered his ears, his elbows pointed straight out. He made a face with the corners of his mouth pulled out and down. Mitch thought it kind of looked like he was caught in the middle of a huge windstorm.

The safety clicked. The hammer clacked. The Beretta blazed and popped. Glass crunched in the distance, and the top half of a Bass Ale bottle tumbled to the table in pieces, the bottom of it tottering three times and settling back into place.

"Yeah!" Matt said, clapping his brother on the back.

"Nice shot," Mitch said.

Kevin just smirked at his dad. Mitch looked upon his son's face. He knew the boy had no idea how happy, how relieved he was to have his son show him up like this. No idea.

"My turn?" Matt said.

Mitch looked at the gun, looked at the boy. He tried to picture the firearm in those tiny hands, and he couldn't.

"Maybe not yet," he said.

Matt smirked. Mitch thought he looked a little disappointed but not surprised.

"You'll get your turn," he said. "But we need to go visit with your grandparents now."

Travis

He thought there was no way the dog would go inside with him, not after being trapped indoors like she was, but she did. She showed no concern, following him everywhere, seeming to trust him entirely. Still, he wanted her to be able to do what she liked.

The back door lay in the yard, balanced on a pair of saw horses. Popping it off the hinges had been easier than he anticipated, just a well placed chisel and a few hammer taps. Now he taped the paper template from the doggie door package to the bottom of the door, a double wide perimeter of green painter's tape to help him see things better. He was pretty drunk after all.

At first, he thought it'd all be down to hand tools and elbow grease without any power for the drill or circular saw. No worries, he figured. Time was the one thing he had. However, the batteries in his dad's cordless drill had enough juice to help him get started. No such luck with the saber saw. Either the battery was dead or the EMP fried it. He wasn't sure. Still, the drill was better than nothing.

Thinking about it now, the only electronic devices that seemed to work — the drill and a small flashlight — had been stored in his dad's metal toolbox. Maybe the metal shielded them from the pulse somehow. He felt like there was a name

135

for this concept that he couldn't remember.

A cigarette hung between his lips, smoke drifting into one eye. The drill whirred, cutting a pilot hole in each corner of the rectangle the hole would soon occupy. It felt crazy, hearing that little electric sound after going so long without anything like it. He went back over each hole, grooving them out a bit to better fit the saw inside, to give him a little room to work.

He paused, reaching over for the mason jar of warm martini and taking a slug. Movement caught his eye just then, and he glanced over his shoulder at the dog sitting on the back steps, mouth open, chest heaving, looking around. He smiled when he looked upon the beast. She had so much energy, was so enthusiastic that it couldn't help but become infectious.

He plucked the cigarette from his mouth and flicked the ashes on the ground. Now came the elbow grease.

He figured the foldable sliding saw was probably designed for pruning shrubs or small tree branches in a garden. It would work, though, even if the going was rough. Maybe when the hole was bigger, he'd dig around for a tool more suitable for the job, something with finer teeth, but he kind of doubted it. The jagged edge would be covered by the plastic lip of the doggie door anyway, so why bother? Just plow through it, he thought.

He worked the saw up and down, slowly etching the first line in the door. The sound and the feel fell into a rhythm right away that lulled him into a distant state. Saw dust clumped in the gap where the saw slid, little tufts of it falling to the sides. His eyes took these things in but he barely noticed them, his mind drifting away to another place.

He wondered sometimes if the raiders broke down his door and killed his parents because they'd seen him hauling cigarettes or booze. He couldn't think of why else they'd target his family. As it happened, they didn't get his supply. At that point, he'd stored it all under the floorboards in his bedroom and the guest room, a hiding place which apparently eluded their search. He still had a decent amount under the floor now, though his collection had grown too big, and he felt secure enough to move the bulk of it to reside behind the locked oak door of his parents' room now that he hardly saw anyone around town.

Still, the idea nagged at him, that perhaps he could be responsible for their deaths in a more direct sense. It was hard to say with any real certainty, but it wasn't like these guys went door to door and killed everyone. They must have selected his house for a reason, right?

Maybe.

He finished the first cut, only making it about a half an inch into the painter's tape perimeter before he noticed, which was a touch better than he expected of himself. He drank again, eyes closing as the booze plummeted down the drain. He imagined himself ordering this concoction:

"I'll have a dry martini. Room temp. Not stirred."

Erin

Presto, Pennsylvania
29 days after

She was frozen in front of the pantry door when the voice came from behind her.

"Language."

Erin whirled around to find Izzy poking her head through the banister from below.

"I told you to wait downstairs!"

Izzy waggled a finger at her.

"That's no excuse for the potty mouth, missy."

"Fine. Come take a look and tell me it's not Holy-Shit-worthy."

Erin crossed back to the living room and threw open the curtains to let in some light. A beam of late afternoon sun illuminated one side of the pantry, casting a golden glow over the rows of canned goods. And that's what all that food looked like to Erin. Solid gold.

All those cans and only *some* of them were beans.

Izzy hopped up the steps two at a time. Erin waited next to the pantry door with a toothy smile and some florid hand movements, trying to give the impression of a game show model revealing a prize.

Izzy's eyes went wide at the sight of the stocked pantry.

"Jackpot!"

"I know. That's kind of what I meant when I said 'Holy

Shit.'"

Erin held up a hand, and they high-fived.

"You swear too much," Izzy said, then dropped to her knees and slid a few cans around.

"Should I start loading up bags?"

Erin sat down beside her and picked up a jar of salsa.

"Let's eat first. I'm starving."

"Me too," Izzy said. "What should we have?"

Erin reached for a bag of Tostitos and a can of refried beans. It was the first can of beans she was actually kind of excited to eat.

"I'm thinking nachos."

While Erin went into the kitchen to prepare the food, Izzy continued perusing the stockpile.

She heard a gasp from inside the pantry.

"What is it?"

Izzy chuckled. "You'll see."

She waddled into the kitchen carrying a can that was almost half her size. The label read "NACHO CHEESE" and depicted a waterfall of orange goop cascading into a bowl.

Erin looked from the gallon-size can of cheese to the bag of chips.

"I think we're going to need more chips."

While she assembled the nachos, Erin kept trying to do a Julia Child impression, even though she was pretty certain Izzy had no idea who Julia Child was.

"Today we'll be making the classical French dish. Nachos! First, you want a generous amount of roasted corn chips, smudged liberally with refried beans -- always from a can, of course! Next, just to dress it up a bit, we'll layer on a bit of nacho cheese, and finally, we garnish with a bit of salsa!"

After their feast, they began the task of unloading the shelves. Toward the back, Erin found two jars with handwritten labels.

"Hey!" She pulled one out to show Izzy.

"Strawberry rhubarb jam!"

Izzy pulled a plastic shopping bag from her pocket and shook it a few times to unwad it. Grasping it by the handles, she held it open while Erin filled it. In went the jars of jam and a can of chicken noodle soup.

Behind the jam jars was a Christmas tin. Erin pried the lid off.

"There's the real jackpot."

Izzy lifted herself on tiptoe to try to peek into the tin. Erin lowered it so she could see the wad of cash inside.

"Who hides money in the pantry?"

"I think it's an old lady thing."

She pushed the lid back on the tin and dropped it into the shopping bag with a clank.

Erin paused with a can of green beans in each fist. Another variety of bean she didn't completely loathe. She tipped her head back, closed her eyes, and inhaled.

"I love that smell."

Wrinkles formed across Izzy's nose.

"You're weird."

"You're over here talking about zombie poop, but *I'm* the weird one?"

The kid grinned and shrugged.

"My Grandma had a pantry just like this. And it had this exact smell." She sniffed again.

"When I was about 12, I found a bag of peanut M&M's in it. The expiration date was from a few months before I was even born."

"What did you do with them?"

"I ate them. Duh."

Izzy laughed.

Erin tossed a box of crackers into the last bag.

"That's the last of the food. I'll go scrape together whatever else I can."

She unfurled a bag and plucked the rings and bracelets from her hands. They'd only get in her way carrying all this crap back. But she left the necklaces on.

She found a pack of batteries in a linen closet, as well as five rolls of toilet paper. That was how to get rich in the post-apocalypse. Toilet paper. If you stockpiled TP, you could probably make a killing.

Izzy was crossing the handles and tying the last bag closed when Erin met her back at the threshold of the pantry.

Erin added her bag to the row and counted them quickly.

"Six bags. Not bad."

"What about the cheese?"

Erin followed Izzy's gaze to the can on the counter. They'd barely put a dent in it.

"I guess we have to leave it. Too much to carry. And it probably wouldn't keep anyway."

"Seems like such a waste, though."

"I know," Erin said, then stooped to pick up her lot of the bags. "Oh well."

The bags swished and rustled with every step. The handles

dug into the fleshy parts of Erin's fingers and arms, threatening to cut off the circulation. She had a bag in each hand and another strung over each arm. She lowered her arms so that the bags slid down from the crook in her elbows and landed in the middle of her forearm. A deep purple line circled her arm where the bag had rested.

It was over a mile back to the house, and they'd made it about half way when Izzy stopped. Erin kept going a few paces, then turned back to see why she was dawdling. Erin flexed her fingers, trying to keep them from going numb.

Izzy's chin was tucked to her chest, and Erin could see her eyes moving back and forth.

"What is it?"

Izzy lifted her head.

"Do you hear that?"

She told herself Izzy was probably just talking about something harmless. A bird or a grasshopper. But her heart knew the truth and started pounding a little faster. It was never something harmless.

"What?"

"Listen."

Erin held her breath and waited.

And then she heard it, too. It was far off (the farther the better) but it was unmistakably the hum of an engine. Car, truck, or motorcycle, she couldn't tell. Not that it mattered. Engines meant people, and people were to be avoided at all costs.

"Shit," Erin said. "Run!"

To their left, the road shoulder dropped into a rocky creek. To their right, the wooded land rose steeply. There was really only one choice.

She veered into the tangle of grass, chicory, and Queen Anne's lace at the side of the road, heading for the woods. Dust kicked into the air as she tore across the ditch.

It was an uphill climb through the overgrowth. Good for a hiding spot. Pain in the ass for climbing with four heavy grocery bags. But the panic lit a fire under her, and she almost forgot about the bags as she scrambled up the hill. She heard Izzy's voice behind her, but there was no time to stop and chat. They had to move.

When she reached the top of the ridge, she dropped over the other side, just to be sure she was really out of sight. She sat, red-faced and huffing, assuming Izzy was right behind her. It was three breaths before she looked back. Izzy was still at the bottom of the hill, trying to rescue the cans and jars and boxes that had burst from one of her bags. The torn remnants of the bag hung from her wrist, flapping in the wind like a flag.

"Izzy, hurry!"

The engine sound was closer now. Erin disentangled herself from her own bags and scurried down the hill.

"Just leave them!"

She half-ran, half-slid down the incline, taking the one good bag from Izzy and pushing her toward the top. Back in her hiding spot, Erin let her head fall forward to rest on her knees.

She couldn't believe she'd just left Izzy behind like that.

"I didn't mean to drop the bag," Izzy said. "It got caught on a branch and then the side ripped open."

"I'm not mad at *you*…" Erin rubbed at the spot between

her eyes, the way her mom used to do when she was stressed out. "But the next time I tell you to run, don't stop for anything."

Izzy started to say something, but Erin held up a hand. "I think it's getting farther away."

They waited another half a minute to confirm that the sound was fading away into the distance.

"It's gone," Izzy said.

They trudged back down the hill, sidestepping like mountain goats to avoid sliding down the incline.

Erin stooped to collect the cans and boxes that had exploded out of Izzy's bag, distributing the goods between the remaining bags before continuing on their way.

Every few minutes, she paused to listen, to make sure there were no new sounds approaching. She couldn't stop imagining what would have happened if they'd come this way. What if they'd seen the food spilled on the side of the road like that? Decided to search the woods. She and Izzy had no way to defend themselves.

And if they had to run, then what? She had zero survival skills. She'd never started a fire. Never hunted. The closest she'd come to gardening was watering a houseplant.

She was barely fit to take care of herself. How the hell could she hope to keep both of them alive in this awful, new world?

There was something else bothering her, too. Something her dad used to say.

He said that you often found out who someone really was by how they responded in a crisis. Maybe Erin was starting to find out who she really was.

At the first sign of danger, she had left the kid behind.

Mitch

The car weaved its way across town. Mitch watched the boys in the rearview mirror, their faces blank, eyes watching the world flicker by through the windows in the back seat, one screen for each of them. He selected a path that would avoid all of the busy streets, figuring them the most likely to burst into violence. They passed mostly working class residential areas, houses all packed together, paint chipping, porches sagging, a couple of brick school buildings the color of sand.

"Dad, what's ring around the collar?" Matt asked.

Mitch's eyes flicked to the mirror, looked into his son's. The kid's forehead wrinkled as he tried to puzzle it out.

"Huh? What do you mean?" Mitch said.

"Jimmy Douglas told a joke today," Matt said. "It said 'ring around the collar' in it."

"Let's hear it," Mitch said.

"OK," the boy said. He cleared his throat. "There are five things wrong with the penis. It has a hole in its head. It has a ring around the collar. It hangs out with a couple of nuts. It sleeps next to an asshole. And when it gets excited, it throws up in a plastic bag."

Everything in the car went quiet.

"Yikes," Kevin said, his gaze not breaking from the world

146

outside the window.

"So I don't get it," Matt said. "What does 'ring around the collar' mean?"

Mitch scratched his chin.

"Well... I don't know, man," he said. "Look, let me try to call your grandparents again."

He pressed the button and the phone dialed. He brought it to his ear. No one answered, but at least it got him out of that conversation. Kevin locked eyes with him in the mirror after he hung up the phone. Mitch shook his head, and his son went back to looking out the window.

Silence settled on the car, everyone staring at their screen, their faces blank. At a stoplight Mitch watched the heavyset girl in the lane next to him sing along with her stereo, closing her eyes and tipping her head back to belt out the high notes.

He wondered what Janice would say about this, what her sarcastic comment would be, and then he remembered that she would never comment on anything again. No more jokes. No more complaints. Ever. She was gone. It didn't quite seem all the way real yet, but in that second, it was real enough to make his breath catch in his throat. He hunched ever so slightly as if reeling from a body blow. God, it was so weird. And he'd never even have time to get used to it, to heal even the slightest bit. He would just suffer for another 30 some hours, and then get pummeled down to his own death.

He swallowed, and his throat felt tight and dry and strange. Was that a sign of the sickness? Probably not. He thought about peeling back that sleeve, finally getting a look at the bite on his wrist, but he couldn't do it. Not now. Not in front of the kids.

He gazed off to the right to peek through the clearings at the intersections. Smoke plumed in the sky in the distance, a dark cloud twirling over the big offices and apartment buildings downtown. If the city was still burning... He wasn't the only one experiencing the death of a loved one today, though knowing this didn't really make it any better.

He thought about how people react to death on TV. Their emotions all came spilling out. Their faces twisted and contorted. They wore their grief in the set of the shoulders, the tilt of their chin, the water pouring from their eyes. And yet, in some sense, it was a safe version of grief, a shallow version that washed right off when you were ready to be done with it. The musical cue swelled. The somber melody soared above the grief montage, tugging at the heart strings for as long as the focus groups said it felt right, and when the montage ended, and the tears were all jerked off, the sad music faded out, and the audience could be done being sad and move onto the next adventure and watch more commercials and buy more fries and Coke.

It wasn't like that, though. Not in real life. The weight of it settled on him in fits and starts, a crushing heaviness on his neck and shoulders and chest. And in real life, the feelings of it came and went in waves. Anger, grief, nostalgia, denial. They swirled around like the ice and booze and cola when he mixed up a whiskey and Coke with a butter knife in the kitchen. And perhaps that was a fitting metaphor as he was mostly drunk on denial for now, he thought. He didn't have full access to his feelings, just periodic flashes of the torment down in there. Mostly his mind did some sleight of hand to keep him numb to it. When he looked in the mirror his face was blank.

He had no time for grief anyway, though, no time to feel sorry for himself.

They drove the last eight blocks in silence, pulling into the driveway at Janice's parents' house. The bungalow sat on a hill, so the driveway was steep as hell. He parked just shy of the garage door and put the emergency brake on.

With the car off, he craned his neck to look up at the house. It was small, but a nice place, cream siding with brick red shutters. They'd spent a small fortune on the matching red aluminum roof on top two years ago. Looking closer, he noted the lack of light in the windows. The grass looked a bit shaggy as well, and Janice's dad was a lawn freak. One of those nuts that loved mowing and sometimes did it twice a week.

His eyes drifted to the glove box, and he rubbed his thumb against his fingers. He wanted to take one of the guns with them, but he didn't want the boys to know he was scared. He'd have to tell them some of this at some point, but not yet.

Not yet.

He opened the door and stepped out, and the kids followed suit. The ache and stiffness he felt in his lower back and the arches of his feet reminded him that he hadn't really slept last night, that aside from a nap of sorts, he'd busied himself shuffling around and buying guns and killing zombies instead.

Sweat greased his palms as they walked up the two sets of concrete steps to the front door. He could feel his pulse banging away in his neck. The bushes running around the porch smelled like pine, and he always felt like he could smell the humidity in the air here, some dank odor that lingered around this porch.

His arm rose, his hand balling into a fist that rapped at the door. He stepped back, eyes watching the peephole for signs of darkness, his shoulders squirming a little as though his jacket suddenly felt too tight. The boys looked disinterested, fidgeting, staring off. He thought about how he should pretend he left something in the car and go grab one of the guns, but he didn't do it. He pounded at the door again. No flicker of darkness came to the peep hole. No sounds or signs of movement.

Nothing. Nothing. Nothing.

Fuck. What was he supposed to do? Their only living grandparents were nowhere to be found. Who the hell was he going to leave these kids with? Where were they going to go?

Fingertips dabbed at the place where his nose and forehead met, smearing at the sweat now pooling there. The skin of his face felt clammy and slicked with grease. The words "all greased up with no place to go" popped into his head.

He didn't know what to do, so he knocked one more time and thought it over. Could he leave them with some of his and Janice's friends? Faces flashed in his head. Most of them were divorced couples he hadn't seen in a long while. At some point, he and Janice settled into their own routine without a lot of outside socializing, and that only became more pronounced after they moved. No one sprung to mind. No one within hundreds of miles.

He felt an itch like a tick crawling on his wrist and went to scratch it. And as his fingernails unsheathed a bit of his forearm, he saw the swirls of black lines crisscrossing out from the bite like some evil roadmap running beneath his flesh. He angled himself away from the kids to shield them from seeing and gazed upon it for a moment. It almost seemed to pulse, but he couldn't tell if it was a trick of the eye since he stood in the shade under the awning.

The black tendrils were no trick. Of that he was certain. He traced one snaking black path with the tip of his index finger.

At least he knew for sure now.

"Dad," Kevin said.

He looked up, pulled his sleeve back over his wrist. In some part of his mind he was aware that this wasn't the first time his son had addressed him just now. He'd zoned out and not heard.

"No one is here," Kevin said. "Let's go."

The boy's shoulders already faced the car, ready to move on.

"Wait," Mitch said.

He riffled his fingers through the back of his hair. They needed the key to the cabin. One way or the other, they weren't leaving here without it.

Travis

Hillsboro, Michigan
54 days after

He'd pissed the bed the night after his parents were killed. He woke up wet and cold sometime before dawn, the smell of stale urine like a cloud hanging in the air in his room. It followed him when he walked out into the hall to get clean sheets. It followed him as he built a fire to heat water to clean himself. Even after the sponge bath, it clung to his skin. He could smell the acidity to it, a bright odor, an astringent citrus note that made it all the grosser somehow. It made him picture a glass of lemonade with those scummy piss bubbles floating on top.

He sat in it all afternoon, piss and shame wafting into his face, stinging his eyes, before he finally heated another pot of water and washed again. The smell seemed mostly gone after that, though he didn't feel much better about it.

He smoked cigarettes and wondered if that was why cowards were called yellow. Because they pissed themselves of fright every night. Later, he drank enough to forget everything, and the rotation was born.

When he pissed the bed this time, some weeks later, he didn't care. Maybe that was the good thing about staying fucked up through the night and into the next day. He was still drunk enough to be confused, to find the circular piss stain on the sheets and blanket vaguely amusing.

It's a good feeling, he thought, *to wet the bed and not care. I bet the great poets have never attempted to describe that one.*

A smile curled his lip, and he rolled over and went back to sleep.

Some hours later, he crawled out of bed. The piss was dry now. He couldn't smell it full on, though he got whiffs now and then. Was his urine less smelly this time for some reason, or was he that used to it from sleeping in it for so long?

The dog lifted its head to look at him from its blanket pile in the corner.

"Hey Hannibal," he said and she wagged her tail. He named her while drunk, only later realizing the dog wasn't a cannibal exactly. It ate its human family, though. Close enough.

He walked downstairs and out into the backyard to urinate. Apparently it'd been long enough for his bladder to reload. Steam coiled off of the ground where his urine slapped and wet the dirt. The cold had returned to vanquish that final gasp of summer a couple of days ago. Just standing out here long enough to pee made his shoulders quiver for a second with the chills. The dog galloped out to the back of the yard to pee along the wood fence.

When they went back inside, Travis caught his reflection in the mirror. It wasn't his face anymore. It was some guy with a broken nose, crusted blood draining down from the nostrils to surround his mouth in red. He brought a finger to his flattened snout, and it was sore.

In the kitchen, he opened the cupboard and fished an off-brand cereal bar out of the box. He ate and tried to think back on the prior evening, but nothing came to him beyond mixing up rum and lime juice and sitting on the porch with Hannibal. After about three strong drinks, he didn't remember anything. Could he have fallen on his face? That's supposed to be hard to do, though it's certainly not impossible, he supposed, when you drink enough to black out. That must be it. He'd probably find a little pool of blood somewhere in the house. The scene of the accident.

He finished the cereal bar and grabbed another. His mind continuing to wander as he ate.

Maybe he didn't fall. Maybe Sean decided it was high time to reestablish the social order of jocks ruling stoners and punched him in the face. That notion made him laugh. The idea of popularity and social order seemed funny all on its own with the town empty, the whole world empty so far as he knew. He thought about the two of them running for Mayor, putting those dumb signs in their yards and chuckled again.

Today was supposed to be a mellowed out day of smoking weed, but he felt like changing things up. Pills. It would be a pill day. Rotation be damned.

With heaven inside of him, he walked around town. It felt more like he was floating, though. His vision held so tranquil and steady, like a shot in a movie that pans and zooms in slow motion, a shot from within the clouds, rolling puffs of white billowing across the frame, everything hazed in a soft focus.

He wasn't in the clouds, though. He walked on the railroad tracks behind a row of convenience stores and gas stations. Brick buildings squatted to his right, and beiged-out husks of tall grass stood to his left, rasping against each other in the wind. The whole place smelled like soot somehow. It reminded him of how his hands smelled when he got home from the factory, all blackened from handling metal parts all day, some of the dust worming through his gloves to coat his palms and fingers.

This section of the railroad was where he used to collect bottles when he was a kid. With a refund value of ten cents each, he could often gather enough to get a candy bar or play games at the arcade. And the search for bottles itself was its own adventure, he thought, at least when you're as poor as his family was. Maybe some kind of nostalgia brought him here now. He wasn't sure.

Sperm congealed in his shorts again, and his eyes crossed once in a while, usually when the jizzy feelings came over him. He thought about all of the billions of people who lived and died and never felt this feeling, never took these pills that pressed that button on the brain that made a grown man come a little bit just walking around. He felt sorry for them. They had no clue what they were missing, and maybe that meant they had no clue about much else. This level of pleasure brought life itself into a strange focus. It made him feel separate from everyone, made him understand that was the nature of things, that we're all stranded in our own skulls, all trapped and isolated from each other, never to fully intertwine with any other, and when he was on it, that was just fine and dandy. He walked around alone and somehow still felt complete. When the bliss died down, though, the heightened sense of loneliness was somehow more intolerable than before, more final.

He moved down the tracks past the place where the

buildings running alongside them gave way to trees and brush, soon reaching a point he'd never gone past as a kid. No bottles this way. Just plants. Today he kept going, though. Nothing to lose or gain now. Just a whole lot of time to kill.

He stepped from plank to plank, his feet landing with rhythmic thuds. He sipped from a water bottle as he moved. He had plenty of water, he'd filled 13 tanks that held 100 gallons each while there was still pressure in the pipes and stored them in the garage. The water tasted a little funny after sitting in plastic for a while, though. Not bad but not good. Flavorless. Dead. That's what he thought when he drank it. It tasted dead. Somehow the bottled water he'd looted from the store tasted better. He took another sip. Yep. This water wasn't stale. Maybe these bottles were sealed better? He wasn't sure. He didn't have many of them, though, so he only drank one a day to make them last.

He wondered what the dog was doing. He'd made her stay on the porch when he left. The dog had been trained well. He was sure Hannibal was wandering around the neighborhood by now. Maybe someday she would wander off for good. He hoped not.

As he moved away from the city, the soot smell faded out, and he smelled trees and grass and fresh air. It smelled like the time the whole family went camping when he was 17. Before his dad's stroke. It wasn't all that extravagant. They borrowed his uncle's camper and set up at one of those campgrounds where a grass field full of RVs are hooked up to plumbing and electricity. It wasn't what he imagined when his dad mentioned a camping trip. He pictured a tent out in the woods. A big fire. Privacy. The silence of nature. He got none of these things.

Still, it wasn't terrible as far as vacations with the family went. It was the first time his dad offered him a beer, and then the second, third, fourth and fifth times his dad offered him a beer. They all got drunk and played cards by lantern light. His mom got the drunkest of all of them and laughed herself to tears on multiple occasions. He felt close to them. Plus, they lucked out in that their plot was right by the woods, so it at least smelled like they were really camping.

Now he passed steel paneled buildings set here and there in the woods and grass fields along the sides of the rails. The large structures looked like factories, maybe, though it was hard to tell much. No windows or doors on the sides he could see. Just ribbed metal walls.

He thought about taking a look inside of one, pictured the exposed rafters above, the large machines spread about over concrete floors, all of them fallen silent and still, the layer of dust coating all things, the small break rooms with candy and pop machines.

He couldn't quite bring himself to stop the churning momentum of his feet, though. His knees swung forward, his feet kicking out from under them, landing, pushing off, repeating. Something about the repetitive nature of the motion, the feel of it, the rhythm of it, lulled him into a trance that he didn't want to end.

Somewhere in the distance an engine growled. Based on the pitch and cadence, he could tell it was a diesel, something pretty big. Even so, he thought nothing of it at first. And then the thudding pound of his feet stopped as its meaning sunk in. People. People driving a car or truck. How long had it been since he'd seen a car in town? How long since he'd seen one go anywhere aside from the grocery store? He wasn't even sure how long it'd been since he'd seen any living soul aside from Sean. He saw a fat man on a dirt bike driving away from the grocery store. That might have been eight or ten days ago. Maybe longer. Time got weird when he was fucked up like this all the time. Days seemed to divide up in strange ways in his memories. He lost count.

He remained motionless for a moment, listening to the grind of the motor ring out over the silence that stretched out around him in all directions. It was getting louder, getting closer. He was excited and a little bit scared at the same time.

He walked on, heading toward the noise, thinking maybe there was some crossing ahead, that maybe he'd get a look at whatever vehicle was passing by. The thuds picked up, their tempo growing more and more upbeat.

As he raced forward, the sparsely wooded fields alongside him morphed into cornfields at some point, he wasn't sure exactly when. Other matters occupied the bulk of his conscious thoughts. He could still hear that diesel out there, and it sounded closer than ever.

And then he saw the arms of the metal frame rising above the tracks in the distance, the railroad crossing gates pointed skyward. That meant there was a road, and when he saw the little shimmer of the light reflecting off the blacktop, he knew for sure. He ran now, feet still careful to land on the planks rather than the gravel, and that care slowed him some.

Pictures danced in his head, different versions of the truck barreling down this road. First he imagined a military truck with soldiers on the back ready to administer some vaccine shots, and every patient also got a big chocolate chip cookie. Then he saw a dump truck full of corpses headed to some mass grave out in the boonies, the soldier at the wheel letting his left arm dangle out of the window, his hand half-cupping the wind. Then he saw one of those extended cab pickup trucks, the bed piled high with scavenged bits and pieces: a mattress, a wood pallet stacked with cases of Lucky Charms wrapped in plastic, a pair of big tanks, probably nitrous but maybe O2.

His breath burned in his throat. His lungs ached, two pulsing throbs of flame in his chest. He knew it must be pretty bad to be able to feel it through the infinite numb of endorphins, but he kept running. He fought through it.

Just as he reached the point where the road and rails intersected, the truck bounded around the corner somewhere between a quarter and a half of a mile away, the grill of the military cargo truck swinging to face him. For one second he froze, wide eyes staring at the moving hulk on the horizon, chest heaving. And then he ran down off of the rails, pounding down the gravel slope into the corn husks where he dropped down to his knees.

The truck rolled up on him at a leisurely pace, slowly but surely gaining speed. He crouched farther, broken shafts of corn plants stabbing at him with their pointed bits, rasping out bitter warnings at him whenever he stirred. It wasn't much cover, but he was hopeful they weren't paying too close of attention.

Part of him wanted to flag the soldiers down, see what they were up to, but he dare not risk anything. It seemed strange to be so excited by and scared of people at the same time. He felt the blood pulse everywhere in him now, felt it pound in his cheeks, twitter in that soft skin around his eyes.

The smell of dirt surrounded him. He longed for the odor of the diesel exhaust to fill his nostrils, but he knew it wouldn't until the truck had passed. His eyes crawled over the vehicle as it got closer and closer, watching through the bars of corn husk in front of him. From his vantage point, he couldn't make out what was in the back as the cabin blocked his view, so he focused on the driver. Looking through the windshield was like trying to gaze through dark water, cold and shiny and murky. Impenetrable. Then he saw the arm dangling out of the window just like he'd imagined it, the cupped hand and all. But wait. It wasn't the same. A cigarette rested between the fingers, and, more importantly, this arm lacked a soldier's uniform. Instead a tattered flannel sleeve adorned it, a plaid comprised of red, navy blue and black.

Raiders.

The world slowed down as the truck passed. More raiders sat in the back, two rows of them with assault rifles and shotguns in their hands. Greasy hair hung down into their eyes. Blackened fingertips smudged at noses and brows. Cigarettes bobbed in and out of mouths. Wrists jerked to flick ashes away. A shine came off of them, the glimmer of scars and scabs and zits and yellow teeth. He'd seen plenty of their kind looting the grocery store, though never so many at once.

But he hadn't just seen their kind. He'd seen two of these men before. In his kitchen. They had the same blank looks on their faces when they killed his parents. One was short with wide-spaced eyes and a fat face that reminded him of a frog. The other had overgrown brown hair hanging over his eyelids and curling out from the back of his neck. His face was sallow except for the bunched up puffs of flesh around his eyes.

The truck zoomed, cresting a small hill and dipping down on the other side so just the top was visible. Black smoke splooged out of the stack, looking like liquid somehow.

The heat of rage flushed his face, hot blood beating through his neck, his cheeks, his eyes, his temples, his forehead. His vision fluttered once as he stood. He didn't know if he was on the verge of fainting from standing so abruptly or blacking out in some kind of rage. Being high on pills made this animal process his body was progressing through seem very distant and strange.

He rose to follow the truck, jogging in the direction it went. Out here in the fields of dead corn, he could tail them from a safe distance, at least for a while. He could follow the only sound that rang out over the empty world.

Baghead

Rural Oklahoma
9 years, 126 days after

The Delta 88 eased up next to a small cinder block building set off by itself. Thistle sprouted through every crack in the asphalt parking lot, standing a good three feet high in most places. The Delta 88 toppled them, the bumper knocking them over, splitting some of the stalks.

Bags turned toward the building itself, a small cement cube that looked windowless from his vantage point. The bushes looked to have gotten out of hand and then died, leaving oversized brown husks that crowded the front door.

"Place used to be a veterinary clinic," Delfino said. "Not a lot of frills, but I liked the location, the lack of windows, and the secure front door."

They got out of the car, and Bags stretched. An ache set in behind his knees upon standing, and his calves felt like there must be anchors attached to them. His legs already felt dead after just an hour in the car. He couldn't imagine how they'd feel at the end of their trek.

They elbowed through the bushes to the front door, a heavy steel thing, and Delfino unlocked it. A hinge squawked as he pushed it open, and they hesitated a moment before that threshold. Bags looked into the shaded interior, unable to make out much detail.

The light from the door revealed a wood paneled front

counter, where people must have checked in before having their dog's balls chopped off years ago. Shadows shrouded everything else.

"After you," Delfino said, his upturned hand waving toward the doorway.

"I guess chivalry remains alive and well in the post-apocalypse."

Bags entered, stale smells coming upon him right away like a mixture of dried spit and raw potatoes. The air seemed different inside. He felt the dry of it in his nostrils. He opened his eyes as wide as they'd go, making out a doorway behind the counter but little else.

The soles of Delfino's shoes shuffled over the tile floor behind him, and he turned to see the driver's silhouette still framed in the light streaming through the doorway. Delfino sidled past him and walked through the doorway behind the counter, disappearing into the dark.

"Should I shut the door?" Bags said.

"Nah, leave it. For the light."

"You can actually see back there?"

"Well enough. I don't want to light any lanterns. We'll be in and out in a couple minutes."

Something thudded to the floor in the backroom, something heavy, and after a beat, it scraped over the floor. Bags watched the black doorway as the sound crept closer.

Delfino took shape in the rectangular opening, stooping to slide a large metal cooler over the floor. It looked like it would have been an antique when Bags was a kid.

Delfino stood, his back jerking on its way up and a grimace pulling back his lips to flash his teeth for an instant.

He put his hands on his hips.

"I've got enough water in here for us to make it the whole way. Got a little food, too, but we'll need to get more along the way. It's cool, though. There are places for that."

"So that thing fits in your trunk?"

Delfino laughed.

"Great thing about driving an old car. I can squeeze this big fucker in the back seat. In fact, I can hide it back there."

"Want some help moving it?"

"That would be awesome."

They lifted the metal box and toted it toward the light. Bags expected it to be heavy, and he wasn't disappointed. It was a load. They slowed in the doorway to avoid any elbow-to-door-frame collisions and got back up to speed as they moved out into the light, nearing the car.

"Right here is good," Delfino said.

They placed it in the sand next to the Delta 88, and Delfino climbed into the back. He peeled the upholstery off of the bench seat, and one half of the seat itself pulled right out. The front corner of the pad popped off just as easily. Delfino tossed the bulk of the seat out, hanging onto the corner.

"OK, in she goes," Delfino said.

They put the cooler in the back where the seat had been, attached the corner piece of padding to it, and Delfino spread the upholstery over it.

He turned to Baghead, the grin on his face teetering on the verge of laughter.

"Looks legit, don't it?"

"Yeah, it looks good."

"I like to put a blanket over it, too. That way if anyone

searches the car, they'll feel like they're really digging in when they peel that blanket back and see regular old upholstery underneath."

"Smart. But will anyone be searching the car?"

Delfino's grin faded.

"More than likely, yeah."

Mitch

Bethel Park, Pennsylvania
42 days before

They circled around the side of the house, tall grass
mashing under their feet. Mitch ran a hand along the
windows, pushing and testing for something unlocked.
Nothing so far. It seemed so quiet out here. He swallowed
hard, his heart racing like some neighbor would see them and
call the police, but he knew the cops had more pressing
concerns at the moment—riots and zombie apocalypses,
namely.

The backyard smelled like flowers and dust and some
sweet green plant smell he could never identify. A pair of
huge pine trees blocked their view of the alley with a little
stone bird bath in front of them.

"Are we breaking in to Grandma and Grandpa's?" Matt
said.

Mitch looked at the boy. He expected to find his son's face
concerned but instead saw him smiling, his eyebrows raised,
his eyes open wide. He looked more excited than anything.

"Not yet," Mitch said. "We might have to, though."

"Is something going on?" Kevin said. "Something we
should know about."

Mitch sighed.

"Yeah," he said. "I've kind of been waiting for the right
time to lay it all out, but yeah, there is something I need to tell

you."

"Does it have to do with the riot?" Kevin said.

"In a way, yeah."

They fell quiet, taking the step up onto the concrete square that comprised the back porch. Mitch opened the screen door, tried to twist the knob beyond that. Nope. Locked.

He took a few steps back to survey the scene. There was only one window along the back of the house, a small pane of frosted glass that led into the bathroom. He looked back at the pines that penned them in, separating the yard from the alley, giving it a sense of privacy.

"So are you going to tell us what's going on or what?" Kevin said.

"In a minute. Let's get inside first."

He picked up a rock and tossed it through the bathroom window. It put a hole the size of a cantaloupe in the frosted glass, cracks splaying out from there in all directions. Mitch tucked his hand into the sleeve of his jacket and knocked the rest out piece by piece, reaching into the opening to knock as much as he could onto the ground outside rather than the bathroom floor. With the glass clear, he stuck his head in to get a look.

The bathroom smelled stale. He smelled soap, but under that he sensed stuffiness. It took a second for his eyes to adjust to the dimness inside. The toilet came into focus first, a pink carpet seat cover staring back at him. It was about three feet from the window to the floor, he thought. That would work. He popped his head back.

"OK, you're going through, Matt," he said. "Be careful of

any broken glass in there and then come around and unlock the back door."

"Me?" Matt said.

"Yeah," Mitch said. After a second he added, "You're the only man for the job."

Grabbing him by the waist, he lifted his son over his head to stick him through the window feet first. The kid's eyes went wide as he hit that moment of descent when his feet were inside and his torso was still outside. Must feel like hell to be out of control like that, Mitch thought.

Matt supported his weight by propping his elbows on the window frame as it got to the point that Mitch could no longer hold him. The boy eased himself the rest of the way, his back bending like he was limboing the last little bit in. His head disappeared into the house, and all was silent for a beat.

"Everything OK?" Mitch said.

No answer.

Oh, shit. What if he'd just sent his youngest son into some zombie death trap? Nothing of the sort crossed his mind until just this moment. Christ on a crutch. Nobody should be more prepared for something like this than him after this morning, and he wasn't. At all.

He stutter-stepped forward, sticking his head back into the window, hands scrabbling at the place where the aluminum siding and window sill met.

"Matt?" he said into the gloom, waiting for his eyes to adjust again. He blinked, trying to speed up the process of pupil dilation.

No answer. He could feel his heart flexing in his throat again, like a stupid frog inflating and deflating that bubble of soft flesh under its chin over and over again as fast as possible.

Then he heard a sound outside, a crack and a scrape, and he yanked his head out of the window again. He twisted his neck about, trying to find the source of the noise. Movement out of the corner of his eye led him to see Matt propping open the back door.

The boy seemed quite pleased with himself. His smile struck Mitch as glib.

The back door led into the kitchen. They all moved in about seven paces and stopped just short of the dining room. The snack bar stood between them and the rest of the house, a marbled yellow chunk of countertop that looked very 70's with a chrome pole supporting it.

"Hello?" Mitch called out.

No answer aside from the clock ticking on the wall.

He found himself reluctant to go farther, somehow uncomfortable with the idea of pressing into this seemingly empty house. He wondered where Janice's father and stepmother were. Somewhere not answering their phone, apparently. That didn't seem promising, though he wouldn't mention it to the kids.

"Hello?" he called out again.

No reply.

"Should we split up?" Matt said.

"I think we'll stay together," Mitch said.

Matt nodded. Mitch found humor in his son's sudden desire to be some kind of scout, but this wasn't the time to indulge him.

He strode into the dining room, green carpet appearing beneath his feet, taking the place of the kitchen tile. He banked right, gazing into the living room. No one. Only empty recliners and a couch. Kevin took a piece of candy from the dish on the coffee table.

A left down the hall followed by a quick scan of the bedrooms revealed similar emptiness. They weren't here. He'd known when they were standing in the kitchen, but now he was sure. He led them back into the living room and stopped, unsure exactly what to do next.

He looked down, saw the bright white of his shoes against the green carpet. From there, his eyes moved to the TV screen out of habit. It wasn't on, but he could see their reflections there in the plasma screen, the three of them standing in this vacant living room. Something about the image refocused him.

"OK, they're not here right now," he said. "And that's OK. We're looking for a key."

"Now should we split up?" Matt said.

"Yeah, I guess so."

"Hey, wait a minute," Kevin said. "You said you were going to explain what was happening."

Mitch looked at his older son out of the side of his eye. At this oblique angle, he looked more like his mom than ever, a smaller version of her, yeah, but that pissed off look on his face was one she wore often. He was right, too, of course. Mitch needed to tell them.

So yeah. This was going to suck.

"You guys know what zombies are, right?" he said.

They nodded, Kevin throwing in a shrug. Mitch paused. Hm... maybe he was taking the wrong route with this.

"Look, lots of people are sick, right?" he said. "You've

heard about that?"

"Yeah," Matt said. "Danny Turner says that they bleed to death out of their buttholes. He says he saw them talk about it on TV."

Kevin snorted out a half of a laugh.

"Pretty much, yeah," Mitch said. "But it's not funny, guys."

He took a knee. He felt like a football coach rallying the team after a tough series. He would unveil the truth in stages.

"A lot of people are going to be sick," he said. "And a lot of people are going to die. We have to get out in front of this thing as fast as we can. If we get set up now, we'll be OK. That's why we need to find the key. If we get out to Grandma and Grandpa's cabin, we'll have access to water and a wood burning stove for heat."

"Will Grandma and Grandpa and Mommy come with us?" Matt said.

"Maybe," he said. "We just don't know right now. Your mother is afraid that she is sick. I didn't want to tell you, because I didn't want you worrying when we don't know yet."

He could taste the lie, an astringent flavor coating the lining of his mouth and throat like some sour, acidic syrup. He felt a tightening in his gut, the muscles all moving to launch into vomit mode, but he couldn't let them do it. If he started puking now, he was afraid he'd never stop.

Nobody spoke.

He expected more questions. He expected panic and fright and confusion. No. None of these. Blank looks formed on the young faces before him. All of the wrinkles and creases let go until their expressions weren't happy or sad or mad. They just looked bored and cold and distant, and it was somehow the worst possible outcome. He couldn't bear to look at them any longer, so he glanced at their reflection in the TV screen again instead, saw the three of them framed in a black plastic box. To his surprise it seemed to help a little.

He said nothing, rising from his position on the floor, moving to the nearest end table and riffling his fingers through the items in a basket there. A jangly sound erupted, giving him momentary hope, but it turned out to be a letter opener clattering against a pair of scissors and some toenail clippers.

He watched in his peripheral vision as the boys moved out, Matt going right and Kevin left. No one talked, but he was proud of them. He should tell them that. He should make sure to tell them that soon.

Moving to the next end table, he found a stack of magazines, a newspaper and a jar of dry roasted peanuts. It occurred to him, as he shifted these things around, that living room end tables were not a likely storage space for keys to a vacation cabin on a lake 90-some miles away. His hands quit digging at magazines. He thought about where he would put such a key.

Two possibilities came to him: on his primary key chain and a backup copy in his bedroom. The picture of the glass jar on his dresser took shape in his mind, full of extra sets of keys and pocket change and matchbooks from weird bars and restaurants they'd gone to on vacation. He left the living room, headed down the hall for the master bedroom. Maybe there'd be a jar there.

"Here," Matt said behind him.

Mitch stopped, three paces shy of the bedroom door. The jangle of keys filled the quiet in the house. He turned to find his son wielding a big ring of keys, shaking them side to side. The boy stood by the front door, a coat rack to his right and a small table to his left. He smiled, but he didn't quite look all the way happy.

Of course. Mitch remembered it now. The family kept their keys and purses and such on a table right by the front door, depositing them there as soon as they got home. He'd witnessed it multiple times in the past. He had forgotten all about it, though he supposed his thoughts were jumbled for good reason just now.

He approached his son, who handed the keys over. Kevin appeared, too, exiting the hallway so all of them stood in the square of tile floor that comprised the foyer. Mitch picked through the keys. He couldn't be certain that one of them was the right key, but there were so many that he was pretty confident. This key chain had an *all the keys* feel.

He closed his eyes and took a deep breath and closed the serrated metal pieces in his fingers. They had done it, and now the boys stood a chance. Maybe.

Travis

Hillsboro, Michigan
54 days after

The truck didn't go far. He heard the sound of the engine change pitch twice; its fury grinding out some low notes, then whirring into a tenor tone. After a long beat, it guttered out altogether. The ensuing silence felt somehow violent. It spread over the cornfields and roads and made the world feel so naked and empty and lonesome. But he knew what he'd just heard had been the noise of the truck parking. The sound couldn't travel more than a couple of miles, he figured.

The road stretched out in front of him, a faded strip of asphalt gashing its way through the corn. He picked his feet up and put them down, the soles of his shoes applauding each step with loud smacks. He knew the volume of the sound meant his running technique was terrible, that his feet and ankles were absorbing all of the shock, but he was too high to correct it just now. He clopped on with all the grace of a racehorse with a broken leg.

He reached an intersection and trusted his ears, veering right. He felt certain the truck's final destination was in a 45 degree angle from where he was standing at the moment the engine stopped. He'd alternate right and left turns to move in that direction. He considered taking the straight line through the cornfields, but all those choppy steps over an uneven ground would only slow him down. He raised his arm, hand pointed in the proper direction to remind himself where he was headed.

His face felt cold and hot at the same time, the chill of the moving air embedding itself in the outer layer of skin, his nose and lips left especially frigid, while angry red heat radiated out from within. The rush of air pushing at his eyes made them a little wet, though not quite enough to water. His mouth felt dry, his tongue like some thick skinned mollusk squirming between his jaw and palate, uneasy and unwilling to keep still.

He rubbed his fingers at his nose, swiping at the flesh surrounding the nostrils. It itched like crazy, felt damp, though it was so cold it was hard to tell if it was actually running or just numb. His fingers came away dry, settling that.

He looked out at the landscape, not really taking it in. The beige expanse of dead corn sprawled out toward the horizon with the green of the woods just visible in the distance. He passed a boarded up farm house, long abandoned. The roof sported a hole the size of a medicine ball. Cracks splintered the brick facade into loosely held together shards. The paint around the windows peeled away to reveal rotten wood going black and green underneath.

He thought about how most houses would look like this within a few years. Dilapidated. Decaying. On a long enough timeline, they'd all cave in or collapse in some way. Maybe a few would make it a long time. Maybe some would get taken care of by the few people left. Or maybe some would outlast the people, if the humans wiped themselves out the rest of the way. Empty houses in an empty world.

Left turn now. He raised his arm again, adjusting the angle so his hand pointed in the right direction once more. He tried to find landmarks to help him mark the way mentally, big trees or buildings or anything, but it all looked the same. Endless fields with the life all sucked out of them, so everything left over was the color of straw.

What was he actually going to do if and when he found these guys? He didn't know. He didn't care. He had no choice now. He just moved toward them like there was some invisible magnetic force that pulled him that way. Some wave in the air that drew him in.

A few turns later, he knew he must be close. Another row of factories and machine shops had taken shape in the distance and grown and grown as he dragged himself toward them with cloppy steps. Now they were just in front of him, no more than a couple hundred yards out. His lungs felt like closed up balls of mucus in his chest that could no longer breathe. They could only burn. But he kept going anyway, most every muscle aching, though he had prepared, he supposed, by dulling all of the pain ahead of time. A preemptive strike.

He jogged past the first of the industrial buildings. Empty. All of its windows were busted out. Weeds shrouded the front door in green along with much of the lower half of the building.

He clopped on, suddenly convinced that they weren't here. These buildings were all empty. He'd misjudged the sound. He couldn't even be certain they'd parked somewhere now. He couldn't trust his own memory being that he was high as hell. They probably drove on to some bigger, better city, to live out their days taking anything and everything they wanted by force while he pissed the bed into oblivion.

And then he spotted the truck parked at the next building. His heart clambered up into his throat, jittering there in double time like a damn humming bird. He stopped running. It felt so strange to just stop, to stand, to let his aching legs and ankles and feet rest for a second. It felt like holding his breath.

Now what?

He hobbled off of the road, down into the tall weeds in the ditch. His eyes didn't leave the truck except to look over the building where it was parked. Were they stopping here? Staying here? He wasn't looking where he was going and one foot sank ankle deep in muck, the middle of the ditch being a mud puddle with more mud than puddle. He pulled his foot free, the ground giving off some suction sound that reminded him of a plunger sucking turds free of the toilet hole.

He crouched down. Waiting. Watching. Nothing much moved. Periodically he heard some swell of voices, their words indecipherable, but it didn't tell him much other than confirming that the bandits were here. There were no windows, so he couldn't discern much about what they might be doing in there.

Time stretched out, and he remained steadfast. He squatted among cattails, adjusting his legs periodically, straightening them out to relieve the growing tension in his joints. The sun got lower in the sky, evening closing in. He wondered if he should start home before the dark set in. It was a long walk. He had two lighters on him, but no other way to light his path.

Then the voices got louder. The door opened, and the men piled into the truck once more. They talked over each other as they moved, snippets of dialogue that bled together so he couldn't make out any individual lines.

He crouched lower when the diesel engine roared to life, settling into a steady churn. The truck jerked out of its parking spot, tires grinding over rocks and kicking up puffs of dirt that looked like smoke the color of sand. Then the vehicle eased back onto the road and took off.

He stayed down until after the taillights had vanished over a hill in the distance, until the sound got quieter and quieter and faded out altogether, and then he stood. His legs felt dead, the muscles somehow rubbery and inflexible. He climbed up the slope, his hands scrabbling at the spots where grass held the loose earth together enough that he could get some traction and help his dead legs make the ascent.

When he got to the top, he dusted himself off and listened for a second. He couldn't hear anything coming from the building. Could one or two have stayed behind? There was no way to be sure. For the first time, he didn't like going into this with pills coursing through his system. He wished he had a clear head.

The light dimmed in the sky, and the shadow cast from the building seemed darker than it did when he'd arrived. He walked into that shade now.

From here he couldn't tell how big the building was. It was only one level, but he got the sense that it covered a lot of ground. Some of these factories stretched on and on. He wouldn't know until he was inside. Blue steel siding covered everything, though, with very few windows. One of those places where you could never tell what time it was inside because, without natural light intervening, it always looked exactly the same. He wondered if they did that on purpose for the sake of their third shift workers, to help them forget that it was the night.

His feet grit stray gravel from the parking lot into the sand as he walked the last ten feet to the front door. Lukewarm water squished in the shoe that had been submerged in the mud puddle.

His hand gripped the knob. His pulse did a drum roll in his temples. He tried to imagine what he would do if someone were in there, but nothing sprang to mind. He didn't think he could run at this point.

He twisted the knob and pushed. The door hinge squawked like a seagull demanding a French fry. He froze, the half opened door in front of him leading into darkness. He waited for the sound of the footsteps closing in on him, the butt of the shotgun cracking him between the eyes and turning everything black. Instead, nothing happened.

He stepped forward, crossing the line from light to dark as he entered the factory. For a second he swore he could actually hear himself sweating, hear the high pitched sound of liquid seeping out of the pores in his skin like a ringing in his ear, but then it was gone.

The light streaming in the open door lit things up enough to see a yellow line painted on the concrete floor. He followed it for the first five or six steps, and then he was in the dark. He pulled a lighter from his pocket, lit it and held it out in front of him. His eyes squinted involuntarily. At first he could make out only the flame itself, but then the squint let up and he could see.

Looking around, he was in a foyer with four snack and cola machines all busted open and lying on their sides with their guts torn out. He followed the yellow light up two steps to a steel door. Going through it, he found himself on the main floor of the factory. The light was a little better here. At first, he thought it was because of a window on the far wall, but then he realized it wasn't a window. It was a hole. The air was heavy in this room. Thick. A little sticky. It reminded him of being in a basement, tacky, wet air clinging to his exposed skin.

A smooth concrete floor painted gray sprawled in front of him and just kept going. The size of it reminded him of looking out at the untouched top of fresh snow on a field. The concrete wasn't without flaw, though. He could see indented spots lacking paint here and there in the floor where huge machines must have sat once.

Between the lack of machines and the hole in the wall, he realized this place must have been empty before the plague killed everyone. So why would they stop at an empty factory? Why would they stay in one?

He moved forward, his footsteps echoing, the scuff of rubber soles on concrete reverberating all around him, each new step piling on the fading echoes of those that came before.

Then he saw the piles of goods. Cases of vegetable oil and Coca-Cola and flour were loaded onto the front row of wood pallets with many more square sized loads trailing away behind them. All of these congregated near the big garage doors where semi-trucks used to pick up shipments, and just like that, it all made sense. They were organized. This was their distribution center. The group of men he'd seen looted all day, brought it back here and prepared it to be picked up, probably by another group, probably taken back to a bigger encampment. These were loading bays. He wondered how big this group could be. Did they have other groups of looters out doing the same thing? Probably. Jesus. That could be something bigger than an encampment. That could be a town.

If he didn't know any better, he'd maybe even see some hope in the idea of something like that, some town of people out there stockpiling supplies, but these guys had kind of, you know, killed his parents in front of him in the kitchen. He knew who they really were.

He walked toward the pallets, observing a cardboard box filled to the brim with bags of different brands of rice, next to that a couple of cases of Kraft macaroni and cheese. Bungee cords held these sloppily stacked items together. Looking elsewhere he saw bottles of motor oil, cans of soup, cases of flour and sugar, 40 pound bags of salt, a bunch of red plastic gas tanks that he presumed were full of gasoline, oil drums that might contain more fuel of some type. They had quite a setup here, quite a collection of useful items.

He walked on, moving to the door on the far side of the room from where he'd entered. This part of the building was carpeted, finished – a lobby and some offices. The air in here felt different, dryer, less dank. This was surely where the human resources people and secretaries and managers all worked. And sleeping bags were everywhere. The first one was laid across a padded bench in the lobby. Others sprawled across office floors, nestled under desks and countertops, and one lay atop a long meeting table.

So the men were staying here, at least for now. Good to know.

He walked back through the cavern, once more feeling that oppressive air in the great empty room. He slowed down in the dark of the foyer, moving through the shadows toward the rectangular opening of light in the distance, feeling along with sliding steps until he found the pair of stairs and navigated them.

And now he was outside, the air morphing yet again, the fading light of day still clinging to the sky. He stretched and began the walk home. He pictured the men at night, nestling into their sleeping bags like this was some kind of camping trip. He couldn't decide whether or not he'd torch the offices after he killed them.

Mitch

North of Pittsburgh, Pennsylvania
42 days before

The boys cradled cardboard boxes on their laps in the back seat, and a stack of frozen pizzas sat on top of two cases of bottled water in the passenger seat next to Mitch. More boxes filled the trunk, and plastic bags piled up on the floors and in any other nook or cranny they could squeeze them, filled with more food and clothing and any other useful item they could load up from home.

He merged onto the highway, joining the stream of cars rocketing north. It was a high speed burn from town to the lake, 96 miles, a straight shot. He figured it'd take them another 80 or 90 minutes if traffic didn't pose a problem. Not too long in one sense, but his life was a clock ticking down to zombie time, and this would eat up a significant chunk.

He adjusted the rearview to look on his sons. They stared out of their windows again, eyes flicking to keep up with the things speeding by. A triple decker stack of partially loaded laundry baskets in the middle of the back seat separated them from each other, isolating each of them with their own glass screen through which to watch the world.

They looked bored, he thought, or perhaps mildly concerned, but there was something about kids that always looked optimistic to Mitch. Some smoothness in their complexion, some perpetual hint of enthusiasm in the set of their eyelids and mouth. Something there told him that life hadn't beaten them down. Not yet, anyway. And knowing that reminded him that it didn't matter that his clock was ticking down.

They raced down the backstretch now, barreling down the final straightaway to the place that offered these boys some hope. There were still obstacles ahead of them, but they'd given themselves a real shot.

He looked at his eyes in the mirror and blinked a few times. He looked tired, he thought, but he was still here.

The traffic flowed alongside them, seemingly growing thicker as they went on. It was moving, though, and that's all Mitch cared about.

The car coiled off of the highway, following the curled path of the exit out to Helmer Road, which was lined with a mix of pines and maples. Green protruded everywhere along the roadside, branches reaching out for the vehicles whizzing by.

They'd made it. The cabin was less than three miles out now. They'd take a right off of Helmer onto a dirt road. He couldn't remember the name just now, but he'd know it when he saw it. It didn't seem real. They'd actually done it. It was the first thing that had gone off without a hitch since all of this started. Yeah, traffic had picked up a little, but it never became a problem.

He glanced at the mirror, watching the reflection of his sons staring at the glass panes before them. A feeling came over him that he didn't quite have words for. Something to do with life being a miracle we have no idea what to do with.

Something about this miracle sitting right under our noses for the duration of our time on this plane, like some valuable antique we don't know how to use so we tuck it away in a closet. These boys were his miracle, and even now he had no idea what to say to them, even when the feelings flooded him until they overflowed, he didn't know what to say. He just watched their blank faces, the way their eyes flicked to observe the images before them, finding himself on the verge of tears.

But he should say something, right?

"You guys know I love you, right?" he said, eyes still locked on the rearview.

"Yeah, Dad," Kevin said, still looking out the window.

"I love you, Daddy," Matt said. He looked up, met his father's eyes in the mirror and smiled, which Mitch could discern in the wrinkles forming in his son's eyelids.

They were good boys. He may not have been the best father ever, he thought, but his sons turned out right despite his mistakes.

There. He saw the dirt road up ahead and slowed to make the turn. The ride felt less smooth as they transitioned from pavement to dirt, leaving the modern standard for the older ways. But that wasn't so bad, he thought: the remoteness of the locale promised safety.

The car shook a little. Rocks shifted under the tires, making a noise something like coffee beans grinding in slow motion, Mitch thought, a crunch and a whir.

"Almost there now," he said, watching them in the mirror again.

They seemed to wake then, squirming in their seats in a

185

way that reminded him of a pile of newborn kittens writhing and mewing after their mother has left them to get a drink of water. They looked around, eyes dancing from window to window to take in the scene, their foreheads wrinkling to break up the blank expressions they'd worn for so long now.

The car juddered over the rocks and divots in the dirt road, and clouds of dust kicked up behind them, a trail of what looked like brown smoke screening the view of where they came from.

Mitch's heart hammered in his chest. He was excited and at the same time paranoid that something would go wrong at the last minute. Maybe they didn't get the right key. Maybe the hand pump was broken and they'd have no access to water. Maybe the whole house had already burned to the ground.

But no. He knew none of these things made sense. They'd done it. They were there.

He pulled into the driveway, and his heart fluttered even faster. He wasn't worried now, though. It was a good flutter. Oh, black sludge might be flowing in his veins, might be killing him a little more with each passing moment, but he had found a place for these boys to stay. He had done one thing right. The biggest thing.

He craned his neck to get a good look at the cabin. There it was. The wood exterior, the stone chimney jutting out, the windows angling up against the roof to reveal the vaulted ceiling within. It was a small building, yes, but a very, very nice one. He glanced out into the backyard, fixing his eyes on the hand pump atop the well. It looked fine, too.

Christ on a crutch. Was it real? Could all of this be real?

He knew it was. He knew it must be.

He turned off the car and gathered the pile of frozen pizzas into his lap, securing them under one arm while he dug the big key ring out of his pocket with the opposite hand. His cheeks stung in a way that reminded him of tasting something sour, and he realized that he couldn't stop smiling, that the muscles in his face verged on cramping up.

As soon as he opened the car door, the crack of gunfire rang out. A single shot. Before he could react, the bullet ruptured the windshield, the tinkle of the metal ripping through the glass reminding him of ice shaking around in a stainless steel tumbler. The slug made a soft tearing sound and then a FLOOF as it embedded itself in the headrest of the passenger seat next to him.

Mitch slammed the door, started the car and skidded back onto the dirt road in a flash. The gun fired again, apparently missing as they moved out of view of the cabin.

"What was that?" Matt said, the bullet lodged about three feet shy of his face.

His father said nothing. He was too nauseous to speak. The tires rolled over the rocks and potholes again as they drove into the brown cloud hovering over the road, into the sandy fog of the unknown.

Travis

Hillsboro, Michigan
54 days after

He lay in his bed that night, cold feelings bubbling around inside of him. Crickets chirped outside, little black things sending shrill sounds into the black. He missed his fan, the white noise that drowned everything out so he could sleep. At least all of the jogging and walking had tired him out. His back ached in a way that somehow felt pleasant now that he reclined. He felt the muscles around each vertebrae let go and somehow tingle and hurt at the same time. His legs felt too tight to offer any pleasure in their relaxation, but there was at least some relief in letting the joints go limp and floppy.

The dog exhaled loudly in the corner on its pile of blankets. That was a good sound. Even if he didn't have the white noise of the fan, he had something: the sound of a companion.

The walk home had been hellish. Once full darkness fell upon the day, he could see nothing. A wisp of clouds blocked out the moon, and the starlight was not enough to help. He never realized how much he'd miss the streetlights until they were gone. He used the lighter just enough to navigate, the flint still getting hot enough to blister his thumb even with limited use. He could kind of see the white line on the side of the road if he didn't stare right at it, so he followed that much of the time.

At some point early in the return trek, he noted that he didn't feel high anymore. His head felt a little funny, but it wasn't pleasant now. It was just dull, a little flutter behind his eyes.

In the dark it felt like he'd never get home; he'd never actually get anywhere. He'd just pump his legs and flick his lighter off and on forever in alternating flashes of brightness and emptiness.

Walking up the front steps felt so strange. He heard the dog's nails clicking across the boards as it moved across the porch to greet him. He reached down, touching the peach fuzz layer of fur coating the beast's head, and it snarfed out some happy sound somewhere between a sneeze and a dry heave. He felt like a dead thing somehow moving, somehow returning to life to go through these old motions once more, pushing the key into the lock, turning it, stepping through the doorway, smelling the familiar odor of home, stale cigarette smoke and some note of cedar that he thought might be from his mom's linen cabinet by the stairs. The dog's nails clacked on the wood floors, somehow fuller sounding than on the porch.

He felt around until his hands clasped the lantern. He flicked the lighter one last time for the night, the flame igniting near the oil chamber, and he lit it. He brushed his teeth by lantern light, spitting off of the back steps into the grass, and he chugged a glass of water before and after the act of hygiene. Then he made his way to bed, peeling off his clothes and pulling up the covers. The blanket felt just heavy enough, resting on him. Like a hug.

His mind circled around the same few thoughts for a long

time. He knew that if he fucked up even slightly, they'd kill him, but he didn't care. His thoughts came back to that landing point over and over again.

I don't care.

I don't care.

I don't care anymore.

To Hell with it.

He dreamed of fire suspended over a lake. A ten foot wall of orange flames the size of a football field that hovered 25 feet above the surface of the water. It lit up the black of the night. He watched the glowing ring a long time, tendrils of flame twisting around each other. Looking above it, flashes flickered on and off in the dark heavens like the fire might reach up at any second, orange fingers stretching out to touch the face of God.

With two bare feet sunk in the sand along the shore, he could see the shimmer of the heat in the air all around him, but he couldn't feel it. He couldn't feel anything at all.

The next morning, he walked out to the fire pit. He crumpled old newspapers into balls for kindling, sitting on a blue and white plastic lawn chair that he believed had been in his family since the 1980's, some terrible heirloom from relatives he'd never even known. Years of sun bleached the once royal blue to a powder blue on the front. Not so much on the back.

He made a teepee of sticks, lit the newspaper and stoked as needed to get flames going before putting a bigger log on. Then he hung the pot of water over the flames. Coffee was a lot harder to make these days, but it would be worth it this time.

No booze today, though it was a booze day in the rotation. No pills. No weed. Nothing.

He wasn't using again until it was done, and he wanted to take a few days to get right. Maybe a little target practice and what not. He stared into the fire, flames licking around the bottom of the pan, the whole pit seeming to hiss out a never ending breath.

The coffee was Maxwell House. Instant. Flavor crystals. Pretty good considering the circumstances. Hot as hell, though. He blew steam across the top of it and sipped it slowly. The drink stung his tongue and the roof of his mouth in a way that made his head jerk and all of the parts of his face twitch one by one.

Looking at the fire, he remembered his dream. The cylinder of flame in the sky that he could see but could not feel. It seemed strange, in a way, to dream about all of that bright light when the nights were so black now. Maybe it was some kind of wishful thinking.

When the coffee got cool enough to drink, he chugged one down and stirred up another. Instant coffee always had a dark chocolate note for him – very bitter, sort of fake, but sort of tasty in its own way. He had grown to really enjoy it, though he didn't have the patience to make it every day. Better to savor it, anyway. He had a lot of it on hand. Three cases of Maxwell House and some kind of generic brand he couldn't remember the name of. Still, it would go quickly if he guzzled nine cups a day.

Of course, he had a few pounds of real coffee beans, too,

but he hadn't come across a hand grinder yet. Maybe that'd be something to save for a special occasion. He didn't have a lot of things left to look forward to in that sense.

Life would be weird now that the novelty of having endless products to try would be over. No more would he sample new flavors of Mr. Pibb or Doritos or blast through the drive through to try new Taco Bell concoctions. He'd plow through the products he had now, maybe unearth a few oddities in houses around town, but that was it. There weren't armies of people manufacturing mass quantities of Spaghetti-o's out there anymore. No farmers remained to coax fruit and grain and vegetables from the soil. He pictured the fertile fields out there, overgrown with weeds, branches and stalks heavy with unharvested crops, so much fruit spoiling on the vine.

A world of convenience and novelty would have almost none of either soon. But it was better to not think of that.

He sipped at the second coffee to make it last a while, watched the fire burn down to coals that seemed to blink off and on depending on when the wind was blowing. Smoke twirled into the air, braids of white that twisted up above him and came uncoiled into nothing.

And he thought of the dream again. Somewhere in the back of his mind, he knew. He knew that in one way the dream was right; that when death came, he wouldn't feel anything.

Erin

Presto, Pennsylvania
29 days after

Erin undid the clasps at her neck, coiling the gold chains into the palm of her hand, feeling how the metal held the warmth of her skin. She dropped the jewelry into the suitcase and watched the chains slither down the pile like shimmering snakes.

The suitcase wasn't fully packed yet, but she figured it was only a matter of time before she crammed it so full of treasure she wouldn't be able to zip it up.

She dug her hands into the jumble, grabbing a fistful and then letting the baubles fall back onto the pile. She felt like a pirate admiring her booty. Yar!

In some ways, she supposed they *were* pirates. They spent their days plundering and looting, amassing riches.

She wasn't sure what she was going to do with it, yet. But she figured at some point it would probably be useful to barter with. Maybe more than paper money. If they ever interacted with other people again, anyway.

Erin picked through the jewels until she found her favorite piece -- the turtle ring. She put it on and wiggled her fingers so the diamonds sparkled and the iridescent colors in the opal really flashed.

Now that she looked at it again, she wasn't even sure it was supposed to be a turtle, but the way the stones were arranged, it reminded her of one. The opal was the shell and the diamonds were the head and feet and tail.

Izzy came into the room with an old pickle jar clutched in her hands.

"What's this?"

Izzy flipped the jar, revealing a piece of paper taped to it. Scrawled in her eight-year-old handwriting were the words SWEAR JAR.

"Funny."

Izzy set the jar on the kitchen counter.

"According to my calculations, you owe the Swear Jar five bucks."

Erin took a running start, sliding on her socked feet across the tile in the kitchen. She came to a halt next to the sink and reached for the Christmas tin from the old lady's pantry.

"This should keep me paid up through the rest of eternity," she said, pulling the whole roll of money out and stuffing it in the jar.

"What are you going to do with all that cash?"

"Something fun."

Erin laughed.

"Yeah? Like what?"

Izzy wedged her bottom lip between the gap in her teeth, thinking.

"Chuck E. Cheese."

"Good luck with that," Erin said.

She gave one last waggle of her hand, admiring the twinkle of the ring. She pulled it from her finger and tossed it back into the suitcase.

Maybe she'd bury it for safe keeping. Draw a map so she

could find it when she needed it. X marks the spot. She smiled to herself.

Just like a real pirate.

Travis

Hillsboro, Michigan
57 days after

He pedaled his bike, keeping the pace moderate to conserve energy. A canvas bag dangled at his side, long and army green and loaded with weapons that clanked against each other when he rode over bumps. The sound reminded him a little of ice cubes rattling in a glass but bigger and dryer.

The train tracks made two parallel lines running alongside this stretch of road, which he could just make out in the darkening sky. It'd been an overcast day, gray sky all the while. And now that the light drained away to night, the gray blackened above him like charred meat.

He hardly noticed these things, however. His mind tumbled other matters. Visions of the near future and visions of the past intertwined in his thoughts.

When his dad heard about the incident at the convenience store, the one where Travis got punched and ran home crying, he told his son that violence was the way Neanderthals solved problems, that walking away was the civilized response, that he had nothing to be ashamed of as a man. They sat in the living room, just the two of them, and his dad's eyes looked all wet. Not like he was on the verge of tears, exactly. Just moist like a dog's eyes.

Travis fidgeted with a lighter while his dad talked, spinning the wheel in slow motion so it wouldn't actually

196

spark, and he hated himself more and more as his father tried to comfort him and tell him that being a huge pussy is somehow still manly. He shifted his legs periodically, the springs in the seat of the chair creaking and groaning. A strange feeling came over him as his father droned on, like his identity had retracted, and all he could do was look down at his pants and play with his lighter and feel the warmth creep into his cheeks, the heat swelling as the talk wore on. He wanted to combust, to vanish into a wisp of smoke, but he sat there and listened and nodded.

And then his mind shifted gears, and he pictured himself kicking open the door to this factory, stalking back to the office and shotgun blasting these guys in the face one by one until the blood stopped flowing and their hearts kept still and their bodies went cold and rigid.

The warmth surged into his face once more, but it was different this time. He would go for it. To hell with the risks. He might die trying, but to hell with it. He thought maybe that's what a man really said, what men like him and his father stopped saying somewhere along the way, but he had it back for the moment, and it felt good.

To hell with it.

He pedaled harder and reminded himself to slow down. No rush. Better to arrive just as it gets dark and wait. Wait until the dead of night when they nestle into their bags. Kill them in their sleep. Of course, he knew it could go any number of ways. Much was left to chance here. If he could find a way to isolate any of the men away from the group, it'd be perfect, but he didn't know a good way to do that.

He followed the blacktop away from the tracks, riding

along country roads spider-webbed with cracks and cratered with potholes, problems he was certain existed before all of this, though now they had little chance of ever being repaired. Not in his lifetime, anyway, he thought. He passed fields of green pocked with the beige of those plants already withering. He wondered how much food out there was going to waste, how many millions of pounds of grain in all of those states that seemingly do nothing but grow wheat and corn. Right now, it didn't matter so much, but food wouldn't be so easy to come by before long. He could already imagine revisiting this thought, these millions of pounds of food rotting unpicked, the first time he got truly hungry. It was a matter of when, he thought, not if.

And then he thought that was a funny thing to think about on a night that he might very well not survive. Hunger could wait for another day, hopefully. For now he needed to concentrate on murdering a bunch of people in their slumber.

When he rode up on the factory, the truck wasn't in the parking lot. A sheen of sweat sprouted all at once across the surface of his skin. Shit. What if they're done here? What if they've moved on, and he missed his chance by a day or two?

Shit. Shit. Shit.

OK no need to panic yet. He circled back about a tenth of a mile to stash his bike in the corn where they wouldn't see it if they returned and speed-walked to the building to investigate. The light was mostly gone from the day. He could still see, but if he stared straight at anything too long, it got all hazy as he strained to make out detail. He found it best to look at things out of the corner of his eye and only in quick bursts.

The pavement transitioned to gravel and then to dirt under his feet as he made his way to the door. He adjusted the strap on the gun bag, trying to simultaneously stop it from digging into his shoulder so much and slide his hands into position to rip a gun free should anyone be inside.

He paused at the threshold, a feeling of déjà vu becoming unavoidable, but at least this time he knew the terrain pretty well. He eased open the door to find the foyer just as he'd left it, dark and empty. He made sure to close the door behind him and followed the yellow line up the steps.

With his nose inches shy of the next steel door, he listened for a long moment. Nothing. Just the thud of the blood banging along to the beat of his heart in his ears, which reminded him of the sound of wind whooshing off of a ceiling fan just now. Even with no sound on the other side of the door, he unzipped the bag and fished out a handgun. Better safe than sorry. That's what everyone always said about heading into a demented killing spree, right? Or maybe they said "brandish 'em if you got 'em." He couldn't decide.

He eased the door open, the little click as the knob reached the end of its rotation making him flinch a little, his shoulders jerking and his muscles stiffening so the top half of his body went rigid. His eyes snapped to the circle of half light where the jagged hole formed a mouth in the far wall. The gray light reflected off of the concrete to somewhat illuminate the rest of the chamber. Nothing moved. He felt the muscles along his spine release, and he took a breath. Still, he wouldn't know much until he got a look in the office area.

He walked, his heart hammering out an angry beat in his

ribcage. Even though he stayed light on his toes, only letting the balls of his feet contact the floor, the scuff of his shoes echoed everywhere around him. The sound fluttered around the room like bat wings, he thought.

He kicked open the door to the offices, arms extended, clutching the gun. It was darker here, but he thought he saw the black rectangle of an empty sleeping bag on the floor. He snaked his forearm into the bag again, this time wrenching free a flashlight. He pressed the button. It clicked, and a circle of light appeared. His eyes needed a second to make sense of things. Yes, a sleeping bag sprawled on the floor before him, and, yes, it was unoccupied.

Interesting.

That likely meant they were still staying here. If so, they'd be back tonight. Meaning he could wait here. He could hide in the shadows, and he could come out when the time was right.

He smiled.

Mitch

North of Pittsburgh, Pennsylvania
42 days before

Nobody spoke as the car trekked south on the highway, going back the way it came. The traffic was much denser now, and they slowed to a near stop every few minutes. The progress coming in bursts and lulls made Mitch think of the vehicle as a salmon fighting its way upstream to lay its eggs. That was something like what he was doing, he guessed. Depositing his offspring somewhere before he died. Not the safe place he wanted to take them, though.

The cracks in the windshield looked like a firework explosion frozen in place, and every line led to the bullet hole in the center. Someone had taken the cabin, had shot at them. He felt sick when he thought about it. He'd failed. How long could these little kids make it on their own without even having long term access to water?

He'd tried to call the grandparents several more times. No answer.

"Dad, who was it?" Matt said.

"What?" Mitch said.

"Who was it that tried to shoot us?" Matt said.

Mitch tried to think about how to answer it.

"Some bad people must have moved into Grandma and Grandpa's cabin," he said. "They thought we were trying to take it from them."

"Are you going to call the police?"

"Yeah, I might. Once we're home."

"Cause you should probably call the police."

The conversation trailed off, and the boy went back to looking out the window. Soon enough Mitch's thoughts swelled once more in his head to assail him.

How could he let this happen? How could he have spent his whole life coasting toward this ending? He thought maybe that's how life worked. You waste time and get comfortable and get soft and just when you fully relax, fully let go, fully take existence for granted, time sucker punches you in the throat. It dry gulches you. And you gasp for breath, but it's too late, fuckhead. It's too damn late. You don't get time to say goodbye. You don't get time to collect your thoughts and process what's happening. You blink a few times and life winks out, and it's gone. You're gone.

And that's it. And that's all.

The traffic slowed again. They stopped next to a minivan, the driver's arm dangling out of the window with a cigarette between his fingers. The man brought the smoke to his mouth, wrinkles forming around his lips as he hit it. What an idiot, Mitch thought, and then it occurred to him that this smoker would outlive him without a doubt. That all of the safety he'd felt in his life was a lie, all of the times he looked down on other people for their poor choices came with some sense that he would be OK, that the bad things would happen to other people. But the bad thing had happened to him, to his family, to his wife already gone and him fading away.

Acid crept up into his throat. It tasted like a mix of vinegar and vegetable broth on the back of his tongue. He was going to die. Death swirled inside of him even now, black tendrils snaking their way ever deeper into his flesh, into his being.

The loss was inevitable. Life would deny him even the ability to set his boys up in a place where they might have a chance. It would humiliate him, smear his nose in the piss of his own failures and snuff him out. He guessed that was always the case, though, wasn't it? Life counted down the hours until it could kill him from the moment he was born, the sad ending etched in place all the while. Life is a game that nobody wins. We all die. We all lose.

Shit.

All of the cars lurched into motion again, the still nature landscapes on the side of the road slowly blurring once more as they gained speed. He watched the boys in the mirror for a long time. They seemed lost in that trance again, each staring out their own glass screen at the never ending stream of images out there, lulled down into that waking stillness usually reserved for people who have been hypnotized.

He looked away, and the desperation gripped him around the chest, squeezed his rib cage, constricting the air flow. Pain throbbed in the middle of him. His mouth popped open then, shallow breaths rasping in and out.

Was he going into shock? Was this a panic attack? He thought this was a panic attack. But what else was there to do but panic?

How could he live out these last few hours? How could he keep going? Shouldn't he just implode? Just evaporate into nothing? How could he still be here, still exist for these next few doomed hours? Shouldn't the weight of it crush him, the desperation overwhelm him and erase him?

He caught part of his reflection in the mirror. Purpled up bags of flesh puffed beneath his eyes, and the whites were all bloodshot. He looked like shit, but he was here. He was still here. Still breathing. What was he supposed to do, though? How could he fill the time in any kind of way that made sense?

How could he pretend everything was OK for a while more yet? Shouldn't he do something drastic or meaningful here and now? And if that proved impossible, why wouldn't he just curl up in a ball and wait for death? Should he pretend everything is fine and dandy right up until the moment he turned into a flesh eating monster? Should he distract himself with ice cream novelties and reality shows until the end? Why carry on the charade that things were OK?

For the kids? Maybe. He didn't know if it was really for them. It certainly wouldn't do them any good in the long term. Just so long as they didn't panic right up until he died and became a zombie, right? That'd be a big help to them.

He craned his neck, his face actually pointed toward his children for the first time in a while, no piece of glass between his eyeballs and them. It seemed intense. Uncomfortable. Unfamiliar. Air passed in and out of his open mouth in ragged bursts, drying out the mucus membranes, and he felt patches of skin on his cheeks and forehead going hotter than the rest. He could picture the red blotches decorating his face. Matt glanced over at him, his head wheeling his way in slow motion until their eyes met.

"Watch the road, Dad," he said.

He turned back, the road ahead again filling his vision

through the windshield. His breathing seemed to slow to a normal pace as they barreled down the highway. He knew that some moment had passed. Something that happened here was over, for better or worse. Something he didn't understand.

Fast food and hotel signs blossomed in the sky in the distance, jutting up from the ground to tower above the tree line.

"You guys hungry?" he said, eyes finding comfort in watching them in the mirror's glass.

Travis

Hillsboro, Michigan
57 days after

He hugged his knees to his chest, the shotgun snuggling between his legs and belly, the bag with the rest of the guns touching his right hip. The dark and the quiet squeezed themselves against his person, made his head feel like it was going to burst.

It was sometime after midnight by now. Way after. It had to be. Didn't it?

He couldn't be sure. Time became an imaginary thing here in this dark closet all alone. The rivers of sweat draining down the sides of his face were real. Each breath was real, the inhale and then the exhale, hot air passing through his nostrils and mouth. Everything else, everything outside of this three foot by three foot cell wasn't all the way real. It was just an idea.

He'd heard the men return at some point, the rumble of the diesel engine, the slam of the door, the baritone drone of male voices chattering on. He found it impossible to decide how many there were. All of the voices bled together. It almost sounded like one person talking, pausing, interrupting himself. Only when they laughed could he hear more than one voice.

And of course, he probably wasn't listening to the whole group. There were maybe a handful or less in the room connected to his closet. Others were surely elsewhere, stretching out with their sleeping bags pulled up to their chins.

What had he been thinking upon hiding in here? How could he possibly kill them all?

He thought about the shotgun. Two shots and it would need to be reloaded. Jesus. What kind of odds did that give him? He would have to discard the shotgun after two blasts and switch to the handgun. Or perhaps run and try to regroup.

He breathed through his mouth now, his breath all hot and sticky. He felt his eyes straining to see in the darkness and closed them. This was a death sentence. It was impossible. Should he just run away? Should he cower in here until they leave again?

Two droplets of sweat ran down his back, one then the other a second later, thick beads that felt like they were the width of quarters. His shoulders twitched at the tickle of the liquid's movement.

No. No, he couldn't run. He couldn't hide. Better to die like a man than live his whole life a coward, a worthless bed-wetting crybaby coward. Is that what this was all about, really? Some way to be a man after a lifetime of never quite getting there? He didn't know. He didn't care. In the dark, his reality filtered down to one idea: he wanted something, one thing, and he would get it or die trying.

He closed his mouth, his breath feeling awkward and choppy and insufficient in his nostrils, but he kept at it, held off that low level panic and focused on his breathing. Slow and even. In, hold it, and out in slow motion.

Nothing stirred in the room beyond. Nothing moved but the heave of his chest and the beat of his heart, both growing controlled. Steady. The dark felt infinite now, just blackness and emptiness stretching out around him forever.

In time, a calm came over him, though it wasn't quite a calm, truly. It was some animal feeling that made his arms feel strong and his blood feel hot surging through his veins. Some primal hatred that extinguished his fear, made him believe once more that he could and would kill them all.

To hell with it.

Mitch

The hungry animals all crowded around the counter to get their scraps of red meat. Maybe it was some weird perspective granted by his impending death, or maybe the energy in the room turned restless and hostile because of the spreading diseases and riots and so forth outside, but the routine experience of getting burgers at McDonald's seemed strange. Unfamiliar. A little scary.

Scowls adorned fleshy faces all around them. Generally speaking, there seemed to be a fake tan glow prevalent among this bunch, that bronzer shade of orange that glows in broad daylight, so it almost looked like they were surrounded by unhappy jack-o'-lanterns. He kept the boys close. Knowing the black marks had spread from his arm over his shoulder and onto his chest, he feared nothing in terms of harm coming to him. He did worry for his sons around these rabid pumpkin heads, though.

The people writhed in the lines ahead of them. Mitch thought they looked like a mosh pit or maybe like sharks jockeying for position in the swells to get their piece of wounded surfer. He and his family waded through the thrashing consumers, making their way to the front and ordering their food. Matt got a kid's meal, Kevin got a Quarter Pounder meal, and Mitch got a Big Mac meal.

Fighting through the crowd in the lobby wasn't part of the plan. The line at the drive thru had been horrendous, however, and Matt wanted to eat inside anyway, so here they were. Maybe it was a waste of time, or maybe it was a final real meal with his boys. Like being on death row. Greasy burgers and fries washed down with Coke -- a fitting end, perhaps, to a life where he never really tried. Never tried to accomplish anything great, anything meaningful to even him, let alone anyone else. It was a fast food life, lived for convenience, lived without regard for much beyond finding comfort, shoving empty calories into his face to try to feel better about the emptiness all around. And it was too late to take any of it back now, he knew, so he might as well wash it down with cola instead. If he could wash death itself down with cola, he would do that, too.

Christ on a crutch. Was he having an existential crisis while ordering a Big Mac at McDonald's? Fucking ridiculous.

The clerk loaded their food onto a plastic tray, and he carried it, elbowing through the crowd to find a place to sit. Matt picked a counter space with swiveling chairs running along a window to their right. Good enough. The tray flopped onto the tabletop, the burgers hopping upon landing, the fries shifting in their sleeves, ice cubes rattling against the sides of the paper cups. They sat and went to work. Wrappers peeled away, and boxes popped open, and ketchup packets squirted their contents into the appropriate places.

Kevin worked at his burger first, taking large bites, chewing a couple of times and then slurping some Coke in with the half chewed food, sometimes shoving a fry into the mix before the drink. Matt swiveled back and forth endlessly in his chair as he scooped up huge wads of ketchup, using his fries more like spoons than anything, periodically pausing to suck down cola. Mitch went back and forth from burger to fries, picking up strands of loose lettuce strips from the bottom of the burger box to mix with his bites of Big Mac.

The food was so bright. Acidic. The cola had acid, and the ketchup had acid, and the special sauce had acid, and the pickle had acid. Every bite packed a punch that made his palate tingle. He wanted to look down on the food, to use irony or some other form of ridicule to put himself above this chain restaurant, this sandwich built on an assembly line and fries mass produced factory-style, these people crawling all over each other for their share. He wanted to tell himself he was better than all of this, but he couldn't. He thought it was delicious. For some reason he was ashamed of that just now, but it was the truth.

None of them spoke during the meal, each of them once more falling into a trance. It wasn't the same as watching the world through the windows. The stimulation here proved more visceral, flashes of pleasure released from the brain as the sugar and fat crossed their taste buds and seeped into the bloodstream. Endorphins.

And Mitch got some nostalgic sense just then, some feeling that if he could stay in this moment, he could be OK. That so long as he was eating, filling that basic animal need and attaining the biological satisfaction that comes with it, he couldn't actually die, that food could somehow comfort him forever. It was an irrational thought, he knew. If only he could find a way to eat ground beef eternally, all of his problems would just go away.

He sucked fizzy syrup from his straw, the sweet, bright fluid rolling over his tongue and cascading down his throat like a miniature Coca-Cola waterfall. He glanced to his right, the savage swarm of pumpkin heads snapping him out of the momentary escape from anxiety over his impending death. The people looked so agitated, aggressive, unhappy. It reminded him of watching the riot, watching the men club the zombie on the sidewalk, watching the people bust out windows and haul away armfuls of merchandise.

He ate the last bite of Big Mac, getting one final burst of that comfort that seemed capable of washing everything else away, feeling it fade out seconds after he swallowed. Of all the stages of death, denial was his favorite, he decided. He just wished he could make it last.

Baghead

Rural Oklahoma
9 years, 126 days after

Sandy ground spread over the flatlands around the Delta 88, with nothing but weeds and the periodic dead tree to break up the monotony. The most plant-less areas evolved rapidly at the whims of the winds, forming dunes and valleys that shifted day by day.

The road looked faded, a light gray like a man's beard right on the cusp of going pure white, with two darker grooves in each lane where the tires wore the asphalt down. The car juddered over cracks and Delfino weaved around potholes the best he could.

"People control the roads between here and there," Delfino said. "And we have to deal with them to get where we want to go."

"So they're going to extort stuff from us."

"Well, I guess you could say that. They call it paying a toll."

"What's the toll, then?"

"Depends on what you have."

Bags scrunched his brow, feeling it rub against the canvas.

"So they dig through your stuff and take what they want?"

"Yeah, pretty much."

"And they call that paying a toll?"

"Right. You get it."

"Have you considered ways of getting around them?"

"Oh, lord no. They're quite diligent about enforcing the toll and quite well armed on top of that. A ruthless bunch out here, but they do take good care of the road."

"So you let just them take whatever they want?"

"Cost of doing business, Bags. They take your stuff, but if you keep in line, they don't kill you. That is one of the things I've always liked about them."

They fell quiet for a while. Bags closed his eyes and listened to the hum of the engine, the tires spinning on the asphalt. They hit a pothole, and the car shook.

"Well, what kind of stuff do they usually take?"

"Weapons and ammo are the first to go, which is why I don't bother bringing any past their checkpoints."

"Wait a minute. You're not even armed? Our deal was for secure transport. Secure. Weapons are strongly implied."

"Relax. I have a stash of guns along the way. More than one stash, in fact. Trust me, we'll have access to more than enough firepower to handle anything we come upon. I've been at this a long time, and I'm still here."

Baghead leaned back in his seat and closed his eyes again. Air puffed from his nostrils, and it took him a second to realize how frustrated he'd grown. He didn't know why. He'd traveled far and wide on his own without weapons, though he mostly stayed off of the road. It must be something about this group that controlled the roads.

"Wait," he said, opening his eyes. "You said they take care of the roads. What does that even entail?"

Delfino smiled.

"See how chewed up all of this out here is? All these

potholes and big ol' cracks and shit. Well, they fill all of that in, mostly with well packed dirt, and it's a constant effort with the traffic and the rain, when it bothers, eating away at it. It ain't perfect, but it's a lot smoother sailing than this junk. Anyway, that effort comes at a price. I just accept it."

"I see."

More bumps throttled the car as if to cement Delfino's point. He looked out at the dust flying around and wondered how long it'd be until they made it somewhere greener, somewhere that actually got consistent enough rainfall to support life beyond weeds. It'd been a long time.

"Like I said, though, this is a ruthless bunch. I mean, they're full on cutthroats. You keep in line and you're fine. But beheadings are real common around these parts if you mess around. I've seen it myself. Just WHACK through the neck and the head pops clean off."

Delfino shook his head before he went on.

"I know how to talk to these types, so it might be best if you don't say anything. Got that?"

"Yeah, sure. When will we get there?"

"We'll hit their territory in about an hour."

Baghead nodded, and then he nestled his head back against the headrest. Within three minutes, he was asleep again.

Travis

Hillsboro, Michigan
57 days after

He moved in a still night, the only thing awake. In fact, he felt like the only thing alive, and maybe that would be true soon enough. His pulse banged in his neck, quaking just below his jaw, a gushing thrum inside of him, hot and wet and red. He clenched and unclenched his teeth, feeling the muscles ball up and release over and over just in front of his ears.

He shifted his weight from foot to foot in a squatted position, coaxing his legs back to life after so long holding still. His feet flexed, lifting him up and setting him back down on the opposite leg. The weight of him rested on the ball of each foot. Everything felt good – his feet, his legs, his back. He felt alive, awake, electricity jittering in his skull, opening his eyes up wide, even in the dark.

This was it.

He pushed the closet door open, his motion slow and careful and confident. The bottom of the door hissed a little against the carpet as it moved, but something about his motion was so fluid that it didn't sound unnatural. It sounded like that little sigh of someone exhaling in their sleep, he thought.

To be sure, he held still in the open doorway, waiting for a long moment. The air in the main room felt cooler than that

216

of the closet, a shock of chill against the sweat dampened skin of his face.

He slithered across the threshold, something the size of a sparrow fluttering in his chest, his feet gliding over the carpet without sound. It almost felt like he was floating, some angel of death hovering toward his victims, teeth all exposed in a sick smile.

He brought a hand to his face to check that. The fingers poked at his lips, swabbed at his teeth. Yes. Yes, he was smiling. It felt almost evil somehow, and maybe it was. He was excited. He wanted to hurt them.

His hand retreated, returning to its place on the shotgun, ready to rack it, the other ready to squeeze the trigger. He pressed his elbow against his belly to feel the bulk there, ensuring the handgun was still stuffed in his hoodie pocket. Good. He did the same with the opposite elbow to feel the rounded bits and ensure the shells were in the other pocket. Indeed.

His glide proceeded into the room, the silence around him changing as he moved into the open. Even with seemingly no noise, he could differentiate the sound of the open office versus that of the closet.

He took another step, however, and there was sound. Air puffed in front of him, the slow respiration of someone deep asleep. It was hard to tell how far away it was. He thought it sounded louder and more detailed than it should, exaggerated after so long in the quiet.

Again his hand left the shotgun, fumbled under the zippered flap of his hoodie to the inside pocket. Something about the size and shape of a cigar found his fingers there, and he pulled it out. He felt along the plastic tube, realized it was backward and turned it so the fatter end faced away from him. Once more his fingers searched its surface. About three quarters of the handle felt rough to the touch, the smooth quarter was the top, and that led the tip of his thumb to the button.

Click.

Light. Too bright. He squinted his eyes down to the narrowest slits, unintentionally closing them a few times before he could get the squint to stick. First he could only see a dark shape on the floor, and then it came into focus, a sleeping bag the shade he believed to be called pewter with a blurred face sticking out of it. He scanned the rest of the room, finding two similar shapes off to his right by the doorway. None of them moved, so the light hadn't woken them.

He brought the flashlight to his mouth and clamped it there between his teeth, his hand going back to the gun, which he raised now to ready it. His eyes winked shut a couple more times, and still, the face was too washed out by the light and the blur to see. He concentrated, grimaced, sweat gushing down the sides of his face and onto his neck, and the picture finally came clear.

Damn. There he was. The dirty blond stubble. The haircut somehow shagging down from the top with the sides shaved. The gaunt cheeks that seemed to tint yellow around the mouth.

It was him. The one who had strangled Travis's mom. What were the chances that he'd be the first one he'd come upon? He didn't know. It almost seemed a bad omen, some sure sign that he may get some form of revenge, but he wouldn't survive the encounter. He didn't care.

He closed one eye to line up his shot, and time slowed down. The gun felt right in his fingers, and he found himself smiling again, beaming out some darkness through his teeth. He wiped his trigger hand on his pants, waited a beat. His breath flowed out of him all slow, and he racked the shotgun. The clickety clack was loud as hell. Shit. The body before him stirred. He didn't wait for the eyes to open. He pulled the trigger.

The boom throttled his ear drums, made his breath catch in his throat.

The face protruding from the pewter sleeping bag exploded, a cavern of red left in its place. It felt like he stared into the face hole for a long time, locked eyes with the emptiness. It reminded him of watching a butternut squash get blown to bits by an m-80 when he was a kid. But it must have been a fraction of a second that somehow stretched out for a long time, because the spray of bloody bits hit him then like a gigantic warm sneeze. Flecks spattered his nose and cheeks and lips.

He saw something jerk to motion out of the corner of his eye, and then the flashlight fell from his teeth, clattered along the floor and spun under the desk to his right to plunge the room once more into darkness.

Erin

Presto, Pennsylvania
32 days after

Erin cracked one eye, saw that the long gray fingers of dawn were just barely poking through the cracks in the curtains, and closed her eyelid.

So far that was one of the few upsides to the way things were now. No alarm clocks. Even if there were, there was no reason to wake up at a particular time anymore. There was no school bus to catch. No morning bell to beat. No teachers recording tardies in a little notebook.

A sound filled the air then, and Erin's forehead crinkled as she struggled to identify it. In her half-awake state, the closest she could come was someone slamming raw chickens onto a counter top. The noise cut off just before two bony heels slammed into the small of her back.

"Damn it, Izzy!"

Erin yanked the covers over her head, remembering all too well that you didn't need an alarm clock when you had an eight-year-old around.

"Sorry," Izzy said, but Erin didn't have to see her to hear the smile on her face.

"Also, language. That's another five bucks for the swear jar."

"I'll give you five hundred if you never do that again."

"I'm hungry."

"So eat something."

"All we have is beans."

Erin sat up, blinked a few times, and let out a long, slow sigh.

She stumbled to the kitchen. The cupboard door opened with a creak. Garbanzo beans, green beans, black beans, dark red kidney beans. She hefted a can of baked beans.

"You know, in England they eat these for breakfast."

Izzy squinted at her dubiously.

"What?"

"On toast."

Izzy just shook her head.

"They probably have some kind of nickname for it, too. Like Bangers and Mash. Or Bubble and Squeak."

"Now you're just making stuff up!"

Erin set the can on the counter.

"I'm not."

She played a game of cupboard Tetris, shifting the contents in the front row off to the side to see what was hidden in back.

"Looks like our best option this morning is going to be Fruit Cocktail in Heavy Syrup." Erin paused and waggled her eyebrows at Izzy.

"Yummy."

She tipped another can into the light.

"Or Sliced Pears. Wait, scratch that. *Lite* Sliced Pears."

She wondered who started that stupid-yet-intentional misspelling. Had they known it would catch on like it did?

"Pears," Izzy said.

The can didn't have a pull tab, so Erin had to resort to a

can opener. Old school. There was a *thunk* as the opener bit into the lid and then the grind of metal on metal as she spun the handle.

Izzy crowded close, reaching to get a pair of forks from the silverware drawer. Erin got a whiff of something, and it wasn't death. It was kid-funk. Sweaty kid pits and stinky kid feet.

Erin was sure she smelled, too. Showering and being powder fresh wasn't high on the priority list at this point. But she at least made it a point to clean up a little every evening. The water from the rain barrel was usually still a little warm from sitting all day in the sun. All Erin had to do was fill the little bucket she kept nearby. A few quick splashes and a scrub at the armpits and she was not-quite-Zestfully clean, but better than nothing. Anything was better than walking around feeling like the death-stink of the world was clinging to you.

But a real bath? The closest she'd had to that was the shower back when they first got to the FEMA camp. And she'd rather not think about that.

Over their breakfast of mushy white blobs, formerly known as fruit, Erin pondered the beans on toast enigma.

"One of them is called S.O.S."

"Huh?" Izzy crammed a pear into her mouth.

"Shit on a Shingle."

"Language!"

"But I think that's some kind of chipped beef or something. Whatever chipped beef is."

Pear juice dribbled down Izzy's chin. Erin watched as she wiped it way with her hand, then smeared her hand on her pants. Yeah, the kid definitely needed a bath.

"You're already up to ten dollars, and you just woke up."

"Turds on Toast."

"That's what they call it?"

"No, that's what I'm going to call it from now on."

After breakfast, Erin pumped water from the well to wash the dishes in. When she dipped her hands in to scrub the bowls, she gave a little shiver. The water was frigid. Way too cold for a bath. Even the rain barrel water wouldn't be warm enough.

She needed a way to heat a lot of water, and a fire seemed like the only way. She had yet to build one. They hadn't really needed it so far. Most of the canned food they ate cold, and the rest she heated on the propane grill next to the deck.

OK, so she had to build a fire. That was the easy part. Cavemen did it, and they didn't even have matches.

At first she imagined herself heating a big pot of water and then hauling it to the bathtub in the house. She'd only probably need to repeat that fifty times to fill the damn thing. No, that wouldn't do. Too much work, plus by the time she boiled the second pot of water, the first one would probably have gotten cold.

There had to be a way to heat it all at once. An image came to her then. An old Bugs Bunny cartoon, where Bugs is in a giant cooking pot over a fire. Elmer Fudd or some other antagonist is fixing to make rabbit stew, but Bugs is chillaxing in the pot like it's a hot tub, using the ladle to spoon hot water over himself.

She smiled to herself. Now she just needed to find a human sized soup pot. And she knew exactly where to find it.

The barn sat on the crest of a small hill, standing watch over the rolling terrain of the property. They'd taken a quick look-see when they'd first arrived. Just enough to get the sense that there was a borderline hoarding situation going on inside.

A few flakes of red paint peeled away as she unlatched the door. The iron was warm under her hand, and she just stood for a moment, admiring the tremendous piles of crap laid out before her. There had to be a vessel suitable for bathing somewhere in there.

"What are you looking for?" Izzy asked.

"You'll see."

She couldn't stop picturing the giant Bugs Bunny cauldron, even though she knew that was out of the question. But with all the junk heaped around her -- furniture, bikes, farm tools and machinery, moldering boxes, lumber scraps, tires and other automotive odds and ends -- she was confident she'd find something that would work.

Her dad always liked Bugs Bunny. One of the cable channels used to play old cartoons during the day, and Erin always wound up watching them when she was home sick from school. Her dad would pass by the living room, pausing in the doorway, transfixed by the images on the TV screen. Caught by some feeling of nostalgia from his own childhood, probably. Eventually, he'd be sitting on the floor or couch with her, laughing when Yosemite Sam's ass caught on fire, and he started screaming about how his biscuits were burning.

He had a funny laugh, the kind that was more inhale than

exhale. Almost a reverse-laugh.

He didn't laugh the last time they watched Bugs Bunny together. He was too sick by then. In too much pain. She bought the Looney Tunes DVD, thinking it would cheer him up. Maybe remembering how they'd laughed together watching it when she was the one that was sick. He smiled then, but he didn't laugh.

He didn't look sick. Not even once he was in hospice, and just getting up to go to the bathroom winded him, so most of the time he just sat in bed in his robe.

She spotted a 55 gallon barrel wedged behind an antique sewing machine on one side of the barn. That could make an OK tub. Sure, she'd have to fold herself into a pretzel shape to fit in it, but that was a small price to pay for hot water. For Izzy, it would be the perfect size.

She hopped onto the sewing machine table and gazed down into the barrel.

"Fuck," she said, quiet enough that Izzy couldn't hear and scold her for it. Probably would have charged her double for using the mother-of-all swear words.

Someone had cut a big rectangle out of the side, to convert it into a burn barrel, she supposed. The hole made it useless as a tub.

Erin climbed off the sewing machine and resumed her search, brushing the dust from her hands and knees.

Izzy's voice came from the other side of a pile of bicycles. "I'm bored."

"Go outside and play then."

"That's what grown ups always say," Izzy said, and Erin had to chuckle.

It was true. Her mom used to say it to her all the time. She bumped into the wheel of one of the bikes, and she stopped to watch the spokes go round and round. They were both gone now. Mom and dad. For the first time, it occurred to her that she was an orphan.

But then anybody that was left now probably was.

Everyone who's anyone is an orphan, she thought, then laughed because her first instinct was to get out her phone and post it on Instagram.

#foundling #AllTheCoolKidsAreDoingIt

But there was no more Instagram. No more Twitter. No more internet. And yet she still carried her phone around in her pocket. Not quite willing to let it go yet.

Sometimes she pulled it out and pressed the button, trying to get it to power up. But the battery was long dead. And ever since that night with the weird bright flash in the sky, it wouldn't even flash the low battery warning anymore. The rumor at camp was that it was something called an Electro-Magnetic Pulse, but Erin didn't know if that was true or just someone talking out of their ass.

A stack of terracotta planters caught her attention. They ranged from tiny pots, only three inches in diameter, to larger ones that must have been three feet across. Some of them were even vaguely cauldron shaped. But they all had drainage holes in the bottom, and even the largest pot wasn't big enough for her to sit in.

Moving toward the back of the barn, her foot caught on an uneven floorboard. She stumbled forward, almost toppling headfirst into a horse trough. There was a beat where she contemplated her own clumsiness before she realized that she was staring into her new bathtub.

Someone had stacked a pair of old dining room chairs in the basin, so she pulled them out and set them aside.

"Hey Erin." Izzy's voice came from outside the barn.

Erin lifted the handle that was welded to one side of the steel trough, testing the weight. Not too bad.

"Erin?"

Erin heaved the tub over her head and side-stepped her way out of the maze of junk into more open space.

"Erin!"

She let the tub fall to the ground with a clang.

"What?!"

"Come here," Izzy said.

Erin inhaled deeply, trying not to lose her temper. Was this what it was like having a kid?

Mom. Mom? MOM! I'm bored.

Mom. Mom? MOM! Come here!

Mom. Mom? MOM! I'm hungry.

She let the breath out slowly, puffing her cheeks with air.

"I'm busy."

"But you have to come see this!"

She sounded different this time. Not quite scared, but something. Something that told Erin she better go look.

The tank dragged behind her as she made her way to the white rectangle of light that was the open door.

At first all she could see was white. She squinted and blinked, waiting for her eyes to adjust after the murky gloom of the barn.

Izzy's finger pointed at the sky, off toward the horizon. A plume rose there, like a black feather sticking out of the ground, the end listing to the right because of the wind. At first she thought it was a tornado, but that didn't make sense. The skies were clear and blue. That and it didn't actually look quite like one. In all the pictures she'd seen of tornadoes, the sides were sort of smooth. You could almost tell from looking at a photograph that it was a sucking, swirling vortex.

But this… this had the almost fluffy looking sides of a cloud. Finally it dawned on her that she was looking at a column of smoke. The base looked almost solid. From this distance she couldn't see the roiling movement of the plume. But toward the top where the smoke thinned into lighter wisps, the haze swirled slowly, caught by the air currents.

"What do you think it is?" Izzy asked.

"I don't know. A house maybe, or a building. Something big."

Neither of them spoke for a moment. Izzy broke the silence.

"Maybe we should try to get closer. To see."

Erin almost considered it for half a second, her curiosity piqued. But then she shook her head. Bad idea.

No, terrible idea.

First, because she had no idea how far away it was. She had no sense of judging a distance like that. Was it two miles? Or ten?

But second, and more importantly, that smoke was visible for miles around. There was no telling how many people it might draw. Like moths to a porch light. It could even be a trap, couldn't it? She imagined the sound of the bug zapper her grandparents had in their backyard when she was a kid. The blue glow luring bugs in and frying them in a buzzing flash of light.

"What's that?" Izzy said, gesturing behind Erin.

She craned her head to look over her shoulder, following Izzy's gaze. She was still holding the galvanized water trough in one hand. The metal clanked as she dropped it to the ground, all thoughts of building her own fire evaporating at another glimpse at the sky.

"Nothing," she said.

Mitch

North of Bethel Park, Pennsylvania
42 days before

The car crested a hill as they approached town, the road winding around a bend with a sheared wall of rock to their left. Turning to their right, they looked down upon the city in the valley below, upon the big buildings downtown and the rows of houses and businesses. Black smoke billowed everywhere, an ever roiling cloud hung up above the streets, concealing the tops of the high-rises. Mitch smelled the char after a few seconds of staring at the smoke, like burnt popcorn mixed with a chemical odor. Jesus. What was he driving them into?

"It's on fire?" Matt said.

"It's from the riot," Mitch said.

A glance in the mirror showed no fear on his son's face. He looked engaged, perhaps even a little excited.

Mitch angled to get a look at his eldest son. Kevin's eyebrows scrunched together, that wrinkle forming between them. He looked hateful, Mitch thought.

"Dad, what is going on?" he said. "Where's mom?"

"I told you-"

"Bullshit. You didn't tell us anything, like always. You never said where she was. You told us the softened version, all mushed up like baby food. Where is she? For real."

Mitch adjusted his grip on the wheel, a film of sweat

greasing the surfaces of his palms like two oil slicks. He wiped them on his jeans, one then the other. His heart battered away in his chest, not fast so much as particularly violent beats.

"Well," he said, drawing out the moment as though he could find a way out of it if he stalled. "If you want to know the truth, I think she's dead."

Matt's mouth dropped open and he clapped a hand over his eyes.

"You *think* she's dead or you *know*?" Kevin said.

Mitch craned his head around to face them again, that clammy feeling from his palms crawling over all of him now, leaving its greasy trail everywhere it touched. When his eyes looked into theirs, he blinked a few times, a rapid fluttering of his eyelids, something just shy of flinching. His head felt swollen, and his face felt too hot and too cold at the same time. In no way did this seem like a thing he was actually doing. He felt outside of it, like he was watching it happen rather than participating.

"Guys, I'm sorry. I didn't know how to tell you," he said. "She's gone."

He turned back around, and silence fell upon the car. That thoughtful quiet one encounters in waiting rooms at doctor's offices, emergency rooms, and abortion clinics, places where people mull lists full of bad options, and pain, and unhappy endings.

The sun shimmered in the sky to their right, an orange ball of fire. Mitch opened his mouth, stretched his jaw, felt some amount of soreness in the muscles in the sideburn region on both sides. What the hell? He rubbed his fingers at one of the knotted up spots. Could this be a result of the black gunk spreading through him? A gland there or something? He didn't know. So many things he didn't know just now. Important things. He would never know most of them, he figured.

He wondered... If Janice was right about how it all worked, did that mean he would go to Hell? Would he pay forever for the choices he made? Right now it seemed like a kind of justice to him. Just cover him with gas and set him on fire and be done with it. But it couldn't be so simple. He had two other people depending on him.

"Where the fuck is she?" Kevin said. "Stop bullshitting us. What's going on? Just tell us."

Mitch's hand dropped from his jaw.

"Just look around, kid. The world is going to shit in a hurry," he said. "A bunch of people are going to die. Maybe most of the people if things go as wrong as they possibly can. Hell, maybe even all of the people."

"Answer the question, Dad. Where is mom? Why can't you just tell us the truth?"

Mitch spoke into the mirror, making eye contact with the furious pair of eyes there. It felt safer that way.

"The truth is that I'm going to die, too. I'm sick the same way your mother was. I don't have long. I'm trying to find a place where you guys can be safe once I'm gone, and I don't think I'm doing a very good job. The truth? The truth is that I don't really know what I'm doing. I'm not sure I ever did."

The quiet returned after he spoke. Mitch looked away from the mirror, avoiding its gaze to watch the other cars instead. A semi passed on their left, mud flaps wobbling behind the sets of tires. The branches of the trees all drooped along the side of the road here. Even the plant life was withering away.

The tires thumped over cracks in the road. He followed a line of cars onto the exit ramp, felt the centrifugal pull as they curled away from the highway, slowing down all the while. They came to a stop at the light, and Mitch braved a glance into the mirror. He wasn't sure what to expect, but he found them staring out their windows as always. Maybe they looked scared, just a little bit, he couldn't tell. Mostly their features looked smooth and calm, he thought. Blank as ever.

After waiting at the light, they turned right onto West Main, moving back into town. They were almost home now.

Teddy

69 days after
Moundsville, West Virginia

The empty road ran out ahead of him and disappeared over a hill. From his vantage point, it looked like the woods swallowed the highway up, but he knew that wasn't true. The woods couldn't actually do that.

He stalked down the side of the road, walking in that strip of dirt and rocks that separated the green of the woods from the blacktop. Little clouds of dust kicked up with each footstep. The air was still, and the smell of death was everywhere. Flies circled around him, around the duffel bag hanging at his side. The rise and fall of their collective buzzing reminded him of radio static, that endless swirl of noises piled on top of each other that somehow added up to a big nothing.

He watched his shadow walk along beside him, the black copy of his torso and arms stretched comically long over the asphalt, angled so the head of the shadow cheated out ahead of him to lead the way. He was tall, a touch over six feet and three inches. His shadow was more like nine feet tall just now, he thought, most of it torso.

A fly landed on his cheek, and he shooed it away with a flutter of his hand. Touching his face, he realized his mouth was open, jaw hanging wide, so he closed it. He didn't like that. His mama always yelled at him for it, said the kids at school would make fun of him, and she was right. They called him a mouth-breather and a retard. But that was over now. He'd been out of school for a long time, and all of those people were dead and gone, his mama included.

The sun beat down on the back of his neck, the peeling pink flesh there perpetually sunburned. He touched it, felt the sting of the burn and the wet of the layer of sweat lingering there. His elbow touched the hatchet holstered at his side. Always there if he needed it.

There wasn't much traffic. Not anymore. In town, he hadn't seen any passing cars in weeks. But out here on the highway they went by every so often. Enough for him to get what he wanted, apparently.

He got a whiff, a strong one. Freshly dead meat.

And then he saw the black shapes on the road up ahead. They looked like crooked hooded things from here, three of them, their backs all hunched over to feast on the dead. He ran at them, waving his arms and yelling as he got close.

The vultures turned their backs to him at first, two of them splaying their wings to try to intimidate him. Their beaks opened up, and they stared at him with their dead eyes. He kept running, and they took off one by one, doing some reverse swoop that lifted them into their circular patrol of this spot. They had no intention of leaving this meal. Neither did he.

He stood in the dusty spot the birds had just vacated, licking his lips in excitement. A dead raccoon lay at his feet. The animal's belly had swollen up so big that it pushed all of its legs straight out. He thought it looked funny, like a volley ball with limbs and fur.

He knelt to gather up the road kill and shove it into the

duffel bag with the others. He'd always loved animals.

Mitch

Bethel Park, Pennsylvania
42 days before

The sound of video game violence blared from the next room, the boys finding solace in blowing off heads with shotgun blasts. He sat at the kitchen table making calls. Nobody was picking up. He stared into the circle of light reflecting off of the wood tabletop with the phone pressed to his ear, listening to it ring, knowing the person on the other end wouldn't pick up since none of them did.

He'd returned home, a place he never thought he'd be again. Something about it reminded him of an injured dog crawling under the porch to die.

He tapped his toe at the linoleum, swished the other socked foot back and forth. Janice always hated when he did that. It turned the bottom of his white sock black. Nothing to worry about now. The phone rang and rang and rang in his ear, and then it cut off, and a robot voice asked him to leave a message. He hung up.

He and Janice had never really made friends in Bethel Park. Not really. He'd moved them here for a job, and the family had kept to themselves. He regretted that now. Being retired, her dad and his new wife had moved in nearby when the kids were born to do all of the babysitting and the like. Outside of work he didn't know anyone, and he certainly didn't know anyone that he'd be comfortable leaving the kids with aside from the grandparents.

The only people he could think of were the parents of Kevin and Matt's friends, but none of them had answered, and he wasn't all that comfortable with the notion to begin with. It didn't seem right to set the fate of his family into the hands of people he barely knew, but he had to try something. Maybe one of these families could watch them until the grandparents were tracked down. That'd be a start.

He hung up on another voicemail greeting, thumbed through his contact list to find another number, selected it. As it rang, he ran his finger along the smooth wood before him, tracing along the perimeter of the circle of light there. His touch skimmed along the surface, just barely making contact so it tingled in his fingertip.

He switched hands, holding the phone with his left now. His right index finger dragged along the table, just as the left had, but no tickling occurred. He had jammed this finger into a car cigarette lighter when he was a kid. The first two times he did it, he'd waited until it faded from red to black and it was still hot but not incredibly so. Just hot enough to feel interesting, to almost sting. The third time, it faded to black very quickly, and touching it sent a poke all through him. The pain shot like a bolt from a crossbow from his finger to his elbow, gave him that spinal reaction where his hand withdrew and dropped the lighter to the floor before he even felt it. He held his finger up to his face, seeing a blackened version of his fingerprint in place, ash which smeared off along with the rest of the tip when he wiped it on the seat. It didn't truly hurt until after the smear. He cried for hours, though he never really noticed a lack of sensitivity in that finger until just now.

No answer again. Of course.

Daylight faded outside, the sky achieving those gray shades that set in just before the sun goes down. He couldn't see the black smoke looking out the window from this vantage point, just a clear sky. Staring into the blank heavens a while, he could almost believe society wasn't collapsing out there, that his body wasn't betraying him from the inside, disease conquering his innards piece by piece. Sitting here, he could glimpse how things used to be, when it felt like he had no real worries, like he could look forward to movies and football games and beer forever.

If you block out most of the view, you can live in paradise, he thought. Not for long, but for a while. It's not real, of course, but what you see is what you believe. Is that the best anyone can do, though? Construct a false paradise to live in for a little bit?

Anyway, none of it mattered. Not anymore. He shifted in his seat, and the black smoke became visible in the corner of the window.

His thumb swiped through the contacts again. He'd run through them all now and would need to start retrying. It felt hopeless.

Movement caught his eye. The circle of light reflecting off of the tabletop flickered, dimming down to a faint glimmer that pulsed like a strobe. He looked up at the fixture above as the illumination swelled back toward full power. Just as his eyes connected with the orb of light glowing down on his head, it winked out.

Shade overtook the room. The house went silent aside from the ticking of the grandfather clock, the video game gun noises suddenly cutting off.

The power was out.

Teddy

69 days after
Moundsville, West Virginia

He pulled the dead animals from the bag one by one and laid them in the grass. He'd learned not to dump them out all at once. The burst abdomen of a groundhog taught him that lesson the hard way. Its slimy gray guts slid out and spread over the rest of the road kill like a puddle of gore. He was used to bad odors, but that smell made him vomit immediately. Never again.

Decent haul today. He'd landed three squirrels, though one was flattened, a rabbit and the raccoon. These should work well, he thought. People had always told him not to pick up road kill, not to play with it, not to put it in his locker at school. But everyone was gone. Nobody could tell him what to do anymore.

Funny to think back and know how much trouble animals had nearly caused him. Back before everything went to shit, he was a garbage man. Manned the back of the truck for four years, and he never lost his fascination with the rear loading machine. He threw in bags of garbage, pulled the lever and the blade would come swinging down to pull all of the trash together and squish it into something tiny. Then the tiny bit would get pushed off into the pile.

He could throw anything in there and watch the machine make it tiny. Some things, tall things like the pole from a

241

basketball hoop, would take a few runs. The machine would bust off a piece of the pole and crush it, then another and another. In the end, though, it'd be tiny like all the rest.

He loved his job, loved to watch the garbage water squish everywhere once that blade did its thing, loved the sound of different items being destroyed. He lived to throw in new things: lamps, recliners, big screen TVs, microwaves.

One day he watched a black and white cat paw at a garbage can up ahead. It got scared of the truck's noise and ran into some bushes as they got closer, but he called it over. He kneeled down and cupped his hand to make it look like he had a treat for it. The cat hesitated for a second and then trotted to him. The fact that he reeked like garbage juice might have helped, too. He wasn't sure.

He felt a tingle run up and down his entire body when he tossed the cat in and pulled the lever, a surge of energy that made all of his hairs stand on end. The blade swung down. This popping noise was different than any of the others. It made him hard right away. He had to put his jacket in front of it before they went to the next house, and he barely stopped giggling the whole rest of the day.

Even now, he laughed thinking about that sound. It was like something from a cartoon. Like Wile E. Coyote splatting against a rock wall.

He got three cats and two dogs that week.

And now he handled more dead animals, picking at the pieces of road kill he'd gathered and laying them out in their proper spots, waiting for them to help him find new pets to play with.

Erin

Something dark stirred in the front yard. A big, black dog. She could tell something was off, though. It wasn't moving right. It was writhing. Twitching. Erin grabbed the back of Izzy's t-shirt to stop her. They did not tangle with dogs.

"What is it?" Izzy said, and even though she'd said it quietly, it was enough.

It burst toward them, but at the same time it exploded, breaking into half a dozen pieces that flew into the sky. Erin pulled Izzy backward a few steps before she realized it wasn't a dog at all, but a group of buzzards.

They swarmed overhead in a low circle, not ready to give up their meal just yet. One of the birds broke from the flock. It swooped down and perched on the top of a white pickup truck parked in the driveway, head angled sideways to better watch them.

Erin moved forward, but Izzy didn't budge.

"I don't like them."

"It's alright. They only eat dead stuff."

"But they're huge!"

Erin didn't deny it. At this proximity, they seemed pretty imposing for giant garbage-eating chickens.

For some reason, she thought of the time a seagull had shat on her head. It was on a school field trip to the museum,

243

and they were outside eating lunch in a little courtyard. She felt the wet splat hit her skull, felt the ooze of liquid seep through her hair and drip onto her scalp. And her first thought was that she hoped no one had noticed. For some reason, it made her feel embarrassed. And vulnerable. Like at any moment, the whole class would turn toward her so they could point and laugh at the white splotch on her head.

As calmly as possible, she made her way to the bathroom. She grabbed a wad of the crappy industrial-grade toilet paper and pressed it to her head. Her face was bright red in the mirror, and standing there staring back at herself, tears started to form in her eyes. It seemed like a bit of an over-reaction, and yet there she was. On the brink of crying because a bird pooped on her.

Thinking back on it now, all she could think was that she'd let a hilarious, once-in-a-lifetime situation go to waste because she'd been too self-conscious. Too worried that someone would laugh at her.

She took a deep breath and announced it to the world.

"One time a bird crapped on my head."

Lines formed on Izzy's forehead. "What?"

"Yep." Erin held her fist over her head, then spread her fingers, mimicking an explosion. "Plop!"

Izzy laughed. And Erin laughed.

"My grandpa always said that was good luck," Izzy said.

"Really?"

"Yep."

Erin tipped her head to the side, considering it. "I accept."

The path to the front door took them close to whatever the vultures had been feeding on. Only the ribcage remained, and the surface had been shredded by the beaks of the carrion birds. It looked more like it was made of frayed rope than bone.

"Don't look," Erin said, but Izzy was already staring.

For once the door was unlocked. Not a complete shock, since it seemed the former occupant had wandered into the front yard to die. Erin did a quick sweep, and then she and Izzy started their inventory.

The house yielded a few things to add to their stockpile: more beans, a couple rolls of toilet paper, some candles and batteries. She pocketed some cash in a purse they found in the foyer. But it was the garage that got Erin's blood pumping.

It was brand new, still in the box. 4000 watts. She didn't know anything about generators, but that sounded like a lot of watts.

This was it. The solution to all of their problems. She imagined a ray of light piercing the clouds, a perfect beam coming through the singular garage window to shine on the black and yellow box. A choir of angels began singing the Hallelujah chorus.

Lights. Hot water. Television. She didn't figure any of the channels still worked, but they could watch DVDs. Play video games. Listen to music. All because of a beautiful thing called electricity.

"Thomas Edison, you beautiful bastard," she said.

Izzy pressed her lips together, and before she could even say it, Erin cut in.

"Yeah, I know. *Language*. But this is fudging awesome."

Erin tried to pick up the box but only managed to scoot it across the floor. She adjusted her grip and tried again. It didn't budge. It was too bulky for her to get her arms all the way around, so she couldn't get a good handle on it.

"Help me out."

Izzy set down her bag and stooped at the other end of the box.

"One, two, three-"

They both grunted under the weight, but the box lifted. It soared a whole three inches off the ground before Izzy's end started to teeter. The thud of the box hitting the concrete floor echoed around the garage.

"It's too heavy," Izzy said, clenching and unclenching her fists, trying to relieve her hands after the strain.

Erin noted the text printed on the bottom right corner of the generator box: NET WT. 94 LBS.

Why the hell was it so heavy?

She scratched at a mosquito bite on the back of her arm, annoyed. They'd never be able to carry it all the way. She needed a way to transport it that didn't require brute strength. But how?

Might as well start with the easiest and most obvious method. She opened the screen door that separated the garage and the house, Izzy following close behind.

"We need keys." As the words tumbled out of her mouth, her gaze fell on the table next to the door. Or more accurately, the purse resting on top of the table. She thrust a hand inside, rooting around until she removed a triumphant fist clutching a key chain.

"What do we need those for?" Izzy asked.

Erin stepped outside, disrupting the vultures again. The beasts flapped back into the air.

"For our truck."

Her feet crunched over the gravel. The door opened and she climbed up to the driver's seat.

As she settled into the fake leather, the stink of new car smell wafted over her. She remembered people remarking that they liked the scent of it, but she never understood the appeal. To her it smelled like plastic and rubber. A sickly sweet chemical combination that made her stomach hurt.

Izzy hopped onto the running board and poked her head inside.

"But we already tried this. It never works."

"This time it will," Erin said.

"How do you know?"

Erin watched Izzy reach overhead, grappling the roof of the truck with both hands. She lifted her feet and dangled from the truck like a monkey.

"I just do."

Erin put the key in, closed her eyes, and turned the ignition. Nothing happened.

Erin's eyes opened. She let go, tried again.

Nothing.

She punched the steering wheel and the horn blared, scaring the shit out of her, Izzy, and the buzzards, who had just settled back in on their buffet.

Izzy dropped from her hanging position, stumbled backward in the gravel. She bumped into the door of the truck before catching her balance. Erin looked down at her, their momentary fear dissolving into a fit of laughter.

"Well the horn still works," Erin said.

She scrambled down from the seat, slamming the door.

She barely even knew how to drive, so maybe it was for the best. She'd only done the first half of driver's ed. Not that her lack of a license mattered a whole lot now.

Back in the garage, she looked for anything that might help her move the generator. The best she came up with was looping some rope around the box. She handed one end of the rope to Izzy.

"What am I supposed to do with this?"

Erin wrapped her end around her waist, yanking until the rope was taut.

"We're going to pull it. Like a dog sled."

She surged forward, straining against the weight of the generator.

"Come on! Mush!"

They got as far as the door before needing a break. She plopped down on the box, wiping sweat from her face and trying to catch her breath.

Izzy handed her the water bottle they'd brought along. Erin took a warm swig and almost spit it out, expecting the water to be as cool as it was fresh from the well. She forced herself to swallow it. Better than nothing.

Through the screen of the front door, she watched the vultures pick at the corpse in the yard. The sun was just kissing the tree line. It would be dark before long.

Erin clenched her jaw, not wanting to give up yet and knowing she had to. They'd only managed to drag the box twenty feet before they collapsed in exhaustion. It would take them hours to haul it back to the house. And it was an uphill walk.

That night she lay awake in bed for a long time. She knew

she was tired, but she struggled against it, desperate for a plan that would solve the generator problem.

Maybe a wheelbarrow would work. They'd need to figure out how to get the generator into it, to start. Assuming they succeeded in that, it was still going to be a long, slow walk back to the house, toting almost a hundred pounds.

She felt the pull of sleep urging her to close her eyes. It reminded her of standing on the beach when she was a kid, and how the waves would lap over her feet. As the water retreated, the sand around her toes drained away with it, and the magnetic draw of the tide tugged at her feet.

Erin's eyelids drooped closed and she let go, allowing the current of sleep to drag her under.

Travis

Hillsboro, Michigan
57 days after

Scuffs and grunts and scrapes and thuds echoed about the room. Travis shuffled to his right, toward the place where he could see the muffled glow of the light on one wedge of the floor. He reached under the desk, hand bouncing along the carpet, and then he found the cigar shaped tube of plastic, scooped it, pressed the button, and returned it to his mouth in the dark.

He kept moving, sure they had a good idea where he was based on the light moving and clicking off. He moved toward them, hoping that would come as a surprise.

His cheeks stung from smiling so hard. The grin itself felt less evil now, more like an involuntary expression of this level of stimulation, so much adrenalin that in most ways he felt numb. He wasn't scared. He wasn't anxious. He was vaguely excited and otherwise empty.

He heard a metallic sound, someone doing something with a gun, he thought, but he couldn't tell based on the noise. Immediately he racked the shotgun. Even the second time, the noise was shocking in its volume. The scuffling on the carpet sounded panicked now, and he heard the zipper of a sleeping bag followed by the patter of footsteps on carpet. Someone ran away.

Well, that might be good. He'd heard about that before,

the sound of a shotgun making people run away. Thinking about it, it only sounded like one set of feet, though. If so, that would mean someone was still here with him, waiting in the dark.

He reached up, clicked on the flashlight, wheeled toward the figure standing to his right. The beam glinted on the metal of the gun and flicked to the man's eyes. He squinted, and his nose scrunched up in the light. The guy's arm jerked, the pistol in his hand blazing and popping. The shot missed high, the bullet buzzing over Travis's head and piercing the wall behind him.

And then he squeezed the trigger in turn. BOOM. Another face gone. Glop slapped the wall behind the guy, like a can of red paint splattered there. The figure tumbled to the ground, folding in all of the places possible.

Now feeling came rushing back to him all at once, heat and blood and hatred roaring through him, flushing his face. He looked down on the corpse, the head like a bashed in red melon, the back of it all blown out.

Yeah, fuck you.

His throat tightened up, and his eyes hurt from being open so wide. He wanted to shoot the dead body again, shoot it until all that was left was a blood and bone smoothie in a thick puddle on the floor, but he couldn't do that. He turned out the light, dropping the shotgun and squat-walking toward the doorway as he pulled the handgun free from his pocket. He hated to leave the shotgun, but holding still long enough to load it didn't seem wise, especially adding in the noises the shells would make.

Not done yet. They all die.

As he moved into the hall, he felt a twinge of fear, a flash of how impossible this was, that he would stalk through these offices and kill another handful of murderers who were all armed and waiting for him. Fucking impossible.

But no. The hatred was stronger than the fear. The heat poured into his face again, made it feel like he was submerged in scalding water.

He knew they were scared now, too, and he liked that. He moved toward them, toward where he knew they must be, his body still gliding along, his weight still bounding from the ball of one foot to the other without sound.

The dark seemed less empty now. Somehow all of the hurts were right there with him, all of the pissed beds, and all of the kids laughing when he ran away from a fight, and all of the girls who didn't want him, the ones who accepted his gifts but never really got to know him, and his dad telling him it was OK to be a pussy. They were all right there in the dark, all around him. Not to be scared of. Not to be ashamed of. There to be burned out, to have their faces disintegrated into a bloody spray.

Because the world was empty now. Life and death were all that were left, and he chose death. He wielded death, dealt it from the barrel of his gun. He had become death, the destroyer of worlds. Faces just disappeared if he wanted them to, and he did.

A glow spilled out of the doorway ahead, a rectangular glimmer that crawled across the floor of the hall. It moved a little, the sides of the rectangle slanting. So they were in the next office, at least some of them, handling a lantern or a flashlight.

Good. He liked knowing where they were, and he smiled harder.

His feet padded forward, and the sweat drained down everywhere, and the air felt cold against the wet sheen all over him, like all of his skin was an open mouth in the winter. And for a second he thought maybe he had gone a little crazy at some point in here, that maybe all of the booze and pills had messed him up somehow, and he remembered reading about how insane certain pills could make you. They messed with the sleep part of the brain, the hypnotic part, so the affected person is almost dreaming while awake. But no. He didn't think so.

Things made sense, he thought. This all made sense.

The light moved again, the rectangle's sides slanting the other way, and then he heard footsteps. He stopped walking and aimed his gun at the illumination, waiting for the shadow in the shape of a man to step into the hall. Time slowed down again, and his heart punched away in his chest, trying to beat its way through ribs and sternum.

Something dark flickered in the light, but whatever it was, it didn't quite come into the hall. He stared down the gun, finger not quite twitching on the trigger, but he felt like it wanted to. He breathed in through his nostrils and out through his mouth, the air thick and warm on his lips. The rectangle of light was the only thing that was real.

And then it fluttered a moment, shimmering on the floor like a strobe light, and guttered out. Black filled in the rectangle, and he got a momentary whiff of smoke. So it was a lantern, and someone must have blown it out.

Footsteps clattered out into the hall. Damn. Travis backed

up against the wall, fired two shots and belly smacked the floor. A man yelled in the distance, his voice wild in the darkness like the scream of some wild animal. Apparently he'd hit one of them. Based on the sound, it seemed they were running away from him.

Interesting.

They didn't bother firing back either. That surprised him. He got to his feet, fired two more shots and ran toward them, dragging his hand along the wall to guide him, hearing the door into the main chamber close somewhere in front of him. The echo of the footsteps dropped off at that point, reduced to just his.

Shit. They were getting away.

He clicked on the flashlight, still clenched in his teeth, and the hall lit up in front of him. He stepped over the corpse, two red holes in his chest. The door wasn't far. He got to it, fumbled his free hand over the steel to the handle, opened it. He shut off the light to avoid making himself an easy target.

No clouds tonight. Moonlight glinted through the hole in the factory wall, a soft glow that reflected off of the shiny paint on the floor. He could see them running for the next door, and he realized that he was still in shadow in the doorway. They couldn't see him.

He raised the gun, fired, cocked the hammer back, fired again, cocked the hammer back, fired again. He moved without thought, like his hands just knew what to do. In the distance two of the bodies dropped to the ground, the head on one and the neck of the other spilling blood on the way down.

Vibrations rattled through his arms as he fired four more times. The char of gunpowder filled his nostrils. Pink splotches throbbed in his field of vision in the shape of the flash from the muzzle. The heat undulated in his face, a living, thrashing thing, angry like the surface of boiling water.

Only one person still moved in the distance, the black silhouette of a man hunched down, his movements frantic. What the hell was he doing? Was he hit? Travis fired three shots. Missed. The man still did whatever he was doing, working at something on the ground, maybe.

Travis wiped his palm on his jeans and fired three more times:

Miss.

Miss.

Click.

Shit.

He fired a couple more times, though he knew it was useless. Click. Click. The clip was empty. He reached into his hoodie pocket and found only shotgun shells. Had he packed an extra clip in there? Had he dropped it? He wasn't sure anymore.

Fire roared inside of him, the fumes of it spilling out of his mouth when he exhaled. He wanted to throw the gun down in frustration, but he didn't. He held it.

The shadow rose, turned toward the door. Travis sprinted after him. It was the first time in a while that words had formed in his thoughts:

Not going to fucking happen.

The shadow disappeared through the door, a jangling sound momentarily ringing out around him. Keys. That's what he'd been doing. Stooping to get the keys off of one of the dead guys.

Oh shit, the bodies.

Travis tripped over a limb, an arm he thought, stumbling forward for eight paces before he crash-landed on the floor, his chin hitting along with the heels of his hands and his ribcage slamming down after that. Fuck. His head went swimmy. He couldn't think right, but he dragged himself up onto wobbly legs.

He knew walking out the front door would be dumb, that anyone with brains would wait for him there and kill him on the spot, but he did it anyway. He couldn't run now, not with his legs like two columns of custard somehow propping him up.

He limped into the doorway and walked through it. The night air pressed its chill against his wet flesh, his sopping shirt. Moonlight lit up everything tonight, the road and corn stretched out in front of him.

A gasp inhaled, and Travis swiveled his head to find the man sitting in the driver's seat of the truck. The keys jingled against each other. The man struggled to find the key or the ignition or both, Travis thought.

He stalked toward the truck, feet beating at gravel, and the bandit drew his weapon, the gun shaking in his hand. He could see the fear coming off of him like steam. In that moment, the idea of seeing the fear made perfect sense.

Travis jolted forward like a pit bull going in for the kill, he slammed the truck door on the guy's arm just as the guy fired at him, the bullet flying off into the corn, the gun wrenching free from his hand as the door snapped bones near his wrist. Travis kicked it under the truck.

The guy ripped his arm free from the door, his wrist all

limp. He flopped it once and screamed like a dying cat. So scared. Travis smiled. He wondered what kind of waves came off of him. What was this guy seeing come off of his body that terrified him so?

He peeled open the car door, reached into the truck and ripped the guy out by the collar of his t-shirt. The body slumped straight to the ground, flopping in the rocks in an awkward heap. In the moonlight, Travis saw that the guy was still in his sleeping attire – boxers and a white t-shirt. He seemed small, his torso shivering against the rocks.

Travis moved without thought now, falling on the man, pinning his arms under his knees. He closed one hand around his throat and clubbed the face staring back at him with the butt of the pistol. The first strike split the flesh open red, and it grew more wet from there. The crunch of metal striking bone entwined with a wet slap like bare feet pattering through a mud puddle.

He couldn't really see the human in the thing beneath him anymore somehow. He looked on the injured pieces, the split nose, the broken teeth in the mouth, the eyes open wide and scared, but they seemed more like disconnected body parts that didn't quite form into a man's face. He never got that flash of recognition, that moment when it all made sense.

The body underneath slowly went limp, but he kept slamming away. And the heat came over him again, bubbling and frothing just beneath the surface of his skin.

By the time he stopped beating at it, the man's face was destroyed. Two bulging eyes looking in different directions set in a mess of red pulp with a skull vaguely discernible underneath. The puddle below grew like spilled fruit punch on linoleum, seeping outward in all directions, dark liquid filling in the spaces between the rocks. He sat there a second still breathing hard, looking at the face but somehow not really seeing it. Blood dripped down off the gun, gummy droplets clinging to the metal for as long as possible before they finally let go. He tucked the weapon in his belt and stood.

He walked out into the road, the soles of his shoes clapping against the asphalt. Moonlight shined down upon him, and the air felt thick and damp and cool against his sweat and blood soaked skin. He held his arms out and closed his eyes and let the chill of the night sink into his flesh to finally cool the heat inside of him. The endorphins were there, the ones that come with this kind of primal victory, though the rush wasn't all that impressive compared to the oxy, he thought.

A breeze kicked up and goose bumps raised along his outstretched arms, the tingle running in a wave from his wrists to his shoulders. He took a deep breath and let it out all slow.

Now what?

The restless part of him felt no satisfaction. It already wanted more. More of what, he didn't know.

He opened his eyes and looked down the empty road, the black nothing that stretched out in front of him for as far as he could see, moonlight glinting off of the gooped up patches of tar. And the heat receded another notch inside of him, and the cold gripped something in his chest and made his shoulders quiver for a second. He brushed frigid fingertips at his brow, felt the skin of his face gone clammy instead of burning. The night air was so thick he thought he could see it taking physical form in the distance, a black mist twirling at the horizon.

Now what?

Erin

Presto, Pennsylvania
38 days after

She dreamed she was riding a horse. It galloped at full speed beneath her, tearing across an open plain. She didn't know how to get it to slow down. There was no saddle, so she had to lean forward to clutch the horse's mane to keep from falling off.

The wind in her face stung her eyes, making them tear up.

They broke through some low grass and the horizon came into view. She squinted, not taking her gaze from where the land met the sky.

The landscape ahead dropped away to nothing. They were approaching a cliff.

She panicked, tugging at the horse's mane, lightly at first, and then harder, trying to get it to stop. They continued on at the same pace, heading for the edge of the world.

She thought about jumping off the horse, but she was scared. With her luck, she'd roll right under the hooves and wind up pummeled to a jelly.

The edge came to meet them faster than she'd anticipated. There were only a hundred feet or so left. Looking over the edge, a body of water took shape below.

This was her last chance -- her choice was to jump from the horse or jump with the horse. Her palms began to sweat, but she held tight to the horse's mane, her decision made.

The horse leapt, plunging into the emptiness, and Erin had a brief moment to consider the water hundreds of feet below. She wondered at her choice to stay on the horse before sheer terror took over and her thoughts devolved into pangs of panic.

She felt herself falling, falling, and then she was twitching herself awake in the bed.

She laid there a few minutes, letting her heart rate return to normal, reorienting herself to reality.

Thinking back over the dream, she wondered how many times she'd even ridden a horse? Only once or twice, and yet her subconscious must have recorded and cataloged every detail because the dream had seemed so real.

When she was younger, she and Kelly used to ride around the neighborhood, pretending their bikes were their steeds. Kelly's aunt was a horse trainer, so she always had a specific breed in mind.

"Mine is an Andalusian," she'd say.

Erin didn't know anything about horses, so she'd just pick a color.

"Mine is black."

"It should be a Friesian," Kelly said.

"Whatever," Erin said.

They'd ride their horse-bikes to the crabapple tree at the end of the road and pick a whole bucket full, pretending they were foraging for food. They always snuck an apple or two to feed to the "horses," and after a long ride they made sure to pause at the creek to let their horses drink. Then they'd collect water at the spring and mix it with dirt to make mud pies. They gathered mint to make poultices. All those hours playing at survival. She wondered if that version of herself would have almost thrived in this new world. Maybe that was why Izzy seemed to have such an easy time adjusting.

She sat up in bed, suddenly, realizing that her dream had solved the riddle of the generator. Had that been the whole point? Had the part of her mind that struggled with words and concrete ideas conjured the image of the horse instead?

She crawled out from under the covers and stepped into her shoes. Izzy stirred.

"Where are you going?"

Erin paused in the doorway.

"To find a steed."

Erin returned to the jumbled pile of wheels and spokes and handlebars in the barn. One by one she wrenched the bikes free, marching them into two neat lines. Two didn't have kickstands, so she laid them on their sides. In total there were twelve fully assembled bikes, plus a few extra frames and orphan tires, and the pièce de résistance: one of those bike trailers that functioned as a child seat. She was pretty sure the generator would fit in it.

Erin took her time, deciding which bike looked most promising. The one she settled on was black. A Friesian, she thought, then snorted to herself.

Like everything else in the barn, it was dusty, except for the hand prints she'd left on it when she pulled it from the pile. She wiped a palm along the frame, revealing the glossy finish underneath.

Walking it around the barn, she bounced the tires a little and squeezed the brakes, testing to make sure it wasn't a dud.

The chain looked to be in good shape. A sturdy horse, indeed. Satisfied, she rolled the bike to the door and rested it against the outside wall.

Izzy banged through the screen door of the house, only half-dressed. While she walked, she pulled her t-shirt over her head. Instead of the neck hole, her face found a sleeve, and she had to stop walking for a moment to extricate herself.

"Hey Iz."

Finally her curly head popped through the correct hole. "What?"

"Do you know how to ride a bike?"

Izzy rolled her eyes. "Uh... duh."

"Well, excuse me. Come pick one out, then."

Izzy ran her tongue over her lips as she surveyed the options in the barn. She wove between the rows of bikes and gripped the handlebars of a steely blue ten speed.

"I was thinking something more like that one," Erin said, pointing to a smaller kid's bike with streamers coming out of the handles. "Look, it already has a basket on it so you can carry stuff."

Izzy wrinkled her face into a snarl.

"That's a baby's bike. And it's pink." She turned back to the ten speed. "I want this one."

"Have you ever ridden a bike like that?"

"What's the difference?"

"It has gears for starters."

Izzy toed the kickstand up and walked the bike toward the door.

"I'll figure it out."

Erin sighed and followed her out.

263

"At least let me lower the seat so you can actually get on the damn thing."

"Language."

After adjusting the seat to the lowest position, Erin steadied the bike while Izzy climbed on.

"OK, you can let go," Izzy said, scooting forward a little.

"Are you sure?"

"Yes."

Erin hesitated.

"Erin, let go!"

She released her grip, putting her palms out flat in front of her in a defensive position.

Izzy took off down the drive, wobbling a little and then righting herself. She looped onto the grass and headed back toward Erin, standing to get more leverage on the pedals.

"Why is it so hard to pedal?"

"That's what I was trying to say about the gears," Erin said, turning in a slow circle to follow Izzy as she wound around her. "Keep pedaling and hit that little thumb trigger with your right hand."

The bike wobbled again as Izzy readjusted her focus on her hands, but she kept it under control. There was a pop and a grind and Izzy made a little alarmed sound, but then the gear shifted and she was riding smoothly again.

"Ha! I did it!" She changed gears a second time. "So what's the point anyway?"

"The lower gears make it easier to pedal. Like if you're climbing a big hill, when it gets hard to pedal, you can switch down to a lower gear and then you don't have to do as much work. The higher gears make it harder to pedal, but then you can get going faster on flat ground without pumping your legs like crazy."

Erin turned back to where her bike was propped against the barn.

"We can ride around a little so you can practice some more."

"Whoa!" Izzy shrieked. "You can pedal backward!"

Erin stopped and pivoted to face her.

"Right, that's the other thing. This kind of bike has hand brakes," she pantomimed braking with her hands. "Squeeze the little levers on the handlebars."

Izzy wrenched on the brake and the bike let out a metallic squeal, throwing her forward and off the seat a little.

"I guess they work."

Erin swung her leg over the bike and pushed off the ground, propelling herself forward. The wind rustled through her hair and she smiled. When was the last time she'd ridden a bike? She couldn't even remember. She'd forgotten how fun it was.

When they weren't pretending their bikes were horses, they were cars. They'd put a bag of chips and a can of Coke in Kelly's mailbox, and then pretend they were pulling into the drive-thru at McDonalds.

"I want to try the hill thing," Izzy called back.

"What?"

"The thing where you change gears and it makes going up easier."

"Alright. I guess we can go down to the road and ride up the hill," Erin said. "But watch for traffic."

"Ha. Ha."

They bumped over potholes as they snaked around the final curve of the driveway and then banked onto the blacktop.

Erin could hear the clunking of Izzy shifting gears behind her. It was a long winding ride up the hill, and before long, she was panting for breath. After a few more pedals, she swung the bike around and dropped a leg down to hold it steady, waiting for Izzy to catch up.

"Think you got the hang of it?"

Izzy nodded. "It's pretty cool. I wonder who came up with it?"

"Bike gears?" Erin said. "I don't know."

She looked across a clearing to her right. Below them, she could see where a bend in the highway cut across the green of the valley. Beyond that, the white steeple of a church rose from the trees.

"Ready to head back down?"

Izzy took off down the hill in response, building speed and making car engine noises.

"Brrrrrrrinnnnnnnnnnn-ninnn-ninnnn-niiiiiiiiin!"

As they approached the driveway, Erin realized too late that Izzy hadn't slowed down. And then everything happened in an instant.

She saw Izzy's legs pedaling backward in vain, trying to engage a foot brake that didn't exist.

Erin yelled, "Brake! Brake! Brake with your hands!"

Izzy took her eyes off the road to look at her fingers, but it was too late. The bike swerved off the road and the last thing Erin saw was Izzy and the bike sailing over the edge and into the creek below.

Travis

Hillsboro, Michigan
57 days after

He rode home in the dark, not pedaling much, just letting the bike coast over the craggy road for long stretches. The tires hummed along the asphalt. The sound of the bike reminded him of the noise of fishing line unspooling in double time as the lure is cast, except a never ending version of that sound that rolled down the road along with him.

Otherwise the night was quiet. He could hear the wind rustle the plants in the fields around him once in a while, and the collective chirp of the insects swelled enough to become audible over the bike sound from time to time, but that was it. He could see a bit, though, compared to the last time he made this trek. The moon reflected off of the surface of the road, lighting it up gray, the cracks marbling it with veins of black. He couldn't discern any details of the plants in the fields to his right and left, but the silhouette was there, the blackest places forming odd shapes so it almost looked like the field had tightly cropped curly hair.

He rode on, and the night stretched out a long way. It felt like the quiet and the dark would never end. The empty world would sprawl endlessly in front of him, peppered with the scattered and the dead.

When he rolled up to the house, the dog waited on the

porch. She stood when she saw him bank around the corner, her head down, her shoulders hunched, her tail wagging too fast to see in that half light just before dawn. He dismounted the bike, leaning it up against the porch rail. Hannibal approached, and he set the bag of guns on the deck to kneel and greet her. He rubbed the beast's ears with his fingers, his palm cupping the back of her head. The skull felt small in his hand, the flesh warm. The dog looked at him for a second, eyes squinted in an expression he took as happy, and then she looked away.

It felt weird to have a being care when he got home, like a tiny version of the way things used to be. He didn't know how to describe it, but that was OK. She didn't care. He liked that you didn't have to talk to dogs. You could just be.

They went inside, passing through the doorway into the gloom. He lit a lantern, the dog's nails clicking on the wood floor behind him as she sniffed around near the bottom of his recliner. Ah, she must be hungry, he thought. Out to the kitchen, then. He scooped some kibble into her bowl, and she ate, lifting her head periodically to look at him as her mouth crunched food.

Travis eyeballed the doorway to the steps for a moment, considering bed for a bit, but no. He was much too tired to sleep.

He stirred up a rum and Coke and made his way to his chair in the living room. The dog followed alongside. He sat and sipped and stared at nothing, at the walls and the floor and the shade outside the window that the candles couldn't defeat. It wasn't a relaxing stare. Exhausted as he may be, he found no sleepy idleness in sitting still. Electricity thrummed through him, held his eyes open wide. He felt it all over, a tingle in his hands, a clenching of his jaw, a churn in his gut. His thoughts somehow stayed remote, though, at least as far as remembering the violence he'd carried out just a couple of hours ago.

It came to him in little flashes. The silhouette of the bodies sprawled along the factory floor. The squeal of the truck door as he opened it. The copper smell of the blood. The way the red seeped to fill the spaces in the gravel like a miniature version of a flash flood flowing through city streets. But it didn't seem real. Not all the way. It seemed like a dream or maybe a memory of something that happened in a movie. And it seemed like it was a long time ago.

He slurped warm rum and Coke. He was almost used to drinking room temp booze now. He didn't think he preferred it yet, but he didn't mind it. He thought that if he kept at it long enough, he would eventually favor it over cold, if cold became an option again someday. That would be weird. He imagined himself at a bar ordering a lukewarm whiskey sour, the bartender making a face.

He reached down to pet the dog, and Hannibal pushed her cold snout into the palm of his hand as it approached. Then she lowered her head so he could pet her and blinked a few times. She was a good dog, he thought.

The booze caught up with him then, his head going lighter and lighter, taking on that almost dizzy euphoria of the first stage of drunkenness. It had been several days since he'd had a drink. He wasn't sure how long anymore. Anyway, the time off had resensitized him to this first rush, when the alcohol first elbows in there to kill some brain cells and loosen things up a bit. It felt like old times. Old memories. Old places where old feelings vibrated in the air and echoed down the halls.

He remembered sitting on a couch at a party, talking to a strange girl with severe bangs about old sit-com theme songs, the conversation barely audible over the music, laughing, drinking, being young and drunk and alive. It felt more like thinking about some other person than a memory of himself. Someone he used to know and had forgotten all about until just now. Someone he liked and felt embarrassed for at the same time.

Time got away from him somewhere in there, and then the world went to shit, and all of the people died, even the people he used to be. So who was he now?

A killer. A murderer.

The words didn't come to him with any sense of shame or pride. They rang out in a matter of fact tone in his head. He was a killer, a person who had murdered other people, rightly or wrongly. That was who he was. He could never take it back, and he didn't want to.

He took a big drink of rum and Coke, swiped the heel of his hand across his lips. His shoulders nestled back into the recliner, and he stared out the window, waiting for the sun. To hell with sleep. To hell with it.

Mitch

Bethel Park, Pennsylvania
42 days before

He sat at the table and listened to the grandfather clock tick. Gray shrouded the kitchen, shadows blackening along the edges of the fridge and the countertops, softening the edges of everything, the fading light from the window unable to compete. Shit. The riot must have knocked the power out. For a second he thought maybe that would be it, maybe the electricity would just never come back on as society disintegrated. But no. Things were still together somewhat for now. They would get it back on for a while at least, though he may not live to see it.

The boys made their way into the kitchen.

"Power's out," Kevin said, not making eye contact.

"Yeah, I think it's from the riot," Mitch said. "I'm sure it will be back on before long."

"But why would they want to do that?" Matt said.

"I doubt anyone intended to kill the electricity," Mitch said. "But fires get out of control. Powerlines melt. Transformers fry. It spreads from there."

"What if it never comes back on?" Matt said.

"It will," Mitch said. "There's work to be done and money to be made. Trust me, they'll keep fixing it until there's no one left to fix it."

"That can happen?" Matt said. "There can be no one left

to fix it?"

"Well, no," Mitch said. "I mean, yeah, I guess it could happen, but I just meant it more like a figure of speech. Don't worry, Matt. They will keep on fixing it."

"OK," Matt said.

"Shouldn't we do something?" Kevin said. "I mean, like, aren't there things we should be doing?"

"I've been making calls," Mitch said. "Hopefully I'll be able to get a hold of your grandparents as soon as possible. That's probably the most important thing. What did you have in mind?"

"I don't know. Should we try to stock up on food and stuff like that?" Kevin said, still looking at the floor.

"Maybe you're right," Mitch said. "It could get busy with the power out, but it's probably not out everywhere yet. We could grab food, ice, maybe some flashlights. Bet those are flying off the shelves."

Mitch made a quick list, and they piled into the car again, though nobody had to hold any boxes on their laps this time. Headlights lit up the night all around. The traffic seemed thick. Cars packed together at intersections like herds of cattle jostling along their fence, looking for some way out. As they waited at a stoplight, the other cars surrounding them, he thought this could be a mistake. That they'd get stuck out here, engulfed in the riot and the traffic somehow and never even get home, encased in the car with zombies closing in, the other cars so close they couldn't open the doors or climb out of the windows. But the paranoia faded when they got moving once more.

The gun on the passenger seat made him feel a little better

anyway. He'd already decided that he'd tuck it in his belt on the way in. Nobody was going to be enforcing any right to conceal permits with half of the city on fire. They'd gotten caught with their guard down outside of the cabin. It wouldn't happen again.

For a few blocks they saw no signs of electricity, dead streetlights leaving the sides of the road in blackness, but then a glimmer of color took shape in the distance. The golden arches and the Burger King logo glowed yellow, red, and orange. Good. Hopefully the grocery store down here had power, too.

Streetlights and traffic lights returned as they rolled on, though not all of them were up and running. It seemed a little hit or miss. Still, there was enough light to see there was no smoke anywhere too near, no masses of humanity kicking and thrashing and knocking down doors and windows. It looked a little busier than normal, but that was it.

"Damn," Mitch said as they approached the unlit Kroger sign.

Darkness shrouded the parking lot, the open space made to feel foreign in the gloom. They pulled in, advancing slowly into the shadows, and it felt like creeping across some African prairie, Mitch thought, the way you could see the flattened land stretch off with the occasional lightpost rising up like a tree to interrupt the flatness. The cars were just a texture along the horizon, their details invisible apart from the silhouettes of their tops.

"There's a light on inside," Kevin said.

Mitch looked up at the front doors before them and saw the headlights reflected off of the glass there, but only darkness behind the glass. Glancing back at his son, he following the trajectory of the boy's outstretched finger. Ah. The lights on the other side of the store were on.

"Nice," he said. "They must have a generator going to power the half of the store with the groceries."

They eased over to that side of the lot. The businesses along the street walled them off from the traffic, so the night felt silent and empty after all of the time surrounded by traffic. The other half of the lot throbbed with activity, though. Mitch saw the headlights of minivans and SUVs pulling in and parking. Another movement flitted among the shadows. It took him a moment to realize that droves of people flocked toward the store, some streaming out of cars while others arrived on bike and foot.

Shit. He licked his lips, tongue dragging over sharp chapped spots in the corners, almost crusted. The phantoms shifted in the dark places, their faces scrunching when the headlights hit them. He didn't like it. Too many people. Too much chaos in the air tonight. He swiped fingers at his forehead, felt a little sweat there.

"Can I ask you something?" Matt said, his head appearing at Mitch's shoulder, in the space between the seats.

"Me? Yeah."

"Can we get some Oreos?"

He looked at the boy, his face dead serious in the glow from the dash lights.

"Yeah, sure," Mitch said. "My boy wants Oreos, he'll have Oreos. You want anything Kevin?"

He tried to find his older son's face in the rearview, but he saw only the faint red glow of the taillights bleeding through the rear windshield. The boy's voice piped up from the gloom:

"I don't know. I'll think about it."

The disembodied voice sounded thicker than Mitch remembered. His son was getting older, but he'd never get to see him become a man, start a family of his own. To him, both of his sons would be boys forever, and forever might only be a few more hours.

The despair of the thing settled upon his shoulders as he parked the car. He closed his eyes and put his head down on the wheel, heard the sound of the back doors open and close as his sons exited the vehicle. He sat there for a moment, head touching the rounded top of the wheel, eyes drifting open to stare into the black nothing where his feet must be.

He picked himself up, grabbed the gun and tucked it in his belt as he opened the door and stood. He thought one of the kids might ask what took him so long or perhaps even see him handling the gun under the dome light and confront him about it, but they were distracted. They looked upon the streams of people moving toward the glow of the glass storefront, many picking their way through the narrow pathways between the parked cars rather than braving the aisles where additional cars still roamed.

They joined the throng of foot traffic, following the zigzagging path between the vehicles. The movement all around made Mitch uptight, and yet something about traveling along with this large group felt social, almost on a primal level, some shared experience in a stressful moment. Like nomads pressing toward a watering hole, maybe.

The square of glowing glass before them seemed to get bigger and bigger on the horizon as they advanced. It burned incandescent against the night, not quite a white light, somewhere toward the shade of egg nog. The traffic pouring into the lot let up, and in the ensuing silence Mitch heard a motor growling in the distance like an idling lawnmower, perhaps the generator out back, he thought.

His heart rate picked up as they got close, the fist shaped muscle in his chest squeezing tighter and tighter, rattling the walls of his chest with each beat. He felt kind of dumb about it, about getting jacked up over arriving at the store, but he couldn't help it. He was awake now. Alive.

Stepping through the doorway, the light was everywhere, white and bright and glaring. Mitch couldn't help but smile at how overwhelming it was, his eyes squinted down to stinging slits. He pressed his forearm against the gun in his belt to make sure it was still there.

"Dang," Matt said. "Too bright."

They toddled forward, half blind, legs staggering out choppy steps as they struggled to keep pace with the crowd around them, all of the people making their way into the open.

Baghead

Rural Oklahoma
9 years, 126 days after

A black dream. No lightning this time. He moved in shadow, walking into nothing, the dark surrounding him, swallowing him up like he wasn't all the way real. He didn't mind that idea of himself, his physical being, reduced in some way, still here but not all the way.

He chose his steps carefully, his feet picking their way over obstacles, somehow able to navigate the roughage even without seeing it. It occurred to him that his movements seemed assured, seemed to have purpose that he wasn't quite aware of. That didn't make sense. Did it?

He stopped walking. Some feeling here struck him as familiar yet new. Like he'd been in a thousand different versions of this place, wherever it was.

Could it be a dream?

He reached for his face, unsure if he'd find the old or the new. He braced himself for either result – the rough feel of the canvas bag or the smooth flesh of his old face restored. His fingers closed in and closed in and found nothing where the bag should be, where the jaw should be, where the cheek should be. Nothing at all. Empty space.

His hand flailed around, looking for anything solid, finally descending toward his torso, feeling along the collar bone to the place where the skin went vertical, climbing the warm flesh along the jugular and finding it sheared off in a stumped neck. His fingers sank into the hole, a jagged bone surrounded by flaps of throat flesh all opened up and wet.

He woke in the Delta 88, recognizing the sound of the engine first and then the uneven throb of the tires rolling over rough patches of road. He adjusted his bag so he could see, the car weaving back and forth over both lanes to avoid the worst of the potholes.

"You awake?" Delfino said.

"Yeah. I am now."

"Good. We're almost there. About five minutes out, in fact."

Bags nodded, the canvas pulling taut against his forehead and releasing.

He looked out the window, noting that the land had flattened out again, and that there were more weeds here, though still nothing like the grass and clusters of trees he'd been hoping to see. Patches of dirt still showed through everywhere. This land was balding instead of bald.

Life was rougher in the places where food still grew, though. The green places. Out in the desert, things were quieter. You had to have money to make that drier climate life work, or you had to be craftier than most. Finding the spot by the river helped a lot in that regard.

"Here we go," Delfino said.

Figures formed on the horizon, distorted by the blur of the heat rising off of the road. Seven of them. The silhouettes looked like men holding assault rifles, but something about it looked off, something that Bags couldn't place. They stood around a metal gate of some kind with a bunch of stop signs attached to it in haphazard fashion, all uneven and some tilted at odd angles. It struck him how clearly he could read their body language and discern their movements, even from a great distance and through the haze rising up from the road. They milled around, shifting their weight from foot to foot, adjusting their grip on their guns or moving them from shoulder to shoulder, leaning forward to spit on the ground.

"Remember, our primary objective here is to not get our heads hacked off. I'll talk. You'll do the opposite of talk. Got it?"

"Got it."

Delfino let off of the accelerator as they got close, the Delta 88 drifting to slower and slower speeds. The haze seemed to clear, all of the details sharpening into focus little by little. They seemed a scrawny bunch, all gaunt faces and stretched-out limbs with deltoids being the only visible muscles among them. Was that what looked so weird from a distance? The rifles rose before Bags could ponder it much, one after another, aimed at their car. A precaution, Baghead hoped.

One of the men in front lowered his weapon and raised a hand, palm out. He wasn't sure if that was a sign for them to stop or if he was communicating with his people via hand signal. And then he got a better look at the man's face. Or the boy's face, he should say. He couldn't have been over 15, a pale stick of a boy with sandy hair and a single black line painted under his eyes. He looked around at the others, all of them sporting the black paint from cheek bone to cheek bone.

And all of them children.

279

Teddy

Moundsville, West Virginia
69 days after

With the traps baited, he walked back to his room to kill some time. This was the hardest part. The waiting.

The ground crunched and scraped with every step. Broken glass littered the sidewalk along with shards of brick and another building material he couldn't place. Most of the front windows of the shops downtown were busted out. It looked like the city was a pinata and someone had taken a stick to it to get all of the candy out. Not much to look at, but this area was a good place for his traps. It had served him well.

As he walked, he remembered getting called into Lewis's office, not three weeks after that first cat got squished by the blade. His boss sat him down in one of those chairs where the upholstery feels like rough carpeting. He knew something was wrong based on Lewis's demeanor. His puff of dark hair looked more frazzled than usual. Extra creases formed around his mouth. His eyes seemed more wet than usual but more fierce, too.

"Teddy, I need to ask you somethin'," he said. "And I need you to be straight with me."

"Yes, sir."

"Rico told me you've been loading cats and dogs into the back of the truck," he said. "Is that true?"

Lewis always sounded like a deep-voiced preacher to

280

Teddy, like some smooth talking character on TV that knew how to make his words sound all nice. His voice had that quality now, but a hushed version, an angry version.

"Yes, sir," Teddy said.

His hands trembled. A warmth crawled up onto his face, and he tucked his chin down to his chest. It felt like being in school when the teacher made him read out loud. His words came out slow and choppy and the kids all laughed, little chortles all around. They laughed like he couldn't hear, like he wasn't a real person.

"Dammit, Teddy. You can't be doin' that," Lewis said. "You can't be doin' stuff like 'at."

Teddy didn't say anything. He knew he did something bad, something worse than he knew at the time.

"Why the Christ would you wanna go and do somethin' like 'at, anyway?" he said. "They lock people up for animal cruelty, you know that?"

Teddy remained silent. Lewis leaned back in his seat and went on.

"Look, Rico is trying to put the screws to me over this," he said. "Says he's going to the cops unless I give him a raise. Says it'd be terrible publicity for us, some whack-job smashing puppies in our trucks, and he has a point there, I expect. A fair point."

He drummed his fingers on his belly.

"It stops now," he said. "I know you. You're not a bad guy. I figure you don't know any better. Other people don't know that, though. Keep fuckin' around, and you'll go to prison. You got that, bub? You can't do it ever again."

"But won't he tell on me?"

281

"Nah," he said. "Shoot, Rico just wants a raise. If he had evidence, he'd have shown it to me to get what he wanted."

Teddy shook the memory off as he turned right into the driveway, closing in on the garage door. He pulled the key to the doorknob, the wire cable unspooling from his belt. With the door unlocked, he released the key, and the wire snapped it back to his waistband. It reminded him of the cord of his mom's vacuum cleaner. He'd lost too many keys, though. He had to keep them attached, right next to the holster that held his hatchet.

From the garage he went through another doorway into the house and then down a flight of steps. He rented a room from an elderly couple, a basement bedroom with two cinder block walls facing two with roughly installed drywall. All bare. Not a single coat of paint on anything. The mattress on the floor was the only furniture there.

The ceiling was also unfinished. He liked to lie on his back and look up at the exposed pipes and heating ducts and wires and joists. It felt like he was seeing the underneath of things, seeing how it all really worked. And he liked to listen to the squeal and thump of the wood when someone walked over the floor above his room.

Nobody walked overhead now, of course. They were all gone. Nobody around but the periodic cars going by out on the highway. He lay down anyway, and his feet dangled off of the end of the twin bed like a child's.

Travis

Hillsboro, Michigan
62 days after

His head dipped as his consciousness slipped away and bobbed back up as he shook himself awake. Oh, shit. Where was he?

He looked around. Sun shined through the windows, bars of light slanting across dirty plates and glasses on the floor all around him. He sat on his bed, his shoulders leaned up against the wall. Right. Yeah, he remembered being in here. A yearbook sat on the bed next to him with a razor and a rolled up dollar bill on it. Yes. He had snorted pills, some odd mixture he hadn't tried before. It was... Wait. What was it again?

He thought about it, and his eyes closed, and he drifted, drifted... Out. His chin slumped to his chest, his whole body gone limp, arms turned to two noodles at his sides. The whole world went deathly still.

And then his breath sucked in with a creaking sound like a swimmer surfacing for oxygen. He popped back up, hands patting around on the comforter. Oh. Bedroom. Right.

Jesus, he was so high. He couldn't think quite right, but he felt good as hell. He knew that much. Pleasure beat in his heart and throbbed in his veins and fluttered in his chest. He had to concentrate to see straight, and once more semen crusted his boxers.

He got a whiff of vomit then. It smelled old, he thought. Can vomit get stale? Wait. Did he puke or did the dog puke? He should remember puking probably, but...

His eyes meandered around the floor, looking for congealed throw up or dark patches on the carpet. There. He saw an orange looking foam with chewed chunks of green bean in it in front of his dresser. Definitely not dog puke. It looked pretty dry, too. It had been there a while.

How long had he been in here now? He wasn't sure.

The rotation was no more. It seemed now he was in a race to snort these pills as fast as he could instead, mixing them together with wild abandon. Some of them fucked his memory. He could remember that. He'd been pretty drunk when he started along this path, so he couldn't quite recall which ones had which effect.

He laughed, not really vocally producing sounds but his body shaking and mouth opening as though to laugh nonetheless. He didn't know what was funny. The puke? Not that funny, he thought. Just more shit he'd have to clean eventually. Still, he laughed on silently, his abs contracting and relaxing over and over so his rib cage quivered in a way that made him hunch. It didn't hurt, but he couldn't stop, and the rib throb became overwhelming. He needed to lie down, to try to sprawl out and hope that'd help it subside.

He pushed his bare feet under the blankets, still shaking out soundless chuckles. Wiggling his toes against the cool of the sheets made him realize that he was dressed for bed. It seemed to be the late afternoon now. Had he been snorting pills in here since the night before? Longer?

The laughing died in time, and he lit a cigarette and stared at a glass on the night stand smudged all over with finger smears. He imagined his fingers pressing against the cup, leaving oily residue with every touch. He looked at the ceiling and breathed smoke as he imagined this, his eyes creeping closed.

He didn't notice the cigarette fall into a fold in the blanket, the cherry pressing its red into the cotton poly blend until it plunged through to the sheet and then the mattress, all of them flickering to brown before going black. His eyelids fluttered. He smelled a smell like burning hair, like the time when he was 12 and he flicked a lighter right next to his ear to listen to the grind of the flint. A strand of his hair vanished into a sizzling sound and a terrible odor. This smelled like that.

The blackened spot on the mattress spread outward like a spilled cola. He felt something in his fingertips in the hand right next to the burning puddle, some shock of warmth. But he rolled away from it, and then the numb roiled up in him again, waves of painlessness and perfection and bliss, and he forgot the smell and the heat and drifted under once more.

The inside of the mattress burned hotter and brighter than the sheet or blanket. The flames licked out and cracked a little, violent snapping sounds like broken ribs and tree branches. The fire hissed its endless exhale.

His eyelids fluttered again. He knew that sound, but he couldn't place it. It reminded him of the back yard, of sitting in the sun bleached chair, boiling water to make coffee.

And then there was a new sound, a sizzle that reminded him of sitting at the kitchen table, his mom standing at the stove with her back to him cooking breakfast. Scrambled eggs, fried potatoes, toast, and bacon. His dad sat across the table, somewhere behind the sports page, his giant mug of black coffee giving off swirls of steam.

For a moment he was aware these images were memories or maybe dreams. Some flash of clarity glimmered through, the notion that he must be asleep, and he wondered if maybe this was what it was like to be in a coma. Then his dad turned the page of the newspaper, and he could see his hair and his forehead, could almost see his father's face, in that second when the pages came together before they fanned back out, and he smelled the bacon again, and he wondered how long it would be until breakfast was ready.

Sleep and pills anesthetized him. He didn't feel the flames crawl over his back, charring the t-shirt, blistering the flesh. In his dream, he smelled the bacon stronger, worrying that his mom might be burning it. Her back stayed to him, her right arm working a spatula at the pans. Maybe it smelled that way on purpose. She liked it crispy to the point that it shattered into dried chunks when you bit it, he remembered.

The dog whined on the other side of the bedroom, high pitch bursts of sound. In his dream, he saw her sitting under the table. He knew, somehow, she wasn't supposed to be there, that her presence didn't quite make sense in some way he couldn't figure, but he was glad she was there. He would give her some of the bacon. He thought she would like that.

He felt nothing when the fire shot up the curtain next to him, engulfing his face in the process. His eyes half opened for a split second, saw some impossibly bright light and closed again. He snuggled back down into the blankets. Too early. He didn't want to go to school today.

And the dog barked, a lone shrill scream, her front paws bouncing up and slamming down with the force of the cry. The sound somehow returned him to the dream, to the kitchen table and the sports page and his mom's back. He reached under the table, his fingers brushing back Hannibal's ears, trying to calm her. He realized he'd never heard her bark before. What could she be so upset about?

She barked again, paused, tilted her head back and barked four more times in a row, each time raring up and jamming her front feet down. She fell back to the sing song melody of a consistent whine, a pleading tone, periodically working her jaw as she whimpered as though she were trying to talk.

Fire roared on the whole mattress now, Travis an unmoving lump in the middle of it. Burning drips of polyester rained down from the curtains, hissing and spitting where they landed on his arms and chest. The blanket melted and fused to the skin of his legs. His boxers did the same.

In the dream, the smoke finally got to him. She was burning the bacon so damn bad that the whole kitchen was smoked up. Must be what the dog was so worked up about.

He tried to tell her, but he could only gag and cough now. He sat up in the bed, melted fabrics congealing with blistered skin, flames dancing around him and on top of him, his face blackened like a burnt rotisserie chicken. He hacked a few times, trying to cough, but the smoke kept catching in his throat, taking his breath away. Finally he lay back, slumping down to the bed in a heap that kept still. His final exhale seeped out, swallowed up by the fire's hiss.

The dog waited a long time in case he might get up, whining periodically as though it might get her master's attention in a way that would bring him back. Once the mattress burned out, the fire died down to a smolder, embers glowing on the floor, smoke spiraling away from a blackened circle on the wall. Eventually, Hannibal thumped down the steps, pressing her snout through the doggie door and walking away from the building.

Erin

Metal clanged against asphalt as she threw her bike to the road and ran toward the spot where Izzy went over the edge.

"Izzy!"

There was no answer.

Gravel skidded under her feet as she came to a stop at the banked lip of the ditch.

Izzy's head and half a bicycle tire protruded from the brown water. A wet mat of hair covered her face, so Erin couldn't tell if she was OK or not.

"Are you hurt?"

One of Izzy's hands appeared from beneath the water to part the curtain of hair. Then she grinned up at Erin.

"I'm OK."

Erin let her eyelids fall closed in relief. All of the air she'd been holding in her lungs exhaled through her nostrils, and then she shimmied down the embankment.

Izzy grunted.

"Except…"

"What?"

"I'm stuck."

"What do you mean?"

Izzy had both arms in the air now, and she wriggled from side to side.

289

"This mud. It's like trying to swim in chocolate pudding!"
Erin started to laugh.

"It's not funny! What if it's like quicksand, and it starts sucking me under?"

Erin scooted to the edge of the bank and stuck out a hand. "Here."

Izzy extended her arm but couldn't quite reach. Erin leaned a little farther until their fingers intertwined and then she pulled. But the mud pulled back, and Erin went toppling into the muck head first.

She floundered under water for a few seconds before righting herself. As she broke the surface, she opened her eyes. At first, all she could see was brown. She had to use her fingers like windshield wipers to clear the mud from her face. Even through mud-plugged ears, she could hear Izzy cackling. At least she was amused.

She shook her head to clear her ears. Bits of mud flung from the ends of her hair, splattering onto Izzy's face in a polka dot pattern.

"Hey!"

Now it was Erin's turn to laugh.

Izzy splashed at her in retaliation.

"You don't want to start this," Erin warned.

Erin cupped her hands together and squirted a stream of water the way her dad had taught her.

"Oh, I'm real scared," Izzy said. Or started to say. She drew out the hard vowel sound in "scared." Taunting, with her mouth wide open.

The jet of water hit Izzy's gaping maw like a bullseye, hitting the back of her throat. The spray cut off the last word and turned it into garbled, sputtering nonsense.

It came out more like, "Oh, I'm real scaaaaAAGGLAGLARGH!"

Erin snickered, reminded of one of those Midway games where you have to spray the clown with a water gun to fill the balloon.

She threw her hands in the air and gave her best impression of an old school carnival barker.

"We have a winnah!"

Izzy coughed and spat and tried to look angry, but it was hard to pull off with her giant gap-toothed grin.

"You're dead."

Erin dodged the softball sized wad of mud flung in her direction.

"You're playing with fire, my friend."

"No, *you* are!"

Erin shot another stream of water at her, trying to get her in the mouth again. Izzy was ready for it this time, snapping her mouth shut and closing her eyes.

Izzy's fist rose from the depths, clutching a gob of mud the size of a grapefruit.

"It's payback time."

Erin ducked under water this time, narrowly avoiding impact. When she resurfaced, before she could even take a breath, a sticky mass of river muck rocketed into her forehead.

"Yes! Eat it!" Izzy said, and then produced a laugh fit for a maniacal cartoon scientist.

An all out mud war ensued, and by the time they called a truce they both looked like swamp creatures.

Erin hooked a finger through the wheel spokes of the bicycle and inched it toward the creek's edge. It really did feel like trying to swim in pudding. Each movement felt like someone had pressed the slow motion button on a remote control.

She slithered up onto the bank and tugged on the bike. The weight of the bike coupled with the suction of the muck made it difficult. Izzy stood a few feet away, smearing the mud on her arms in circles.

"Help me, mudbutt," Erin said.

"I'm not a mudbutt! You're the mudbutt."

Izzy took the front wheel and Erin grappled with the few inches of frame sticking above the water. They heaved, almost falling backward when the swampy mire finally released its grasp on the bike with a *squelch*.

Erin sat on the bank, watching clots of mud drip from Izzy's clothes and hair.

"If you didn't need a bath before, you definitely need one now. Filthy little mudbutt."

With a flick of her fingers, Izzy sent a spatter of muddy droplets at Erin. The sludgy spray plopped against the coating of goop already completely encompassing her person.

Erin ran the flat of her hand over Izzy's arm like a squeegee, scraping several cups of mud away. She repeated this motion over the rest of Izzy and then herself. By the time she finished, the remaining layer of mud had started to dry in the sun. It felt tight on her skin, and when she moved, little cracks appeared, like in pictures she'd seen of Death Valley.

"You know what I could go for right now?" Erin asked.

"What?"

"A Tootsie Roll."

Izzy wrinkled her nose in a scowl.

"No way! That's the crappiest kind of candy!"

"I know," Erin said, lifting her bike from its prone position on the ground. "But for some reason, I want one. My mom used to give me one of those cardboard and plastic Tootsie Roll banks in my stocking every year for Christmas. I threw so many of those away without eating a single Tootsie Roll. Such a waste."

"You're nuts," Izzy said.

"You're telling me that if we found one Tootsie Roll on our next shopping trip, what could be the *last* Tootsie Roll in the whole world, you wouldn't fight me for it?"

Izzy cleared mud from the seat of her bike.

"Milky Ways are better. And Three Musketeers."

"Why don't you just wish for a unicorn while you're at it? I'm not talking about what candy is the best. I'm talking about the weird but unique, semi-chocolatey, taffy thing that is the Tootsie Roll. They're not the best. But there's nothing else like them."

"I guess I'd have a bite."

"Ha! Like I'm sharing."

Back at the house, they took turns filling a watering can at the rain barrel and then holding it over the other person's head like a mini shower. It wasn't a bad setup, except that they ran out of water pretty quickly. Erin tried using water straight from the well, but it was so cold, she actually screamed when Izzy dumped it on her, her torso jerking with that spinal response that reminded her of touching the handle of a hot pan.

She scratched her head. She could still feel the grit of the mud on her scalp.

Now that she'd solved the puzzle of how to move the generator, she felt less urgency to do so. It wasn't going anywhere. And so her thoughts returned to a bath.

Her eyes flicked over to where she'd left the horse trough next to the barn. The idea of a fire still made her uneasy. Whenever that image of smoke on the horizon came to mind, she got bubbleguts again.

Still, they'd have to build a fire sooner or later. Maybe she'd start small, with a test fire to see how much smoke it made.

After a lunch of jam on crackers and green beans — "more like gray beans," Izzy said — they got back on their bikes. Erin led the way back to the rhubarb house. It was a good distance away from their place, probably at least a mile, and Erin remembered seeing some wood stacked out back.

The grass closest to the house was nearly up to her waist, but as she swished through it and got closer to the shade cast by the woods, the grass thinned out. She hadn't noticed before, but there was a ring of cinder blocks next to the woodpile. A fire pit. Perfect.

Izzy hopped onto the circle of cement blocks and walked around it with both arms out, like it was a balance beam.

"Don't fall in. You'll get all sooty," Erin said.

"I won't."

Izzy bent her knees and dismounted.

Erin pulled three logs from the pile, upsetting a spindle-legged spider that went scurrying deeper into the pile.

Squatting next to the bricks, she arranged the wood in a teepee shape, the way she'd always seen on TV. She'd never actually made a fire before, but how hard could it be? Make a teepee, crumple up some paper for kindling-

Oh.

She hadn't thought about that. Hadn't planned much at all before leaving the house, other than grabbing a lighter. She'd been so proud of coming up with the idea of a test fire that she kind of just rushed out without thinking too far ahead. Idiot.

She patted her pockets and came up with a wadded up Kleenex. Izzy sat next to her, snapping the twigs from a fallen branch.

"Got any paper?" Erin said.

Izzy shook her head. But then her eyes went a little wider.

"I can go get some from inside."

She hooked a thumb over her shoulder.

"Oh, right."

Of course there'd be paper in the house. Maybe she wasn't such an idiot after all.

The green bucket was still in place by the window, but they went around front to enter. Erin never locked the doors after they were finished. Seemed pointless.

It was odd being back inside one of the houses. There was still some of the same uneasiness. A sense of being a trespasser. But at the same time, there was a feeling of familiarity since they had been inside before. Erin stood just inside the door, absorbing the sensation. Izzy bounded past her, up the steps.

Erin followed, pausing in the kitchen to peer into the can

of nacho cheese.

"Gross."

Izzy's head popped up from behind the breakfast nook.

"What is it?"

"That huge thing of nacho cheese."

"Is it all moldy?"

Erin shook her head.

"No. It looks exactly the same. It must be indestructible, like Twinkies."

Izzy laughed.

Erin heard rustling and then Izzy was waving a stack of newspapers at her.

"Will these work?"

"Does a bear shit in the woods?"

"Language!"

Back at the fire pit, Erin slid a sheet of newsprint from the pile. Her hand started to crumple it, until the front page headline caught her eye. She stopped, eyes flicking left to right over the letters.

US Death Toll Reaches 16 Million.

A sub-headline read - Pandemic Swells Worldwide.

She stared at it, trying to imagine 16 million people dead. And that was just the beginning.

"What are you reading?" Izzy said.

"Nothing."

Erin scrunched the paper into a ball and nestled it under her wood teepee.

"I was just thinking about how I didn't think anyone got the newspaper anymore. The paper version, I mean."

Erin added more paper balls to the pile. She got to the

Sunday comics and paused. She pulled that sheet free and handed it to Izzy.

"Here. This was the only part of the paper I was ever interested in reading."

Izzy took the page, face already glued to the colorful images.

"My parents used to wrap most of the Christmas presents in the old Sunday comics."

Izzy wrinkled her nose.

"Were you poor or something?"

Erin laughed.

"Maybe that was part of it. But I think they also thought it was less wasteful than buying fancy wrapping paper that was just going to get torn off and thrown out after a few minutes."

She found another section of comics and set it aside. It seemed wrong to burn the comics pages for some reason. She wasn't sure if it was nostalgia or just that it was so much more colorful than the rest of the paper.

"Plus, they are pretty festive."

Izzy chuckled at one of the strips.

"I forgot to warn you. I don't know if they still print it, but beware of Family Circus."

"Why?"

Erin pantomimed sticking her finger down her throat and made a gagging sound.

The button on the lighter clicked under her thumb. She held it under the paper, watching the orange flame scorch the paper black. The flames spread, engulfing the pile of paper and sending fiery tongues to lick over the logs.

Erin rocked back on her heels, proud of herself. She'd

started her first fire. And then the flames died, sputtering out as the last of the paper was consumed.

"Damn," she said.

"L-A-N… however you spell Language!"

"Well, the fire went out."

Izzy peered over the edge of her comics pages.

"You didn't use any of the kindling I made."

With one toe, she kicked at the pile of twigs she'd broken from the dead branch.

"Oh," Erin said. She'd been thinking Izzy was just tearing the branch apart for fun. "Have you done this before?"

"Not by myself. But breaking the sticks into kindling was always my job when we went camping."

Erin started over, scrunching the paper into wads, tossing them under the wood. Here and there she added some of Izzy's sticks. She lit the pile again, crossing her fingers.

As the flames grew higher, she added more of the twigs, watching the outsides blacken. It was working. The smaller pieces were actually burning now. She threw on more paper and more of the wood caught. The fire crackled and popped, one of the embers exploding into sparks.

Erin took a few steps back from the heat and observed that it really wasn't creating a lot of smoke. She went back around to the front of the house, watching for any wisps above the roof line, but there were none. It wasn't a huge fire, but really, the smaller the better for their purposes.

Still, she wanted to test this right. What if it rained for a few days and they had to burn wet wood? Back at the fire, she threw on more wood, hoping a bigger fire might make a bit more smoke. It didn't.

"Try some leaves," Izzy said, not even looking up from the comics page.

"What?"

"My neighbor used to burn leaves every fall. It made a ton of smoke."

Worth a try, Erin thought.

She scooped a bundle of dry leaves into her arms, waddled to the fire, and dumped them on top, dusting her hands together. Almost instantly the leaves began to smolder and smoke. She went back for another two armfuls, trying not to think of all the bugs and worms and other creepy crawlies inside. When she was satisfied with the amount of smoke, she pulled at Izzy's sleeve.

"We should go hide. Just in case."

Crunching through the dry leaves littering the forest floor, they walked deeper into the woods. They found a fallen tree to perch on and waited. Izzy was still perusing the newspaper.

"Ew," Izzy said.

"What?"

"Family Circus."

"Told you."

Erin noticed that the trees over the fire seemed to disperse a lot of the smoke, keeping it from rising in one concentrated column. Worth keeping in mind.

Minutes passed, and the flames died down. When it was only embers left, Erin decided to call it a success.

She kicked at the dirt next to the fire pit, trying to smother the remainder of the fire. The last thing she wanted to do was create some kind of monster forest fire out here.

"Go see if you can find something to put the fire out,"

Erin said, and Izzy took off toward the house, the comics pages flapping behind her like a cape.

Erin expected her to return with a pot filled with water from the toilet tank. Or maybe a fire extinguisher. What she did not anticipate was Izzy lumbering around the corner of the house with the giant can of cheese.

"Nice," she said, rolling her eyes.

"Well, we're not going to eat it, are we?"

"Just be careful. Don't cut yourself on the lid or something dumb like that."

Izzy upended the container over the fire and a viscous orange liquid oozed out. The top had formed a skin, and that came out first, followed by a slightly lighter hue of cheese goop. It slopped into the pit, sizzling as it hit the embers. The heat caused the cheese to boil and bubble, like the mudpots she'd seen when her family took a trip to Yellowstone. It made a wet noise like someone blowing raspberries.

"Cheese farts!" Izzy said, giggling.

Steam rose, imparting a smoky-cheesy smell to the air. Cheese farts, indeed. But it worked. The cheese sludge had extinguished the fire.

Erin turned to Izzy.

"We made history today, Iz."

"Because now we can have a fire?"

"No. Because I guarantee you that's the first time anyone has ever used nacho cheese to put out a fire."

She held up her hand for a high five.

Mitch

Bethel Park, Pennsylvania
42 days before

The white light shimmered off the pale gray tiles. Mitch looked down to avoid the brightness, but he found orbs of illumination staring back at him every few steps anyway. The brightness proved unavoidable.

They straggled past a couple of racks of shitty DVDs and the horde around them splintered into segments moving left, right and straight. Mitch and the boys veered right, squaring their shoulders toward the produce department. Mobs of people swarmed the displays of plant life. From what Mitch could see, the fruit was already gone, the black racks picked clean aside from a stray grape and a lemon, shriveled and moldy. People shuffled around the empty shelves in small groups, skittering in all directions. They looked haggard, a few without shoes on, many with their hoods up and their heads down, like refugees fleeing some kind of genocide. Maybe that wasn't so far from the truth, Mitch thought, more than most of them even knew.

He stopped walking, just planted his feet on a perforated rubber mat near the empty crate where the watermelons used to be. He tried to think. What would make the most sense to buy in this scenario? It was hard to concentrate with people bustling around the way they were, with panic and chaos broadcasting from brain to brain like radio waves. Voices brayed out staccato bursts, nervous chatter like everyone was amped up on 13 cups of coffee. It may as well have all been in a foreign language, like they teleported to some Middle Eastern country he'd never heard of the minute they stepped into the light.

"What are we doing?" Matt said, tugging at his dad's sleeve.

"Huh? Oh, I'm thinking."

"About what?"

"I'm trying to decide what we should grab. I didn't think... I mean, I didn't know people would clean the place out like this."

"Oreos. We're supposed to get Oreos."

Mitch laughed and even that came out neurotic and rushed.

"OK, fine. We'll try to get Oreos first."

"Try? You think people took them all already?"

"I hope not, but look around man. People are going nuts."

They angled left to get back out to the main aisle, working their way through the humanity to get to the Oreos. A squat man rushed past going the other way with both arms clutching hot dog buns to his chest, additional bags of buns dangling from his fists. Mitch made eye contact with Kevin as the bun man passed, and they laughed. He knew his older son was upset, probably a lot more in tune with the reality of the situation than Matt was, so it made him feel better to see him smile. Not that much better, maybe even a sad version of better, but it was something.

That's the trick, right? Find these happy moments, these hopeful moments. Find them and hold onto them. Make yourself believe you're happy for as long as you can, and then slip into oblivion. No amount of thinking can prepare you for death, Mitch thought. You can't brace yourself in some certain way and ease into it. Better to fool yourself for a lifetime and slide into it when no one is looking, not even you.

Empty space occupied the freezer display where the pizzas were supposed to be. Mitch pointed a thumb at the bare freezer as he spoke.

"Damn. The savages ran wild in here. Even took all of the good pizza."

"We still have a few at home," Kevin said. "And who knows how long the power will be out? We should get grain. Rice. Oatmeal. Ice for the coolers. Maybe containers to store water. Stuff for..."

"After," Mitch said.

"Oh, God," Matt said, covering his face with his hands again. Mitch put a hand on the boy's shoulder.

"Hey, you'll be alright," he said. "You're tough, aren't you?"

"What? Yeah, I'm just worried that the Oreos will be all gone. 'Cause of the savages, I mean."

"Yeah, well we're about to find out."

They turned right, stalking into the cookie and cracker aisle. There were still a few things on the shelf here: chicken flavored crackers, off brand chocolate chip cookies, a couple of damaged boxes of chocolate Teddy Grahams. His eyes jumped farther down the aisle, looking for blue packages, the shitty dehydrated chocolate cookies with a layer of hydrogenated white crap sandwiched between them. Or maybe it wasn't hydrogenated anymore. He remembered reading something about it.

A detail from the article sprang to mind: Oreos were as addictive as cocaine. He remembered that. They did a study with rats that found the little guys loved the cookies as much as they loved hard drugs. He could imagine rats here in the store now, scurrying along with the people, fleeing from trouble, gathering supplies to hunker down somewhere.

That would be a weird job, though. Feeding cocaine to rats.

A blue package caught his eye on the bottom shelf some 10 feet ahead. He focused on it, his conscious reality filtering down to the blue exterior, the flap on the side where the front and back pieces crimp together like the edge of a candy wrapper. Subconsciously, his brain must still be telling his legs to put one foot in front of the other, but he didn't feel it at all, didn't think about it. It just happened. From his perspective, he simply glided closer and closer to the package, the sounds around him fading down into something small and way in the background, like the chatter of a school cafeteria full of people heard from several classrooms away.

But no. Not Oreos. Chips Ahoy.

"Damn," he said.

"Here," Kevin said.

He reached deep into the shelf, his hand hovering over bags of off brand ginger snaps that looked more or less untouched. All the way in the back, a package sat atop the snaps. The shape looked right. He pulled the box out of the shadows, and the light revealed blue and white and pink. Pink? Oh, it was the Double Stuf kind.

"Good eye," Mitch said, clapping his son's shoulder.

Kevin handed the Oreos to Matt, who turned them around to read the label, his eyebrows crushed together.

"Double Stuf?" Matt said, smearing a finger over the smooth plastic in front of him.

"Yeah, they have more of the white stuff than regular Oreos," Mitch said. "You OK with that?"

"Uh, yeah. This is going to be awesome."

The boy tucked the cookies under his arm, and it occurred to Mitch that they had forgotten to grab a cart in all of the confusion upon walking into the bright light. That was dumb.

"Should we go get a cart?" he said.

"They're all gone," Kevin said. "The rack up front was empty when we walked by anyway."

Mitch remembered the guy carrying all of the hot dog buns in his arms. Maybe the lack of carts played a role there.

"Damn."

"It's all right, Dad. There are three of us. We can carry plenty."

"I guess."

"This way."

Kevin took the lead. They turned back, weaving through an influx of traffic in the cookie aisle. Looking past them, Mitch saw the dark half of the store in the distance. The generators must only power the grocery side, leaving the department store type area in the dark. Damn. He had planned to grab some things from over there. Should they brave the lack of light? The decision could wait.

They merged into the flow of traffic in the main aisle once more, advancing three rows to find the grain and pasta shelves. Kevin turned sideways to make himself skinny enough to squeeze through a gap between two fat men, and he squirted through to get ahead of his dad and brother. Mitch grabbed Matt's shoulder to make sure he wouldn't do the same.

"Kevin!" Mitch said, his voice rising above the tangle of chatter.

His older son disappeared in the thick crowd populating this aisle, the red hair swallowed up among the shoulders and torsos. Mitch's heart sped up.

Still gripping Matt, he elbowed enough space to maneuver between the stagnant fatties, jostling them out of his way with a little force. One of them, a man with a salt and pepper beard and hair hanging down to cover one side of his face, gave Mitch a dirty look. In turn Mitch stared at him, his forearm touching the gun in his belt once more. The man looked away.

Now he battled his way through the writhing mass of limbs and torsos. All of the people seemed to be jockeying for position, closing in on something ahead that he couldn't see. Some of the people were turning back, fighting their way upstream with goods of some kind in their hands, plastic bags of something.

And then Kevin appeared among those fighting their way back, a smile on his face. Mitch stopped and let his son come to him.

"The stock boy brought out a couple of boxes, but the people tore them open before he could stock them," Kevin said. "I got in there and got some."

He cradled nine pounds of brown rice in his arms.

Baghead

Rural Oklahoma
9 years, 126 days after

Delfino put the car in park, and they sat facing the blockade of armed children.

"So these are the ruthless war mongers you warned me about? A bunch of kids."

Delfino said nothing, but the look on his face seemed to lack any trace of amusement.

"Turn the engine off and get out," the kid in the front said. "Slow. Hands up, too."

"Wait," Baghead said under his breath. "What are we paying the toll with?"

Delfino shook his head, his chin tucked in a strange way. He spoke through his teeth.

"It's taken care of. Just stay quiet."

"But couldn't we pay someone to take out seven kids?"

"This is one squad. They have an army that would hunt us for the rest of our lives and dismember us. And a lot of them are kids, sure, but not all. Please, please just shut your mouth."

He turned the key, and the hum of the engine died out. The quiet swelled up around them, filling the empty space where the motor had churned, the only sound remaining that of the wind swishing fistfuls of sand around.

They climbed out of the sedan, stepping out of the shade

of the car and into the glare of the direct sunlight. Bags squinted, fighting to keep his eyes open in the brightness.

The leader waved his hand, and the child soldiers closed on them. They sprinted forward, their footsteps pounding out a heavy clatter on the pavement.

Two kids moved in on Bags, walling him off from the car, their rifles raised at him. Their lips curled back, foreheads creased, eyebrows clenched up. One of the kids was barely five feet tall with the deadest eyes of the bunch. Bags stared straight into the boy's face without thinking about it, trying to figure him out and finding only hatred there.

Looking over, he saw the same scenario playing out for Delfino on the other side of the car. He noticed that Delfino stared straight down at the ground. Perhaps that was the proper etiquette.

The other two soldiers climbed into the car, one in the front and one in the back. They moved quickly, reaching under seats and rooting their hands around.

Finally, the one in the back peeled the blanket off of the back seat. Bags held his breath. The kid wadded the blanket up, tossed it back down to the seat.

"Back is clear. I'll check the trunk."

The kid in the front worked on, fidgeting in the glove box a while, and then running his hand all around underneath the dash. Something clicked.

"Got something," he said.

"What is it?" the leader said.

He held up a wad of money and a silver chain.

"Some old world cash and a piece of jewelry tucked in a little compartment under the dash."

The leader smirked at Delfino.

"Hiding the valuables?"

"Hey, a guy has to try to make a living out here. You know how it is."

The leader nodded, placing the cash and jewelry in his breast pocket.

"Trunk is clear. A few blankets if we want them."

"No need."

The smallest one with the dead eyes spoke up. Based on the timbre of his voice, Baghead realized he was older than he looked -- probably 14, at least. Just small for his age.

"What's with the bag on this one's head?"

"Ain't no business of ours," the leader said.

"The hell it ain't. What if he's hiding something under there? Why else wear it?"

"You blind? Can't you see his eye? The radiation got 'im, man. Just let it go. They've paid the toll just fine, and they'll be on their way."

Everyone hesitated for a second, and Bags stared into the hateful eyes again. He didn't want to, but he somehow couldn't look away.

"Open the gate," the leader said, and then he waved Bags and Delfino back to their car. "Enjoy your trip."

A couple of the kids ran over to wheel the gate out of the way, but the little one hung back. He rammed a shoulder into Baghead's chest as he moved toward the car. It got Bags just right to make it feel like his lungs had imploded, no longer capable of inhaling.

The kid didn't say anything. He walked away like nothing happened, not even looking back to gloat.

Mitch

Bethel Park, Pennsylvania
42 days before

As they moved into the graying tones toward the dark half of the store, they found an abandoned cart in the pet department. They removed two bags of kitty litter and loaded their things into it. Though the shelves had been ravaged, they'd landed some pouches of tuna, a few pounds of oatmeal and quite a bit of rice as Kevin had gone back for another haul.

"What do we need from over here?" Kevin said, his head gesturing toward the darkening department store around them.

"Buckets or rain barrels," Mitch said. "If the water goes out, you can catch rain water from the downspouts. You can use it to flush the toilet. If you boil it first, you can even drink it."

"That's smart. Do you think they're sold out already, though?"

"I'm not sure, but I don't think people are thinking that far ahead just yet. Anyway, be on the lookout for other useful items."

By the time they got to the hardware department, it was hard to see. A little light glinted its way across the store, but it felt like walking around in a cave, Mitch thought. They walked past cans of spray paint, and another group of shoppers were suddenly on top of them, appearing as though from nowhere, flitting by like a colony of bats headed toward the light.

Mitch's heart hammered away, picking up speed. Sweat slicked his palms and forehead. He left his hand on the butt of the gun, couldn't quite bring himself to remove it. He didn't want the boys to know how much this had spooked him, so he talked.

"You guys see any hatchets? That might be something worth having. A multi-tasker."

"Maybe two hatchets, right?" Matt said. "I'd like my own."

"Sure. Two hatchets, if we can find them."

The cart's wheels squeaked as they turned a corner, moving into an aisle of nails and screws and nuts and bolts. Shopping proved to be difficult in the half light, Mitch thought. They couldn't glance down rows, their eyes perusing wares from a distance. Walking within a couple feet of things served as the only way to see what they were looking at.

They glided past spools of chain to the farthest back corner of the store, and a dark figure took shape at the end of the aisle. Silent. Unmoving. Mitch's tongue jerked, seeming to stick in the back of his throat like a starfish clinging to the reef. He didn't like this.

"What about an ax, though?" Matt said. "Maybe an ax is better than a hatchet, right?"

"Be quiet, Matt," Mitch said, his voice all hushed and gritty like sandpaper.

The figure moved. It was hard to tell at first, but it walked toward them. Something about the silhouette seemed to move in an inhuman way, the footsteps somehow too fluid, the set of its shoulders almost demonic. Mitch drew the gun.

The thing swooped at them, a lunge quick enough that Mitch lost sight of the figure, seeing only movement among the shades of black that he couldn't make much sense of. Things moved near him, ceiling hooks and fixtures clattering to the floor. Total confusion. He kept the gun aimed at the ground, feet sliding him forward toward the commotion.

Matt screamed. No words, just terror torn from his throat. The sound rang out small and pathetic like a lamb being slaughtered, a series of high pitched bleats that reverberated in the silence around them, the echoes somehow otherworldly in the darkness, a filtered ringing quality hanging in the air long after the sound of his voice faded out.

And Mitch closed in, the gun pointed ahead of him now. He crashed into the dark figure, knocking it flat and falling on top of it. A scramble of limbs ensued. Moving body parts bashing into each other. He found himself on top of the being, and he sat up, glancing for a split second over his shoulder to ensure his children were behind him.

And he squeezed the trigger, and the muzzle flashed, lighting everything up. The world went into slow motion. In that instant of light, he found no demon beneath him, no zombie or mutant or beastly creature at all. Just a small man with a haggard look about him. Purple bags beneath the eyes. Pit stains darkening his t-shirt. Stubble giving way to a scraggly blond beard. And then time resumed, and the muzzle popped, and the bullet tore open the guy's gut, and that filtered ring hung in the air again. It was so fast. Just a flash and a bang and the guy was opened up, blood seeping out of him, the dark spot of the puddle spreading around him on the white floor.

This seemed a lot more permanent now that it was done, Mitch realized. A split decision that would change lives forever. What had even happened here? He didn't know, and he knew he never would.

The man howled once, and Mitch put one in his head.

"Let's go," he said, getting to his feet. "People will come looking this way because of the gun shots. Just act natural and keep moving."

Nobody spoke. They rounded the corner, and he put a rain barrel into the cart, and they wheeled back toward the light.

He didn't know what happened, but it didn't matter anymore. Keeping these boys safe was the only thing that mattered now. It was the only thing.

Erin

After standing next to the heat of the fire, the air rushing past as they sped down the road on their bikes felt extra refreshing. Every few seconds, Erin heard the click of Izzy's gears. The novelty hadn't worn off yet, apparently.

When the driveway came in sight, she pedaled a little harder. If she got the fire going quickly, she was pretty sure she could squeeze in a bath before it got dark.

She coasted through the barn door, parking her bike just inside. Izzy buzzed around the yard, still tinkering with the gears.

The galvanized tub clunked over the uneven ground as she towed it along beside her. Where to build the fire? That was the question. Remembering the way the trees dispersed the smoke, she considered building it at the edge of the yard, where the shaggy grass gave away to the oaks, hickories, and pines.

Then again, that was a long walk from the well pump. How many buckets would it take to fill the tub? Her best guess was a shitload.

The only tree anywhere near the pump was a lone scraggly pine. It cast a patchy shadow over the grass, needles twitching in the breeze.

Good enough.

314

She left the tub near the tree and skipped back to the barn, where she loaded cement blocks into the wheelbarrow she found amongst the junk. The tire on it was flat, but it still worked. Just took a little more elbow grease. And it beat lugging the bricks one by one.

She laid out two squat towers of blocks, three wide by two tall. She left a space between the towers for the fire, and laid the tub on top, like a bridge.

Erin paused to admire the setup. Her fingers itched to slide her phone from her pocket, to snap a photo of her creation with the pink sunset in the background, to slap an ironic hashtag on it before posting it for the world to see.

#SpaDay #pampered

Instead she gathered wood and kindling and some paper for the fire.

Izzy glided by on her bike.

"This is a lot of work for a bath."

Erin cracked a twig in half.

"It's going to be worth it. Besides, once we get the generator, we won't have to go to all this trouble. We can just hook up the water heater."

With the fire crackling away, she started to haul the water from the well pump, one bucket at a time. The first bucketful hissed when it hit the hot metal and produced a cloud of steam. She poured in five buckets and then stopped to add more wood to the fire.

She dipped her fingers in. The water was still cold around the edges, but she swore the water in the center was a little warmer.

She continued the back and forth of toting water, pausing

now and then to add more wood or test the temperature. She filled the tub about half way, and left an extra bucket full of water nearby. Then she went inside and gathered soap, a washcloth, shampoo, and two towels.

When she came back out of the house, Izzy and her bike were nowhere in sight. Erin set her bath gear in the grass next to the tub, added another log to the fire, and moseyed up to the barn. Izzy's bike leaned on its kickstand next to Erin's bike.

"Izzy?"

No answer.

Back at the door, she surveyed the property. Could she have gone in the house after Erin, and she hadn't noticed?

She headed toward the house, trailing her fingers along the surface of the bath water as she passed. It was definitely getting warm. Slowly but surely.

Erin crossed under the pine tree and something brushed her shoulder. She whirled around, thinking Izzy had sneaked up behind her from somewhere. But the only thing behind her was her own shadow.

A piece of bark struck the top of her head. The sound came from above: the high-pitched cackle of a tiny witch.

Erin peered up into the branches of the tree and found Izzy sprawled on her belly over a large bough.

"You won't be grinning when I climb up there and hang you from a branch by your underwear."

Izzy slithered down from her perch.

"Can't get me now."

"I can still give you an atomic wedgie."

Izzy chuckled, then stopped abruptly.

"What's an *atomic* wedgie?"

"It's where I hike your underwear so high, I stretch it up over your head. And then you're just stuck like that. For eternity."

"Nuh uh!"

"Yep."

Erin lurched at her, and Izzy took off running for the house, squealing the whole way.

From inside, she pressed her hands and face to the screen, distorting her features. She smeared her face down, catching her nose on the screen so it squashed upwards like a pig.

Erin's shoes thudded up the porch steps.

"Do you want to take the first bath?"

Izzy moved her head side to side, dragging her nose along the screen.

"Are you sure? If you go after me, you have to use my funk water."

Izzy's finger found a hole in the screen and jabbed at it.

"I'm not taking a bath."

"Come on, Iz. You have to."

"No!"

Erin took a half-step backward at Izzy's tone. She'd never thrown any kind of tantrum before.

"Izzy," she started, not sure how to proceed.

"I said no! You can't make me."

With that, Izzy flipped the lock on the screen door and stomped farther into the house.

Erin stood motionless for a moment, trying to figure out what the hell had just happened. Guess the kid must really hate baths, she thought.

Grass swished around her ankles. When she reached the tub, she plunged her hand in. It was warm. Maybe not quite warm enough, but she couldn't wait any longer.

She stoked the fire and added two more logs before kicking off her shoes and peeling away her socks. She unbuttoned her shorts and let them fall down around her ankles before she stepped out of the leg holes one foot at a time. When it got to the point of taking off her shirt, she had a sudden twinge of bashfulness. She reminded herself that she and Izzy might as well be the last two people left on the planet.

She pulled her shirt over her head. The uneasiness uncovered a partially buried memory, from when they first arrived at the FEMA camp. They made everyone coming into the camp undress and go through a disinfectant shower. Not that it ended up doing them any good.

It had been humiliating to disrobe in such a public way like that. They had female guards and workers manning the women's tent, but they just stood there and stared at them. She felt like livestock. She probably wouldn't have been able to do it if she'd been alone. She only got through it because her mom was with her and told her it was OK. Everything would be OK.

Well, shit.

Now she understood Izzy's fit, maybe. It would have been traumatizing enough for a kid to go through that at all, but Izzy had come to the camp alone. She turned her head over her shoulder to glance at the house. Probably best just to leave it alone for now.

She got the rest of the way undressed and climbed in. The

water had warmed a few more degrees while she disrobed, and it felt delightful. She probed at the bottom of the tub that hovered over the fire and pulled her hand away like she'd touched a hot stove. Because that's exactly what it felt like. Something to consider if she ever had to do this again. Lining the bottom with stones could help. Or maybe more cinder blocks. They wouldn't transfer heat the same way the metal did.

She couldn't stop grinning as she lathered the soap and shampooed her hair. After rinsing the suds from her head, she leaned back.

For the first time in she didn't know how long, she actually felt relaxed. Tension eased out of her shoulders and neck. She let her eyes bat closed.

So peaceful.

The screen door banged open and shut.

"I see Erin's boobies! I see Erin's boooobies!"

Erin opened her eyes to see Izzy dancing down the steps, singing the words in a continuous loop.

"Take a good look. This is you in a few years."

"No, thank you."

"I hate to break this to you, but you don't get a choice."

Izzy looked down at herself, crossing her hands over her chest.

"Fine then. Small ones would be OK, I guess. Really small."

"Now you jinxed it. You're going to have huge ones."

"Nuh-uh!"

"Yep. Massive hooters."

"Shut up."

"Sorry, that's just how it works."

"I'll just cut them off."

Now Erin was the one covering her chest.

"Ouch. That's a little extreme, don't you think?"

Izzy shrugged, and picked up a stick from the pile of kindling next to the fire. She jabbed it into the glowing red coals.

"Don't they get in the way?"

Erin laughed.

"Yeah, they kind of do."

"Do they hurt?"

"Hurt?" Erin thought about it. "Not really. I mean, they can get sore sometimes. Like when you jump on a trampoline without a bra."

Izzy spit out a laugh.

"What?!"

Erin pantomimed grotesquely huge boobs bouncing in the air in slow motion in front of her, adding a *BOOMP! BOOMP! BOOMP!* sound effect.

Izzy keeled over into the grass, laughing.

"That's so gross!"

"If you think that's gross, just wait. You've got a whole smorgasbord of puberty grossness ahead of you."

"Pube-erty," Izzy repeated, stretching out the first syllable and giggling.

Erin knew she'd eventually have to have the birds and the bees talk with Izzy. But the thought of broaching the subject scared her almost as much as the thought of running into other people. Or zombies. Or becoming a zombie.

She thought back to her own first lesson about sex. She

was about Izzy's age, and she heard some kids on the bus talking about masturbation. From context she knew that it was something relating to sex, but she wasn't sure what exactly. So that night, she asked her mom.

"When I was a kid, they told us you'd go blind if you did it. You probably won't, though. Anyway, it's a thing boys do."

That was it.

Eventually, she resorted to asking Kelly. Kelly's sister, Liz, was six years older. Kelly always had the scoop on sex stuff from eavesdropping on Liz and her friends.

Sprawled on bean bag chairs in Kelly's basement, Erin spent the better part of *The Princess Bride* working up the nerve to ask. When she finally pressed her face to Kelly's ear and mumbled those four mysterious syllables, Kelly's head snapped back, eye's glowing with the same mischievous spark they always had when they talked about things they weren't supposed to.

Her top lip curled back a little in that sneering smile.

"You don't *know*?"

This was why she hadn't wanted to ask Kelly in the first place. She could never resist lording it over Erin for a little while. Basking in the superiority of her more advanced knowledge of sex.

No wonder she'd been so uptight about sex. She hadn't realized it at the time, of course. She wasn't like Maureen Majors, who took every opportunity to remind everyone that "as far as the Bible is concerned, you will go to Hell if you have sex before marriage." She thought of herself as being open-minded. But she wasn't really.

Like when Kelly lost her virginity to her boyfriend, Erin

remembered feeling disappointed in her. Even though Kelly and Ryan had been dating for two years. Now that she thought about it, that probably had more to do with the fact that Kelly hung out with Ryan more and more and Erin less and less since they'd started dating.

She couldn't have imagined a way to bring it up with Izzy without it being totally awkward. And now here it was, the perfect segue.

"You know what it is, right? Puberty?"

Izzy groaned and poked at the fire.

"I know all about minstrels because of my brother's girlfriend."

Now Erin was the one laughing so hard she bent at the waist, nose touching the water.

Izzy stared at her.

"What?"

Erin tried to stop laughing long enough to explain, but she only got out a strained, "minstrels!" before convulsing in amusement.

Izzy tossed her stick in the fire.

"Why is that funny?"

As the laughter subsided, Erin was able to catch her breath.

"Minstrels," she said, and chuckled one more time, "are like… medieval traveling musicians."

"Like a bard?"

Erin slapped the water, sending a warm spray splashing in every direction.

"Why would you know the word bard but not minstrel?"

"Video games."

"Of course. Yeah, bard and minstrel. Pretty much the same thing. But you were thinking of menstrual."

"Fine, then. Menstruals."

Erin grinned.

"What now?"

"Well a menstrual isn't a thing. It's an adjective, I guess. It would be menstrual cycles. Or menses. Or menstruation."

Izzy plopped onto the ground.

"And boys don't get them, right? Menstrual… cycles?"

Erin shook her head.

"The lucky bastards."

"Language," Izzy said, then after a beat, "Don't they get anything?"

Erin thought about it and smirked.

"Yeah, they kind of get their own thing. It's not exactly the same, but it can be… embarrassing," she said, thinking of the time Kirk Meade got a hard-on in his gym shorts in ninth grade.

She didn't think Izzy needed to know about that just yet. She leaned her head back against the metal rim of the trough and closed her eyes, sinking a little lower into the water. They'd have plenty of time to delve further into the topic later. They had all the time in the world.

Ray

Galveston, Texas
3 days before

The unlit cigar made his lips tingle where it touched them. He adjusted it in his mouth, slid the tube of tobacco from one corner to the other. The itchy nicotine tickle traced this movement after a few seconds delay, swelling to reach that full-on medicinal sting.

He stood on the deck, forearms leaned against the rail. Green grass trailed out in front of him, dropping off into a little swath of sand and then the blue forever-ness of the ocean. Wind whipped off of the water. He lifted his hat to let the rushing breeze touch his hair, muss it up some. His hair had gone all silver young, but he still had a full head of it. He thought about that often and felt lucky. In his line of work, that was important.

He brought a hand to the cigar and held it while he adjusted his lips yet again. He'd given up smoking the things years ago, but he still liked that acrid feel of nicotine seeping into the lining of his mouth. It burned a little if he got it right. He didn't quite get there this time, though, and the end was soggy now, so he pitched it.

He looked back at the house, saw his muted reflection in the sliding glass door. Between the sunglasses, sandals, and cargo shorts, he looked more like a beach bum than a man of God. Then again, that was probably a more accurate description of his lifestyle.

His eyes trailed away to scan across the rest of the house. His mansion was empty now. No staff left. No women. He'd sent them all away. Told them to get out of town sooner than later.

He could barely stand to be inside the place, alone in the quiet. He kept finding excuses to walk around the yard or around the neighborhood. Those locations were empty, too, but when the wind blew in off the water, the landscape moved, and it wasn't as bad somehow. It felt like he'd turn a corner and find a group of people socializing, sipping cocktails, gossiping, laughing.

He'd initially thought he would ride this thing out. Not anymore. Food and water were getting to be a concern already even before he heard, and there was never any sign that the government would get their shit together to repair things anytime soon.

But one phone call from Ted Miles yesterday had eliminated the last of his delusions that he could stay home. By government order, Houston would be erased within two days, disintegrated by nukes. Even if Galveston survived the blast, the radiation could get it. And he planned to be far, far away by the time it happened.

Yet again he felt lucky. How many would die under that mushroom cloud? Millions? And surely Houston wouldn't be the only city being targeted. He had money, and he knew people, and because of those things, he had a chance to get away from it. He'd go north, out into the middle of nowhere, and wait.

He turned away from the house, looked out at the yard

again. It would still hurt to leave this place. His fortress. He'd paid cash for it, spent the bulk of his savings. All of the accountants and money people told him it was a mistake, a bad investment, but he didn't listen. He was the one that built an empire, and they were the ones working for him. He still remembered the conversation he had with Ted, his chief financial adviser at the time, before he moved on to be a lobbyist.

"Tying up all of that capital in real estate just isn't smart, Ray," he said. "It's better to keep that money earning for you. Let me put it this way: There are a bunch of investment opportunities available that are the equivalent of wide open slam dunks. I'm talking about sure things that will put points on the board. Sinking all of that money into a house is like passing up the dunk to heave up a jump shot from half court. You never know what can happen in the real estate market, or what your earnings will look like in two years."

"Oh, I don't know about all of that," Ray said. "I expect my earnings will be just fine. Hope and salvation are evergreen."

He walked across the deck and down the wooden stairway into the yard. The wind rushed at him again, pressing his shirt flat against his chest. It kept at it as he made his way to the garage, but he didn't mind. He liked the way the air moved across his cheeks and nose.

His arm pressed into the door to the garage, and he stepped through, out of the breeze, into the stillness. He flipped the switch, and the fluorescent bulbs hesitated a second before they flickered on.

A fleet of vehicles stood before him: two Jaguars, three

Cadillacs, five SUVs, a matching pair of jet skis and a speed boat. He could only take one, of course. He walked past them, fingers dragging over glossy paint. He knew which one it would be before he even entered the room, of course. The rest had a 50/50 chance to survive the blast, he thought.

A few garment bags hung on a rack to his left. His emergency suits, always ready on short notice. He stripped off his clothes and changed into one. Better to head out this way, right? Everyone trusts a man in a suit.

At the far end of the garage, he knelt before a mini-fridge, reached in and pulled out six bottles of water, hugging them to his chest. These he unloaded in the passenger seat of a Jeep Grand Cherokee. This was his choice, perhaps the most modest of his automobiles, but he figured modesty had increased value now that everything was falling apart.

One more call. One more try, and then he'd leave. The cell phone rang against his ear, his pulse keeping the meter, and the voicemail message came on, and he hung up. It was too weird to hear her voice and have no idea if she was OK.

Maybe she wasn't dead, he thought. Maybe she just didn't want to talk to him. The two possibilities seemed about equally likely.

And so he drove out away from his compound, leaving behind all he'd built and all he'd owned, bringing nothing but a few bottles of water along for the ride. Well, those and the handgun in the glove box. He knew he'd be fine, though. He may not have had faith in many things, but he had it in himself. He was an earner. A charmer. Always had been. He'd find his way like he always did.

Teddy

Moundsville, West Virginia
69 days after

He drank long and deep. The Mountain Dew was warm, but he'd always liked it that way. He set the bottle down on the floor next to his bed, still feeling the acidic tingle on his lips and tongue. He grabbed a handful of cheese puffs out of the bag resting on his chest and crunched them one by one. When his hand was empty, he sucked the orange cheese off of his fingertips, getting a whiff of death for a split second as his ring finger entered his mouth. He lay there and breathed for a moment, his hands folded on his belly like paws, the plastic bag rising and falling with his chest. Then he went back for another handful.

Here he was, in an otherwise empty room, in an otherwise empty house, in an otherwise empty town, indulging in a private all-you-can-eat-buffet of his favorite food and drink. It felt like a dream, a strange dream.

In some ways he missed the people, the sound of them, knowing they were out there. He missed TV. He missed meat, too. That one he really missed.

Sometimes the old lady that owned the house would give him their leftovers – salisbury steak, meatloaf, roasted chicken, Swedish meatballs, barbecue ribs, and even clam chowder once. The cheese puffs were good, but he missed all of that, missed the sensation of biting down on a well cooked piece of protein and feeling the texture of it as he chewed it up.

And that made him think about the garbage truck again, about the cats and dogs. It never made much sense to him that people would get so worked up about some animals and not others. Why was it OK for cows to get massacred by the thousands in slaughterhouses, but bad for him to throw a few cats into the truck? Why could people like his uncle hunt and kill deer but hurting a dog was bad? Why did the other kids think he was sick for picking up road kill, but when the lunch lady slopped beef stroganoff onto their tray, they ate it all up? None of them thought twice when they went to the grocery store and saw all of the little plastic packages of meat in the meat department. It made no sense.

He liked putting the cats in the truck the same way he liked eating meat. Both made him happy, stimulated, excited. Both made him feel some primal satisfaction, made him feel powerful in some vague sense like he could wrestle the world under his command if he needed to. He knew other people liked meat a lot. He didn't know why they didn't like the other.

It was bad, though, what he did to people's pets. He knew it must be a bad thing, but he couldn't understand it. Not all of the way.

He crumpled the top of the cheese puff bag closed, rolling it up and setting it down on the floor in such a manner that it would stay closed. It was time to check his traps.

He licked his lips, and they tasted like fake cheese and salt and Mountain Dew.

Ray

"Giving people something to believe in is the best gift you can give them," he said, his fingers tapping at the steering wheel. "That's what I tell people I do for a living. Sounds a hell of a lot better than 'televangelist,' you know?"

She smiled and nodded and looked out the window. She wasn't much of a talker, but he didn't mind that. Her black hair sheared off above her eyebrows, a severe line of bangs. It was an uncommon haircut for a woman of her age but one that highlighted the shape of her face.

They sat at a red light, the city around them bustling as usual, people driving and walking and eating their fries and drinking their Coke, no idea that they'd be incinerated before long. He hadn't even explained that to his new companion yet. Wasn't sure how to bring it up. He looked at her again.

Her breasts were enormous. Probably fake. He didn't mind that, either. As far as Ray was concerned, breast implants ranked among mankind's greatest achievements, one of the clearest symbols of capitalism's strengths. For a price you could reinvent yourself to any degree, even physically. Any dream could come true if you scratched and clawed and earned your way to it. If you paid the price, it was yours.

In this world, everything had a price. He saw great

opportunity in that. Endless possibilities.

He ran into her outside of a Texaco station that the raiders had already sucked dry, a phenomenon he'd only heard about on the news until now. All across the South, these sons of bitches were stealing gas, and the police were too occupied with the riots to do anything about it.

She was standing by the pumps, just outside of her Sebring, the tank apparently empty, and he pulled in to ask if she needed any help. She recognized him from TV. If any magic truly existed, Ray thought, it was the magic power of fame, of television. When your face gets broadcast into someone's home, they tend to feel like they know you, like they can trust you. Apparently a certain portion will even send you their life savings if you ask for it, and he did ask for it. Often.

"So where are we headed?" she said.

"We've got to get out of town," he said. "Some crazy shit is about to go down. You're lucky you ran into me, you know that?"

She smiled and nodded and looked out the window again. It struck him that she may be on drugs of some kind, probably pills. He'd taken her slow, medicated feel as an aloofness until now. But heading out of town with a stranger without a second thought was a little weird, even if she did know him from TV.

What was her name again? Debra? Diana? Started with a D, he thought. Maybe a B.

His cell phone itched in his pocket. He wanted to try another call but not in front of his new guest.

Still, already he wasn't alone. Already he'd found a

follower not 15 minutes out from his home. He knew he was going to be just fine.

Baghead

Rural Oklahoma
9 years, 126 days after

The car rolled through the place where the stop sign fence had been moments before, and then they accelerated. The engine hummed. The sand and weeds alongside them returned to their former state of blurriness. It felt good to get moving again.

Bags watched in the rearview as the gate rolled back into place, and the soldiers went back to standing around, just their heads visible above the fence. They shrank and their features darkened until the horizon swallowed them up.

Delfino smiled in the driver's seat, his eyes opened wide.

"You wanted them to find the money, didn't you?" Bags said.

"You're finally starting to figure me out, smart guy."

"Making them work to find it makes them assume they've found your big stash."

"Righto. And I like to throw in something shiny that they probably don't see too often. Today it was the necklace, but anything with an air of fanciness will do the trick."

"So all of your best stuff is actually in the cooler?"

"Now don't you go worrying your baggy little head about that."

"Rough bunch of kids there. Not what I was expecting when you said they were ruthless, but…"

Delfino squinted.

"I can't tell if you're making fun of me or not. They really are ruthless, though. One of them bit me once! Look at this."

He rolled up his sleeve to reveal a jagged oval of a scar just at the spot where the triceps and deltoid met.

"You ever seen what it looks like when a human bite gets infected?"

"Never."

"It's hellish, man. It's truly hellish."

The conversation trailed off as Delfino rolled down his sleeve.

Bags checked the rearview again, as though the hateful kid might have reappeared on the horizon, but no. The road trailed away to a point like it always did. Nothing to see.

"Was that true?" Delfino said. "What that kid said about your face, about the radiation?"

"Yeah. Yeah, that was true. At least, I'm pretty sure that's what happened."

"There wasn't supposed to be no fallout, but the government fucked it up, right?"

"Yeah, something like that. The radiation should have dissipated in the air. If all of the bombs had airburst, like they were supposed to, the fallout would have been negligible. It didn't happen that way. Not in Miami, anyway. It's all dead cities out that way, from Atlanta or so on south."

"Miami? You been all the way down there?"

"Yeah, I've been all over. Haven't traveled as much this past year, but I've been around."

"That's juicy butt crack country."

"What?"

"The humidity down that way, man. Makes my ass all sweaty, and it won't evaporate, so I'm running around with a soggy ass crack all day. Wearing a pair of boxer shorts you could ring out like a dishrag."

They were silent for a beat. Baghead pressed his hand into the bag, trying to smash down his beard so it didn't touch the canvas anymore.

"Well, that's good to know," Bags said.

Delfino pulled the tin out of his pocket and lit a cigarette. He spoke again as he exhaled his second puff.

"Not to pry, but you ever get a doc to take a look at it? Your face, I mean?"

"No. I never figured there'd be much of a point. If it's cancerous or whatever, there's nothing to be done about it. No chemo or radiation or surgery exists that's going to fix it. Not anymore. And it's not like there are any plastic surgeons out there to pretty me up."

Another beat of silence overtook the Delta 88. Smoke rolled out of Delfino's nose and ascended, coiling around above his head.

"I'm still here, right? Still walking around. That's all that matters for now."

Delfino nodded, smoke still spinning out of his face.

"Mind if I ask you one more question?"

"Go ahead."

"The Hand of Death. Did you get the card?"

"I did."

"Do you, you know, have it on you?"

"I do."

Delfino licks his lips.

"Might I take a look at it?"

Baghead turned his shoulders and looked out the window. "No."

Erin

It wasn't until they brought the generator home and unloaded it that Erin realized they'd need fuel for it.

She looked down at the box, and scratched the side of her nose in agitation. It took every ounce of her willpower not to let loose a string of obscenities. But Izzy would give her hell for it. So she kept her mouth shut and let every swear word she knew echo inside her skull.

She'd been so preoccupied with the idea of having power that she just glossed right over the specifics. She'd imagined them hauling it back to the house, pressing a button, and boom -- let there be light.

OK, so they'd have to find gas first. It shouldn't be that hard. There had to be tons of gas just sitting out there.

They hadn't ventured into the nearest town since they found the house, but Erin knew from road signs that the village of Presto was only four miles down the road. She filled a water bottle for each of them at the well and tossed a gas can from the barn into the carrier.

Erin watched Izzy mount the bike.

"A little refresher course for you: the brakes are located on the handlebars. You wanna slow down, you give those hand brakes a squeeze."

Izzy pedaled by, sticking her tongue out.

"Or you could just stop the old-fashioned way by riding into a swamp. Up to you."

The water bottle sloshed around as the tires of Erin's bike bumped over a pothole where the driveway met the road.

It was mostly coasting downhill to town, and the wind at their backs made the ride seem even easier. Almost more braking than pedaling.

The first several houses they passed were familiar: the Slim Jim house, the rhubarb house, and a few others they'd been through, scavenging for food and supplies. But after about half a mile, it was new territory.

In one yard, someone had placed a white and blue sign that said "Stop the Gravel Pit - Vote No on Prop 4." Well they'd gotten their wish. There would be no gravel pit.

A long stretch of uninhabited road sprawled before them. It was all green on either side. The whisper of leaves in the breeze and the sounds of the birds and crickets and cicadas made it feel like they were in the Amazon. Jungle explorers entering uncharted lands.

Amongst the greenery, the back of a truck came into view, tire tracks leading off the road and through the brush. The front end wrapped around the trunk of a maple. Like the truck was giving the tree a crumpled metal hug. She could just make out the silhouette of the driver slumped over the wheel.

Out of the corner of her eye, she sensed movement in the cab. A little pulse of panic shot through her. Was he still alive? Was this a trap? And then she saw the tiny shapes flitting about and realized it was flies. Hundreds and hundreds of flies.

Erin turned away, redirecting her focus back to the road.

They slowed at the first traffic light at the edge of town. In the center of the intersection, half a dozen vehicles lay motionless in a pile-up, a knotted mass of plastic, metal, and glass. It looked like someone had taken a bucketful of toy cars and dumped them onto the road, except they weren't toys. And those weren't Lego people fused to the road in gory globs. And that wasn't ketchup smearing the shattered windshields.

It was a slap-in-the-face reminder of how things were now. They were sheltered from most of it at the house. Sure, they saw bodies in houses. There was no power. They were alone. But this display of destruction was a wake-up call. This wasn't a camping trip. This was the end of the world.

Erin released her grip on the handlebars one at a time to wipe the sweat from her palms. This was the closest they'd come to a densely populated area in weeks. She couldn't stop imagining a sniper shooting at them from the top of one of the buildings. Or a mob of zombies staggering out of an alley at the smell of fresh meat.

She glanced over at Izzy, hair dancing in the wind like coiled snakes. Maybe she should have come alone. Entering the town would be dangerous. And she couldn't do a sweep the way she did for the houses. At the same time, she knew she would have been too chicken to come by herself.

Main street rolled into view, and they veered right.

"A playground!" Izzy said.

It jutted out from an oval of sand in the middle of a park at the end of the street. The jungle gym was blue and yellow, a cone-shaped turret on each end giving it a castle-like appearance. A red slide curved around the front, looking like a giant tongue. Beyond the sand, Erin could see the shimmering surface of the river.

"Can I go check it out?"

The breeze loosened a strand of Erin's hair and sent it fluttering over her face. She tucked it back behind her ear.

"Maybe after we get the gas."

"Why can't I go while you get the gas?"

"Because I don't want you going off by yourself."

A bank and the post office appeared ahead. Both had their windows mostly smashed. The bank Erin understood. Someone figured the apocalypse was the perfect chance to become a "self-made" millionaire. But the post office?

"I guess someone really wanted their damn mail."

The next building was the public library, which appeared to be without a scratch.

"Figures," Erin muttered to herself.

The squeal of Izzy's brakes sounded ahead of her.

"Hey, look."

Izzy pointed across the street from the library, and Erin turned her head to check it out.

The gas station windows were busted out, trash littering the ground. Glass shards and convenience store flotsam and jetsam were scattered about the parking lot like confetti. Erin imagined people looting it, arms loaded up so heavily with Snickers bars and cases of Budweiser that bits and pieces inevitably fell from the pile, stomped by the herd. A body sprawled in the middle of the lot, face down with one of the arms at an impossible angle.

Maybe he died of natural causes, she thought. Or as natural as was possible when the apocalypse was happening.

Like maybe he was sick, but he decided to pop out to grab a bag of pretzels. But as her bike rolled nearer, she saw the blood on his shirt and the crater in the back of his head and the black stain spreading out on the concrete beneath him.

They'd seen so many bodies now, she hadn't anticipated anything would be able to shock and disturb her anymore. But this was the first victim of violence she'd seen since they left the camp. Or the first obvious one, anyway.

Thankfully, Izzy seemed to have glided right by it without noticing, fixating on the gas pumps. Erin swooped in next to her, hopped down from the bike, and lowered the kickstand. While she retrieved the gas can, Izzy lifted the nozzle from the cradle of the pump labeled #2.

"Can I pump the gas?"

Erin unscrewed the lid from the can.

"I guess so. Have you done it before?"

Izzy nodded.

The can made a hollow sound like a drum as she set it on the ground. It was one of the red plastic deals, pretty standard.

Izzy bent over it, inserting the nozzle. She squeezed the trigger. Nothing happened.

Her fist clenched as she squeezed it again, but still the gas didn't flow.

Erin's eyes followed the fuel hose from the nozzle back up to the pump. The little windows that usually flashed a price per gallon were dark. She pushed at the button labeled PREMIUM anyway. Izzy wiggled the nozzle and shook the hose to no effect.

Erin's molars pressed together, harder and harder until

her jaw ached and the muscles actually started to shake. Why couldn't anything go as planned? Why did everything have to be such a goddamned ordeal?

The frustration made her want to flop onto the cement and throw a tantrum, like she was a toddler in a store, one that had been told, no, she couldn't have the toy she wanted, the shiny box ripped from her pudgy fist.

She tipped her head backward until all she could see was sky. The clouds spread in a rippled pattern, like white caps on a choppy sea. At this angle, it felt like the world had been turned upside-down. Her eyes drifted closed, the sunlight glowing pink through the capillaries in her eyelids.

It was too hard. All of it. The food and the fire and gas and taking care of a kid. She wanted things back the way they were.

Izzy's voice cut through her silent outburst.

"I bet we need the key."

Erin blinked, head swiveling back down to peer at the kid. "Huh?"

Izzy crooked a finger at the gas pump, drawing an invisible line to a shiny circle bumping out from the surface. Taking a step closer, Erin saw the slice cutting through the circle like a little mouth. A keyhole.

"If we unlock that, maybe there's a switch or something we can flip under this panel so we can pump the gas without electricity."

This snapped Erin back to reality, and she felt stupid for having her little mental meltdown. Here she was, supposed to be the elder in the situation, and the eight-year-old was the one keeping her cool, taking the problem one step at a time, thinking critically.

Erin ruffled Izzy's curls.

"You're a pint-sized genius, you know that?"

Mitch

Bethel Park, Pennsylvania
42 days before

The headaches started on the ride home, flashes of pain, bright and hot and, above all else, sharp. As he drove, he pushed his index finger and thumb into that pressure point where the nose and forehead met. It seemed to help a little.

This wasn't the constant throb of a normal headache. His head felt fine much of the time with a periodic stabbing pain on one side, like someone peeling back the front left quarter of his skull and jabbing a serving fork into the slab of brain there every 45 seconds or so. He knew what it meant. Time was running out. Even faster than he'd thought. Would he make it until lunch time tomorrow? Probably not.

Christ on a crutch.

They sat at an intersection, headlights shining all around, taillights tinting trunks and rear windshields red. They inched their way up to the front of the pack. Things moved slower with the streetlights out. Their progress came in little fits, all of the cars lurching forward and jerking to stops over and over again, their vehicular body language aggressive, defensive, hostile.

Inside the car, it was too quiet. Mitch didn't like it. He reached down into his brain and grasped around for words, for ideas, for any coherent thoughts to share aloud. What are you supposed to say at a time like this? Shouldn't he say something to his sons? Something that would encapsulate a little bit about what this experience of consciousness is supposed to mean now that his was nearly over, some sense of what being alive is all about, or what purpose we're supposed to serve here? Shouldn't he have some wisdom to share from his time here? Some perspective now that he was dying? Shouldn't he have found some route to redemption he could tell them about?

As the car got to the front of the line and moved on, he stirred around in his brains and found nothing solid to be had. No wisdom. No perspective. Nothing to share. He didn't even know what he thought or felt about any of it. But they were moving now, so forget it.

Go. Just go.

Don't look back.

Teddy

Moundsville, West Virginia
69 days after

He smeared the back of his hand across his brow, his head shaking back and forth of its own volition, which he didn't realize until he touched it. The first two traps were empty. He was getting nervous.

He hated waiting. He always did.

He crunched over the broken bits downtown again, that sound of glass screeching and grinding against the sidewalk filling the air. He walked past the barbershop he used to go to as a kid. The windows were broken, but the barber pole was untouched. He guessed nobody felt that to be worthy of destruction. Why all of the other glass and not the barber pole? Made no sense to him.

The ground gave way to a sloping grade, his feet slapping their way down the hill. When the sidewalk flattened out again, he could see the chain link fence in the distance. Inside, green grass led up to the sandy ovals worn under each swing on the swing set as well as the place where the slide ended. He couldn't tell anything for sure yet, but this might be his best hope.

Please. Please just let one be there. His chest heaved once, a single deep breath, and he strode on.

At first he thought the smell of the rotting meat drew them in, the putrid aroma that filled the air even where he walked now, but lately he'd wondered if the collective sound of all of the buzzing of the flies might be what did it. He wasn't certain how it worked, but the road kill attracted them well enough, especially if he put it in what was once a well populated area. Could they actually smell or hear or both? He didn't know. They didn't seem to be all the way there. That was for sure.

He smeared his hand over his brow again and felt the faintest ache just behind his left eye, a brewing headache. They came when he got stressed out like this. His mama said it was from high blood pressure. He remembered all of the things she said, and sometimes that made him feel like she was still there with him, cigarette perched between her lips, leaned against a wall somewhere always just around the corner from him, just in the next room.

He saw movement in the distance, within the walls of the fence, and all of the nervousness drained out of him right away. A figure stumbled, a man stepping this direction and that, arms limp at his sides, no discernible goal in mind. He was short and stocky, maybe five foot eight and 180 pounds, Teddy figured.

He'd caught one.

Erin

Presto, Pennsylvania
40 days after

Erin took a meandering route to the door of the gas station, wanting to keep them as far from the broken body on the pavement as possible. Where the blacktop of the parking lot met the lighter gray concrete of the sidewalk, she hopped over a bag of Utz potato chips. It had been trampled so badly that one end had burst open, leaking a pale yellow powder of pulverized potato onto the ground.

Bells jangled as she pulled the door open. She was somewhat surprised it wasn't locked. Not that it mattered. With the windows gone, there were plenty of points of entry.

Something crunched under her foot as she stepped inside. From the sound, she imagined she'd just stepped on the world's biggest cockroach. Tipping her shoe to the side to get a look at it, she saw that it wasn't a bug but a lighter. A pair of cheap yellow Bics lay there, the plastic case of one cracked in half.

The shelves were picked clean of anything remotely edible. No gum. No jerky. Even the jar that once held the disturbingly pink pickled eggs next to the counter was empty. Only the fuchsia liquid remained. There was a shelf of windshield wiper fluid that seemed mostly untouched. A spinning rack of sunglasses leaned across one aisle like a fallen tree.

"Clean up on aisle four," Izzy said.

One of the doors of the refrigerated section had a big green splat in the center of it. Erin's gaze followed the drips down the glass to the floor, where a dented container of mint chip ice cream oozed the remainder of its contents onto the floor. A dried puddle of creamy goo, speckled with black dots. She'd never been a huge fan of mint chip — it always felt kinda like licking at a scoop of frozen toothpaste — but man, it sounded good right then. It had been so long since she'd had anything colder than room temperature.

Lottery tickets were strewn about the counter. Erin stooped and picked one up, studying it. Sure enough, some of the silvery foil had been scratched away with a coin, revealing a tiny image of a pot of gold underneath. She grabbed a handful of the cards, confirming that they had indeed all been scratched off. Some moron, in the midst of the world going to shit, had actually stood in this gas station and done a bunch of scratch offs. Where did they think they were going to cash those in?

She released them, the rectangles of cardstock swooping and floating to the ground like autumn leaves.

Izzy was already poking at the buttons on the cash register. Next to that was a touchscreen with a row of stickers along the top: PUMP 1, PUMP 2, PUMP 3, and so on. Erin ran a finger over the screen, depressed the power button, but nothing happened. No surprise there.

She scanned the area around the counter, on the lookout for a key. Or a ring of keys. Or even an empty hook for a set of keys, so they'd at least know they were on the right track.

Izzy kept punching at the cash register. Whether she was

actually trying to accomplish something or was just playing at being a cashier, Erin wasn't sure.

She turned to face a door behind them. A blue and white sign proclaimed, "EMPLOYEES ONLY."

As she pushed through the door, a wave of stench hit her. The room was windowless, pitch black except for the wedge of light from the open door. She let the door fall closed, knowing what the smell meant. Goddammit.

"Language."

She hadn't even realized she'd said it out loud until Izzy reprimanded her.

Her shoe connected with the door, toeing it open again. The minuscule amount of light from the store wasn't enough to penetrate the smothering darkness inside.

She sure as hell wasn't going into that room without a light of some kind when she knew there was a body inside. No effing way.

She imagined stepping into the pitch blackness and the door swinging closed behind her and everything going dark. A prickle ran up her spine.

The Dracula's Dungeon debacle came to mind just then. The summer she turned ten.

Erin and Kelly begged their parents to let them go. There was a sign out front of the building that rotated around in the breeze, and they created a little chant to go along with it that they repeated relentlessly any time they rode by. "Haunted... HOUSE! Open... TODAY! Haunted... HOUSE! Open... TODAY!"

After several weeks, Erin's dad caved. The door chimed as they entered and whooshed closed behind them. Goosebumps puckered over Erin's arms from the air conditioning.

It smelled like wet paint inside. A kid, maybe seventeen, lounged behind the counter reading a skateboard magazine. When her dad inquired about the entry fee, the kid's eyes wandered over to Erin and Kelly. He pressed his lips together.

"We don't really recommend the haunted house for kids under 12."

Now it was her dad's turn to study them. Erin and Kelly affected looks of pure, wide-eyed enthusiasm. They couldn't really get this close only to be turned away, could they?

Her dad leaned into the counter.

"They've been hounding me about this thing for weeks."

The kid shrugged.

"Hey, man. It's up to you." He pointed at a set of steel doors. A handpainted sign above them read, "Point of No Return(s)!"

"They have to be accompanied by an adult, and once you step inside, no refunds."

Her dad gave them one more inspection before he pulled his wallet from his back pocket and forked over the fifty bucks- $15 each for kids under 16, $20 for adults.

Erin and Kelly grinned at each other, bouncing on their feet. It was finally happening!

The kid pecked at the cash register. It jangled as its jaw unhinged and slid out. He deposited the bill and slammed it shut.

Kelly squeezed Erin's arm, digging her nails in a little. "Scary!"

Erin swatted at her.

"Quit, we're not even inside yet."

The kid banged a fist on one of the steel doors and a half second later, it opened. A man in a black stovepipe hat and tailcoat stepped through the door. His face was painted a ghoulish gray, darker around the eyes.

"What's this? Ah! Fresh bloo-" He cleared his throat. "I mean, new guests! How marvelous."

He smiled, showing off a set of fangs. Erin tried not to laugh at the atrocious Transylvanian accent he was trying to pull off.

"Please come in and make yourselves at home. It's been ages since I had anyone… for dinner."

He threw his head back and cackled. A cascade of white ruffles flowed down from the neck of his shirt, and the flounces of fabric shook when he laughed.

Erin leaned closed to Kelly and whispered, "Nice blouse."

Kelly snickered.

Vlad led them into a room lit by candles. They passed by a coffin, and he quickly shut the lid.

"Silly me, always forgetting to make the bed!"

There was a door at the end of the room, and he stopped in front of it.

"Why don't you have a look around my humble abode while I make dinner preparations?"

He turned the knob and opened the door. Nothing was visible beyond the threshold. It was a black void.

"I think you'll enjoy this part of the tour. It's my lightless labyrinth, a pitch black maze of my own design!"

As they passed by him, he lifted his arm to stroke his chin with a white gloved hand.

"You know, it just occurred to me that the last visitors I

had went into the maze… but they never came out!"

Vlad chuckled.

"Oh, but I'm sure you'll make it through just fine!"

The door closed behind them, smothering them in darkness.

"Christ, that's it?" her dad said, somewhere in front of her. "Alright. Erin, you hold onto my belt with one hand and hold hands with Kelly with the other."

She held onto both with an iron grip. For the first few moments in the blackness, Erin felt only the thrill of excitement. But with each step, she couldn't stop imagining that they'd get stuck in the maze forever, unable to find their way out. Or worse, that she'd get separated from her dad and Kelly, and she'd be stranded by herself. The walls, even though she couldn't see them, felt like they were closing in.

They inched forward. She could hear her dad's hand slide along the wall as a guide. There was a hollow bumping sound and then an annoyed puff of air.

"Dead end. We have to turn around."

After they hit two more dead ends, she started to convince herself they were going in circles. They could literally walk around in here for hours and never find a way out.

Her legs got heavy, feet dragging along the floor. And then they stopped.

"I can't," she said.

"What?"

"I want to go back," she said.

"We can't go back, honey. It's a maze."

"I want to go back!"

She started to hyperventilate.

Her dad's voice called out, echoing between the narrow walls of the maze.

"Hello? Whoever's out there that can hear me, we're having a bit of a problem. If you could turn on the lights, or bring a flashlight."

Silence.

His voice boomed, "Turn on the lights, goddammit!"

Adrenaline flowed into her hands, turning them to ice. She started to shake.

Fluorescent lights jittered to life overhead, flooding the space in blinding light. Erin squinted.

Unfinished plywood walls. Paint spattered cement floor. Not scary at all.

Footsteps approached, and Vlad rounded the corner. But he wasn't Vlad anymore. All the theatrical energy he'd displayed before was gone. Even his posture had changed with the loss of his vampiric essence. He stooped forward, looking like a deflated balloon.

"Might as well go back through the front," he said, the faux Transylvanian accent long gone.

He led them back out the way they came.

It was so long ago. Why did it still bother her? She breathed in, long and deep, then let it out slow.

An idea came to her, and she clicked her tongue against the roof of her mouth. She skirted around the counter, eyes scanning the ground. The candy yellow plastic caught her eye, and she scooped up the uncracked lighter.

Her thumb flicked the wheel, emitting a spark but getting no flame. She tried again, the lighter making it's raspy sound that suddenly reminded her of a cricket. Flame sprang from the end, and she held it in the air triumphantly, like an Olympic torch.

Back at the door, she turned the handle and propped it open with her foot. She scooted farther into the darkness before she ignited her tiny flame. The room lit up with an orange tint, and she had to fight her instinct to flee.

It wasn't just one body, but a pile of them. Heaped on top of one another like curbside junk on bulk trash day. She thought of the photos she'd seen in her history books of the mass graves at Nazi concentration camps. All the limbs and skulls and torsos tangled up that way looked so wrong. The flickering light on her hand danced over the corpses, casting shadows, making it seem like they were moving. Writhing.

She let the flame go out and backpedaled out the door.

"What is it?" Izzy's voice came from over her shoulder, startling her.

"Nothing," Erin said. "Just a body, I mean. Stay here."

She put her hand on the door, not wanting to go back in.

She thought of Dracula's Dungeon again and how after they got back to the lobby, they tried to get her to go back in.

Her dad got down on one knee.

"You wanna try again?"

Erin shook her head, worried that if she stepped back into the maze, she'd panic again. It was embarrassing enough to have it happen once. If it happened again, she might as well just wander further into the maze and die there.

She had to do it this time, had to beat the fear. Again she shoved through the door and held the lighter high. She scooted as far as she could while still holding the door with her foot, but it wasn't enough. She had to let go of the door.

The light from the lobby winked out. The brightness of the lighter left squiggly pink blind spots that danced over her field of vision.

Her feet slid along the floor more than walked. She was scared of tripping over something in the gloom.

She held her breath and tried to let her focus soften so that the mound of human flesh in front of her lost the harsh detail. Still, she could make out the dark stains on the clothing. Skirting around the edge of the pile, she knew that just like the trampled body in the parking lot, these people had not died of natural causes.

Something reflected the glow of the lighter, and Erin hunched over to get a better look. A key ring, dangling from the belt loop of one of the corpses.

She forced herself to take a step closer. Just as her fingers brushed the keys, she realized how hot the top of the lighter had grown under her thumb. She tried to stop herself from letting go, but reflex took over and her thumb released the button. The light flicked out, and the darkness closed in.

Teddy

Moundsville, West Virginia
69 days after

The zombie wandered around the perimeter of its pen, too dumb to find the gate and move on. The feet skittered along the grass, not so much lifting for legitimate steps as sliding forward in uneven jerks that made the torso above wobble and lean at odd angles. Its clothes were tattered. Red covered the shriveled flesh around its mouth, but its eyes didn't convey any malice or viciousness or much of anything at all. They stared out at nothing, blank like all of the others.

Teddy smiled. This wasn't much of a trap, but it worked well enough. In fact, it proved more effective than some of his more elaborate contraptions. If he put a piece of road kill in this fenced-in park with all but one of the gates closed, he could usually pen one in long enough to get here before it found the way out. They were pretty good at getting to the meat, but not great at finding their way out.

He watched it veer off to the left, wandering past the swings and seesaw, its limp arm flopping against the side of a slide. Memories came to him as his eyes traced its meandering path under the monkey bars.

The other kids beat him up on the playground when he was really young. Mostly it seemed to be about humiliating him – pushing him down, smacking him around a little – but the meaner kids took it beyond that sometimes.

357

Scott Melvin. That was the kid who punched him the hardest. He was a year older than everyone else, held back because of emotional issues. He had red hair and saggy looking cheeks, and he wore metal t-shirts of bands that Teddy had never actually heard. It all just sounded like noise to him anyway. Metal and all the rest of the music the kids listened to. Meaningless ticking and tocking and wailing.

He remembered watching Scott's pudgy fist loop in on his forehead in second grade, seeing everything go black with flashes of red when it connected. He came to face down in the red wood chips under the swings. He wasn't sure how many times he was struck. Just once? Were all of those red flashes times he got hit? His fingers scanned his forehead, locating a single lump at the edge of his brow that sent a twinge of pain through him when he touched it.

He brought himself up to his knees and brushed flecks of wood off of cheeks and shirt. The kids laughed at that, a semi-circle of them laughing their stupid heads off. It felt like time had passed, like he'd gone somewhere else and come back, but he wasn't certain. Had he really been knocked out? Or did he psych himself out into fainting? He didn't know.

Now he entered the gates of the park, his hand fidgeting along the handle of the hatchet as he moved toward the hunch-backed figure shambling away from him. He was ready to play.

Mitch

Bethel Park, Pennsylvania
41 days before

Mitch sat at the table in the kitchen. A lone candle burned there, and he watched the flame flicker atop it, a river of wax seeping down the side. The boys had gone to bed, but he knew he couldn't sleep, not like this, so he didn't bother trying. He could feel the sting of tiredness like sand gritting at his eyes, could feel the fog in his head obscure pieces of his thoughts, but even so, he couldn't make his brain stop, couldn't even slow it down. He didn't know if he even wanted to.

He thought about what they would do now. Should he take them to their grandparents' house in the morning? At least that way some kind of guardian would have a chance to find them, assuming ol' Grandma and Grandpa were still alive anyway. They hadn't answered the phone or been home, so it was hard to say. On the other hand, they could stay here and make calls. They'd be in a familiar place, with a decent amount of supplies.

Pain stabbed through his skull again, the headache's blade entering the top of his head about four inches behind his left eyeball, jabbing about in there, and then leaving for a while.

He reached out for the phone where it sat on the table, fingers brushing at the screen which did not respond to his touch. He had turned it off to save some of the battery for the daylight hours tomorrow. It was tempting to check it now, but no. Not yet. He removed his fingers from the device, leaving it off.

With the power still out, the house felt so still and dark. He thought about Janice down on the basement floor, the scrap of tarp covering her face. He saw her in his mind, his wife, the love of his life, now a corpse laid out on the concrete slab with bullet holes running through her. In some way remembering the physicality of her final resting place made her death seem more real, which made his own impending demise a touch less scary. What was he still doing here anyway? What could he hope to do without her? He was nothing on his own. He was no one. Death made sense with her gone, he thought, as much sense as it can ever make anyway. From other angles it was terrifying still, some voyage into the unknown, maybe a drop off into nothingness, but when he thought of her, he felt prepared. He was good to go.

He looked up to the spot above the candle where the light flickered on the ceiling. It was hard to imagine that this used to feel like a safe place, he thought. It used to feel like home. For years that was the way of things. Not anymore. No safe place existed. No home existed. Not for his wife, and not for him. Maybe for his boys it still could be, but deep down, he didn't think so.

He stood and opened the window over the sink for some fresh air. The cool undulated in through the open rectangle, ballooning across his face and the bare flesh of his arms. He closed his eyes and inhaled, felt the chill enter his nostrils and pass through his throat into his chest. It seemed weird, just then, all of the animal things people do to survive, all of the bodily functions. Eating, sleeping, breathing, pissing, shitting, etc. He didn't consider these things often, so much so that they felt foreign and far away now.

He stood at the window a long time, staring at the blackness out there. No streetlights. No driveways lit up. Just black along the ground and stars in the sky. Stars that hung up there like impartial judges, that looked down on him the same way they did on his wedding day and the day his wife passed and now the day he would do the same. Stars he had gazed at throughout his life, full of wonder for what the universe might have in store, what life might have in store. With all of the endless possibilities, this is what he got.

He craned his neck to stare at the stars full on, and for a moment, regret welled in him. Regret for the days gone by, the time wasted, the attention never paid. But it passed. This was how life worked. He knew that.

It must be quite late now, maybe around 2 AM, he thought. The neighborhood was dead still. He put his hands on the window sill, felt the cool roiling around his fingertips, thought about closing it. The quiet outside made him uncomfortable, a foreboding feeling that made him hold his breath and wait for something to happen over and over again, but he left it.

He walked back to the table and sat once more, forearms resting on the edge. His abs felt tight, flexed, holding him upright in a manner that struck him as aggressive, almost ape-like. His diaphragm squeezed breath in and out of him.

They would stay here, he thought. He couldn't risk further travel, not for his sons, at least, not without knowing for sure the grandparents were out there somewhere. No, they would try to make it here. At home.

He could feel the cool air from the window roll across the back of his neck. Not a breeze, just the faintest movement of air. It made the hair there stand up, a prickling feeling that spread across the brain stem region in slow motion.

He closed his eyes. He knew what he had to do now. He didn't want to do it, but he knew he would.

Baghead

Rural Oklahoma
9 years, 126 days after

Waves of sand skimmed over the blacktop before the Delta 88. Endless streams of grit that twisted and changed directions. Baghead thought it looked like a miniature flock of migrating birds.

"Shit," Delfino said. "This doesn't look good."

He pointed farther down the road. Spirals of sand stood tall against the horizon. Three funnel cloud-looking towers. Billowing dust draped over the road beneath them.

"A sand storm?" Baghead said.

"Yeah. Blowing in from the south from the looks of it."

Delfino lifted a little in his seat, putting more weight on the accelerator. The car lurched forward, snuggling Bags' shoulder blades back into the seat.

"We might be able to outrun the worst of it."

Without soil management and irrigation and people to look after it, the first long drought had turned most of the Great Plains to dust. The plant life withered, and the topsoil blew away.

Looking out at the crags and the cracks and the sand, it was hard to imagine that crops ever grew here. The earth had shriveled, had dried out like the dead bodies still sprawled in the ghost towns up and down the highway.

"Will it short out the car? The sand, I mean."

Delfino's eyebrows reached up for his hairline.

"Might. Guess we're about to find out."

They barreled down a hill, and a wall of brown smoke engulfed them. The cloud seemed to hang in the air all around, almost appearing motionless like fog until Baghead stared at it long enough to detect the swirls and eddies and the current of the wind.

Delfino eased back down into his seat, letting up on the accelerator a bit.

"Shit."

He pulled the car over, easing it halfway onto the shoulder and cutting the engine.

"We'll have to wait it out."

Delfino dug in his breast pocket for a cigarette.

With the engine noise gone, they could hear the wind whistling over the vehicle. Something about it seemed lonesome and cold, Bags thought.

He leaned back in his seat and closed his eyes. His sleep was dreamless.

The wind roared over the car. It moaned and hissed and whimpered.

Dust clouded all things. It blocked out the sun. Turned everything inside the car the color of ash.

Delfino's lighter scraped and clicked, the glow lighting his face from below and turning the tip of his cigarette red. He flicked the lighter closed with another click, and the flame cut out. The color drained back to gray.

"How long has it been?" Bags said, sitting up from his sleep spot.

Delfino exhaled before he spoke, smoke coiling out of his nose.

"Not long. Maybe 45 minutes. Maybe less."

Bags nodded. He looked out the window at the swirling plume of dirt around them. This was not the nearly motionless cloud they sat in before. It jerked. It pulsated. A throbbing black mass that engulfed them.

Sand whipped against the car. It tinkled at the windows and rasped over the roof above.

Clods of filth were visible now and then. Beach ball sized clumps of earth torn from the ground and tossed about.

"Can I ask you something?" Delfino said.

"Sure."

"Do you believe in souls?"

Baghead raked his fingers over the canvas shrouding his jaw before he answered.

"I don't know. I guess sometimes I do. It scares me, maybe, if we don't have souls."

"Scares you?"

"Yeah. The idea that we are just strange apes. Here for no purpose. Deluding ourselves into thinking that there's meaning in our endless drive to consume things. Doesn't that scare you?"

Delfino stubbed his cigarette butt out in the ash tray, the red cherry going black with a little hiss.

"Well... no. I mean, it would, maybe. But I do believe in souls. I never quite made the jump to religion, you know? But I figure if all of those old Greek philosophers believed in souls, there must be something to it. Bunch of people that are a lot smarter than me, you know?"

"The ghost in the machine."

"What?"

"That's what they call all of the old beliefs. A lot of the old philosophers all bought into the idea that the mind and body are fundamentally separate, which, if accepted, sort of proves the idea that there is a soul – a ghost in the machine – that makes the whole thing go. But now it's used as an example of modern people accepting fallacies from more primitive times. I mean, we now understand that our brain functioning is the mind. It's not fundamentally separate from our physical beings after all, right?"

They sat a moment without talking.

"The ghost in the machine. Has a ring to it, anyway," Delfino said.

The wind moaned in the seam along Baghead's door, almost like a tea kettle flipping off and on. Periodically bigger gusts rose up, the pitch of the noise against the car deeper and more powerful, enough to rattle the metal body.

Delfino squirmed a little in his seat.

"I was wondering. Since we're just sitting here a while," he said. "Might I see it now?"

Baghead thought about it a second, nodded.

"I suppose."

He plucked the Hand of Death from his pocket, passed it over. Delfino handled it gingerly, fingertips making sure to only touch the edges. He gasped a little upon turning it toward himself, seeming to hold his breath.

They both looked upon the image for a long moment without speaking.

The red background held its hue even in the half-light.

The black hand stood out that much more, and the skull in the palm contrasted even further.

"Do you know what the symbols mean?" Delfino said.

He hovered a finger over the ornate markings, one hovering above each black finger.

"It's some ancient occult language. Reading right to left, it spells 'death.'"

Delfino nodded. He looked at the card a while longer before he handed it back.

"Never thought I'd actually see it," he said. "Man, I bet looking at that thing makes you want to believe in souls, don't it?"

Ray

Houston, Texas
3 days before

Dark surrounded the Grand Cherokee like the night was trying to swallow it up. The daylight had faded fast while they were stuck in traffic, and they were still here. Still in Houston. Not good.

"You were right," she said.

"How do you mean?" he said.

"You said some crazy shit was about to go down," she said, gesturing to the standstill traffic around them. "It sure is."

She smiled. She didn't seem alarmed to a level that seemed appropriate for an impending nuclear holocaust, but that was probably for the best. She didn't know about that anyway, of course. He decided he'd tell her after they were out of town, if they ever found a damn way out.

All roads out of Houston had military roadblocks in place now. They'd tried to get onto the interstate, either 45 or 69, but soldiers turned them away both times. Armed guards directing traffic, waving everyone away. One yelled that the terror levels had been raised and everyone was to stay in town by order of the Department of Homeland Security. He added that it'd probably be lifted in the next day or two.

Now Ray wrestled with the steering wheel and searched the nooks and crannies of his mind for the remotest routes he could think of. The backroads that seemed least likely to be guarded, and even if they were, the privacy might give them options.

The sounds of the engines rose and fell in a way that conveyed restlessness, Ray thought. Headlights shone all around, the cars advancing in fits and starts, all the traffic lurching forward and jerking to a stop in unison like some herd of cattle. That's just what it was like, he knew. All of the people piled up on top of each other like cows getting funneled into the kill chute at a slaughterhouse.

He wished he had a cigar to chew on, but he hadn't brought any.

Mitch

The basement stairs creaked beneath his feet, and the wood sagged a little with each step. He felt it bend and contort under the strain of his weight. He wasn't scared, but he walked slowly, deliberately. It felt like an act of reverence in some way, a show of respect.

The flashlight nestled into his fist like the hilt of a sword, its glowing blade carving a tunnel of light into the darkness. The circle of illumination bounced along the concrete floor below as he made his way down the steps. It looked like a spotlight beaming onto a stage, the lights turned down so only the star of the show was visible, but he couldn't quite bring himself to shine the light on the star of this production. Not yet.

At the bottom, the sag of the wood gave way to the solid cement. He planted his feet there, took a breath. It was cool down here, dank and a little chilly as it always was in the basement, he supposed, but the sweat poured out of him anyway. It seeped out of his forehead and lubricated his palms. He smeared the back of his hand over his brow, left to right, felt the perspiration sluice down the side of his face, clinging to the stubble at the corner of his jaw.

He stepped forward, again moving with care. The light inched toward its destination, toward the big reveal. The feet came into view at the edge of the spotlight, still and grayed out like they were being broadcast in black and white. He stopped there, looked on the sole of the lone remaining tennis shoe. The tread looked fairly new, not beat and scuffed to hell like his shoes. Jan always took better care of her things like that.

Air rushed into his lungs with a click and a scraping sound, and he realized he'd been holding his breath. He stood and just breathed a while, his eyes dancing away from the feet and moving back toward them, like he wanted to look away but couldn't. He closed them for a moment, though, and that stuck.

The stab of the headache ruptured in his brain again, and he saw a pink splotch within his closed eyes from where the hurt seemed to occur. He brought a hand to his left eye and pressed on it. It didn't help, but the cool of his fingers against his eyelid felt good. The headache was worse now, the pain sharper, bigger, coming on more frequently. That wasn't good, but it was no surprise.

The Sickness. The sickness unto death, he thought. Those words had banged around in his head in this very basement last night, before she was gone. He didn't know why he thought them or where they came from. He did know that last night, sitting on the lawn chairs in the basement with Janice, chugging Red Bull and beer, seemed like 50 years ago.

He opened his eyes, and the feet returned to his field of vision. They were entirely motionless, of course, still and dead like mannequin legs, but it still somehow felt like they'd popped up the moment his eyelids parted. Like they were gone, erased until he looked at them.

He took a step forward, hesitated, took another stride. Now color flowed back into the shoe, vanquishing the gray. The pale pink canvas contrasted with the white sole. A little dirt scuffed the left toe, but otherwise no one would know it was six or seven years old. Maybe even older than Matt.

Still, he kept his distance. He stopped a couple of paces shy of the sprawled figure on the floor, but he let the flashlight drift forward, its glow creeping up the body in slow motion, revealing the faded jeans that flared slightly at the ankle. Boot cut jeans for someone who never wore boots, he thought. The bottom of her hoodie covered the waist of the jeans, an oversized blue one that used to be his. It stretched to the point that the fabric was almost worn thin enough to see through at the elbows, all slack and sagged, and she wore it almost like a snuggie. Finally the tarp came into view, light reflecting off of the gray plastic surface, her face sheathed somewhere underneath, her shattered head, her broken body that could never be fixed, all wrapped in plastic.

He brushed his fingers over the stubble on his upper lip and thought about how he would go about this. Should he scoop her up, tarp and all, lugging her over one shoulder? He turned back to glance at the steps. Getting up those would be rough, but he thought he could do it. She wasn't heavy.

Wheeling back toward the body again, the light caught on the toppled lawn chairs off to his right. Her purse lay there on its side, the pack of cigarettes protruding halfway from the open zipper. The impulse made no sense to him, but he couldn't resist. He walked to the chairs, knelt, picked up the pack of smokes and shook one loose, resting it between his lips. For a second he just sat there, his nostrils full of the smell of the unlit cigarette like expensive coffee with an extra tang to it, and then he remembered what he was supposed to do next. He braved a hand into the black of the purse's interior, swimming it around in there, feeling the jumble of items rattling against his palm and knuckles until his fingertips found the lighter and secured it.

The flashlight wobbled on the floor as the lighter's flame lit up his face from beneath. Only half of the tobacco lit, so he puffed the cig a couple times to get the cherry even. It tasted pretty bad. He'd never acquired a taste for tobacco smoke, but he knelt there and smoked it anyway. He still didn't know why. Maybe because it was hers.

He picked up the flashlight again, holding it so it pointed to the ceiling and watching the second hand smoke drift through its beam when he exhaled. The idea of lung cancer crossed his mind, and he almost laughed.

It was weird, he thought. In so many ways he'd lived like he would live forever. He'd taken his time for granted on one hand and simultaneously not fully indulged, not fully embraced his passions on the other. It was the worst of both worlds. Maybe this would be the lesson he'd try to teach his boys – that their time is precious and they should use that as a motivator to do something awesome, not a reason to fear a death that's inevitable -- but then maybe not. He didn't know if you could learn this lesson without experiencing elements of it, and if so, he didn't know if he could be the one that could teach it to them.

He stubbed the cigarette butt out on the floor. The red tip crushed into a smudge of black soot with a muffled hiss. He stood then, his eyes returning to the tarp covered body, and he knew how he needed to do it.

Baghead

Rural Oklahoma
9 years, 126 days after

As soon as the sand cleared enough to see, they got moving again. The engine seemed to cough a little as it started up, choking on dust. But the sound evened out, and they rocketed forward.

The car seat vibrated beneath Baghead, and when he stared straight ahead long without blinking, he got a weird sense of how fast they were moving. He almost had to let his mind go blank, let his eyes go unfocused to get there, like looking at a magic eye picture in a mall years and years before.

"Can I ask you another question?" Delfino said.

That shook Bags out of his state of concentration. He tried not to sound annoyed when he responded.

"Go ahead."

"Do you have a real name? I mean, I'm guessing your birth certificate didn't say 'Baghead' anywhere on it."

"I did. I don't anymore."

"I see. You want to tell me what it was?"

"No."

Delfino's brow wrinkled for a microsecond, but it smoothed out just as quickly.

"That's fair enough, I guess. What's a name even mean out here?"

The conversation died, and the silence in the car got more and more comfortable, Bags thought, like lying in bed, feeling the sheet do that slow motion swell from cold to lukewarm to toasty. It was almost like an anesthetic, a thing that numbed him and calmed him and cleared his head.

They drove past a barn, the roof all caved in, the whole structure leaning to one side like a well-timed sneeze by either of them would take it down once and for all. Even in this state of decay, the structure was an odd sight in the middle of this barren landscape, sand all drifted up along one side of the building like snow. Barns had populated all of this land not long ago, he knew, but almost none were left. The drought and the dust storms changed everything so fast.

His tongue moved to comment upon it, to say something to Delfino to wash away the feeling that prior conversation had surely left, but something held it. The momentum of the silence won out. After a couple of minutes, he was happy for that, to have kept hold of the hushed feeling in here.

The sound of the road lulled Bags into a tranquil state. The rhythmic thump of the tires rolling over the cracks here almost sounded like a horse's gallop, and the engine's hum steadied until it felt like a held chord on a background organ, low in the mix, just there for ambiance.

He stared straight ahead, not thinking, not looking at anything, his muscles limp. Asleep with his eyes open. Drool pooled in his mouth, threatening to spill out of the corners of his lips.

"Uh-oh," Delfino said.

Bags' eyes blinked a couple of times and then drifted to Delfino's before finally following his gaze to the road ahead. It took him a second to make sense of what he saw there.

A bloody stump sat in the left lane of the highway, only vaguely looking human. It appeared limbless, though somehow sitting up, the face covered in red.

Delfino slowed the car a little, and they craned their necks to get a better look. All time seemed to slow down for the moment.

The closer look revealed that it wasn't a bloody stump after all. It was a little girl with her arms and legs tucked into her t-shirt, squatting in the road. Maybe 11 years old. The blood made her facial expression hard to read, but Bags thought it seemed pretty catatonic. Her total lack of acknowledgment of the Delta 88 seemed to back up that assertion. She gazed off at nothing.

She wasn't dead, however. She blinked, and her blank expression didn't convey any pain. Hopefully the blood was someone else's, Baghead thought.

They passed her, and the car picked up speed again. Bags whirled to watch her through the back windshield as she began that process of shrinking, of her discernible features folding up into a black speck that the horizon would devour.

"Pull over," he said.

Delfino sucked air between his teeth and then spoke.

"We can't."

Baghead turned to face him.

"Pull the car over."

"Can't do it."

"I'll jump out of the moving vehicle if you want me to."

"Look, that kid might be in trouble, might desperately need our help, or it might be a trap. We can't know."

"Unless we stop and find out."

"And knowing will do us such good after we're beheaded, won't it? We'll be so happy about it, we'll gush blood out of our necks and roll our heads around on the asphalt a while in glee."

Bags didn't say anything.

"I told you. That's what they do out here. I've seen it myself."

He scratched his chin before he went on.

"For all you know that kid back there is the work of one of the five. So go rolling out that car door to your funeral if you want, but this car ain't stopping."

Bags sat back, his jaw all clenched up, and they rode in silence for a while. He angled himself away from Delfino and looked out the window.

Wisps of sand flitted around in the wind atop the dunes, the sunlight catching on the grains in the air so it almost looked like handfuls of glitter being tossed around.

The ride grew bumpy once more, and the Delta 88 slowed in anticipation of a big crack in the road up ahead where the dirt fill had gotten washed out by the rain. The change in momentum made both of them lean forward in their seats, heads pushed out over their knees.

When the car got down under 30 miles per hour, Baghead opened the door and jumped.

Mitch

Bethel Park, Pennsylvania
41 days before

He peeled the tarp back from her face, and there she was, the broken being he'd sworn to have and to hold. He guessed he would hold her once more after all.

From the brow up, her head was mostly gone, a haggard concave dome of bone with dried blood gummed up all over it. Beneath that it still looked like her, though, especially after he dragged a hand over to her eyelids to close them. He dipped a rag into the bucket of warm water next to his leg, and went to work washing her face. Grime wiped away from her cheek, a second swipe clearing that crevice where the nose and face meet.

He knew this gesture wasn't for her. She was gone. It was for him.

As he dipped the rag again and wrung it out over the bucket, the water made sounds that reminded him of taking a bath as a boy, of giving his sons baths when they were young. It was a happy sound and a calm one. He brought the rag to the opposite cheek and repeated the process.

As the smudges of black faded away, her skin beamed so clear and smooth. She looked like herself again. Strange how a person's face comes together, the pieces form into something that looks so intentional, like a painstakingly crafted sculpture instead of the random chance of genetics and biology.

He thought this task would be an unpleasant one, but it wasn't. It was important to him somehow. There would be no tarp as he carried her now, and he wouldn't sling her over his shoulder like a bag of rock salt. He would do it in a way that made sense to him. He didn't know if it was a way she would've wanted, but he hoped so.

The rag navigated the jagged edge where her skull cleaved off, scrubbing there, clearing away most of the blood, though he knew he couldn't get it all. Again his hand dunked into the warm, the rag soaking up fresh water to help clear away the blood. Again he twisted the piece of cloth, and again the water dripped down into the water in the bucket, the sing-song melody of its impact reminding him a little of wind chimes.

Her dying wish was that the boys not see her like this, not see her as a zombie, especially one with her brains blown out. He would make sure that was the case. He could do that. Time was short, though, and digging a grave six feet deep wasn't an option.

He and his wife would need to take one last road trip.

Teddy

Moundsville, West Virginia
69 days after

Teddy's hatchet hacked hard enough at the thing's neck that with just one stroke its head flopped down, dangling along with the tatters of black t-shirt draped over the sickly gray skin of the chest. The thing hissed, and when it tottered toward him, the head swung back and forth like a pendulum. Teddy laughed. It seemed too funny, like something in an animation, the way it hissed and dangled at the same time.

It was never quite right killing them, though. They never whimpered or looked scared how they were supposed to. He liked those sounds the animals sometimes made in the back of the truck, little feminine mews and cries. The noises made his heart flutter, made his teeth grit, made his cock so hard it throbbed.

It wasn't like that killing the zombies. They didn't show any feelings beyond a mindless aggression. There was only one thing that really made them seem to suffer, but it was involved. He could only do it so often.

He raised his hatchet again. He knew another whack at the neck would finish the job, most likely, as decapitation did the trick. He aimed, but he couldn't do it. Not yet.

He changed his grip and swung at the arm twice. The skin split open like the scored slash on a seared duck breast and black goo oozed out. He guessed that was old blood of some kind. These things didn't make much sense. Even after he cut them open and looked at all of the insides, they didn't make much sense to him. Just black globs and gloop and shriveled bits.

He backpedaled, letting the thing come at him, that dark substance seeping down its arm, the head grunting and hissing and clattering its teeth upside-down in its dangling position.

Something cold brushed at his back, and he jumped. He could picture the second zombie creeping up on him, its arms gripping around his waist as its teeth sank into the curve where the spine and neck meet. But no. It was just the chain of one of the swings.

The surge of adrenalin rendered his hands cold and shaky within a second of the contact, excitement and fear and life flowing through all of him. He took a breath and hurled himself at the zombie, hacking and slashing with great gusto.

The head flopped to the grass, but he leapt again for the body, falling with it as it tumbled to the ground. He straddled it and bashed away at it for a long time after it was still, his arms and chest and face wearing a spatter of thick black blood. Gummy drops mixed with sweat trailed down from the sides of his brow, flowing into the creases between his cheeks and mouth.

He realized his mouth was open, so he closed it.

Lorraine

Houston, Texas

3 days before

Houston rolled by on the sides of the street, the endless urban sprawl. Fast food signs and streetlights cut arches and wedges into the swelling shadows of dusk. When she looked up at the lights, she could almost believe things were normal, that everything was the same as it had always been. No plague. No zombies. No riots. None of it.

Then movement in the driver's seat caught her eye, and she turned to see not her husband, Greg, but Ray Dalton, the televangelist, manning the wheel, taking his cell phone from his ear and hanging it up. So things were not normal. Not at all.

She didn't know why she got into the car with Dalton. Not really. She was out of it, standing at the gas station with nothing left, pretty far gone on prescription pills, and then he showed up. Of all of the people in the world, the multi-millionaire snake oil salesman pulled up in an SUV. She knew he wasn't a good person, knew all the rumors about his whole operation being a money making scheme, that he talked more about attaining wealth than scripture, that studies showed he spent 70% of his time on TV asking for money rather than preaching, that he didn't even read any of the prayer requests sent to him, just had grunt workers remove the checks from the envelopes and throw the rest away.

Still, she needed to get out of town fast, and his car seemed to have gas in it. Maybe she would stick with him for a while. Hell, if anyone would survive a nuclear blast, it'd be the cockroaches and Ray Dalton, right?

She thought about telling Dalton what Greg had been told by his boss, that several major metropolitan areas in the South would be nuked, Houston among them. She looked at him in the driver's seat, though, his chiseled jaw, his thick head of silver hair, and she couldn't bring herself to do it. He'd already said they were headed out of town. That was good enough for now.

She couldn't tell him what her husband had known or what had happened to Greg.

Mitch

Bethel Park, Pennsylvania
41 days before

With her face clean, he looped one arm under her knees and the other under her neck. He lifted her that way, like a sleeping child, her broken head resting on the edge of his pectoral and shoulder. After hours on the concrete basement floor, she felt like cold meat against his torso, the way a leftover Thanksgiving turkey gets that chill to it after a few hours in the fridge.

He adjusted the bulk in his arms before moving out, staring down a moment into that black chasm where her brain used to be. The smell of the congealed blood wafted in his face, a familiar odor. Not a rotten smell, at least not yet. It smelled the way pennies tasted, he thought, recalling putting one of the coins in his mouth as a child and getting yelled at by his mother.

He walked across the basement floor, and the legs dangled from his arm, the head flopping and bouncing against him with every step. He had expected to find her muscles stiff with rigor mortis, but perhaps the rigidity had already passed, or perhaps the zombie virus sped it up or prevented it in some way. He didn't know, and he guessed it didn't matter much.

Once more the steps groaned and sagged under his feet. He mounted them slowly, with care, his spine arched back a little to help balance, keeping the weight of her body leaned up against him and letting his legs do most of the work.

He thought it would be disturbing to handle her dead body like this, but it wasn't, at least not that much. Maybe he was in shock, or maybe he had accepted the way of things more than he'd realized, and he was OK now putting her to rest, putting his life to rest. A reverence had come over him as he cleaned her up, a feeling that this was important, that it was special, and the feeling remained as he held her now, this tiny being pressed against his chest.

He felt like he was still with her in a way when he carried her in his arms, an irrational way, of course. He thought it would be more disturbing when she was all the way gone, when the physical being before him was no longer visible, and she was just a gray memory that crept along in his imagination. Of course, she wouldn't exist in that state for long since his imagination was coming up on its own expiration date.

The hardest part of the physical labor was almost over. His feet advanced, taking each step with care and hesitating before moving to the next one. He was halfway to the top when the stair shifted under his weight, and he wobbled, his balance slipping away from him. His shoulders leaned too far back, and he could feel the emptiness behind him, the way nothing was holding him up, like that split second when he'd leaned his chair too far back in pre-algebra in seventh grade. He knew his seat was about to go crashing down, knew he'd gone too far, and a moment of queasiness overcame him, a moment of weightlessness and dread that must have only been a second but seemed to stretch out for a long time.

His right hand shot out to grab the rail at his side, and the broken head flopped away from his chest, sliding down to the crook of his elbow. He fought to right himself like a listing boat's buoyancy stopping it from capsizing, and the weight of the body shifting forward helped his cause. His torso flailed twice, and then he jerked his weight back over his knees, regaining control of himself. The weightlessness vanished, the ground made solid under his feet once again.

He stood there a moment, taking a deep breath and letting the electrical excitement tingling in his head and chest die down a little. It felt so strange for that queasy feeling to not pay off in a crash landing, almost anti-climactic. He didn't fall, though, and he didn't drop her. This was good.

He gathered her head up against his shoulder again and climbed the last five steps to the kitchen.

The car stood before him, the trunk gaping like an open mouth. Mist descended upon him, upon the night, tumbling through the beam of the flashlight without a sound. Its damp slicked his arms, and he felt droplets drain down from his hair to run across the back of his neck. His shoulders twitched, and he began lowering her into the darkness there, but he stopped himself. He retracted his arms, hugging the corpse against his chest once again, feeling the chill through his t-shirt.

He couldn't do it. He couldn't put her in the trunk.

He rounded the corner of the car, tottering more than walking now, the toes of her shoes scraping against the fender as he moved. With the flashlight occupying his left hand, he had to duck down to one knee, dipping her head to get his right hand to the door handle. Then he had to scramble back a couple of paces to get out of the path of the door so he could swing it open. It took a couple of tries to feel for the cracked opening, to hook his fingers onto the metal well enough to fling it wide, but he got it.

He lay her body in the back seat, tucking the knees up toward the torso in a semi-fetal position so he'd be able to get the door closed. Stepping back, he looked down on her. From this angle, standing at her feet, he couldn't see the way the top of her head was blown off. It looked like she was sleeping, like they'd gone out to a party tonight, and she decided to lie down in the back on the ride home and fell asleep there, like he should wake her up now, and they could go in and go to bed.

Christ, it was late. Was he being noisy out here? His focus zeroed in on her so much that he hadn't thought about it once during this process. His head swiveled. He looked around, peered out at the blackness shrouding the neighborhood. He saw no signs of light out there, no candlelight flickering behind curtains or flashlight beams moving about. He couldn't even see the houses across the street.

With the dome light shining down on the corpse, and the flashlight in his hand, anyone looking on would be able to see him, though. He was the light for the moment, and that notion made a shiver run down his spine.

He eased the door closed, the click seeming loud now that he felt on display out here. He turned off the flashlight and walked backward a few steps, trying to ease into the safety of the shadows until the dome light turned off.

His torso shimmied, a chill crawling through him, and he realized how cold and humid it was out here, the air almost as heavy as it was in the basement. While he watched the light, he considered what time it might be. He didn't have a great guess. It must be somewhere between two and five AM now. Dawn was a ways off yet, most likely.

Just as the panicked part of his brain expressed certainty that the interior light wasn't going to turn off, that he didn't get the door closed all the way or something, it clicked and faded to black. Well. Good.

He walked toward the car, feet kicking through grass thoroughly saturated with dew. He clicked the flashlight on and pressed it close to the window, looking down upon the back seat. He couldn't see her very well, just a vague shape. That was good, but he knew it wasn't good enough.

He went inside for blankets.

Teddy

Moundsville, West Virginia
69 days after

He wiped at his face over and over on the walk home, sliding his palms and then fingers over his forehead, bringing the loaded hands down to his side and flopping them back and forth one after the other to fling sheets of black gunk away, a move somehow reminiscent of a wet dog shaking itself dry. He smeared whatever was left onto his t-shirt before going back for more.

The sky grew darker now, dusk closing out another day. Shadows fell long in the dimming light, draining the color out of the brick facades and awnings plumped up over the storefronts down here. He thought about checking the other two traps but figured leaving them would give him that much more incentive to get up in the morning. With his hand in his face much of the way, he stumbled along on the sidewalk, treading on the broken bits of his town once again.

Weirdly, he thought the moment of fear, when the chain of the swing touched his back, made this one more satisfying. He could still feel it, the cold metal pressing between his shoulder blades, and that electric shock of fear coursing through him, that moment of total panic. That got him good. Usually cutting them didn't do that much for him, but today it felt right. It wasn't like with the animals, though. This was something different. It was more like back in school.

After a few years of being a playground punching bag, he grew up, swelled up into something bigger and stronger than the rest of them. He weighed 180 pounds by the time he was 12, little to no fat on his body. Just an out of control ball of muscle. No discipline. No impulse control. He bounced around all day, finding it increasingly difficult to sit still. Starting in sixth grade, they put him in special education, which segregated him from the general population of the school. That wasn't so bad. It was a place with a peaceful energy, and the teachers knew how to calm everyone down.

In high school, he ate lunch with a chunk of the general student population, though, and things veered back toward the way they were before. They called him a retard and did crude arm motions to mock some of the other special ed kids. All of the bad feelings flooded back up to the surface, the feeling of plucking wood chips from divots in his face while everyone laughed.

So he waited for the right time, and it came.

He swirled his chicken nugget in a paper cup of honey, just vaguely aware of the other four hundred people in the room because of the low level chatter droning in all directions like a TV on in the next room. Someone clapped him on the back, and he looked back and up over his shoulder into the face of Chuck Wentworth, a kid with gerbil teeth and a terrible poof of curly blond hair that somehow looked too greasy and too dry at the same time. It reminded him of a Chia Pet. He didn't know Chuck other than by name, so this touching wasn't normal or welcome.

A semi-circle of giggling jagoffs stood behind Chuck, and Teddy knew something was coming. Some laugh riot, Friar's

Club Roast of the retard variety.

"How's that chicken nugget treatin' ya?" Chuck said.

Teddy didn't wait for the hilarity to ensue. He turned to the side, getting one leg out from under the lunch table so he could get some torque into his punch. His body coiled and uncoiled in some violent way reminiscent of an ape, and he landed a short, straight right hand right to the kid's throat. His knuckles connected with a heavy slap and then some hollow throat sound came out of Chuck's mouth. Teddy could feel the Adam's apple shove straight back in. It felt like it lodged there, cinching his wind pipe closed. Teddy hoped that it did.

The kid brought his hands to his neck, gagging, fingers crawling up the sides of his throat like flailing spider legs as though that could help him breathe. His friends stood motionless for a beat, and then they moved in as though they could aid in his attempts to breathe or talk him into it by yelling at him. None of them made eye contact with Teddy.

Chuck's face turned all red and then went a little purple. It looked, Teddy thought, like it might explode, that blond Chia poof bursting to spread its fluff everywhere like confetti at a parade. He pictured the swarm of children excitedly picking up wads of Chuck's hair along with the candy, fat little kid fingers gripping flecks of his scalp and palms cupping bloody shards of bone from his ruptured skull. He laughed so hard that he cried, barely able to finish eating his chicken nuggets, and no one in the cafeteria would look at him.

Erin

Stuck in the dark again. Erin flicked at the lighter in a panic, but it wouldn't catch. She couldn't feel her thumb right from the burn. Her movements were clumsy.

She staggered backward, toward the door. But when she swung her hand to try to catch the handle, she came up empty. She was back in the lightless labyrinth again. Set afloat in pitch black space. Doomed to be lost forever.

Her breath came short and fast, and she started to feel dizzy. She was hyperventilating. On TV they always made you breathe into a paper lunch bag if you started to hyperventilate. She didn't know why. And she didn't have a bag. So she imagined one instead. Imagined the paper bulging as it inflated with her breath. When she inhaled, the bag crinkled.

She did this again and again until she got her breathing back under control. She put the lighter in the opposite hand and lit it, keeping her thumb away from the metal. She reached out, disconnected the key ring from the corpse, and scuttled to the door, throwing it wide and lurching through it.

She took big greedy breaths of the fresh air.

Relief filled her, and then saliva rushed into her mouth, and a bitter taste rose in the back of her throat. She tried to run for the door, but didn't quite make it, spewing watery, half-digested fruit cocktail onto the gray tile.

Back at the bikes, she rinsed her mouth, swishing the water from cheek to cheek before spitting it out. Another squeeze of the bottle shot a spray of lukewarm water into her mouth, and this time she swallowed it.

Her thumb ached. When she poked at it with her forefinger, she could feel the blister there.

The keys were all labeled. She found the one that said PUMP 2 and inserted it into the lock. The rest of the keys tinkled together like bells as she turned it. She tried not to notice the dark red crust on some of them.

The little door swung open revealing a whole lot of electronic equipment. Nothing that seemed to turn the pump on for manual use. Erin stared at it a long while before taking a step back.

"I give up. You still want to check out the playground?"

Izzy rested a fist on one hip.

"No, I decided I'd rather go to the library and read a bunch of books instead."

Erin gave her the side-eye.

"Wait a minute. Did you just figure out how sarcasm works?"

They rode through another intersection partially blocked by a collection of crumpled cars. The ground around the crash looked like it was studded with diamonds, bits of glass glittering in the sun. As they wove around the destruction, something red caught Erin's eye.

She did a double-take, slowing her bike on the second glance. Izzy pulled ahead.

"Slow down for a second."

Erin left her bike on the sidewalk and walked into the center of the street. There was a dark brown El Camino in the wreckage. The wrinkled metal reminded her of the outside of a raisin. But she was less concerned with the condition of the vehicle and more intrigued by what lay in the rear bed.

It was a red plastic gas can, just like the empty one in her bike carrier.

Wrapping her palm around the handle, she gave it a shake. The muffled sound of sloshing liquid met her ears. She lifted it, feeling the weight of the gas inside.

"No way," Izzy said. "What are the odds?"

Erin got that feeling she got in the houses sometimes. Even though she'd been prepared to take gas from the gas station, that somehow felt different. This act of pulling the can out of someone's car felt more like a violation. Like stealing. Maybe it seemed too easy. She knew it was silly, but she found herself craning her neck around, on the lookout as if she were a kid shoplifting a candy bar from the corner store.

She nestled the new gas can into the carrier with the old one, tucking it in like a baby.

"I'll race you to the swings," Izzy said, then took off before Erin could even get back on her bike.

"Cheater!"

Erin ran after her, pulling the bike along to get a better start. Izzy zoomed out ahead, already crossing the bridge stretching over the river. Erin pumped at the pedals to catch up, less because she was concerned about winning the race, and more because she didn't want Izzy to get too far ahead. She still couldn't shake the uneasiness of being around all the houses and cars.

Sunlight filtered through the trees above. The wind rustled through the leaves, casting quivering shadows on the sand at Erin's feet. The river babbled in the background, a sound that made the world seem a little less empty.

Erin sat in one of the swings, her back to the jungle gym. She wasn't really swinging so much as pushing her legs back and forth in a swaying motion. Like a rocking chair.

She and Kelly used to try to see who could swing higher, pumping their legs back and forth, leaning in and pointing their toes at the top of the arc.

There was always talk about the kids who had managed to swing all the way around, completing the circle. Of course now she knew that was all bogus. Made up by older kids probably. But back then, when she sort of believed it might be possible, she wondered what would happen if she did keep swinging higher, higher, higher, until finally the swing inverted, flipping her upside-down, chain wrapping around the metal bar. Half of her wanted to do it, and the other half was scared shitless at the thought. What if she got to the top, reached the pinnacle, and she just fell out of the swing, gravity ripping her back down to the ground?

"Erin! Erin, watch this!"

She spiraled around to face Izzy, the swing chains twisting into an X.

Sand kicked up under Izzy's feet as she got a running start at one end of the sand pit. When she reached the structure, she flung herself in the air like a gibbon and latched onto a zip line. The metallic whir of the wire filled the air. Izzy dangled from the handle, kicking her legs in the air. At the end of the line, she let go, hovering in the air for a beat before she landed the perfect dismount.

Erin lifted an imaginary scorecard over her head.

"Ten-point-oh! Perfect score!"

Izzy bowed and then ducked into one of the slides and climbed up the wrong way. Erin could almost remember what it was like to be that age. To be able to pretend it wasn't a jungle gym, but a castle, and half-believe it.

She lifted her feet and let the chains over her head unwind. The world spun around her in a blur, and then she was back facing the frozen traffic jam across the sidewalk.

Everything was so quiet now. So still. It felt like walking around in a photograph or a painting, almost. For a moment, Erin pretended that the world hadn't ended. Someone had a remote control for the world, and they just pressed the pause button at the exact moment all those cars piled up in the intersection. In two seconds, they'd press play again. And the door of the smashed up Lexus would open, and the driver would get out. He'd be pissed off. Shaking his fist at the kid in the blue Volkswagen. An old lady would come out on the porch of the bungalow across the street to see what all the commotion was about. A fisherman would float down the river in an aluminum rowboat.

If it weren't for the subtle movements of the grass and the leaves and the little ripples on the surface of the river, she could almost believe the world was just paused.

It made more sense in some ways. How could the world just end like this, with no notice? Yeah, things had been bad with the outbreak of the plague. The death toll on the news, climbing higher and higher each night. The riots. The power outages.

Some people even said it was the beginning of the end. But the people on TV — the talking heads and politicians — they all said it was under control. No cause for panic. Her mom repeated it. And she bought it. Because she wanted to.

Erin wondered if they'd known all along where things were headed. They had to, on some level, right?

It didn't matter, though. Not really. She knew from experience that even if you knew the worst was coming, you still found ways to lie to yourself. To trick yourself into believing that everything was OK.

Like when her dad died. She kept anticipating some kind of final moment. The kind they always showed in movies. The family gathers around the bed, pearls of wisdom are exchanged. But that was the movies and not real life. In real life, people were there one second and gone the next. You might not even notice. You might be sitting on the floor in the corner, doing your trig homework, while your mom napped on the cramped little couch.

She didn't even know how long it had been when she looked up and noticed something was off. Thinking back, she couldn't even identify what it was exactly. The stillness that told her he wasn't breathing? The way his mouth hung slack? The opaqueness of the skin? Whatever it was, she crawled toward the bed without thinking, her math book sliding to the floor, secants and cotangents forgotten.

Erin didn't know how many minutes she stood there, but eventually her mom's voice broke her trance.

"What is it?"

Their eyes met. Erin's mom unfolded her legs from their

scrunched position on the love seat. Her gaze moved from Erin down to the bed, and she saw for herself that he was gone.

And then she said, "Why are you just standing there? Why didn't you wake me up?"

There was a note of accusation in her voice, and even though it was probably just the grief talking, Erin still remembered it, still felt it. She probably would for the rest of her life.

Her mom ran off to find a nurse then. Like the nurse was going to come in and do what? Wake him up? Pronounce him dead? What did it matter how fucking long she stood there?

Stage one, denial. Her mom was an expert at that one.

Tears welled in her eyes, and she pulled at the shoulder of her t-shirt to wipe them away.

Izzy's voice suddenly came in a tight whisper. "Errrriiinnnnn!"

She glanced sideways at Izzy and noticed her body language: stiff and upright, like a rabbit that's just spotted a wolf.

Before Erin pinpointed what Izzy was looking at, a sound startled her.

"Well, hello there!"

On the opposite side of the river, standing just shy of the water line, was a man. It was hard to tell from this distance, but from the graying beard and the way he was dressed — faded jeans, flannel shirt, and a Pittsburgh Pirates hat — she guessed him to be in his fifties. Maybe a youngish sixty.

A fishing pole extended from one hand. In the other, he held a blue Dixie cup, presumably filled with worms.

Izzy scurried back to stand next to and slightly behind Erin.

"Hi," Izzy said from around Erin's elbow.

Erin nudged Izzy's foot with her own.

"What are you doing?" Erin growled the words through her teeth.

"I don't know," Izzy hissed back.

The man craned his neck around, surveying the girls' side of the river. "Are you two out here all alone?"

Before Izzy could say anything stupid, Erin called back.

"Don't worry about it." She turned to Izzy. "Don't say anything."

"No need to be hasty. I didn't mean to scare you. It's just been so long since I've seen anyone," he said, and licked his lips.

Erin beat down a pang of sympathy for him. It was that stupid beard. Her dad had always worn a beard, and every time she saw an older man with a beard, she got a little sad. Like when he died, it left a little wound in her that got opened up at the sight of some salt and pepper scruff.

"I'm Clay, by the way," he said. "May I ask your names?"

"Thelma and Louise," Erin answered. To Izzy, she whispered, "Go get your bike. We're going."

"Please, I only want to talk to you. I know you must be frightened, two young girls out here on your own. I can help you."

Erin couldn't help it. The condescension got her hackles up.

"We don't need your help."

"Look, there's a bridge a little down the ways, why don't

we head thataway and meet up there? I have a nice place.
Food. Water. I could keep you safe."

"No, thanks."

His voice raised in pitch and volume as he realized he was
losing them. He sounded a little frantic.

"It's not safe for you to be out here alone! There's bad
people about. Killers. Rapers."

"Thanks for the update," Erin called as they rode away
from the park.

She cranked her head over her shoulder, half-expecting to
see him wading across the river to follow them. But each time
she looked back, he was still rooted in the same spot,
watching them roll away. After a few blocks, he was out of
sight completely.

The bike bumped over a curb, reminding her to watch
where she was going.

The guy talking to her like she was some frail waif-thing
pissed her off. What the hell did he know? They'd done just
fine so far. Not to mention the fact that she was well aware of
the potential threat of murderers and "rapers." Was she just
supposed to trust that he wasn't one or the other? Fat chance,
old man.

And yet there was a part of her that was almost tempted.
Not for her sake, but for Izzy's. It would be nice if someone
else was responsible for the kid. Someone else's job to make
sure she brushed her teeth, to hound her about taking a bath.
Someone else for her to elbow and kick in the middle of the
night.

Izzy spoke up.

"Is it always going to be like this?"

They coasted down a small hill and Izzy kept pace alongside her. They rode into the wind now, and the button-down shirt Izzy wore flapped behind her like a cape.

"Like what?"

"Being scared of everyone. Having to hide or run away from any other person we ever see."

"I don't know," Erin said. "Probably."

Izzy quirked her mouth like she was sucking on a sour piece of candy.

"That stinks."

"Bored of me already?"

Erin joked, but she knew what Izzy meant.

"No, it's just… we can't be the only good people left. There have to be other good people out there."

Erin tried to picture it in her head. She imagined the old man taking Izzy by the hand, leading her back to his little cottage. Smoke puffed out of the chimney, and his wife waited by the white picket fence out front. A little old lady with white hair pulled into a bun and reading glasses perched on her nose. She dried her hands on her apron and then extended her arms, wrapping Izzy in a hug.

Erin blinked the daydream away. It was all fantasy. In reality, it was more likely for the guy to be some kind of predator. The kind of creep that used to peep in windows and break into sorority houses to steal panties.

She watched Izzy gliding down the empty road, hair fluttering around her head, and wished the world could be the way Izzy wanted it. But deep down she knew, the meek did not inherit. The meek got eaten by the monsters, until eventually there were only monsters left.

Ray

Houston, Texas
3 days before

This roadblock looked dead. Just the two soldiers standing there. No other traffic. It would have to do.

Ray stopped the Grand Cherokee just shy of the men and turned to the woman, placing his hand on her arm.

"No matter what happens here, just stay calm," he said. "This is life or death."

He licked his lips before he went on.

"A lot of people are going to die in the next day or two, and we're not going to be among them. I'll do whatever it takes to make sure that's the case."

Her eyelids fluttered, and she nodded. For the first time he thought she seemed to be grasping the gravity of things, at least a little.

Ray put his window down.

The closer of the two soldiers approached, leaned in, his head hovering in the open threshold of the driver's side window.

"Sorry, sir. These roads are closed by order of the Department of Homeland Security," he said.

"I understand that. It's just that we're a little lost," Ray said. "And the GPS seems to be as confused as we are. I don't suppose you have any idea where Paradise Cove Bed and Breakfast is?"

The soldier shook his head.

"Never heard of it. Sorry."

"You think your buddy over there might know?"

Ray gestured at the other soldier, still standing in front of the barrier, squinting into the glare of the headlights.

"Spence, come here. You ever heard of a bed and breakfast called Paradise uh... what was it, again?"

Now both soldiers leaned toward the window, their heads floating before him like talking heads on a TV screen.

"Paradise Cove."

The second soldier shrugged his shoulders.

"Nah, man."

"Well, shoot," Ray said. "Is it just the two of you here? There's no one else around that might know?"

"Just us, sorry."

The talking heads shook around in the frame, their eyebrows raised in matching expressions that Ray thought looked like sheepish cartoons, so sorry to disappoint him. Christ, they were just kids.

"OK, good."

Ray raised the handgun then and fired twice, the crack echoing off the windshield with a ringing tone, and the muzzle blazing, and the force rattling his arm. Both of the heads burst open and tumbled out of the frame. One of them whimpered a couple of times like a puppy before he went silent.

Ray moved the barrier, and they pressed on, moving out away from the doomed city, the headlights shining down empty roads that seemed endless.

Erin

Presto, Pennsylvania
40 days after

Erin knelt next to the generator, plucking the cap off the end of the gas can spout. Just to be sure, she lowered her head until her face was only about an inch from the spout and sniffed. She only meant to get a little whiff, but the astringent benzene smell filled her nose.

Yep, definitely gas. Her shoulders shuddered. Gas fumes always made her feel an odd combination of giddy and nauseous. She was glad she hadn't needed to resort to siphoning gas. Just the thought of the stuff in her mouth made her spit.

The lackadaisical breeze from that morning had grown stronger throughout the day. A gust of wind rushed into her, ruffling her hair and the hem of her shirt. The generator manual lay in the grass next to her, and the pages flapped and fluttered like a goose trying to take off. She had to slap a hand on it to keep it from flying away. She found half of an old brick a few feet away and used it to anchor the manual to the ground.

The clouds were thicker now, too. Less scattered than before. They huddled together, forming larger masses that blocked out the sun for a few seconds at a time before blowing past. The daylight faded and brightened, faded and brightened, like someone was playing with a dimmer switch connected to the sun.

She didn't want to overfill the gas tank, so she only emptied the can halfway. Her finger traced over the words on the manual, reading the instructions out loud as she performed each action.

"Fuel cap vent lever: on. Choke lever: closed. Engine switch: on. Pull starter grip."

She pulled but too slow. She needed to stand for more leverage. On her feet, she tugged at it again, putting her back and legs into it this time. The starter rope whirred as it unraveled, but the engine didn't catch.

A single dot of rain splatted on her nose. Clouds blotted out the sun completely now. Off to the west, the sky touching the horizon was a charcoal-black smudge.

She stooped back over the generator, renewing her efforts. She tried yanking with both hands, balancing one foot on the generator for a stronger pull.

Izzy bounced into view.

"It's raining!"

She tipped her head back and stuck out her tongue, trying to catch a few drops.

Erin wiggled her fingers, giving them a moment's break.

"I know. Go inside, I'll be there in a minute."

She grasped the handle and tried again.

"Maybe it doesn't work. The generator, I mean. Maybe it's dead like all the cars."

Erin dug her teeth into her bottom lip to keep from screaming.

"It's going to work."

She measured each word carefully, struggling to stay calm.

The intermittent sprinkle grew to a more steady rain.

"Go inside," she repeated. Izzy shrugged and turned toward the house.

Before Erin began again, she wiped her palms on her shirt. The rain was making them slippery.

She worked at the pull start until her shoulder and arm ached.

It had to work. There was no way it couldn't work. She'd spent so much time trying to figure out how to move the stupid thing. Dragging it here. Finding gas. It had to work.

She only gave up when she started to shiver, her clothes soaked through and clinging to her skin. She threw the starter handle down after her last pull, and the generator sucked it up like a piece of spaghetti. She wanted to kick it but knew it would hurt her more than it would hurt the generator.

Hot rage tears dribbled down her face, mixing with the colder droplets of rain. She let the frustration and anger burn hot for a few moments before she let it go. She took a deep breath. And then another one. She didn't want to go inside crying. It would probably freak Izzy out, and she didn't want that.

Her hair formed sopping tentacles, drip-dropping water onto the porch while she waited for it to pass.

Finally she wiped the tears away, not that it mattered with the rain. Inside, she peeled off her wet clothes and left them in the bathtub in a soggy wad.

As she slid on a pair of dry jeans, she tried not to think about how she would have put them in the dryer to warm up if the generator had started. And then she could have thrown in the wet clothes. They'd have dried in less than half an hour.

Izzy hadn't made a peep since she came in. She must have sensed that Erin was in a mood.

"You hungry?"

Izzy nodded. When Erin opened the cabinet door, she was greeted by a very limited array of edibles. They hadn't gone picking for food in days. She'd been too fixated on the generator.

"We have beans, beans, and beans."

They ate cold kidney beans and Saltines for dinner. The unheated food was another reminder of her failure to get the generator running.

She felt drained. Empty. Like someone had taken a cork out of her head and tipped her over, letting her insides spill out.

The storm sucked the light out of the sky, so even though the sun was just setting somewhere behind the heavy curtain of clouds, it was almost as dark as night.

Her hair was still wet when they went to bed. She pushed the damp strands away from her neck and face, sick of the cold. Soon the warmth of sleep overtook her.

Erin dreamed they were scavenging in an old, dusty house. Weathered wood creaked under her feet, and her eyes traced gouges that cut pale lines into the dark floorboards.

She didn't think she knew the house at first, but then she rounded a corner and saw all the flowers. They were dead now. Drooping and dried into colorless skeletons.

This was the house they had her dad's funeral in.

She became aware of a noise. Something familiar, but she couldn't quite place it. She followed the sound, skirting around a shriveled fern that reached out from its vase like a papery brown claw.

The noise got louder, but she still couldn't identify it.

Izzy squeezed her hand, and Erin turned to look at her. Had Izzy been there the whole time?

The kid's eyes opened wide, and she whispered, "Scary!"

Just like Kelly in Dracula's Dungeon. This time, Erin shivered.

They came to an opening that led into a living room and saw it finally. It was a TV. An old one. The sound was the static that went with the fuzzy snow when a channel was out. Erin smiled at the familiarity. It was probably the first time anyone had ever been glad to see TV snow.

She found the remote wedged between two of the couch cushions and started flipping channels, hoping to find something that still worked.

Izzy danced in front of the TV, and Erin leaned around her.

"Hey Erin."

Erin gestured with the remote.

"Move."

"What's in there?"

Erin glanced where Izzy was pointing. There was a door across the room.

She went back to channel surfing in the snow.

"I don't know."

She didn't know how much time had passed when she realized Izzy was gone. And the door at the end of the room stood open. Not all the way. Just a few inches. Enough that Erin knew Izzy had slipped through it.

That was when she noticed the sign over the door. The one that said, "Point of No Return(s)!"

It hadn't been there before, when Izzy first asked about the door. Erin would have noticed that. She would have told Izzy not to go inside. But it was too late now.

She threw the remote down and stood up, approaching the door. Her whole body trembled as she extended her hand toward the door knob. She took a deep breath and held it.

The hinges whined as the door swung open the rest of the way, revealing a pitch black corridor. The lightless labyrinth.

"Izzy?" she called out, and her voice seemed to get swallowed up by the darkness beyond the doorway.

There was no answer.

She knew she had to go in. She had to find Izzy. But her legs were frozen in place.

She tried calling again.

"Izzy?"

She held her breath, straining to hear over the crashing of her heartbeat in her ears.

Why wasn't she answering?

"Izzy!"

The force of trying to scream in her sleep woke her up. She shook herself awake. Her eyes opened and at first she was surrounded by pitch blackness. Was she in the maze again?

And then the room lit up in blue-white light. Thunder boomed a beat later, rattling the glass in the windows. In the next flash of lightning, Erin looked to her right and noted the lump of Izzy's form under the blankets. She let her head fall back onto her pillow.

She laid there a while, allowing her breathing to return to

normal. But after a few minutes, she gave up on falling back asleep.

The floor was chilly under her bare feet. She pulled on a pair of dry socks and padded out of the room.

At the kitchen window, she looked out into the night and the rain. She could only really see when the lightning flashed.

Izzy was probably right. The generator was likely fried like everything else. Why hadn't she thought about that before?

It seemed so stupid now. Even if she had been able to get it started, so what? She kept pretending that electricity would somehow solve all of their problems, but that wasn't true. They still had to find food if they wanted to survive.

Time passed. She knew it must be getting close to dawn, because there was enough light outside that she could finally see a little without the lightning. Everything looked gray in the half-light.

Her eyes wandered from the water dribbling over the gutters to the dwindling store of food in the cabinet. This was only a little rain. What was going to happen when it was snow?

How much food would they need to have on hand to make it through the winter?

She didn't know.

And how many days had they wasted on the failed generator?

She didn't want to know.

Baghead

Rural Oklahoma
9 years, 126 days after

He flung himself from the car, hitting the road on his side, his hip bone taking the brunt of it. He bounced once and then skidded over the asphalt, the hot tar and gravel concoction grating at his flesh and clothing. He fought the instinct to dig his feet in or claw at the ground, instead lifting his hands and legs the best he could. Better to let momentum carry him to the shoulder.

As soon as he hit the dirt, he bounced again, flopping face down, his vision obscured by the bag. A bunch of sand poured into the eyeholes, the grit grinding at his face like a dry, power wash version of exfoliating beads.

He skidded to the bottom of the ditch, which wasn't far, and finally came to a stop. He held still for a moment, almost waiting for a second round of dirt sliding to kick in, and then rolled over onto his back, taking a deep breath as he did so. A bunch of sand spilled into his nose and mouth, though, and caught in his throat. He rolled back over, unzipping the hood at his chin so he could spit the dirt out. The powder burned, especially in his nostrils, and it dried out every mucus membrane that it touched.

He crouched in the vomit position, on hands and knees, for quite a while. No amount of spitting or retching removed all of the dirt from his throat, and no matter how long he kept at it, each brush of his beard flung more grains of sand to the ground.

Finally, he gathered himself and stood. His chest heaved, and he found the top half of his back sore and stiff. Christ. He was exhausted from trying, and failing, to hack up some sand.

A voice spoke behind him:

"You gonna make it, chief?"

He turned to find Delfino standing on the edge of the road above him, the sun at his back in a way that hid his face in shadow. The blacked out face reminded Bags of looking at backlit photographs when he was a kid and everything was still on film.

He looked past Delfino, noting the lack of any 1973 Oldsmobile Delta 88s in the vicinity.

"Where's the car?"

"I told you, man. It ain't wise to park out here. I found a low spot to park it and jogged up this way. Hopefully the dunes will hide it if anyone passes by."

Bags nodded.

"Seriously, though, are you OK?"

"Yeah. I'm fine. I'll be picking sand out of my beard for a month, but I'm OK."

The wind blew then, and feeling the cool air on his chin, Baghead realized that his bag had been unzipped all this time. He'd forgotten all about it after the sand situation. He turned away from Delfino and zipped it up. A weird tingle rippled in the center of his chest, and a heat crept up onto his cheeks.

He stayed turned away, feeling that warmth in his face, and things got quiet for a moment.

"Should we, uh, go check on this kid? Or do you just want

to wait around for a lynch mob?"

"Yeah, let's go."

Mitch

Bethel Park, Pennsylvania
41 days before

The landscape reflected the glow from the headlights, wet leaves and blades of grass shimmering like ice sculptures. It felt strange to look on this shininess, this embarrassment of illumination, after all of the time he'd spent in the dark so far this evening. The car's clock confirmed the time to be 4:37 AM. He couldn't help but think of turning on the brights in this darkness as the equivalent of shining a flashlight in someone's face, like the whole world was trying to sleep now, and he was just being obnoxious.

The car moved through the outskirts of town, well away from the riots and the busy streets. Here he found shoddy houses and overgrown vacant lots on the side of the road. Various grasses gone to seed stood waist high, waving as he passed.

He glanced over his shoulder every few seconds, though he knew this to be unnecessary. Two blankets and an afghan swathed the corpse in the back seat, the blankets folded to produce enough layers of cover that an onlooker couldn't discern the shape of the body underneath. She wasn't going anywhere or doing anything, but he checked on her anyway. He couldn't help it.

The engine's vibration thrummed through the steering wheel and into his hands. Not much. Just enough to make his fingers tingle. He realized that he liked driving, especially alone. He liked being at the controls of a machine of this size and power. He liked the white noise of the engine's hum against the quiet in the car. He liked putting the window down just a crack and letting the cold air blow along the side of his head, flipping his hair up a little.

Even his headache seemed to get lulled into a stupor as he drove, receding from the off and on throb of stabbing brain pain to more of a dull ache that lingered just above the threshold necessary to be considered annoying. It stayed well below the level of miserable or excruciating, though, so he was happy with that.

As bad as it had tasted, he wished he'd brought along Janice's pack of cigarettes. He could feel the filter adhered to his lips, see the flame burst from the lighter and lick around the paper and tobacco, smell the smoke. He didn't know why he wanted any of this. Why didn't matter in most respects now. He just moved forward. He acted first and saved thinking for something to do to kill time during the lulls.

Now the buildings along the roadside grew more sparse, fields of saplings and brush filling in the empty spaces. He passed a few odd small businesses, a snowmobile dealership, a couple of auto mechanics, a veterinary clinic, but most of the land out here was vacant. Desolate. He hadn't passed another car in a long time.

He didn't quite know how he was going to do this. Knowing that her priority was that the boys didn't see her this way, his first thought had been to find some spot way out of town and put her in a dumpster outside of a gas station or something, but that seemed way too crass. An easy answer, yes, but a disrespectful one. He couldn't see the police digging too deep on something like a Jane Doe in a dumpster anytime too soon with the city on fire, but there was certainly a possibility that they'd identify her in some way. Maybe that could lead to Matt and Kevin seeing her somehow. Torching her within the dumpster crossed his mind as well, but no. She had expressed her interest in cremation, but it was too messy and too attention grabbing. That would get found right away and might drum up enough outrage among the public to warrant an investigation even with the riots and such going on. So yeah, that was out.

Of course, he would've preferred burying her in the yard. At home where she belonged. Not having the time to invest in digging a deep grave, though, he worried a heavy rain might unearth her. Or maybe his sons would get curious about the mound of dirt out back and poke around. Kevin would probably know a shallow grave when he saw one, but would that make him leave it be or even more apt to check it out? Yeah, that was a no go.

He drove on, engine whirring, air sucking through the crack in the window and floofing his hair around. He was not certain of his destination, but he would know it when he saw it. He let his mind wander, let it go blank to the point that he almost forgot about his headache, almost forgot what he was doing out here at all. He watched the dashed line rush past in the middle of the road, the way the yellow paint reflected the glow of the headlights.

The car descended a small hill, picking up speed with gravity's help, making his stomach feel that twinge of excitement like being on a roller coaster. Without thinking, he floored it, butt lifting off of the upholstery, foot pressing all of his weight down on the pedal. The engine roared, and the car rocketed through the emptiness, lighting up the black nothing all around.

His heart thumped, though he didn't perceive it as rushing so much as a more powerful beat, a more confident one. He felt alive, and that notion occurred to him. Feeling alive. Shit. He didn't feel alive until he was about to die. Better late than never, though, he thought.

He looked down at the speedometer, saw the needle thrust back and forth in the realm of three figures, and let up on the pedal some. Probably not wise to do 116 mph when you've got a body in the back seat. He pictured a yellow bumper sticker affixed to his back window that read, "Dead body on board." Then he pictured getting pulled over for speeding, the cop thrusting his nightstick into the mess of blankets. For whatever reason these images struck him as funny, though. He knew the police were too busy to be worried about traffic violations just now.

He dropped it down to 80 as a compromise and pressed on. The scenery had changed while he sped along. More and more trees populated the sides of the road now. Sparsely wooded grass fields slowly thickened around him as he sped by. Pines intertwined with oaks and maples, blotting the landscape with fuller and fuller foliage like adolescent peach fuzz becoming a fully fledged man beard.

Well, this would do, he thought. He didn't know why, but it felt right.

Lorraine

Houston, Texas
3 days before

She stared out the window at the blackness, shoulders squared away from the driver. Something about the dark out there intrigued her just now, like if she stared into it long enough, something would have to take shape in the gloom, something would have to make sense of all of this.

Ray hadn't said a word after the confrontation with the soldiers. Did it even count as a confrontation, she wondered? It was less like he confronted them and more like he sucker punched them with bullets. Not that she was judging him. Life and death were the only judges that mattered for now, maybe.

If she was honest with herself, there was almost something exhilarating about watching Ray put bullets in the soldiers' heads. The fury of that blaze of the muzzle, the crack of the gun. The violence of that first entry wound, that hole torn in the forehead. The force of the bloody spray exiting the back of the skull, knocking the head toward them on a limp neck as though the man was sneezing. The decisiveness of Ray's arm swiveling the gun to the second head and firing again. It was brutality. It was carnage. It was flesh separated from bone, brain separated from skull. Life extinguished faster than stubbing out a cigarette butt.

There was a horror to all of that, of course, but she found

herself numb to it just now. She'd seen too much death up close to feel it at all. (And maybe the pills played a role in that numbness, too.) Instead she merely sensed the kind of primal awe one felt when watching a knockout punch in a heavyweight fight, when watching a lion pounce out of the weeds to snag a zebra, when watching a shark thrash around to tear up a seal.

The soldiers died quickly, at least. She couldn't say the same for her husband.

Erin

Izzy held a book horizontally across her chest while Erin stacked more on top, right up to her chin.

"Are you sure you've got them?"

Izzy's tongue protruded through the gap where her front tooth was starting to come in. She nodded, all seriousness.

Erin lifted her own pile and followed Izzy into the house. The books clattered onto the carpet in the living room.

Izzy nudged a drug reference book with her toe.

"Why do we need all these again?"

"Because this," Erin gestured at the cluster of books that looked like fallen dominoes, "is the old school version of the internet."

The blank expression on Izzy's face told her that wasn't enough explanation. She bent and picked up a book on wilderness survival.

"This one is going to teach us how to make fire by rubbing two sticks together. Hopefully we won't ever need it, but matches and lighters could run out at some point. You never know."

She traded the wilderness book for a gardening book that was as thick as a phone book.

"We can read this and learn how to grow vegetables."

She dropped it back into the pile and selected a title on

prepping.

"This book will tell us how much food we need to store for winter and how to preserve the stuff from our garden."

Izzy still had a puss on.

"What?"

Her lips pouted out.

"I don't like tomatoes."

"I see," Erin said. But she didn't. "I don't know what you're talking about."

"My dad had a garden. But the only thing he ever grew was tomatoes."

"Oh. Well, we can grow whatever you want. Corn, potatoes, melon, squash, lettuce."

"Strawberries?"

"Sure. Why not?"

Erin settled into the carpet and slid the books around into piles: camping and survival books in one stack, gardening in another, miscellaneous in a third.

It was funny that the library had been left untouched, really. Aside from a handful of things like food, water, and gas, the library probably had some of the most valuable things left at this point. Erin didn't know dick about survival, but she'd found dozens of books there that could teach her. That was worth way more than their pile of pirate loot.

Mitch

Bethel Park, Pennsylvania
41 days before

Falling from a crouch to his knees, he brushed away dead leaves with his fingers, crispy papery bits and soggy flaps alike. Black soil stared back at him, clumps of it clinging to his hands. The earth was moist here. Not wet enough to be mud, but damp enough to have a clay-like consistency rather than a sandy one. He wished he'd brought a shovel, even a small garden spade, but he hadn't. No use fretting over it now.

The woods towered over him, long and tall and dark. He leaned back a moment to adjust the flashlight clenched between his teeth, taking care not to get his muddy fingers too close to his lips. The light shined up into the trees for a moment, the beam revealing crisscrossed branches hung up above him. Though he'd only wandered 20 feet off the road, he felt enclosed here. Encased by the thick green wall he'd trampled through to get under the canopy of trees where the undergrowth wasn't as thick.

This was good cover for the hand dug grave he was about to carve into the ground. When he focused on that part, he felt better about it. It wasn't such a bad resting place. Better than winding up in a dumpster fire, at least.

He scratched out wads of top soil and flung them away, his hands clawing and scooping and flinging with great speed, great gusto. The clumps of dirt rattled through leaves and soon started slapping together into a pile along the edge of the hole. The divot in the ground was small, though, despite his great effort. He knew this would take a while.

He felt the heat build in his face as he worked. The humidity in the air made sure that his sweat didn't evaporate, so the perspiration drained down from his forehead, drizzling from his jawline to the dirt in little bursts. It soaked his shirt until it was a sopping thing that drooped at the collar from the weight of the moisture.

Still his hands flew. The black dirt on top gave way to a sandier color below, more densely packed and not as wet. He probably wouldn't be able to go much deeper, he knew. Maybe a couple more inches if he put in some elbow grease.

His headache seemed to swell from a consistent dull pain to a sharp one, the stabby feelings coming on harder and faster now. It made his jaw clench involuntarily, a little gritting sound ringing out as his teeth ground against the handle of the flashlight like they meant to shatter it.

As the pain faded, his mind began to wander. How many hours did he have left now? Maybe eight? He mulled that a moment. It was OK, he thought. He just had to make the most of it. Had to.

He heard the drops before he felt them, rain pattering against the canopy above, slapping into the dead leaves on the ground with a papery rasp accompanying the smack of the impact so it sounded a little like a snare drum. A fat one finally got him on the back of the neck. Water so cold it almost stung. It clapped into his flesh and spread, wrapping chilly fingers around his neck. He swiped at it with his hand without thinking, caking mud against his skin.

Shit.

He sat up, feeling almost dizzy from the body heat he'd worked up as he dug. In that sense the rain was a blessing. A few more drops dove into his hair, and now the cold felt good as it spread over his scalp. Still his head remained swimmy like he'd stood too long under a hot shower, the bathroom filling with steam. He sat a while, breath heaving in and out of him. He hoped that holding still would help him cool some, but so far it wasn't doing much.

He looked down at the grave. It wasn't deep at all, maybe a foot and a half at the deepest point, but it was going to have to do.

Standing, he wiped his hands on his wet pants, three swipes each, mud streaking over the thighs, and then he took the flashlight out of his mouth. A big drop got him right on the forehead, a blast of cold that didn't really dim his headache, though for a split second it felt like it might, and even the hope of relief was a good feeling.

He trudged to the car, the plants rubbing their wet leaves and stems against his arms. The cool water felt good enough running down his limbs, chilling him to the point that goose bumps rippled across his flesh. But there was something a little slimy about the plants' touch, something off-putting.

He ducked under a branch and took a high step over some prickers, and just like that, he was in the clear along the side of the road. Strange feelings washed over him as he moved out in the open, treading on the grass, legs free to maneuver without picking a path between branches and over logs. He pointed the flashlight down the path of the road and stared off into that opening. The air tasted fresh out here, too, not so thick. The rain had let up to a mist now, which wet him as he walked through it.

The dome light kicked on when he opened the door to the back seat, and for a moment that twinge of fear came upon him, like a flashback to the vulnerability he felt in the driveway. It passed, though. The last building he'd passed was a couple of miles ago, and it was a business that was almost surely unoccupied at this time of night. There may not be any living soul around for miles. Just one dying one, he thought.

He leaned into the back and unpiled the blankets, cloaking her top half in just one -- the afghan she always wrapped around her legs when she sat on the couch. The flashlight returned to its vacation home between his teeth. He grabbed her by the ankles and scooted her halfway out into the night, and then stooped to scoop her in the same fashion as before -- one arm cradling under the knees, the other under her shoulder blades.

Her head rested against his shoulder again, and it felt like her somehow. Maybe the afghan made it seem that way. He wasn't sure. He wondered, as he walked, what his motivation for wrapping her up had really been.

Was he scared of someone driving by and spotting him toting some chick with a shattered skull out into the woods? He didn't think so. Carrying someone wrapped in a blanket didn't look much better in his opinion.

Was he protecting her from the rain, from being exposed? Maybe. He was going to stick her in a muddy hole in the woods somewhere, though. That would leave her pretty exposed.

Did he want to bury her with her blanket? He didn't know

if it was the truth, but he liked that explanation the best. It felt more like she wouldn't be alone somehow with the familiar blue and white knit nestled around her. For a second he thought she wouldn't be as cold, maybe, but he knew it wasn't true. It was cold under the dirt, and there was nothing to be done about it.

He mashed down more greenery, feet tromping the thicket of weeds into the ground as he contorted and squat-walked under branches to make his way back under the tall trees. The ground was mushy now, his feet sinking into the soggy concoction of wet leaves and mud below. It felt like walking on an endless layer of cheesecake with wet leaves on top of it.

Shit. He hadn't considered how hard it might be to find his way back to his digging spot. He rotated his head back and forth as he walked to swivel the light across the ground. The movement was slow and repetitive. Robotic. It all looked the same, though.

He walked, the afghan growing wet and heavy as the rain picked up again, droplets collecting and combining on leaves to spill fat drops that exploded cold water on his head and neck and shoulders. He stayed patient, though. He didn't panic. If he had to dig a new grave, he'd dig a new grave. He had time to do it if it were necessary.

There. The flashlight shone on the rim of black topsoil around the sandy brown hole. It did stick out among the green after all. Maybe the mud puddle collecting in the hole helped. The water reflected his light.

Balancing the body in his lap, he squatted to try to push some of the water out of the hole with his hand. It wasn't much, and he'd rather lay her some place dry. It didn't work, though, so he gave up.

He peeled back the afghan to look on her face one last time. Seeing the smoothness of her skin was a surprise again. He thought maybe her complexion was starting to go now, and he was going on a lot of hours with almost no sleep, but she was still beautiful to him, at least in a way. She was still the person he loved, even though she wasn't.

A lump bulged in his throat, but he didn't cry.

He nestled her down into the grave, wrapping the blanket around her shoulders and up onto her face so her nose peeked out. He didn't think of it as hiding her, as covering her face. He thought of it as a little extra protection, even though she no longer needed that.

He pushed the dirt on top of her, trying to kick the piles into the hole but finding he needed to get down on his knees and scrape it in with his fingers. The mud flopped down, concealing her feet, then legs, then torso and arms, and finally her broken head. He flung a few handfuls of leaves on top of the black, so the spot wouldn't stick out quite so much.

And it didn't feel right anymore. It didn't feel right to leave her in the ground in the woods. The afghan made no difference. It felt like she would be alone. Forever.

But he knew that wasn't real. He knew she'd been gone for more than a day by now.

When he got back to the road, the rain was really coming down. His shoulders shivered, and his teeth chattered, and his clothes tugged at him, the weight of the water making them sag and cling to him.

He shuffled toward the car, his shoes making squishy

noises with every step.

He sat down and put his hands on the wheel, the lump in his throat quivering and wetness clinging to his eyes. Was he crying, or was it just the rain? He wanted nothing more than to run out there and dig her up, to take her home and figure out some scenario that would keep her dry and safe, but instead he started the car and drove away.

Teddy

Moundsville, West Virginia
69 days after

His feet dangled off the edge of the bed again, and he stared up at the skeletal ceiling. A single candle illuminated about a third of the room, a sphere of glow that faded at its edges and gave way to black.

His eyes didn't really take in the ceiling just now, though. Instead, he pictured the gashed open places in the zombie's arm, the way its head swung like a pendulum. He liked to remember them all for as long as he could. He could see the thing's face in his mind now, the droopy eyes, the greasy bowl cut, the flat nose that looked like it had been broken many times. He could picture its every detail for now, but eventually it would all be gone. It would blend in with the rest somehow, and he'd never call it to mind again specifically. He didn't like that. He wished he could have pictures of them to help him remember. Better still, he wished he could keep them all.

He brought the two liter bottle to his mouth and lifted his head enough to drink. The beverage tingled on his tongue, bright and sweet and delicious. It tasted exactly like the shade of neon yellow-green that it looked like, he thought. Just like it. Right now the bottle looked gray in the dark like everything else, but he knew the color exactly every time he took a drink.

He wondered sometimes if he should move, pack up his few things and go some place nicer, some mansion set on top of a hill. He liked it here, liked his room and his mattress and his ceiling, but he could live anywhere now. At some point, he should take advantage of that.

He took another drink and some Mountain Dew spritzed out of the side of his mouth, dribbling down to the place where his chin and jaw formed an angle and falling to the mattress. Shit. He hated to waste it.

He blew out the candle and lay back once more and pictured the part at the end of the encounter when he let his arms go and the hatchet swung freely. The head plummeted to the ground like a dropped soccer ball, and he hacked at the lifeless torso until it was an unrecognizable puddle of black goo in the vague shape of a man.

The pictures ran forward and backward in his head as he drifted off to sleep. He would treasure these images for as long as he could hold them in his skull.

Baghead

Rural Oklahoma
9 years, 126 days after

The girl still sat on the road in the distance, motionless. Again she looked more like a bloody stump from this far out, though Bags thought her back seemed less bloody than her front.

They moved on her, walking quickly, their shoes clomping on the asphalt. Delfino glanced over his shoulder every few seconds, more like a head twitch, a nervous tick, than a natural movement. Bags kept his eyes on the girl.

As they got closer, her details filled in one by one. First, the red spatter on the back of her shirt came into focus. Then he saw the way the blood matted her hair together into one brownish red clump on the back of her head. A bun held together by dried platelets and red blood cells.

He wondered if she'd run from them once they got close, or if she was so far gone that she wouldn't get out of the way even if a car came barreling down her side of the road to hit her. Either possibility seemed plausible.

"This is fucked, man," Delfino said. "It don't feel right."

"Well, I happen to think that it *do* feel right."

"Funny. Make fun of the ignorant man's grammar as you march him to his beheading."

"That's why they call it gallows humor, right?"

"Gallows are for hanging, smart guy."

"Well, that's why they call it head-chopping-block humor. Or whatever. Does that thing have a fancy name?"

"How the hell should I know?"

"You're the one who won't shut up about getting your damn head chopped off. Seems like you'd know a thing or two about the process."

"I don't know every detail. I grasp the gist. That's enough for me."

"Quiet now."

They slowed as they closed the last ten feet toward the girl. Bags resisted the urge to hold his breath and tiptoe the final five paces. He forced himself to walk normal, though something vibrated in his chest. He circled around in front of her and kneeled, not far off but not too close, either. Delfino stayed back, head snapping around to see if any cars were coming.

She looked smaller up close, like a baby bird out in the street, confused, waiting around to get saved or splattered. Then again with the amount of blood on her, maybe she was the one that administered the splatterings rather than receiving them. She showed no signs of being aware of either of them.

"Well," he said. "You gonna say something to her or did you jump out of the car just to gawk at her?"

Bags turned toward him, whispered.

"Maybe you should do the talking," he said. "She could be scared of the bag, right?"

"Does she even see us?"

"I don't know. Just saying."

"It's possible she'd be scared, I guess. You do sort of look

433

like a super villain."

Bags shrugged, hesitated a moment, nodded.

Delfino reached into his pocket and pulled out a sandwich baggy full of jerky.

"Why don't you try giving her some of this?" he said, handing it over. "Venison jerky. Good as hell, too. That should win just about anybody over, way I figure it."

Bags looked down at the dried out hunks of meat in the bag. The smell managed to penetrate the canvas over his nose, a peppery odor, and his mouth got all juicy right away. He didn't eat much meat these days by choice, but this smelled delicious.

He squat-walked over to the girl again and kneeled before her.

"Are you hurt?" he said.

Her face remained blank.

"Are you hungry?"

No response.

He reached into the baggie and pulled a strip of jerky out, the individual strands visible within the red. He reached toward her slowly, palm up with the venison protruding from his fingers as though he gripped the stem of a wine glass.

Still she made no movement aside from blinking.

Bags turned back to Delfino.

"What do you think?"

"Give it a second. The smell might perk up her appetite, snap her out of it."

The dried meat hovered a few inches shy of her face. He fidgeted with it a little, trying to figure out a way to advance it toward her nose without feeling weird.

434

Delfino spoke up from behind him:

"The good news is that we've yet to get decapitated. The bad news is that you are taking for-goddamned-ever."

"Shut up."

"Do the airplane-flying-into-the-hangar thing. Kids love that."

"That's for infants. Maybe toddlers. This girl is at least ten."

"Oh, well I'm sorry. Excuse me for having not studied up on how best to appeal to the appetite of a bloody kid in the middle of the road. I guess your way is best. Please continue sitting there with your thumb up your ass."

Baghead looked at the knotted up strip of meat in his hand. He rolled it between his fingers, gave it a little test dip like the thing was hitting some turbulence, thinking about whether or not to let it take flight and head for that hangar.

"OK. I'll try it."

"The airplane thing?"

"Yep."

"Mind her teeth, though. You don't want to get bit by a kid, man. Trust me. Not cool."

Bags looked at her mouth, finding it too easy to imagine those lips parting and her teeth latching onto his wrist. He shuddered, took a breath.

"OK. Here goes."

He brought the piece of jerky up to eye level and started bobbing it up and down, weaving it in a serpentine path that meandered toward her mouth. No reaction showed in her face or eyes. Again Delfino spoke up:

"Whoa. What's with the silent treatment?"

435

Bags stopped the flight midair.

"Huh?"

"If I'm a kid, I want to hear some jet engines rumbling through the sky, man. Start over and do it right."

Baghead sighed, his shoulders sagging. He returned the piece of venison to the starting point. This time he pursed his lips and growled out a sound that he thought probably sounded more like a car engine than a jet. He didn't know if jets changed gears regularly in midair. This one did.

The girl's eyes locked on his right away and then flicked to the jerky, still blinking often. Her breathing changed, deeper breaths, though not any slower, and her chest fluttered in a way that made her head sway a little. It reminded him of a move that a baby would do when they finally stop crying, their body jerking those little choked tremor sounds out every few minutes for a while.

She brought her hands out of the sleeves of the shirt, resting the heels of them on the ground, and she leaned back on them, just a little.

He wasn't sure how to read her body language. It didn't seem aggressive, at least.

The jet swooped into its final descent, and the hangar door opened just in time.

Erin

Presto, Pennsylvania
48 days after

The bag of rice shifted in her hands as the grains flowed from top to bottom like sand in an hour glass.

"Five pounds of rice."

Erin said it out loud as she wrote it down on the notepad.

One pound per day per person, according to the prepper book. Technically Izzy didn't need as much as an adult, but she wanted to err on the side of caution. So that meant two and a half days of food.

Her pencil scratched at the paper as she added that to the tally, bringing their estimated food supply to 27 days. Not nearly enough to last the whole winter, but they'd done well so far, scavenging the last seven days from dawn until dusk.

The screen door screeched and slammed. Izzy came in, bouncing from foot to foot.

"You have to come see it."

"What?"

"I'm not telling. You have to see for yourself."

Erin slid the closet door shut and followed Izzy out onto the property, past the barn, and into the big cornfield out back.

"I always wondered what was at the end of the cornfield, but I was too scared to go by myself. But not today. Today I was just wandering-"

"Weren't you supposed to be unloading firewood?"

"I was! But I got distracted."

Erin glanced back over her shoulder at the nearly full pile of wood still in the bike carrier. She tried to think of a way to explain the direness of their situation, but it seemed like no matter what angle she took, Izzy couldn't comprehend it.

Maybe it was an age thing. Would Erin have understood how bad things were when she was eight?

As they reached the edge of the field, the excitement became too much for Izzy, and she blurted it out.

"There's a house! A big one! And I figured it had to have something worth picking. But you have to see it."

She clamped a hand on Erin's sleeve and started pulling her.

"Wait, did you go inside? You're not supposed to-"

The house came into view through the dried stalks then. Izzy released her grip and Erin's hand returned limply to her side.

"Holy balls."

"Isn't it awesome?"

"In the most literal sense of the word, yes. Yes it is."

The house was, well not even a house, really. Even the term "mansion" didn't quite do it justice. Was mega-mansion a word? She didn't know.

It was an ugly sprawling thing, looking a lot like eight or nine houses stuck together. If she was going to have a mega-mansion, she'd want it to look like a castle or a palace or something.

The saving grace was the pool area, complete with a water slide, diving board, water trampoline, and cabana.

438

"I still don't like that you came this close by yourself."

"I did everything you always tell me. I stayed at the edge of the field for a long time, watching. And I didn't go inside."

After waiting a few minutes at the edge of the lawn, Erin judged it safe to move closer.

Izzy gasped.

"Look at the bottom of the pool!"

Erin peered over the edge and found herself looking at a coral reef inhabited by a rainbow of tropical fish.

"Is it real?"

The ripple effect of the water almost convinced her, but Erin shook her head.

"It's just a mural. Pretty cool, though."

Farther out she saw sharks and a killer whale and at the far end, a shipwreck. She got goosebumps just looking at it.

Water splashed, and Erin looked over to see Izzy on her hands and knees, plunging her hand into the water. Her chin tilted up.

"So? Can we?"

"What?"

"Go swimming, duh!"

Erin cast a glance back toward their house, imagining the wood still sitting in the bike carrier. The food inventory incomplete. Then the rippling blue surface of the pool caught her eye. She still hadn't managed to get Izzy to take a real bath. It had been a while now since her own bath. And while a dip in the pool wasn't exactly the same as sudsing up with soap and shampoo, it was better than nothing.

Plus, how long since they'd done anything fun? They'd been working their butts off.

"OK, but the last one in is a rotten egg," Erin said, and dove into the pool.

Erin squeezed the hem of her shirt. The way the pool water ran between her fingers reminded her of the time she made homemade lemonade with her grandmother. She closed her eyes, conjuring the smell of fresh lemons, trying to force the citrus tang to replace the salty chemical stink of the chlorine. Would she ever see a lemon again?

A slapping sound filled the air. Her eyelids rolled open in time to watch Izzy waddle out of the poolhouse wearing flippers, goggles, and a snorkel. A toy boat was tucked into the crook of her elbow.

Erin tousled her hair with a beach towel — another item looted from the poolhouse — and unfolded onto one of the lounge chairs next to the pool.

"Where are you headed, Jacques Cousteau?"

"Huh?"

Izzy's voice echoed out of the snorkel.

"He was a famous oceanog- forget it."

Izzy tossed the plastic boat into the pool and cannonballed in after it. The waves from her entrance sent the boat listing from stern to bow.

"Looks like rough seas."

"Nothing this old girl can't handle," Izzy said, nudging the boat toward the center of the pool.

Erin nestled her head against the back of the lounger.

"That's what we need."

Izzy spit the snorkel out of her mouth and said, "What?"

"A boat."

"I don't think it would fit in the pool."

"Not for the pool, doofus. On the ocean. We'll sail the seven seas!"

"Like pirates?"

"Yar! Like pirates, matey!"

"Where would we get drinking water?"

"Hmm, good point. Maybe a big lake would be better."

Of course, that wasn't the only problem with the plan, once she thought about it. Even if they were able to catch fish, they'd still need other food to survive. Then there was the problem of mobility. If all the car engines were dead, then so were the boats. That still left sailing as an option.

Erin had only been sailing once. Some friends of her parents had a sailboat, and they went out on Lake Erie one summer. The clearest memory Erin had of that trip was passing an island in the boat. It wasn't much of an island, maybe two or three acres at most, with a short rocky beach and a few scrubby little trees. And yet squatting in the center was the carcass of an old house. Just the stone shell remained — a foundation with a chimney at either end.

"What's that?" Erin asked, not able to take her eyes from the ruins.

"That's Gull Island," her dad's friend Bill said. "Used to be a house there, as you can see, but now it belongs to the birds."

Erin squinted as they got closer. Sure enough, the island teemed with them — swooping over the remains of the house, taking off from the swaying grass, perching in the trees.

"People lived there?" Erin said.

Bill nodded.

"Sure. Though now that the birds have taken over, I hear

if you don't watch where you're walking, you're liable to end up neck deep in bird shit."

Erin watched the island until it was just a speck on the horizon, transfixed. What would it have been like to live there? Wouldn't it have been lonely to be out there, all by yourself? And yet despite that, she felt drawn to it.

Maybe the boat wasn't such a bad idea. If they could find an island, they really could be safe from it all. No zombies. No disease. No psycho bad guys.

Abandoning the toy boat, Izzy flipped onto her back and kicked her feet. With the flippers on, she was able to propel herself around the pool at an impressive speed. After two laps, she paused to float near where Erin was sitting.

"Can we still be pirates even if we're not on the ocean?"

"Of course. If we can't be pirates, then what's the point?"

Erin wrapped the towel tighter around her shoulders.

"I like the idea of a lake better anyway. Less scary."

"Scary?"

"Being in the middle of the ocean would freak me out."

Izzy propped both arms on the deck of the pool and wriggled out of the water. Beads of water cascaded off her flippered feet, and she scooted forward on her belly. She looked like a seal flopping out of the water onto a shelf of ice in the arctic.

"Haven't you ever been on a cruise?"

Wet strands of hair bumped Erin's cheeks when she shook her head.

"Nope."

"Well I have. It's not scary."

"It would be scary to me. What if you hit an iceberg?"

442

Izzy laughed.

"You won't be laughing when your cruise ship starts a-sinking."

"Have you ever seen those ships? They're huge! There's no way they'd sink."

Erin clapped her hands together.

"That's what they said about the Titanic! You jinxed it now. We can't get a boat."

Izzy rolled around so she was sitting on the edge of the pool, feet in the water. She churned her legs, producing furious rapids which she then dropped the toy boat into. It lurched, to and fro. Anytime it got close to straying outside of the rapid zone, Izzy plucked it from the water and set it back in the turbulence.

She paused her agitation and said, "But our boat would be small enough that we would just be able to steer around any icebergs."

Erin didn't know if that was logically sound, but she'd already had another thought.

"What about pissed off whales? They'll ram a hole right into the side of the boat."

"They will not!"

"Haven't you ever heard of Moby Dick?"

"That's made up," Izzy said, upending the boat to drain the water it had accumulated.

"Yeah, but it's based on a true story. And you know what happened to the crew? Their boat sank, and they wound up drifting around in lifeboats for months. When the first guy died of starvation, they tossed him overboard. But when the second guy died-"

Erin realized how grim the tone of the conversation had turned. Probably not the wisest idea to be filling a kid's head with this stuff.

"What?"

"Nothing. Never mind."

She ran her hand over the napped texture of the towel so she wouldn't have to look at Izzy.

"Now you have to tell me!"

When she didn't answer, Izzy kicked her legs in protest, fins slapping the water loudly and splashing Erin in the process.

Erin exhaled loudly.

"Fine! When the second guy died, they ate him."

The splashing stopped all at once.

"What? They did not!"

Erin nodded.

"That's so gross."

They were silent for a moment, and then she added.

"I wouldn't eat you if that happened to us."

Erin couldn't help let an evil grin spread over her face.

"I make no such promises."

"That's not funny!"

"In fact, I'm feeling a bit peckish at the moment."

She lurched forward, crawling down the length of the chair toward Izzy.

"I might just have to eat you right now!"

Izzy launched herself into the pool with a squeal, and Erin dove in after her. She chased Izzy around in circles for a few laps, but with the fins on, Izzy could outswim her easily.

Erin paused to catch her breath. Glancing down into the

undulating water, she realized she was floating above the shipwreck. She flapped her feet and propelled herself away from it.

"Goo!"

"Ha ha, chicken!" Izzy called from the other end of the pool.

"That's what you're going to taste like! A chicken nugget. I'll dip you in barbecue sauce."

Erin planted her feet against the side of the pool and kicked off in Izzy's direction.

Mitch

Bethel Park, Pennsylvania
41 days before

Dawn crested the horizon just as he turned onto their street, the sun an orange ball rising through the mist to kill off the rain and burn away the patches of fog all at once. His eyes stung, and his clothes were still soaked, but he was home. It might not be for long, but he was here.

He pulled into the driveway, the car's tires sloshing through the mud puddle in the gutter on the way in. He always thought the sound of the wheels jamming into the potholes of water sounded like cannonballs plunging into the sea in a pirate movie.

He killed the engine, hand resting on the key for a long moment before he withdrew it from the ignition. He jangled it against the other keys, wrapping his fingers around the lot of them and sliding them into his pocket.

Once more, he found himself unsure of what to do next. Oh, he knew how this story would end, knew exactly where he was going, but he didn't know the route he would take to get to that destination.

Maybe he shouldn't even go inside. Maybe he should drive off and handle this himself, leaving the kids now so they wouldn't have to deal with it. He liked this option in a certain sense, but it was problematic in a couple of ways. If he took one of the guns, the kids would have no way to retrieve it.

That seemed too valuable of a tool now. The car itself would also have great value, even if they didn't know how to drive it yet.

He craned his neck to look up at the house through the glass screen of the passenger window. He could leave the car, leave the guns and walk away. He could walk the two and a half miles to the bridge and hurl himself to the river. That would do it, right? A handful of people did it every year. He tried to imagine it, tried to picture what it must feel like to plummet off of the edge, the wind assailing you, the water rushing up at you.

But no. No. Not everyone who jumped died, and even if he did, he would come back, wouldn't he? Unless he managed to brain himself, he would come back. He would bite and kill and spread the disease. He couldn't let that happen.

He lowered his head into his palms, the flesh of his hands cold against his forehead. Even in wet clothes he was burning up like his skull was an oven set to bake his brain at 450 degrees. The kind of heat that made it hard to concentrate, hard to think. Maybe that was why every decision was so difficult just now.

He looked at the house again, the sun glancing across the slats of the porch, reflecting off of a rectangular piece of the white siding. He wasn't quite done with this place yet, he thought. He'd ride things out for a while more. He could still make himself useful, and he would.

He opened the door, stepped out onto the wet concrete and stretched. His arms reached up, one then the other, back extending to uncoil the muscles along his spine. He rolled his neck from shoulder to shoulder a few times, the pain in his head seeming to flop from side to side as he did so.

The headache had evened out into a steady pain, less of the stabbing throbs. It hurt, but he preferred this to the pain blinking off and on. Instead of a series of stabbings, this was more like someone left the blade in finally, and he'd grown used to its presence. Anyway, the disease must be well into the final stage now.

He walked toward the house, feet skimming over the water atop the driveway. His hand clasped the black door handle on the screen door, touching the cold metal he'd touched thousands of times before, but his thumb hesitated to push the button to open the latch. Should he actually do this? Wouldn't it be a risk?

No. He needed to trust himself for once. He needed to believe in himself. He had a few hours left, and he could make them count if he had faith in himself. Maybe he couldn't make things OK for his boys by himself, but he could give them a better shot at it.

The door squawked when he opened it, and as he stepped into the kitchen, he thought about how unlikely all of this would have seemed even three days ago. The reality of the situation bludgeoned him, that this is what his life had become: weighing his options for how best to kill himself.

But first he would get some dry clothes.

He stood in front of the full-length mirror in the bedroom. Shirtless. Black swirls clouded most of his chest now, spreading from one shoulder to just shy of the other. They weren't thick black lines like the ones snaking over his arm. They were small, more like smoky capillaries, the biggest few reaching the width of an earthworm in places, most of the others tiny in comparison. He traced his finger over the flesh, drawing an invisible line above his sternum, but it felt no different than normal to the touch. He turned sideways in the mirror, seeing the same pattern of black webbing over his back.

Wetness still clung to his hair from the cold shower he'd taken minutes before. Letting the chilly water pour over his skull had been overwhelming, hard to get through, but his mind felt clearer now, so he was glad he powered through it.

He slid on a long sleeved t-shirt and made his way out to the kitchen. The phone sat on the table. He'd almost forgotten that that was next on the to-do list. It dinged when he pressed the button, the screen lighting up as it cycled through a few startup screens. There. No new messages. Somehow he wasn't surprised or disappointed. He'd been planning as though this would be the case. He turned the phone off again to further conserve the battery.

He rooted around in the drawer under the oven until he found a suitable frying pan. The thought of eating made him nauseous now, made a bad taste crawl up from inside to linger at the back of his mouth. He was done with meals, he knew, but he would make something for the boys.

He couldn't take the idea of cracking open eggs, watching the yolk and white pour into the pan like globs of snot, watching the clear goo go opaque white as it cooked until it was rubbery like some kind of tentacle material.

No. Never.

He'd make pancakes.

Baghead

Rural Arkansas
9 years, 126 days after

The car rocketed forward once more, grass and small trees beginning to fill in along the sides of the road. The plant life almost felt smothering after all of that time in the open.

Bags leaned back to check on the girl. She slept in the back, curled up in a blanket. Blood still crusted her hair, the strands all woven and matted together like leftover spaghetti. He'd wanted to wash it, but Delfino thought it'd be best to put some distance between them and whatever might have been involved with the blood being all over the girl in the first place, and Baghead agreed.

He was still surprised that she had gotten into the car at all. She seemed like a rabid thing that would freak out at the notion of confinement or at least freak out when the car started moving. But she was fine. Of course, the jerky Delfino had dug out of the cooler had probably made the car a lot more enticing.

She scarfed hers and Bags handed over the last half of his, which she wolfed down even faster. Delfino had dug a rag out of the glove compartment and dumped a little water on it, handing it over so she could wipe some of the blood off of her face. After that, she was out.

"You think she can talk?" Delfino whispered.

"I'd imagine so. It's not like she's wearing a loin cloth, you know? She has a t-shirt and pants on."

"No shoes. But yeah, I see what you're getting at. She seems a little wild, though, right?"

Bags nodded, and they were quiet for a while. The tires thudded over dirt-filled potholes and cracks.

"What are we going to do with her?" Delfino said.

"What do you mean?"

"I don't know. Did you just, like, sign up for a lifetime of taking care of this kid? It's not like we're going to track down her parents. Shit, that's probably her parents' blood smeared all over her."

Bags had to admit to himself that Delfino had just made a good point. He jumped out of the car to help her because it was the right thing to do, but was taking her along on a road trip with assassins trying to kill him the right thing to do?

"I don't know," he said. "We'll figure it out, I guess."

Delfino nodded, but Bags thought his eyes looked far away. The driver licked his lips and then spoke:

"Just… I don't know much about taking care of a kid is all, and there's a damn contract on your life. Do you know what you're doing?"

"We're getting her out of a really bad situation. She is better off than she was 45 minutes ago. For now, that's more than good enough."

"I guess so."

Lorraine

North of Houston, Texas
2 days before

The sun glinted down between the brick buildings, the glare reflecting off of the glossy black plastic bags bulging out of the top of the dumpster. Flies circled above the alley, like vultures waiting for something new to die.

She knew this was a bad idea, knew they needed to get gone faster than this, but he insisted, and he always got his way.

She watched him through the passenger window, her eyes bouncing between his head and shoulders, which she could see above the dumpster, and the ground beneath him, looking for any sign of activity in either locale.

"Hurry up," she said.

"I'm trying. Jesus, Lorraine. Stop pressuring me."

There. She heard it. The stream of urine slapped the blacktop at his feet.

He put a palm on the bricks in front of him for balance and scooted his legs out and back, bending partially at the waist. The position made her chuckle, though after a second she realized he must be attempting to keep the piss off his shoes.

The thing lurched out of the dumpster before either of them could react. She thought it was a dog at first, a dog lunging up from among the garbage bags to tear out his

452

jugular. Almost like a dog draped in fabric.

It clung to his shoulders, and the face part attached to his neck. It almost looked like a baby sloth climbing on its mother.

He screamed. He screamed like a woman. There was no other way to describe it.

He turned away from the brick wall, and the thing came into view. It wasn't a dog. It was a girl in a black hoodie. She was dead, or she should have been. The right side of her face was all chewed off, revealing the skeletal view of her cheek bone and temple and teeth. The remaining flesh on the opposite side of her face was yellowed and shiny like sweaty cheese. Her eyes didn't seem to recognize anything going on around her, but her mouth never stopped reaching out for meat like a baby bird's gaping beak.

He teetered, hands ripping at the thing, screaming whenever the head nuzzled into him, whenever the teeth ripped at his skin. He stumbled backward a few paces, and then over-corrected, lurching forward, knees skidding down in the piss puddle.

And then the thing tore away a pretty good sized neck chunk, and the blood sprayed like the spigot next to her garden. He gurgled three times, throaty sounds like that suction tube at the dentist removing saliva from the back of the mouth, and he was gone, lying still while the thing ate him.

A rabid dead girl. That was how her husband, Greg, died earlier that afternoon. With his cock out in an alley.

She woke. Back in the dark. Back in the Grand Cherokee. Back with the swearing preacher, a human being more like a lizard than a man. More like a snake. He hung up his phone right away as she opened her eyes, his movements rushed. Suspicious, she thought.

She watched him lick his lips as he drove, his big orange face lit up by the dashboard lights. Why did it work this way? Why did a lizard person, con artist get to live while Greg died a horrific death?

She dug in her purse for one more pill.

Ray

Rural Texas
2 days before

The headlights pierced the dark, but the black still seemed to close in on them, pressing against the windows all around. They drove into the dead of night, no one else around, the Grand Cherokee barreling north on backroads neither of them had ever heard of. The signs on the side of the road mentioned tiny towns that were equally unfamiliar.

She slept off and on, her neck going limp to lean her head down onto her shoulder, a single dribble of drool spilling onto the seat. When she was out, he felt like he was navigating some bigger vehicle as it pressed into the void, a ship of some kind hurtling into the black nothing. It almost felt like driving a house.

Sometime after 3 AM, she woke. She rifled through her purse, pulled out an orange container of prescription pills. Her hands moved to twist its head off, but Ray intervened, snatching the pill bottle away.

"What is this?" he said.

The pills rattled in the bottle, and he felt the muscles in his face tense, his brow crease, his jaw flex.

Her mouth hung open, and he thought she wasn't going to say anything, but after a second she did.

"It's my medication."

This was a tone he hadn't heard from her to this point.

The indignance of the entitled rich woman. A housewife, he would guess. The kind of housewife who was very important with little to do, always planning dinner parties and brunches and get-togethers, an endless stream of meaningless interactions all meticulously plotted out and fussed over.

He tilted the bottle toward the light spilling out of the dash indicators. First he saw her name. Lorraine. Lorraine Murray. Huh. Not a D name after all. He scanned farther. Xanax. A powerful anti-anxiety medicine. One of the most addictive and one of the most dangerous, from what he had learned the hard way.

He caught his reflection in the driver's side window out of the corner of his eye, saw the scowl on his mouth, the furrow of his brow, and then something in him softened. Why was he so angry? Why was his instinct to intervene here, to tell a stranger how to behave?

He tossed the pills to her.

"Gotta be careful with that stuff," he said. "Those sedative hypnotics will mess you up bad if you get hooked."

She gripped the pill bottle as though to open it but stopped and put them away instead.

"Your body gets so addicted that it crosses wires in your brain. When you try to quit, you can go into a coma. Happened to my boy. He didn't make it."

He licked his lips.

"But that was a long time ago."

She didn't say anything, and a quiet came over the car, a tension. The black pressed even harder at the windows, trying to get inside and swallow them up.

"I'm sorry," he said. "I don't know what came over me. I

guess with what happened earlier..."

Her head turned, and their eyes met for the first time in a while.

"Don't worry about it," she said, and she put her hand on his arm.

"They're going to bomb it," he said, his voice just above a whisper.

"Bomb what?"

"Houston. The government is giving up on beating the plague. Killing some so others might live. Probably lots of cities in the South are going down."

She didn't say anything, but her grip on his arm tightened.

Erin

An explosive crack echoed across the valley to the north.

Erin reached for the edge of the pool and stopped paddling. She held still, waiting.

The noise came again, twice. It was a sound that used to mean hunting season. Or target practice. Not anymore.

Her heart raced. Gunshots meant people. And people were bad enough. People *with* guns… she didn't want to think about it.

Izzy popped up from under the water.

"How long did I hold it that time?"

"Get out of the pool."

Erin was already lifting herself out. Water dribbled from her hair and clothes onto the ground.

"What?"

"Just do it."

She reached out and pulled Izzy from the pool. Four more shots rang out.

"What was that?"

Erin was too busy scanning the horizon to answer.

"Was that a gun?"

"Put your shoes on."

They wove back through the path in the cornfield. When the house came in to view, Erin crouched down, creeping to the edge. Watching for movement.

She didn't know where they were or who they were, but their presence in their neighborhood felt like a violation. The house had come to feel like a safe place. Maybe the only safe place in the world. And now Erin feared to go inside because she was worried they'd be trapped there if someone came looking.

Almost as bad, the house held all of their supplies. All of their food. She'd completely taken for granted the possibility that someone could come take it. And there would be nothing they could do but sit out here in the dried up corn husks and shiver in their wet clothes.

"It sounded like it was coming from up by the house where we got the generator. That's close."

Erin shushed her. She continued scanning the area, eyes flicking from left to right and back again.

"If we snuck up through the woods," Izzy whispered, "we could get a closer look."

"No, we should stay here."

Izzy let out a little grunt of impatience.

"For how long? I'm hungry."

"Until we're sure they're gone."

Erin thought back to the day they'd heard the engine, and they'd run into the woods to hide. The time she'd left Izzy behind.

They'd been ill-prepared then, and they were ill-prepared now. What if the worst case scenario came true, and they did have to run? If someone rode up the drive right now, they'd have to. And they'd be without food or water. No blankets. No dry clothes. Screwed.

Just like they'd needed to get serious about gathering food, they needed to get serious about security. It was life and death out here. No police or parents were around to protect them. Not anymore.

Every time she thought she was making progress, finally figuring things out, the world stuck out a leg and tripped her as she ran by.

Pain shot threw Erin's jaw. She'd been grinding her molars together in frustration.

She unclenched her teeth and opened her mouth to stretch her jaw muscles out.

Izzy was being uncharacteristically quiet. Erin swiveled around and found herself alone in the field. An electric current of fear jolted through her and made her shoulders jerk. Her mind leapt to the most dramatic possibility first: they had taken Izzy.

OK, no. That was silly. There had to be a rational explanation. Maybe… Maybe she scooted off to pee or something.

"Izzy?"

It came out in a throaty hiss. Not quite a whisper, but not a full projection of her voice either.

The only answer was the scrape of dry cornstalks shifting in the breeze.

She tried to keep from panicking, but her brain fought her for that right, insisting that this was an absolutely appropriate moment to panic.

Again her thoughts went to the time she left Izzy behind. Had she done it again? The events were all jumbled in her head, like a deck of cards someone threw to the ground. Some landed face up, some face down. They were all out of order.

She started at the beginning.

They were swimming in the pool. Izzy was underwater, holding her breath. Erin was supposed to be counting. She heard the first gunshot and froze. It wasn't until the second shot that she knew for sure. She climbed out and told Izzy to get out of the pool. There were more gunshots. How many more? Three or four, she couldn't remember. They slid their shoes on over wet feet. No socks. They made their way through the corn, stopping when the house came in view. And then they squatted there. They. Or had she just assumed Izzy was there the whole time? She imagined Izzy trying to peel the flippers off so she could get her shoes on. Maybe she took too long and Erin rushed off without her. But no. She'd said something while they waited in the field. She was hungry.

Something rankled in her memory. There was something she was missing. Something else Izzy said. Erin closed her eyes, tried to let it come to her. When it did, her eyes snapped open.

A closer look.

That's what Izzy had said.

"We could get a closer look."

Mitch

He watched his sons eat in silence, their eyes still puffy with sleep. It was early for them, and in a way he hated to wake them, but he didn't have a lot of time, something he thought Kevin understood, at least.

Matt's blanket draped around his shoulders at his seat at the kitchen table. The blue bedspread wrinkled when he reached out for his glass of orange juice. It almost looked like a cape flapping behind him in the wind.

"Either of you ever driven a car before?" Mitch said, his voice sounding thick and sleepy even to himself.

Wrinkles creased both of the foreheads sitting across from him as all four eyebrows raised. All of the attention quickly turned away from the food. Kevin shook his head, and Matt followed his lead a beat later.

"I figured not. I thought maybe we'd head out to the backroads when you're done eating, and you could give it a shot."

He shrugged and added:

"Might come in handy sooner than later, I suspect."

"Driving lessons? Me too?" Matt said.

"Yeah, why not? You may as well give it a try."

Matt's eyes were wide open now, early morning or not. He sliced a big wedge of pancake with the side of his fork, smeared it in syrup and chewed it as fast as possible before going back to slice off another chunk.

Kevin rolled his eyes, and Mitch smiled.

"Slow down, Matthew. You'll choke."

The sun reflected off of the gray surface of the asphalt, the rock and tar combination worn smooth by the endless rub of car tires. Mitch put it in park, and the car idled in the middle of the vacant road. He slid over to the passenger seat.

"You ready?" he said, looking at Kevin.

His older son pressed his lips together, but he quit doing it as soon as he knew Mitch was looking. Nervous and trying to hide it, Mitch thought. Better to be a little nervous than fearless, as far as he was concerned. Kevin slid out the back door and banged it shut behind him, a whoosh of the morning air rushing in with the door's movement, still thick with humidity.

Mitch checked the mirror and glanced around as Kevin climbed behind the wheel and buckled himself in. Nobody around for as far as he could see.

"Ready?" he said.

"Yeah, I think so."

"Did you adjust the seat so you're comfortable getting to the pedals?"

Kevin reached down by his ankles and slid the seat forward a couple of clicks.

"OK. Put it in drive and let's do this."

He had Kevin start with his foot off of the accelerator, letting the car crawl forward, so he could get a handle for the controls without the added pressure of speed. The boy panicked a little, jerking them to seatbelt-tugging stops four times in the first 30 seconds.

"Relax," Mitch said. "Just relax. You're in control."

Kevin took a deep breath and let it out slow. He released the brake, and they rolled on. Over the next couple of minutes, something clicked. He seemed to pick up the nuances of the way the brake and the wheel gave him control over the car, that they were tools to be used subtly, not violently.

He loosened his death grip on the wheel and acquired a feel for how the vehicle moved, how it handled. Mitch had him speed up to 25 miles per hour, and they drove a while past fields of soy beans and corn, taking a right turn and two left turns. Mitch directed Kevin to build up speed little by little until they were flying along at the speed limit like it was normal.

"Look how quickly you figured that out. Experience is the only way to learn," Mitch said. "What do you think?"

"I don't know. It's pretty fun."

"Easier than you thought it'd be, isn't it?"

Kevin nodded.

"I want to do it," Matt said. "I'm supposed to get a turn!"

Mitch laughed.

"You will, you will. In just a minute."

He looked into the back seat to see Matt clinging to the door, knuckles white. Apparently he wasn't so comfortable with Kevin's driving, which seemed funny.

They drove on. Mitch had Kevin pull into someone's dirt driveway and back out for a little practice moving in reverse. That seemed to make the new driver uncomfortable. He

464

slammed on the brakes again, giving them all a good shake. Things smoothed out when they got back on the road.

He made eye contact with Kevin at a stop sign, and he clapped a hand on his shoulder and smiled at his son. Even though his eyes hurt, and his head hurt, and the heat rolled off of his skull in waves, and the blackness inside spread until it would break and end him, he smiled so his boy would know he was proud of him.

"Put it in park," he said. "We better give Matt a turn."

Kevin put it in park, a skeptical smirk on his lips. Mitch gave him a look, a tilt of the head and a wry smile.

Matt released his vice grip from the door handle, and the boys exchanged seats. Matt looked so small behind the driver's seat. Tiny.

"How much do you weigh? Do you know?" Mitch said as Matt buckled himself in.

"53 pounds."

"And that's all muscle, right?"

"Pretty much. Well, I guess some of it would be bone, too."

He scratched his cheek.

"How much of it do you think would be bone, Dad?"

"I have no idea. But hey, you can reach the pedals and still see over the wheel, right?"

Matt's feet kicked out toward the pedals, but they came up short. Even in this position, he could barely see over the wheel. When he slid himself down far enough to get a toe on the brake, he was almost laying down on the seat.

"Maybe not," he said.

"Well, that's OK. How about I work the pedals for you,

and you can steer?"

"We can do that?"

"Yeah, you'll just sit on my lap."

"Will I really be steering, though?"

"Of course."

Baghead

Rural Arkansas
9 years, 126 days after

The day fell to dusk fell to night, the dark deepening around them until it achieved full blackness. The headlights cut wedges of light out of the gloom, but they were no help inside the car.

If the Delta 88 ever had dash lights, they must have burned out long ago. Probably well before everyone got sick and died, Bags thought. This feature, or lack thereof, made him uneasy. When Delfino talked, it was a disembodied voice speaking from the shadows, and somewhere in the back a rabid girl still slept, but he was unable to check on her visually. The darkness imprisoned him. All he could do was stare straight ahead where the lights lit up the next section of road that they'd hurtle down.

Would she be confused when she woke up in the dark? Would she look out at the headlights and remember the car and the food and the guy with the bag on his head?

"You thought about a name?" Delfino said, startling Baghead from his thoughts.

"What?"

"Let's say the rabid child back there don't talk. Like, ever. Have you thought about what you might name her?"

"Nope. First of all, why would I leap to that conclusion? I said I figured she can talk when you asked me about that,

467

remember?"

"Well, I've always liked the name Anya is all. Just putting it out there."

Bags puffed an almost silent laugh from his nostrils.

"It's not bad."

"So listen, we're going to be coming up on one of my stashes here before long."

"Weapons?"

"Exactly. I'd hoped we'd get there before dark, but we didn't. It's OK, though. I've got lanterns we can use. Anyway, I'm going to feel a hell of a lot better once we're armed."

"Yeah, I can understand that."

"Going back for the rabid child scared the bejesus out of me, man. I ain't kiddin'. I don't think I've unpuckered since. I believe those guns will help me unclench, and believe you me, I'm looking forward to that."

"Always straight to the butthole talk with you, huh? You realize that's your go-to reference for everything?"

"What are you getting at?"

"Nothing."

The car hit a poorly patched pothole with a bang, and everything shook. Bags felt the impact like a jolt in his ribcage somehow, and he swore he heard the fenders rattle. He wheeled his head around to the back seat, staring into the dark, waiting for some sound or sign of movement back there, but none came.

"Almost expected that to blow out a tire or something," Bags said.

"Shoot. Little bump like that ain't no thang. Not for this tank."

"If you say so."

The quiet came upon them again, the road sounds seeming to drown out Baghead's thoughts, leaving him to stare at the way the headlights hit the foliage on the side of the road. Individual stems and stalks and blades lit up, their stretched-out shadows slowly shrinking as the source of light closed on them.

"Here we go," Delfino said.

It took Bags a second to make out the faintly worn spot in the weeds up ahead to the left. His eyes traced the path as far as they could and found no signs of a building before the light cut off.

The Delta 88 slowed and made the left turn, bouncing a little over the rough terrain. The sound struck Baghead more than the feeling. The hum of the tires cut out, replaced by thuds and squeaking shocks and the sound of the taller weeds tinkling against the bumper and swishing against the undercarriage.

"Reach down behind my seat, would you?" Delfino said. "There's a lantern there. It's partially wedged in the opening between the floor and the back of the seat so it won't fall over."

Baghead squared his shoulders toward the back windshield and reached an arm between the seats. He tried to fight off that little butterfly feeling in his stomach as his hand descended into the void, but he couldn't quite do it. The tip of his thumb found the floor, and he flopped his hand along it like a fish, fingers feeling around on the Astroturf-like carpet and rubber floor mat.

There. He caught the side of the glass chamber with his

469

middle finger and let his hand crawl to the top of the lantern like a spider, latching onto the looped metal handle and lifting. The bottom of the seat tugged on it for a moment before it let go.

"Got it."

"Nice. I'll light it here in a second."

The Delta 88 breasted a hill, and then took a sharp left. The weeds this far out looked to be about waist high, most of them. Their path was clear of trees, but none of those around them looked bigger around than a cigar anyway. This must have been one of the areas recovering some from the worst of the Dust Bowl years. Some of the places farther west would probably never even get this level of growth back.

Without warning, Delfino stopped the car, put it in park, and shut off the ignition.

Bags glanced around and saw no building in the vicinity. He had expected a cabin of some type, something small and far enough off the road to avoid interest. In his head, he saw a ramshackle little place with a single window that'd been boarded up, barely big enough to be called a cabin instead of a shed. Instead he saw only weeds.

"Hand over that lantern," Delfino said.

Baghead did as he was asked. But he wished he could see the driver, to get a read on him. Some paranoia reached up out of the dark and seized him by the throat, making it hard to swallow or breathe. Jesus, what did he really know about Delfino? Why had the guy asked so many questions and then driven him out into a field? Could Father have wanted some kind of interrogation before the assassination? Would he be digging for some particular piece of information?

He stared into the black nothing to his left, eyes straining.

Flint grated against steel, sparks flashed, and the Zippo lit with a click and a whoosh. The flame glowed under Delfino's chin, flickering red and orange hues up onto his face, something about the dance of shadows around his eyes and brow making him look demonic. Then the lighter moved into the glass chamber to light the lantern. The glow started small and swelled.

Bags looked through squinted eyes, searching Delfino's face and finding no maliciousness, no more trace of demonry. He saw a simple man that loved his car, his job, and, apparently, quite a wide variety of pornography.

"It's not far," Delfino said. "Do you want to come with me, or stay here and watch the girl?"

Bags looked back to see the girl sound asleep.

"I think I'll come along. My legs could use stretching."

Ray

North of Canton, Texas
2 days before

The sun came up, everything going gray and then
returning to full color, and the Grand Cherokee rumbled on.
A scraggly mess of trees occupied the roadside to their left, all
stunted and close together, branches intertwined, everything
shrouded in leaves. An expanse of grass lay to the right. Ray
knew that Dallas was somewhere off to the west. Not far,
even, though you couldn't tell when you stared into the wall
of malnourished brush that direction.

A mist descended upon them in the morning, wetting the
windshield and the asphalt below like a can of beer on a
summer day. It evaporated quickly, though the tires still
sounded different rolling over the half-moistened blacktop for
some time after all else seemed dry.

They passed through sleepy town after sleepy town as the
day inched toward lunchtime, and Ray hated every second
that their speed dropped to 25 miles per hour in residential
areas, but he didn't know the best way to get to the interstate,
and he figured it best to keep moving. He knew they'd made
terrible time to this point, picking random roads and weaving
only vaguely in the direction they'd wanted to go. The least he
could do was keep going.

Ray opened a bottle of water, took a sip, plopped it into
the cup holder. His eyes stung like someone had flung sand in

them, those tiny shards of glass ripping up and down every time he blinked.

How far away from Houston was far enough? He wasn't sure. Dallas would probably get hit, too, and they were close as hell to that right now. Maybe better to get out of Texas altogether, he thought, to just keep going, to never stop.

Of course, they would have to stop for gas and a piss break soon. Maybe grab something to eat. The thought made him uneasy. He didn't like to think of their momentum stopping for even a few minutes.

As if on cue, a gas station with a Dairy Queen next door caught his eye ahead, and he decided to go for it sooner rather than later. To get it over with and not stop again until Texas was in the rearview and, preferably, sucking on their tailpipe.

Mitch

Bethel Park, Pennsylvania
41 days before

He stood under the cold water once more, the bathroom light glinting through the frosted door of the shower stall, lighting up powder blue tiles along the walls. He lowered his head, letting the shower's spray blast directly onto the crown of his dome. His fingers alternated between scratching and massaging his scalp. It felt good.

He'd almost blacked out when the cold first washed over his head this time. Everything had faded out for a split second, sound and vision reduced to black nothing. When it flipped back on, a breath rasped into him all loud and choked, and everything had a red tint for a moment. He'd gripped the little built-in shelf for soap to avoid falling down.

He felt better now, though. The cold cleared his thoughts once more, made him feel like himself. He didn't think it would work much longer, but he was thankful that it was working now. And he was thankful to be able to take his sons out for a drive. They would carry on without him, he knew, and if he was helping prepare them a little bit for that, he was happy.

He tipped his head back and now the cold liquid tumbled across his nose and cheeks and brow. Maybe it was just the water's chill, but his headache seemed to have receded to almost nothing. He could only tell it was there now if he really concentrated.

He stepped back, blinking a few times to clear the water from his eyes. The black capillaries on his chest didn't seem to have advanced at all. The black streaks almost looked to have thinned out in places. He had to stop himself from thinking about that too hard, though.

He stood before the fogged mirror as he dressed, pulling on the long sleeve shirt, the tie dyed one Kevin had made him at some day camp years ago. Iron-on letters spelled MITCH across the front.

It had been weird to stand in front of his closet, flipping through the t-shirts on hangers, figuring out which one to die in. This one made sense, though. His boy had made it for him.

"You OK, Dad?" Kevin said. "You look all dark around the eyes."

"I'm fine. Not enough sleep is all, and I probably need to drink some water."

They stood in the kitchen. With the power still out, there wasn't much to do as far as distractions, so everyone milled around, moving from room to room at random, wasting time. The boys didn't seem terribly concerned with Mitch's impending death. He thought maybe it was hard for them to grasp the reality of it, the gravity of it. In most ways, he was thankful for that.

The grandfather clock chimed to mark the half hour.

He took a glass to the sink, letting the water spill over his fingertips until it ran cold and then filling it. He drank. The fluid felt so cold draining from his mouth to his stomach that it was almost like it was burning his throat for a second.

He looked at Kevin and Matt between drinks and realized that he was preparing them for a harsh world, making the intuitive leap to some kind of life after a societal collapse. He didn't know exactly when he committed to that line of thinking. Maybe it was during the riot. Anyway, with the diseases raging like they were, it seemed a possibility, maybe even a strong one, but he supposed there was still some hope they'd be back in school before long, that things would return to normal. He hadn't considered that in a while, and it seemed so strange. Life would go on without him and Janice, perhaps in a totally normal way. Still, he had no regrets as far as his approach. Always best to prepare for the worst, he thought.

Sweat beaded up on the outside of the glass, and his fingers slipped a little as he went to take another sip. How long had he been standing here, staring at nothing, thinking? Thinking about fairy tales where all of this worked out OK.

But what if? What if the worst didn't happen?

He closed his eyes and chugged down the rest of the glass. He tried to stave off the thoughts burbling up from his subconscious, the part of the brain where faith must live, the part that wants to believe in ghosts and Gods and aliens and so forth. He did his best to keep these ideas at bay, but he couldn't.

What if he didn't die? What if he fought the disease off? Surely someone would develop an immunity. That's how it worked, right? Maybe it would be him. His headache wasn't as bad. The black tendrils beneath his skin seemed to be receding. Maybe his immune system was killing it even now as he refilled his water.

"I think..." he said, catching himself.

No. Even if there was some sliver of a chance that he'd survive, he couldn't express that to his sons. He couldn't give them any kind of hope if it might not come true.

"What?" Matt said.

"Huh?"

"What do you think? You started saying something."

"Oh. I forgot what I was going to say."

He took another long drink of water, his eyes drifting closed as he drank. It didn't burn in his throat anymore. It felt cool and nice and refreshing. Was that good?

Ray

North of Canton, Texas
2 days before

"I'll take a Hungr-Buster with cheese and jalapeños," he said.

His hand rested on the gas nozzle where it entered the car, and the vibrations from the flowing gas made his palm and fingers tingle. He looked over to her on the other side of the car, one hand cupped against her bangs to shade her eyes. Her other hand pulled her sweater up over her shoulders. It wasn't cold out, but it was so windy that it almost stung.

"Anything to drink?" she said.

"Oh yeah, I'll take a Dr. Pepper. Fries, too."

"Gotcha."

She went inside to get the food, and he turned back to watch the numbers on the pump ascend. He was pleased that this was going off without trouble, and his mind felt clearer now that his bladder was empty. She'd come back any minute with a bag of burgers and some drinks, and they'd burn out of here, eating on the road.

He didn't note the scuff of the shoes behind him as the gas nozzle clicked off and he returned it to its holster, never had any inkling of foresight as the blunt object swung down into the back of his head. He just felt its impact and a flash of panic as he tumbled to the concrete and everything went black.

Baghead

Rural Arkansas
9 years, 127 days after

As soon as they stepped out of the car, the insect sound surrounded them. The wall of chirps and clicks and throaty sounds reminded Bags that at least one biological community was thriving in the post-apocalypse.

His legs ached, and it only got worse a couple of steps in. Pins and needles throbbed along his inner thighs, the epicenter of the pain pulsing upon his taint, creeping up onto the flesh of the underside of his scrotum. He hobbled after Delfino, struggling to keep up, wandering off of the path so weeds slapped stalks and stems at his pants.

There was something terrifying about the lantern getting farther and farther away, the light withdrawing, leaving him alone in the dark. Like the lit place was the only thing that was real, and everything else was a black hole you fell into forever.

Delfino stopped, swinging the lantern back toward Baghead. He spoke in that gritty tone just louder than a whisper.

"You coming?"

"Yeah. Sorry. My legs are asleep. Well, really it's my crotch, mostly. Total nightmare."

"Aw, damn. Is it getting that under-flap of the ballsack?"

"Totally."

Delfino sucked air between his teeth, a grimace forming

on the half of his face closest to the lantern. Bags presumed the other half grimaced as well, just in the dark.

"That's the worst," Delfino said. "Makes my sack skin crawl just to think of it."

Bags caught up, and they moved forward together, Delfino slowing down to match Baghead's limping gait. He felt alive again to be back in the light, relieved, though his heart still fluttered in his chest from the adrenalin.

The pain in his groin faded just a little, and now Bags could see where they were going somewhat better. A foot path slashed a brown line into the greenery, though it didn't lead to a building, at least not one he could see within the perimeter of the lantern's light. They walked for a while, the taint throb slowly dying away.

The bob of the lantern moved the shadows in unison like Delfino was a puppeteer pulling all of the strings at once, making them stand up and sit down and dance a herky jerky dance. Bags got so focused on watching the silhouette's shuffle that he didn't notice right away when the path split in two.

"Here," Delfino said. "This is it. Hold the lantern for me, would you?"

Bags held the light up as Delfino walked to the apex of the fork in the trail, got down on his hands and knees, and began brushing at the loose dirt right along the line where the beaten path gave way to the clumps of grass. Soon he stopped brushing and seemed to dip his fingers into the earth along that place where the grass and path touched.

"Here we go," he said.

He pulled a rectangular flap of the ground up, maybe two

inches thick with the clumps of grass still sticking out of it and everything. A little dirt fell out as he flopped it open but not much. It was a surreal image, something revealed to be manmade out here in the middle of endless fields. Like something from a magician's act, Bags thought. He held the lantern up to get a look at the bottom of the sheet of earth, finding plastic lined chicken wire there.

"Pretty sweet, right?" Delfino said. "The roots of the grass hold the soil in place in case it rains or whatever. Plus the roots get all tangled up in this wire mesh, so you can peel the whole thing up like a sheet of sod. I saw it on TV a long time ago."

In the place where the flap had been, Bags found another of those old metal coolers like the one in the back seat. Delfino reached down, wedging his finger in the gap to pop the lid.

The driver's torso adjusted then and blocked the light so when Bags tried to gaze down into the open cooler, he saw only shadow. Delfino plunged a hand into the gloom, and when he retracted it, a 9mm handgun appeared in its grasp.

"This one work for you?" he said, tossing the gun to Bags.

Baghead caught it without thinking, pinning it to his torso with his free hand. It almost surprised him that he didn't flinch or try to get out of its path, just snatching it out of the air like a football instead of an instrument of death.

Delfino turned to root around in the cooler again, and Baghead thought about telling him. Telling him what, though? That he hadn't touched a gun in years? Was that a wise thing to share? Delfino interrupted the thought, as usual:

"This one is more my style."

He lifted and held a sawed-off shotgun over his head like an athlete hoisting a trophy.

"Always been more of a shotgun guy, I guess. Just racking one of these things gets me half hard, you know? Anyway, we're armed, finally. Pretty great, right? You want to carry the lantern or this can of gas?"

Mitch

Bethel Park, Pennsylvania
41 days before

The day wore into the afternoon, the boys finding distraction in playing Horse in the driveway. Mitch didn't watch them very closely, but he heard. The basketball pounded against the blacktop, the sound echoing in all directions. Their voices rose over each other, a tangle of words he couldn't quite make out.

He sat at the table, drinking another glass of water, staring at the blue square of sky visible through the window over the sink. His hand rested on his stomach, now full. He'd fished some lunch meat out of the cooler and made a pastrami sandwich with some spicy mustard that was delicious. His appetite surprised him, and handling the meat made him a little queasy at first, but as soon as he tasted it, he felt better. It was like an old friend coming home after a long time away.

He thought he would be gone by now, and he kept the Beretta tucked in his belt in case it became necessary. So far it wasn't. If he had to, he would do it in the shed, he thought. His initial instinct, like his wife's, had been to hide his death away from Kevin and Matt completely, but when he thought on it more, he decided against it. He wanted to be alone for the act itself, of course, but after that? Well, maybe they should see. It would be disturbing, of course, but they would have closure. Plus, they could retrieve the gun, an item of utmost value going forward.

Anyway, with food in his gut, all of that felt far away. His mood was better than it had been since before he ventured down into the basement with Janice in the first place.

He tried not to think about it, tried not to let his hopes breathe, but his faith just grew and grew.

He turned on the phone again, watched it flash through the cycle of screens. Then it vibrated and beeped. Was that...? He had a text. His chest seized up, a breath caught in his throat. The idea that maybe his boys would have a place to stay after this, someone to look after them, fluttered inside of his ribcage like a bird's wings. He tapped the screen a couple of times and read the message from Janice's parents.

"We are both sick. In hospital. I am doing OK, I think. He is not. Would be great if Jan and the boys could visit. Soon."

He closed his eyes. Without looking, he felt around for the proper button with his thumb, powered the phone down, and skidded it across the table to be away from it.

He paced up and down the hallway outside of the bedrooms. The floor creaked under his feet, the boards beneath the carpet squeaking shrill and dry. He tried to run through the options in his mind, but he couldn't think of any. He could keep trying to call parents of friends, but nobody was answering or calling back, and conserving the battery was probably the better option.

What else?

Well, he could pace the floors in his home and wait to die. That one might be worth looking into, he thought.

But no. He shouldn't think like that. He didn't have to die.

If it happened that way, it happened that way. Nobody would know until the thing played itself out, he figured.

He heard the thud of the ball slamming the backboard outside, a long range miss from the sound of it. The sound startled him out of his thoughts for a split second, though.

He stopped walking and drummed his fingers on his cheek. Was he losing it? Was he fooling himself? He'd sat in the basement, napping in a lawn chair, while his wife morphed into a zombie, and now he was telling himself that he was going to be OK. Total nonsense. Some denial thing, probably some primal function, like part of the survival instinct that would keep him fighting and hopeful in dire circumstances.

Then again, he had regained his appetite, and his headache had died out almost completely. He couldn't say for certain that the black streaks running across his chest had lessened, though he thought so. Still, the food and headache were definitive pieces of information. Were they evidence of something or not? He couldn't say.

Without thinking, he walked back out to the kitchen, bare feet pattering over the cold linoleum. It felt good. Refreshing. He felt alive again, at least most of the way.

His hand reached out for the handle to the fridge door, gripping it, and then he stopped himself. He couldn't browse for food now. The power was out, and they needed to keep it closed as much as possible. Weird how ingrained these habits are, he thought. The compulsion to eat and drink whether or not one was actually hungry or thirsty. He didn't know what to think of it.

Letting his hand fall away from the fridge, he turned

toward the sink, light shining through the window above it. Something wasn't right. He knew that, but he didn't know what it was.

The boys? He listened. After a beat, the basketball bounced off the driveway a few times and clanged against the rim. No. They were fine.

Was it-

His torso convulsed, bending him at the waist. His mouth opened, teeth prying wide, and the second wretch heaved chewed chunks of pastrami sandwich from his mouth, spilling them in wet globs that slapped on the linoleum. The smell of puke and spicy mustard crept up his throat to fill his sinus cavity.

He tried to stand up straight, but he couldn't. Two more abdominal contortions tore the rest of the food from him, but that wasn't all. Blood came up, too, in a steaming spray, projectile vomited against the floor, washing over the chunks of chewed meat and bread. Some kind of black goo came up next. It looked about the same consistency as the blood. Thick. Opaque.

So maybe he wasn't fine after all.

Erin

Erin took off, dodging cornstalks. She headed for the path that wound through the woods to the road. She suspected Izzy had gone this way, but she wasn't certain.

How could she have run off like this? Did she really have that little sense of how dangerous things were? Even in the best of times, you don't run toward gunshots. You run away from them.

A tangle of roots caught her toe, and she teetered forward, knees slamming into the ground. She didn't even look down, didn't slow her pace. She could worry about bruises and bloody scrapes later.

By the time she reached the spindly sumac bushes that marked the end of the field and the beginning of the woods, she was out of breath. Oxygen clawed at the insides of her lungs with each inhalation.

She kept moving toward the road, eyes scanning, but Izzy was nowhere in sight.

The trail cut up a hill, winding its way through the trees. Erin climbed upward, bending forward to rest her hands on her knees while she walked.

Maybe she was wrong. Maybe Izzy had gone back to the house. She *had* mentioned being hungry. Maybe she just got tired of waiting for Erin to give the go-ahead. It seemed like a silly explanation, but she was just a kid. Kids could be silly sometimes.

She half-considered turning back to check the house. Just then, the area where the trees thinned to make way for the road came into view. And there was Izzy, standing motionless on the shoulder. She stood so still, at first Erin's eyes missed her.

Another jolt of energy came upon her, and Erin darted forward, taking everything in quickly. Izzy's stillness alarmed her at first. She imagined someone standing just out of sight, pointing a gun at her, telling her to freeze. But her eyes told her Izzy was alone.

Well, alone except for the dead bodies heaped in the road at her feet. They were fresh, the first fresh dead she'd seen since the plague first started. It was different than seeing the near-skeletons. The dried-up husks left in the houses they scavenged. It was even different than the rotting pile at the gas station. This was scarier. It felt wrong.

But she could worry about that later.

Gripping Izzy's forearm, Erin swung her around. Maybe a little too roughly than she meant to.

"What the hell, Izzy? Why would you run off like that?"

Izzy's lower lip disappeared into her mouth.

"I just wanted to see."

Erin's voice went up a notch, incredulous.

"See what? The psycho who murdered these people? What if he — or they — had still been here?"

A knot of wrinkles formed on Izzy's chin. She looked at her feet.

"I don't know."

"Well, I *do* know. They would have killed you, too. Or worse."

Curls fell over Izzy's eyes, obscuring her face. But her hair didn't block the sound of her sniffles.

Christ. Now the kid was crying. It wasn't what she'd intended, but maybe it would get through to her now. Still, Erin hated how much she sounded like her mom.

She lowered her knee to the dirt so they'd be at eye level.

"Don't cry. I didn't mean to yell. But you scared the shit out of me."

Izzy's nose quirked as she sniffed. Her eyelashes were all matted together with tears.

"Language," she muttered, trying not to smile. Just like Erin knew she would.

She squeezed the kid's arm, so skinny she could almost wrap her fingers all the way around it.

"Promise me you'll never run off like that again."

"I promise."

"Cross your heart and hope to die?"

Her head bobbed, yes. Erin reached out and pinched one of Izzy's curls between her fingers, stretching it out until the hair was straight. She released it, the hair bouncing back like a spring.

They turned to head back down the trail, when a noise came from behind.

It was a rasping sound. The sound of air scraping over a dry throat.

Erin instinctively pushed Izzy behind her, peering back at the bodies splayed in the road.

It was coming from the body farthest from where they

stood. A man in his 30s. Maybe 40s. It was hard to tell. He lay on his back, head angled away from them.

"Stay here," she told Izzy, then approached slowly. She was careful to walk well away from the bodies. She couldn't stop imagining one of them reaching out and grabbing her by the ankle, like in a horror movie.

She skirted around him until she could see his face.

His eyelids fluttered, seemingly not sure if they wanted to be open or shut. His mouth moved, too. At first Erin thought he was trying to speak, but when she saw how the jaw moved up and down, almost in a mechanical way, she changed her mind. It was more like a spasm, an involuntary motion. Like a puppet or a ventriloquist's dummy.

There was a bullet wound in his neck and another in his forehead. She didn't know why he wasn't dead, but she figured it was only a matter of time before he would be.

Erin turned away, gathering Izzy and nudging her back toward the house.

"Let's go."

Izzy planted her feet, resisting.

"We have to help him."

"How? Even if we could move him, he'd be dead before we got him back to the house. And if, by the grace of God, he somehow wasn't already dead, I wouldn't even know where to begin. It's not like you can just slap a Band-aid and some Neosporin on a gunshot wound."

"It's not right to just leave him like this."

Erin gave one more glance back at the half-dead man.

"There's nothing else we can do, Iz."

Erin's clothes were almost dry by the time they got back to the house, but she relished changing out of them anyway.

"Hungry?" she asked Izzy.

Izzy shook her head, not looking up from the Calvin and Hobbes book she'd picked out at the library. Ever since Erin had given her the funny pages the day they built their first fire, Izzy had become obsessed with comic strips.

Erin took her silence as moping at first. The kid had been whining about being hungry half an hour ago. And then the grating sounds the dying man made came back to her, and it occurred to her that she wasn't that hungry, either.

She couldn't help glancing at the window facing that section of the road, gaze going beyond the grass and the yellowing corn. She couldn't actually see the road from there, but her eyes were drawn there anyway.

Was he still alive up there? Still breathing those terrible rasping breaths?

She spun away from the window. She needed to think about something else.

Her focus fell on a box of scavenged food on the counter. It hadn't been inventoried yet. That would take her mind off of things.

Except that the crusty red bits around the lid of the half-empty bottle of off-brand ketchup made her think of the almost-dead man's wounds. Jagged holes in the flesh, torn and cauterized by the bullet. She scooted the ketchup into the darkness at the back of the cabinet, out of sight. The next thing her eyes lighted on was the bag of rice. Nothing sinister about rice. Except that they kind of resembled maggots, which would soon be crawling all over the three men on the road.

The cabinet banged shut.

OK, food was a bad idea. There was a shopping bag on the table, filled with a variety of medications they'd found in the their recent shopping excursions. She'd also scored a pharmacology book at the library, which came in handy since she didn't know what half of the meds were. The bag rustled as she plucked a pill bottle from its depths. She shook it in her fist, watching the white pills rattle against the translucent orange plastic. Then she spun it in her hands and read the label.

The name on the bottle was Lucinda Silvie. Below that, the name of the drug was printed: SONATA 10MG.

She cracked the book, heading for the index in the back.

Her thumbnail scratched down the page until she found it.

Sonata, see zaleplon, page 465.

On a blank page of her notebook, she took down the two names, then flipped to page 465.

Zaleplon. A non-benzodiazepine sedative hypnotic. Clinical indications: short-term insomnia treatment.

True enough, she thought. Just reading about it was putting her to sleep.

She skimmed the page, barely able to make sense of half the words printed there. Class: pyrazolopyrimidine. Chemical name: N-[3-(3-cyanopyrazolo[1,5-a]pyrimidin-7-yl)phenyl]-N-ethylacetamide. Empirical formula: $C_{17}H_{15}N_5O$.

A butterfly fluttered past the window. Erin's head snapped back abruptly. How had she wound up in front of the window again? She peeked over her shoulder. Izzy still sat in the window seat at the other end of the room, curled up with her book. She must have gotten lost in thought and wandered back to the window without even realizing it. Jesus.

She paced through the kitchen, not able to sit still. What if he *was* still alive up there? Lying on the asphalt, bleeding out.

He was going to die. She couldn't change that. But there was something she could do. She just didn't know if she had the guts.

The sun was making its final descent of the day, tinting the whole world in an amber light. It reminded Erin of the old sepia photographs from her American History book.

Corn husks bumped and rubbed against one another in the breeze, filling the air with a rasping song that gave her the chills. It reminded her a little too much of the almost-dead man's breathing.

She passed from the field to the start of the forest, climbing up toward the road. She'd made Izzy swear she'd stay in the house three times.

The road came into view, along with the two fully dead men. Erin stopped, having second thoughts. Was she really going to do this?

She thumbed the utility knife clutched in her hand, extending the blade from the case. She still wasn't sure she could do it, but it made her feel a little less scared with the knife ready.

She clambered the last few yards up to the road and stared. She blinked once, twice, then pressed her eyes closed. This wasn't right. It wasn't possible.

The almost-dead man was gone.

Mitch

Bethel Park, Pennsylvania
41 days before

Bare wooden walls surrounded him, beams like ribs and plywood like the flesh surrounding the bone. That put him in the shed's belly, perched atop an upside-down bucket. Maybe that made sense.

When he first sat here and looked at the evenly spaced two-by-four beams around him, he saw them as bars, saw this shed as his cell where he waited for himself to administer the death penalty. But maybe it was more accurate to think of the shed as consuming him. He crawled into its mouth-door, and it swallowed him whole. He would never walk out.

In the belly of the shed-beast, he thought.

He ran a finger along the plastic lip around the bottom of the bucket. It was hard and sharp and scuffed into a rough texture from its friction with the concrete slab below. The gun sat in his lap. Not quite ready to perform its duty.

All of the hope drained out of him along with the pastrami sandwich and the blood and the black goo. He knew it was over at that moment, knew that the end would come soon. In some way, knowing was a relief. His mind no longer tussled with his fate as an abstract unknown it could never quite get a hold of. His fate turned concrete, an inevitability, an absolute. A kind of peace came with that.

Now he was just waiting for the right feeling to come over

him so he could go through with it. It felt like swallowing a pill, he thought, having that mouthful of water and a tablet sloshing around on his tongue, waiting that beat, that momentary hesitation, before sending it over the epiglottis and down the drain. His whole life was like that beat stretched out now, waiting to send himself down a different drain.

He bounced his leg, his shoe scraping a little against the rippled texture of the concrete. It smelled like lawn care products and wood and gasoline here, with other unidentifiable shed odors mixed in. Dried grass caked the edge of the weed whacker and mower, matted chunks of green going brown.

Mitch lifted a mason jar full of water to his lips and sipped, his hand shaking a little. He didn't think drinking did him much good now, didn't think he could really hydrate himself at this point with his body breaking down into black sludge or whatever the fuck, but it was a comfort. He liked the way the cold water felt on his lips and washing down his throat. He figured it might come back up, but hopefully he wouldn't be out here long enough for that to happen.

He touched the gun with his left hand, fingers stroking across it and then moving away. Cold and smooth, the steel vibrated against his skin, made the tips of his fingers tingle. Could that be real? Or was it his imagination? It didn't matter, he thought. Either way, it was too intense, somehow, to maintain contact. For now, anyway.

He closed his eyes and rubbed at the eyelids, pink and yellow splotches exploding in flashes in his field of vision like fireworks. His fingers pressed at puffs of swollen flesh that extended from his eyes to halfway down his nose. It didn't feel

495

like touching part of his face. It felt like touching two fat slugs, fleshy and slimy and firm. And it was tender, the pain swelling to something significant when he applied any pressure.

Something knocked on the wood, shaking him back into the moment. He removed his hand and opened his eyes, waiting, listening. He blinked a few times, turned his head to point each ear at the door for a moment, as though one of them might reveal something, but no.

Only silence.

Was one of the boys at the door? He hoped not. He'd told Kevin to stay away and to keep Matt away, told him he'd only do it if he had to and told him to get the gun after, and that it'd be OK for Matt to see then, so he could understand the thing, that it'd hurt, but in the long run it's better to see it and deal with it. He barely remembered saying these things. The scenes all jumbled together in his head after the puke, a rush of panic and talking and heat.

Just as he returned to rubbing at his slug eyes, another knock came and then another. Except now that he wasn't distracted, he could tell that they were more taps than knocks, and they weren't coming from the door, they were coming from the roof. He knew this sound. Rain. Just a sprinkle for now with a few bigger drops here and there by the sound of it.

Now.

He lifted the gun with his right hand, brought it to his head in slow motion. The metal cooled his palm, and his index finger poked along the side of the barrel, adjusting down and in to find its place on the trigger.

When he had the weapon at chin level, he paused, the

barrel facing up and away from him. How would he do this? He pictured himself putting the muzzle under his chin, but he knew firing through his jaw left a chance for the bullet to glance off the bone and miss his brain or at least do minimal damage to it. It'd tear his face up, yeah, but he'd be alive. More importantly, his brain would remain intact, at least mostly, which made a zombie change possible even if he did die. Same thing with the temple. It could work, but the bone made a fluke ricochet — and thus survival — possible.

He licked his lips and swallowed, the lump in his throat shifting and clicking. His eyes locked onto the gun before him. He watched it twitch and sway along with the muscles in his arm. The more he tried to hold it still, the more it shifted and wiggled and wavered.

Should he put it in his mouth? Blowing out the brain stem was the quickest and easiest way to kill a human, but would that also kill a zombie? He wasn't sure. Should he angle the muzzle behind his teeth and fire up through the roof of his mouth? That seemed like the best option to ensure the most thorough destruction of brain tissue.

He felt the sweat from his palm smearing into the steel, making the gun greasy in his mitt. Maybe he should wipe that off, he thought. He brought the gun down, set it in his lap, a little tension in his neck and shoulders letting go right away. He wiped his palm on his pant leg a few times, checked it. Still moist, almost like a buttery breadstick feeling, but better than before.

The rain pelted the roof now, water thudding off of the asphalt shingles. He hadn't noticed the noise with the gun near his head. In that moment, he heard only his heart

497

slamming in his chest, the blood squishing through his ears.

He pivoted on the bucket, feet scuffing on the floor to square his shoulders to the door. The temptation to look outside filled him. He wanted to watch the raindrops burst upon impact with the driveway, watch the blades of grass bob and weave under the water's assault. Not that these would make great entertainment so much as hearing the rain on the roof without seeing it felt incomplete.

Maybe there was more to it than that, he thought. Water is life, and he was sitting in death, the instrument of its doing resting upon his thighs. Maybe he just wanted to look upon life one more time, to see the rain give life to the plants, to see the worms crawl up from the soggy ground and writhe on the sidewalk.

But no. He turned his head toward the weed whacker, its mouth crusted with green and brown flecks. He wouldn't look out there. It was a waste of time. He would concentrate and be done with it.

He glanced down at the gun. It rested just a couple of feet below his head, but it somehow felt like peeking over the edge of a cliff, that overwhelming tension of looking down on the jagged earth far below. Half exhilarating. Half terrifying. For Mitch, looking over bridges and cliffs served as one of those moments when the notion of his existence came to the forefront of his thoughts. The dread of existing, of not knowing where it was headed or what it was for. Half of him locked up, frozen in fear, watching his toes, keeping them well away from the edge. The other half wanted to hurl himself every time. Not out of great sadness or despair. Not for any melodramatic, attention-seeking reasons. Just as a way to ease that dread of existence, of being conscious of himself and his mortality and the meandering trajectory his life traveled. To turn off the endless anxiety and self-consciousness, to turn the unknown into a known, any known, even death. To turn the in-between into something permanent. Something final. Forever.

He closed his eyes again, searching himself for those feelings now that he needed them. But the fear was so big just now. He felt like a child too scared to get in the deep end of the pool.

It was a weird feeling to know that killing himself was the best option, the only solution to all of the problems before him, and still find himself too scared. But he would wait, and the right feeling would come around. He knew it would come around. It had to.

Teddy

Moundsville, West Virginia
74 days after

All of his things, aside from his food and drink stash, fit into a polyester laundry bag that he slung over his shoulder. It bounced along with his footsteps, the bottom of the bag slapping at his back once in a while.

He walked down the middle of Main Street, feet treading on the parallel yellow lines. Birds darted on and off of the dead power lines above him, not singing but chirping single notes periodically, alarmed screeches that he took as warnings to keep his distance. He'd never liked birds. They seemed so cold hearted. Dead-eyed things. No feelings inside.

The sun warmed the asphalt beneath his feet and reflected the heat so he felt it on the exposed skin of his arms and face. He pictured his cheeks going pink, shimmering like two pieces of salmon in a frying pan, the layers flaking away from each other. He wanted to see if that was real, but there were no windows around to cast his reflection.

He took a right on Walnut Street, heading up a hill. With nothing occupying his traps for the past few days, he'd bided his time scouting houses for a new place to stay. The search turned up many promising options with features he'd only ever seen on TV. Marble countertops. Vaulted ceilings with skylights. One of them even had an elevator, though it didn't work since there was no electricity. Still, he thought that was pretty classy.

The house he picked had none of these things. It was a fairly modest place. Sure, it was in a convenient location, just three blocks from his traps and four from the well with the hand pump where he'd been getting his water every day. But those reasons didn't factor into his decision either. Not truly.

Another right put him on Pinehurst. Green grass and pine trees surrounded houses set back from the road. In this subdivision, the houses had a little space, a little privacy, even though they were right in the midst of everything downtown.

The last house on the right was the one he'd settled on. White vinyl siding with blue-gray shudders that looked to have been sun bleached a few shades lighter over the years. Paint chipped, flaking away from the wood around the windows, and the sills all looked bloated and spongy and rotten. Green mold or mildew of some kind crept up one side of the garage, the jagged edges of the green blob against the white made it look like a land mass on a map, Teddy thought. None of these things concerned him.

He pushed open the door and crossed the threshold, stepping out of the sunlight and into the shade. He paused just inside, letting his eyes adjust. Soon the couch and loveseat took shape in front of him, leather upholstery. Forest green. Berber carpet swathed the floor. Cream with brown flecks.

It felt dry inside, and he found no signs of water damage or mildew on the interior, despite the mold and rotten wood outside. There had been no dead bodies here either.

None of these were factors in his choosing this house, though. The basement was what he liked. It was perfect. The heavy steel door with a clasp for a padlock. Poured concrete walls, all smooth. Just one window, but the most secure one you could get. Glass blocks cemented in place. Not going anywhere.

It was the perfect basement. The perfect place to keep his pets.

Erin

Presto, Pennsylvania
48 days after

Erin crossed around the two remaining bodies to where the almost-dead man had lain. She stared at the bloody stain on the road, the only remaining evidence that he'd been there, and tried to think of an explanation.

She leaned forward, studying the blood in the waning light. She couldn't remember exactly where he'd been positioned, but it seemed like the bloody spot on the asphalt sort of smeared toward the other side of the road. Like maybe the body had been dragged?

Could he have stayed alive long enough, had enough strength to pull himself into the grass?

She hopped around the stain, careful not to get her shoes in it. She scanned the surrounding area, even taking a few steps into the grass to be sure, but he was nowhere to be seen. There wasn't any more blood that she could see, either.

She didn't like this. Not at all. Her fingers squeezed around the utility knife, a reminder that it was there. She looked down and noticed her hands were shaking. They were cold as hell, too.

OK, think. What would the most rational explanation be?

That he turned into a zombie and walked off?

I said rational, she thought.

So maybe whoever killed him came back for the body.

Why? No idea. But it wasn't impossible. Though why they'd only take the one body and not the other two-

She stopped, holding her breath, another icy wave traveling up her spine and over her skin.

Maybe they came back for him because they knew he wasn't dead. Maybe it had all been a ruse. A trick to lure them in.

And then she remembered that she'd left Izzy alone at the house.

Branches whipped at her face and arms, but she barely felt them. She lost her balance at the bottom of the hill, rolling sideways on her hands and knees into the field, re-bloodying the scrapes from her earlier fall. But she clawed her way upright and ran for the house.

She didn't bother scoping out the house before hand, she just barged in, slamming the screen door into the side of the house.

Izzy was at the dining room table, in the midst of shoving a handful of Frosted Flakes in her mouth. She leered at Erin.

"What?"

Erin steadied herself against the door, panting.

"I thought-"

She let her head fall backward to rest against the door.

"Never mind."

Izzy hadn't been kidnapped. So that was good.

But that still didn't explain where the hell Almost Dead Guy wandered off to.

Erin turned and pressed her face to the screen, squinting through the holes and out into the velveteen half-light of dusk. Was he out there right now, watching? Pissed off that they hadn't helped him?

She closed the storm door and locked it, then went through the whole house, double-checking the other doors and windows. Back in the kitchen, Erin set a candle on the table and lit it.

"No lanterns, tonight, OK?"

Izzy shrugged.

"I thought we were going to have a fire today. So you could do laundry."

"It'll have to wait," Erin said.

That night, Erin couldn't sleep. Before she got in bed, she tucked the utility knife under her pillow.

Now she lay there, eyes open. Every time she heard a noise, her body jerked a little involuntarily. Her mind raced, trying to determine the source. Eventually she'd calm herself. Just the house settling. Then she'd snake her hand along the mattress until she felt the cold metal of the knife under her pillow. Checking to make sure it was still there.

At some point she dozed off, because she was awakened by Izzy screaming. Erin's eyes twitched open, and she struggled against the blanket to push herself into a seated position. They were alone in the room when Erin finally got her bearings. It was only Izzy having a nightmare.

"It's OK," she said, squeezing Izzy's shoulder. "You're having a bad dream."

Izzy blinked and rubbed at her cheek.

"I had a dream that we were cannibals."

Of course. Erin knew she shouldn't have told Izzy that shipwreck story.

"We were eating that man on the road. And he was still alive."

Better us eating him than him eating us, Erin thought. But she didn't say it out loud.

Instead she pulled the sheet up to Izzy's chin and said, "You're alright, now. Go back to sleep."

When she closed her eyes, she saw the smear of blood on the road again and wondered, what if?

Ray

North of Canton, Texas
2 days before

He woke to the smell of pickles, that vinegar odor. She sat on the curb next to him, a couple of bites into her burger, a strawberry shake balanced between her knees.

He glanced around the parking lot, getting the vague sense that something was off, something was missing, and then it clicked. The Grand Cherokee was gone. It felt like someone large twisted the heel of their boot into his chest.

He sat up, and their eyes met. She finished chewing before she spoke.

"Police are on their way."

"What? No police. We have to get out of here, get moving."

"You got whacked in the head and your Jeep got stolen. The gas station attendant called it in."

He stood, and the pain throbbed in the back of his head, an ache that spread like a burst of little lightning bolts reaching out toward his forehead.

"No police. It's a waste of time. We're not waiting around here to try to get the SUV back. Plus we had that run-in last night. With the soldiers."

He thought of the gun, the murder weapon, in the glove box as he said it. He was almost sorrier to lose that than the vehicle itself. Almost.

507

"Right," she said.

He patted at his pockets.

"Goddamn. They took my phone, too. Do you have one?"

"It's dead."

"Damn. Well, we can just charge it in the…"

"In the car? Yeah, I thought the same thing before I remembered."

He ran his fingers through his hair, felt his eyes flick back and forth as he tried to think.

"Whole thing's going to hell. But let's get out of here before the police show."

She took a huge bite of sandwich and then hesitated, turning the semi-circle of beef and bread in her hands, trying to figure out a good way to wrap it back up. A few strands of lettuce flopped out of the side.

"Here," he said.

He held the shake while she returned her burger to the waxed paper wrapper from whence it came.

Baghead

Rural Arkansas
9 years, 127 days after

The blackest dream.

He runs through the field with the gun in his hand, weeds grazing him and flicking out of the way, the air thick and black. Heavy with wet. Pressing clammy fingers against his forehead and chest, chilling him. It passes between his lips, touching his throat on the way to his lungs.

The lantern sways in the distance, the circle of light growing smaller as it pulls away from him, leaving him in the dark. He runs faster, as fast as he can, but it's no use. He can't keep up.

His lungs burn, which makes the cold air entering them feel all the more wrong. Too hot and too cold all at once. Like sweating in the winter. That chill that seeps deeper and deeper into the muscle as you work and move and perspire.

He goes to yell, but just as his throat opens to create the sound, the gun slips from his fingers. He stops running, cuts off the cry in his throat, dropping to his knees, hands patting at the dirt and the weeds. How could he drop the gun?

And then the light flickers off and on, twice, three times, and vanishes. And he gasps, and the dank air reaches deeper into his chest, tendrils of wet pressed against the walls of his lungs like tentacles, like flaps of flesh inside of him.

The darkness surrounds him, envelops him, thick and wet

around him like a womb, and then he falls. No ground catches him. No one catches him. Into the void. Into the abyss. He falls.

He thrashes and kicks and flails at the emptiness. And he thinks of the girl, the pit in his stomach somehow growing wider. The rabid child. He was supposed to take care of her, supposed to look after her, but he'd failed. He'd let it slip through his fingers.

And thunder rumbles, and he shakes himself awake in the Delta 88, in the dark, with rain pouring down, rattling against the windshield and slanting through the beams of the headlights.

Mitch

Bethel Park, Pennsylvania
41 days before

The rain beat down harder now, giving off hollow noises so it almost sounded like a steel drum banging out a monotone melody above him. He kept his eyes closed, and his heart slowed down, and his breathing slowed down, and something like a calm came over him. A stillness. An emptiness.

He put his hand on the gun again, this time leaving it there, fingers crawling over the thing and settling in. Not gripping it, just touching it. That's what he needed to do first, get used to touching it, get comfortable with the feel of it on his fingers. Let that become routine, and he could do the rest.

He opened his eyes, found the jar of water and drank. A little liquid dribbled out of the side of his mouth, tumbling to his shirt, soaking into the tie-dyed fabric in a dark oval just above his belly button.

His brain kicked up once in a while, launching into the whir of conjecture, of pontification, of self-consciousness, but he stopped it. Blocked it out.

No more words.

His fingers shifted over the surface of the gun, and he felt the way the metal had gone warm against his skin, felt the line where the heated part gave way to the cool of the untouched steel. His index finger traced up and down that line.

511

The rain hit in staccato bursts now when the wind blew, firing off watery explosions against the wood at the rate of a machine gun or a snare roll. He could tell that it had gotten cooler in the shed since the downpour started. Even with the door closed, the air found its way in to press its chill into the swollen flesh of his face, to blow cold against his sweat-soaked brow.

He closed his eyes again and concentrated on his breathing, drawing every inhalation in slow and even, holding it there for a beat before letting it out. The air tickled when it crossed through the back of his mouth and entered his throat, cool and thick. His ribcage swelled up like a bloated raccoon on the side of the road, and then it deflated, and the muscles in his back released their tension little by little as his shoulders sagged for a moment before he repeated the process. His chest tingled.

His fingers clasped the butt of the gun, sliding it into the crook of his palm, the index finger finding its way to the trigger, and he lifted the gun, felt the heft of it strain against his wrist and forearm, felt his deltoid shimmy a little as it raised the piece of metal, and his elbow bent, angling his hand toward his face, toward his mouth, and the steel grazed his chin, cold and hard, the sharp angles scraping against his stubble and withdrawing, and his lips parted, and his teeth parted, and his tongue smacked a moist sound as it pulled away from the roof of his mouth, and the cold air reached into the gaping hole in his face and caressed the wet places, the pink places, with its icy touch, and his breath blew some warmth back at the cold, and saliva excreted from his glands to try to fight the dry of all of this air-to-mucus-membrane

512

contact, and the clear fluid pooled under his tongue, and the muzzle pushed past his lips, tapping his two front teeth on the way with a sound like dropping a pair of Chiclets on a tile floor, and his breath rushed past the gun, redirecting to pass around the sides of the obstruction, and the barrel hesitated a moment in the opening, and it swayed there, rocking in the empty space between his teeth, and another breath blew against it, almost whistling in the hollow between the steel and the flap of lip and cheek on one side, and he squeezed his eyes shut so tight that it hurt a little, all of the muscles cinching all the way, spasming a little, pinching folds and wrinkles into the swollen skin of his eyelids, and the barrel lurched, the muzzle touching the roof of his mouth, connecting and disconnecting, cold and dry, making his shoulders jerk, and he could taste it now, the taste of metal and grease in his mouth, on his lips, on his teeth, and he pictured black sludge smeared around in his mouth, though he knew that wasn't real, and he tilted the gun in slow motion, bringing the angle of the barrel closer to perpendicular to the roof of his mouth, inching and inching until one end rested against his bottom lip and teeth, and he waited a beat, and he pushed again, and the muzzle scraped over his palate until it dead-ended at the back of his front teeth, not quite forming a 90 degree angle with the top of his skull, but close, and he waited, and the metal quivered against his teeth every few seconds, little rattling shakes that made sounds like when the dentists slid the little mirror around in his mouth, and his nose itched, and his chest jerked for breath, and he realized he'd been holding it, and his finger trembled on the trigger, muscle tremors twitching all along his hands, wrists and arms, and he exhaled, blowing hot air past the cold bulk in his mouth again, and the rain poured and poured and poured on the roof, hollow clanging now like someone beating on the top of a garbage can with drum sticks, and the muscles around his eyes let go, and he grasped after some type of calm, some type of stillness he could hold inside of himself long enough to be able to do this, and the violence of the act felt so huge, so appalling and unfathomable and gruesome, the idea of a bullet ripping through him, and he pictured it, pictured the muzzle flashing, the gunpowder combusting in a fast-motion blaze to create the force to launch a cylinder of metal around 800 miles per hour into his skull, chunks of bone exploding, blood vessels rupturing, gelatinous brain tissue disintegrating into a spray of jelly, the force of the bullet pushing an expanding wad of shattered bone and blood and brain out of the exit wound about the size of a fist, and something chirped to his left, a shrill throaty sound with a ragged texture, and the sound wavered once and then steadied itself, its voice an endless grating thing, inorganic.

Huh? What the hell was that?

He opened his eyes to find the gun and his hand occupying the bottom half of his vision. He let his eyes drift to his left, scanning past the weed whacker and the grass shavings and the gas can. Nothing out of the ordinary. Now he turned his head, the barrel of the gun pressing into the inside of his cheek until he adjusted it to match the new angle of his mouth. His vision crawled over a shelf in the corner covered with tools and cans of paint and cloth rags clouded black with soot.

He saw nothing, but the chirp rasped on, its tiny voice

rattling out a high pitched vibration. It reminded him a little of a buzzing light bulb, but there were no lights here. No electricity at all in the shed, and even if there were, the power was still out.

He swiveled his head back so it was facing straight ahead and looked up at the ceiling in a way that made it so he could barely see the gun jammed into his mouth. Just the faintest black smudge at the bottom of his field of vision.

His back ached between the shoulder blades, and the sting of tiredness crept over his eyes again. The anesthetic of his focus faded out, all of the pain swimming up from the depths. Some moment had passed, he knew. Some spell he'd been under had withered away, the sound snapping him back to reality. He squinted his eyes, watching the world through eyelash-thatched slits, and he pulled the gun out of his mouth. Saliva sheened on the barrel, the drool thickest near the muzzle.

The sense of the gun's absence was visceral. An emptiness occupied his face, tingled in the muscles of his jaw, cried out from all of the flesh of his lips and gums and the roof of his mouth.

Erin

Presto, Pennsylvania
50 days after

Erin lifted and lowered the handle on the old well. The sound of the pump lulled her into almost a trance.

Squeak.

Clank.

Gurgle.

Squeak.

Clank.

Gurgle.

Water gushed out from the spigot and slapped into the bucket below. She continued working the pump until the water sloshed over the top edge of the metal bucket.

She tipped the bucket, dumping out some water so it would be easier to carry. A little more splashed into the grass when she set it next to the grill.

The valve on the propane tank squeaked as she twisted it open and lit the burner. Then she lifted the bucket with a grunt and set it over the flame. When the water got hot, she added the detergent and gave it a stir.

Shirts and shorts went in first. Erin pushed them down into the water with a wooden spoon.

While her vat of clothes bubbled away, she looked out over the landscape. There had been no sign of the possibly-reanimated corpse of Almost Dead Guy. No more gunshots or further evidence of other people in the area at all. Nothing out of the ordinary. But she still half-expected to gaze out one of these days and see his zombified figure staggering toward the house.

When the clothes were well done, she plucked them from the water with a pair of tongs and set them aside to cool off before wringing them out. After that, they went into a second bucket of cold water where she could rinse out the soap.

She may not know dick about survival, but she at least knew how to do a load of laundry.

The stinky socks and crumpled up wads of underwear went into the pot last, being the dirtiest.

Izzy slipped through the back door and hopped down the steps.

"What are you making?"

Erin lifted the spoon, revealing a pair of Izzy's striped undies.

"Underwear soup. Want some?"

"Ew, no!"

Izzy squatted over a soccer ball she'd found in the barn. She looked kind of like a bird trying to hatch an over-sized egg.

"Do you how to play Rain on the Roof?"

Izzy shook her head, and Erin stepped away from the heat of the grill, leaving the underthings to simmer.

She showed Izzy the game, like Erin's mom had shown her all those years ago. They took turns throwing the ball on the roof and then they raced forward, trying to catch it before it touched the ground.

After a few rounds, Erin went back to stir the linens.

"Why don't we just get new clothes?" Izzy's words were punctuated by the ball bouncing over the shingles. "When the old ones get dirty, we can just throw them away. We'd never have to do laundry again."

Erin tapped the spoon on the edge of the bucket.

"I don't know. It seems wrong somehow. I mean, at some point, we'd probably run out of new clothes to wear. We'd each need over three hundred pairs of socks. Over three hundred pairs of underwear. That's a lot."

Izzy snatched the ball mid-air, her hands slapping into the leather.

"Only if you change them every day."

"Well I don't want to walk around in sweaty underwear, so yeah. I'll be changing mine every day, you little crust butt."

Erin dodged the ball Izzy hurled at her.

"I'm not a crust butt!"

"That's exactly what a crust butt would say."

Erin lifted the bag, hoisting it up and down, trying to get a feel for the weight. Was it too heavy?

When she first got the idea, she thought she'd put together one bag. She hadn't necessarily planned on telling Izzy about it, either. Only because she didn't want to scare the kid. But as she mulled over the various scenarios in which the bag would be useful, it occurred to her that it was entirely possible that they could become separated if something went wrong.

So she made two panic bags. That's what she'd been calling them, in her head of course. One red and one pink, both filled with emergency supplies.

"Here," Erin said, handing Izzy the red bag. She'd picked up on the fact that Izzy had an aversion to anything pink.

"What's this?"

"It's a… bag," she said, omitting the word "panic." "There's one for you and one for me. Packed with important stuff in case we ever need to get away in a hurry."

"Like when we left the camp?"

"Exactly."

"I want to go through all of it so you know what you have. The other thing is, there's some good food in here, but you can't eat it. Not unless we really need it. Get it?"

Izzy nodded.

Erin unzipped the top and upended the bag on the rug.

"Dry clothes," she said, holding up a Ziploc bag with a shirt, pants, hoodie, socks, and underwear inside. Anything that needed to stay dry was packed in plastic, just in case.

She lifted another bag containing toilet paper, matches and a lighter, and tea lights. (Erin's had the addition of tampons for her "minstrels.")

"Shit tickets and candles."

A chuckle slipped out before Izzy could stop it. She shook her head.

"You owe the Swear Jar like ten million dollars."

Erin went through the rest of the contents, packing each item back in the bag when she was finished.

Obviously there was food. She'd spent some time figuring out what food gave them the highest calories by weight. Canned goods were out — they were way too heavy, plus they required a can opener. They'd found a few energy bars, so those went in first. The box of Slim Jims wound up being a

519

great find. They were light, individually packaged, and almost all protein. She divided those evenly between the two bags. Lastly, they each got a half-eaten jar of peanut butter and some foil packets of tuna.

There were two bottles of water and a purification kit. They only had one of those, and Erin decided Izzy should have it. She hoped they'd find another one somewhere.

Each bag also had a blanket, a multitool and pocket knife, and some basic first aid: Tylenol and ibuprofen, antibiotic ointment, Amoxicillin tablets, alcohol wipes, and some bandages.

Izzy held the bag on her lap after they'd finished, staring at the canvas fabric. Her head was cocked to one side, and Erin could tell she was lost in thought. She worried Izzy was thinking on the possibility of being separated.

Finally, she spoke.

"So it's a ditty bag."

"A what?" Erin said.

"That's what my dad always called it when we went camping. A ditty bag."

Ditty bag. It sounded a lot more innocuous than panic bag.

"OK then. Ditty bag, it is."

That night Erin climbed the narrow staircase into the small finished attic. Scooting around the desk that took up most of the floorspace in the tiny attic-turned-office, she knelt in front of one of the bookcases lining the wall. She didn't know why she remembered seeing it when they first went through the house, but it was still there, right where she'd left it.

It landed with a thud on the kitchen table, rattling the salt and pepper shakers.

"What's that?" Izzy asked.

She had a pinky finger jammed in one ear, de-waxing or just being a gross kid, Erin wasn't sure.

"Seriously?"

Izzy pulled a waxy finger from her ear and stared at Erin, impatient for an explanation.

"It's a phone book."

Seeing that this wasn't registering, she elaborated.

"Before the internet, this was how you found someone's phone number. The first section here, the white pages, those are personal numbers. People's houses."

"For phones like that?"

Izzy pointed to the black cordless model bolted to the wall next to the refrigerator.

Erin nodded.

"The back is called the yellow pages, and it's all businesses. So here, I'm looking through the G section."

She ran her finger over the thin page and stopped when she found what she wanted.

"Guns. And then it has a list of places that carry guns."

"We're getting guns? Finally. I keep trying to tell you-"

"Please don't start with the zombies again."

"Well how are you going to kill a zombie without a gun? I mean, one zombie, maybe. But a bunch? We need firepower."

She looked so serious, Erin couldn't help but laugh.

"So what are we getting? M-14? AK? .357 Magnum?"

Erin took her eyes from the page to give Izzy a long look.

"What the hell? How do you even know all those?"

Izzy shrugged.

"Call of Duty."

"You were allowed to play Call of Duty?"

She shrugged again.

"Technically, no. It was my brother's."

"Oh, right."

Erin kept her head down like she was still perusing the phone book but lifted her eyes to sneak a glance at Iz. She watched for a sign that bringing up the past and the people from Before might have upset Izzy, but she seemed normal.

They tended not to talk about their families much. It was sort of an unspoken thing, and Erin had just stepped right into it without thinking.

Erin turned the page.

Someone needed to write a book about post-apocalyptic etiquette.

Ray

North of Canton, Texas
2 days before

Dust kicked up everywhere when the wind blew, little clouds of it puffing and scattering all around them, whipping grit into their faces. They walked along the side of the road, still headed north.

"We either have a few hours or about a day," he said. "I can't remember exactly what Ted said as far as the timetable."

"The arrival time of a nuclear blast seems like the kind of thing you'd want to remember."

There it was. The rich lady tone again. He should have known she'd want to twist his nuts up about this. He knew she wasn't wrong to do it, though. Jesus, how could he forget something like that?

"Look, it was a lot to process, and I haven't slept. Maybe Ted wasn't that explicit about the timeframe. I can't remember for sure. Anyhow, I'm not making excuses. I wish I knew."

They walked for a time, the shadows of the taller trees reaching out to brush across their cheeks and the backs of their necks, a little flicker of light and dark playing exclusively on their right-hand side.

His head throbbed along with that flicker of shadow and sunlight. How could he let someone get the jump on him like that? Embarrassing. Worse than embarrassing. They reached into his pocket and took his keys and phone while he was unconscious. He felt violated. He brought his hand up to his forehead.

"Are you all right?" she said.

"Fine. Just my head hurts some."

"Take this."

He turned to her and she held out her hand, dropping a pill into his. Xanax. He turned the bar over in his palm.

"This ain't exactly headache medicine."

"It will help you calm down is all."

He thought it might be a mistake to dull his senses in any way at this point, but he didn't care for the moment. Any relief was welcome. He popped the pill into his mouth and swallowed it dry. It felt stuck in his throat, so he pawed at his neck, wiggled his Adam's apple back and forth as though that might help shake it loose.

"Thank you," he said after a moment.

A truck passed by on the road, and the engine growled, and the air rushed at them, more clouds of dust whipping around everywhere.

"If we had the gun, we'd have a better shot at getting another vehicle," he said. "Any weapon, I guess, would help our cause."

"Wait."

She stopped and opened her purse, digging around a while. This purse was full of solutions, he thought.

"Here."

She pulled a little plastic canister out. Yellow with a black lid. It almost looked like a travel sized can of hairspray or maybe one of those old school breath fresheners that people always squirt into their mouths in movies just before a big date. He took it from her, spun it around to read the label. Pepper spray. Police strength.

Teddy

Moundsville, West Virginia
76 days after

He sat on his new couch now, watching the dust motes drift in the bars of sunlight glinting through the front window. Settling in at the new house was coming along well. It smelled cleaner here, and it already felt like home, felt like his own.

He didn't sleep much that first night, tossing and turning on a new bed, his eyes unwilling to stay closed, but that had already passed. He felt fancy sleeping up high on a mattress not touching the floor, a mattress long enough to support his feet rather than leaving them to dangle off the end. Even the blankets were softer here, no longer scratchy.

He wished he had some ice cream to celebrate the move. A bowl of vanilla bean would be great. Or meat. Meat would be even better.

He stood, gathering a couple of cans of lighter fluid that had rested on the couch cushion next to him, tucking one under his arm and one in his hands. He passed through the kitchen to the basement, pausing outside the door, listening to the sound of shoes scuffing on the cement down there.

He'd already lured a pair of zombies into the chamber, which was exciting at first, but in the hours since he'd secured them, something about it had become disappointing. For all of the effort it took to trap them and have them follow him all the way home and down into the basement, it was anticlimactic. They didn't moan at all in their cell, didn't whimper to acknowledge the power he had over them. They just shuffled from wall to wall, pressing their hands into the concrete and moving on, mostly undisturbed.

It angered him somehow, like a decent movie with a bullshit ending. He knew how to liven things up, though. It'd get messy, but it would be worth it.

He twisted the key in the padlock, opened the basement door and descended into the cell. He let his feet fall heavy on the steps. He wanted them to know he was coming.

The creatures turned their heads toward him, their facial expressions still as dim as ever, mouths hanging open, eyelids all drooped. They were both girls, one with long brown hair, maybe 15 or 20, the other with short salt and pepper hair, probably in her 40s. He tried to picture their features un-zombiefied, but it was difficult. Maybe they were even pretty before all of this. He couldn't say.

Their shoulders squared toward him, their hips twisting around to match a beat later, and the feet now scuffled in his direction, rubber soles sliding over the cement.

He popped the top of one of the cans of lighter fluid, swiveling the red nozzle out and letting the other can fall to his feet on the landing at the bottom of the stairs. He pointed the red tip at the younger girl, squeezed the can.

A burst of fluid spurted in her face, and she didn't even blink. The sides of the can tinkled out a little two tone melody when he let go. He squeezed again, harder this time so he could maintain a steady stream like urine, the lighter fluid trailing down from her eye to her gaping mouth, spraying inside, slapping against the inside of her cheek. The sound of the flammable juice pooling echoed in the hollow of her throat.

Something about all of this satisfied him beyond what he had expected. He'd doused zombies with accelerants before but never in his own home. It just felt right.

He moved to his left, walking around the perimeter of the room like a boxer staying outside, making the opponent chase him. The zombies followed, too slow to ever catch up.

He sprayed the older one, lighter fluid spritzing her hair with such velocity that little droplets flung off in a mist that seemed to hover above her. Then he pointed the bottle lower, wetting her body a little, almost embarrassed to do so at first. He found confidence soon enough and worked the bottle up and down on diagonal lines like a paint roller, soaking their bellies and boobs.

The fumes filled the room now, made him a little lightheaded. Time to end the suspense. Time to give them what they came here for.

He tossed the can of lighter fluid onto the landing with the other and reached into his pocket, fingers fishing around, tumbling and fumbling the little wooden sticks around in there before he finally got a hold of one and pulled it free.

He scraped the match against the zipper of his jeans, and it hissed and flashed as the chemical tip ignited. He held it at eye level as the flash died down and the wood maintained the smaller flame.

This was it. Just about as aroused as he could be.

He flipped the match at the younger one, sent it in a spiraling arc toward her face, trying to land it in her mouth like a three point shot.

Mitch

He stomped his foot, the sole of his shoe pounding into the concrete slab with a smack and a thump. Right away, the endless chirp wavered and cut off like something falling out of the air around him. The silence welled up to fill the shed, and his shoulders tensed, and it felt weird to move, to breathe, to exist at all.

He scratched behind his ear and thought about what this meant. The sound reacted to him, to his stomp, and the nature of the sound guttering out was definitely organic, a living thing. Not a light bulb or some electrical noise. It must be an insect after all.

His eyes darted back and forth, scanning along the place where the floor and wall met. Could it be some kind of cricket? One of those fat cicada-type things with black veins stitched through its wings? What being could possess this shrill, gravel-throated voice? And how could it screech for minutes at a time without stopping to inhale? Did it not need to breathe?

Nothing stirred in the shed, though. No six-footed creature stepped forward to reveal itself, pattering out to the center of the room with one arm raised.

He let his eyes drop to his lap, looking upon his hand resting on the firearm there. He grit his teeth and wished he

530

could do it all in one motion, just lift the steel to his face, pull the trigger and be done with it, a flash and a pop and off to oblivion, off to somewhere else or maybe nowhere, but he couldn't do it.

The sweat seeped from his pores again, beads of moisture glomming together into pools that clung to his skin all over. The wet did nothing to ease the heat inside of him. It just made him feel soggy and sopped into his clothes so he felt like he was wearing wet rags.

He thought that from afar suicide seemed like mostly a sad thing, an abstract thing, maybe even romantic in a tragic way, someone in so much pain that they couldn't go on, someone choosing a time and place to leave because they couldn't do it anymore. But up close it was so violent. Sticking a gun in his mouth and pulling the trigger felt like such an aggressive act now that he stared its reality in the face. How bad did you have to hate yourself to be able to do that? A person didn't just have a streak of sadness or a lack of confidence in that case. The feelings they had toward themselves probably had more in common with the people who shoot a bunch of kids at their school. They wanted destruction. They wanted blood. They wanted bones splintered and brains disintegrated and their face erased into a bloody jelly. Maybe that wasn't true in many cases. He couldn't be sure. But it must be true in some. Up close, that's what felt necessary to be able to do it, to overcome the fear.

Not sadness. Hatred.

Not blue feelings. Red hot fiery ones.

All of the passion and despair and energy that drove people to do all that they do in the world, all of that life force channeled into hatred for one's self that swelled up so huge that it couldn't be contained. Maybe society needed to turn that into a Hallmark card version of what it really was to be able to deal with it. They needed to make it small, a smiley face with the smile turned upside down. But it came from the same place that murder came from, the same place that rape came from, the primal place that seethes and flails and finds satisfaction only in inflicting pain and death and destruction. It was those things turned inward instead of outward.

He rubbed one hand against his neck, feeling the smooth skin give way to rough at the place where the stubble began under his chin. He wondered if the black crept up there now, dark lines threading over the curve of his throat and moving out of view beneath his facial hair.

He thought it strange to be human just then, strange to be a walking bag of meat, the smartest of the apes, strange to live in a world that pretended that the animal part of him was less real than the social constructs all around. When he touched the gun, his fingertips grazing over the metal, he knew that life and death were real, that somehow they hadn't quite seemed real before, back when he wanted nothing more than to kick his feet up and watch TV. Before, all of the fake things seemed real: TV shows and sports and political theater masquerading as policy debate and investment portfolios and real estate deals and picking out new appliances and the hope of trading in the station wagon for something a little sportier once the kids were a little older.

But no. He was a hunk of meat, a group of muscles, a four chambered heart squishing red blood cells loaded with oxygen and nutrients to his oversized brain. And now the scenario had tasked him with destroying the meat, defiling the flesh, blowing a big red hole in the oversized brain so all of the blood poured out like water spiraling out of a bathtub faucet.

He touched his neck again, felt the warmth and the thrum of the pumping blood against his palm. He closed his eyes, and his pulse fluttered against his hand, his ribcage shaking like the walls of a building about to buckle in an earthquake.

Again his fingers took their places on the handle and trigger of the gun, and again he lifted it. He stared straight ahead, his eyes locked on a bottle of WD-40 on the shelf across the room, the gun bobbing and weaving at the bottom of his field of vision. His shoulders twitched a few times, that little quiver like getting a chill.

He closed his eyes and slid the gun between his teeth again.

Ray

North of Canton, Texas
2 days before

Heat shimmered off of the road now, the midday sun making his eyes want to pinch closed rather than look at the bright light reflected off of the white line running parallel to them.

The plaza in the distance became their destination – a mini-mall with surplus clothing shops and a Gamestop. What came next would be pretty simple, he thought. They just needed to pepper spray somebody and take their car. They could even grab some deeply discounted jeans along the way, maybe.

The pepper spray canister bulged in his pocket, not quite visible if you didn't know to look for it, he thought, but he felt his pants tighten around it with each step, a little fabric pinch and then a release. He stared down at it while he walked. Maybe you could see it, if-

"Question," she said.

He looked up, waiting for her to go on, feeling a little self-conscious to have his pants and crotch gazing interrupted. She finished her thought in a deadpan:

"Is that a can of police strength pepper spray in your pocket, or are you just happy to see me?"

He laughed. He hadn't seen that coming from her. It made it funnier that she kept a totally straight face, staring off into the distance, almost looking distracted.

"Real question," she said. "How are we going to pick?"

"Pick?"

"How are we going to... you know... pick a car, I guess?"

"Oh."

His eyes scanned the businesses on the horizon again, swinging down from the red signage of Gamestop to the movement on the ground before it.

People moved to and from cars. Even with the apocalypse upon them, people still wanted video games and ponchos and Skechers. From this distance, they looked small, their shoulders slouched, their movements indistinct, somewhat aimless.

His head swiveled over to take in the mouth of the lot. It stirred with life as well. Minivans and SUVs thrummed in and out in rhythmic bursts like the parking lot was inhaling and exhaling soccer moms.

He zoned out watching these moving parts, his mind going all the way blank for a good 90 seconds, and then he remembered that she had asked an interesting question: how would they pick a car? Better to think of it as picking a car than picking a victim, too. She was smart.

"I don't know. It'll be just like shopping for a new set of wheels, maybe," he said.

Erin

Pittsburgh, Pennsylvania
52 days after

Erin made certain they approached the building from behind. She didn't want to ruin the surprise. They hid their bikes behind a rusting blue dumpster at the back of the strip mall.

"Close your eyes," she said.

Erin watched Izzy's eyelids snap shut. She took a small hand in hers and led Izzy around the side of the building.

"What is it?"

Erin turned back and saw that Izzy had opened one eye a crack. She stopped walking and stuck a finger in Izzy's face.

"Cover those little peepers!"

Izzy slapped her free hand over her eyes. Satisfied, Erin continued around the building.

"It's a surprise. No peeking."

Their feet scuffed over the gravel of the mostly empty parking lot. When they were nicely centered about a hundred yards in front of the building, she took Izzy by the shoulders and squared her toward the facade.

"OK, open them."

Izzy's mouth popped open at the familiar logo, eyes zigzagging over the letters and the cartoon mouse on the sign.

"Chuck E. Cheese!"

"Happy birthday, Izzy."

Izzy clapped her hands together.

"You remembered!"

"You only mentioned it like every day for the past week."

As they crossed the parking lot, Erin scanned the area. She didn't want to linger in the city longer than they had to, but she wanted to do something nice for Izzy. It was her birthday, and she was still a kid. She deserved a little fun now and again. Plus, it made it so their trek into the city wasn't a complete waste of time.

Chuck E. Cheese was one of the few places they'd come across with all of its windows still intact. Erin tugged at the door, but it was locked.

"Still got that bobby pin?" Erin said.

Izzy produced the little twist of metal from her pocket. She kept begging Erin to let her try picking the locks. Might as well go for the full birthday spoil-a-thon.

While Izzy worked at the door, Erin ran through the last few days. For the thousandth time, she bemoaned the fact that they still hadn't found a gun.

First they'd tried the Rod and Gun Club in Presto. With a name like that, you'd think it'd be some kind of firearm cornucopia. But it turned out to be more of a banquet hall type of place, like an American Legion. The only difference was they had targets set up in a shooting range out back.

Next they searched Presto's lone pawn shop, but it had been cleaned out of everything but some older model TVs and an electric guitar with the neck snapped off.

Save for hoping to come across a gun in someone's house on one of their scavenging trips, Erin realized they'd need to brave the city if she was serious about finding a gun.

According to the trusty phone book, Cabela's was the best option. They left first thing that morning, taking along only their ditty bags, food, and water. Erin stowed the utility knife in her pocket, just in case.

They rode out toward Presto before veering onto the highway. As her bike bumped over the rumble strip that marked the shoulder of the road, Erin's eyes followed the serpentine line of cars extending into the distance. It was still now, of course, most of the cars literally bumper-to-bumper. It kind of reminded her of a snake. A big, dead snake.

Several times they had to get off their bikes, walking them around a big pile-up or through a tight squeeze of vehicles. Even though the sporting goods store was only about ten miles away, it was three hours before they arrived.

As soon as she rolled up and saw the jagged hole in the glass out front, Erin knew their chances were slim. But she tried to keep her hopes high.

They entered the store, stepping through the gaping glass mouth. Everywhere she looked, merchandise was strewn about. Like a tornado had gone right down every aisle.

When they reached the firearms section, Erin's shoulders slumped.

"Damn," she said.

The racks were empty. Even the display models had been taken.

A giant faux mountain rose from the center of the store, complete with taxidermy mountain goats, ram, deer, and wolves. One of the stuffed goats was captured mid-climb, legs akimbo. How bizarre that this used to be someone's full time job. Some person dedicated a lot of time to stuffing that goat, but not just stuffing it. Posing it in a very precise manner so that it would look natural. And alive.

The full-size diorama was one of the only areas of the store that looked untouched. They skirted around it, searching for any other gem that might prove useful. Since most of the looting had happened in the dead of summer, the winter wear section hadn't been picked clean quite the same way. Erin snagged good cold weather gear for each of them — coats, gloves, and boots. And just as they were leaving, she spotted a water purifier wedged behind a garbage bin. Someone must have dropped it on their way out.

So it really hadn't been a totally wasted trip. Not by a long shot. But they were still without a gun. Still without a means of protecting themselves. Unless she counted the box cutter in her pocket.

Izzy wrenched the bobby pin from the lock and sighed.

"I give up."

Time for a little vandalism. Or did it not count as vandalism now that everyone was dead?

Erin picked up a grapefruit-sized rock from one of the landscaped islands in the parking lot. She weighed it in her hand for a beat before heaving it at the glass.

The stone thudded into the window, then ricocheted off, springing back like a rubber ball. They stared at the series of cracks spiderwebbing out from the point of impact. Then they looked at each other and started laughing.

"It bounced!" Izzy said.

Erin stepped forward, lifting the rock again.

"Must be some kind of safety glass."

She threw the rock a second time, and it crashed through

the weakened glass, tiny shards tinkling onto the sidewalk.

As usual, Izzy waited while Erin scoped the place out. Inside smelled musty, abandoned. She found a set of keys behind a counter toward the back and pocketed them.

Before poking her head into the kitchen area, she plugged her nose, assuming it would be a mess of rotting food. The emergency evacuation map bolted to the wall next to the door caught her eye, the little hallways and doors marked in black, the sequence of lines denoting a stairwell. The red dot declaring "YOU ARE HERE." Did those disaster plans ever actually work? When the shit hit the fan, did everyone form an orderly line, moving single file to the nearest exit? Or did they run to the doors in a panic, pushing to be the first out, trampling anyone who got in their way? In her experience, it was always the latter.

She kicked the kitchen door open with her foot, glanced around. All was still.

The door labeled "Manager's Office" was locked. She left it alone and called out to Izzy.

"Race you to the ball pit!"

After wading through a waist-deep sea of colored spheres for a few minutes, they headed into the series of tubes above. Erin felt a tingle of static electricity on her scalp. It built as she scooted through the maze.

She slid down into another ball pit and exited the play area, jangling the keys on her finger.

"Hey Erin!" Izzy called out from above.

Erin turned and looked up in time to see Izzy stick her open mouth on one of the little tube windows. She took a big breath and blew out, inflating her cheeks.

Erin raised both fists, two thumbs up.

"Nice. And very sanitary, I'm sure."

The keys clanked together as Erin flipped through them until she found the one she was looking for. She unlocked the little compartment and took a Skee-Ball in hand. Then she swung it behind her like a bowling ball and rolled it up the chute.

"Forty points! Woo!"

When Izzy emerged from the tube maze, Erin handed her a cup filled with tokens. Even though they were useless, there was something about the metallic clink that made the experience a little more authentic.

"I hereby challenge you to a Skee-Ball tournament."

From Skee-Ball, they moved on to the Jump Shot basketball game nearby. A little more imagination was required when it came to playing the more traditional arcade games. First they climbed into one of the race car games and pretended to career around the road. Next up, Erin found a cowboy themed shooting game. She only had the artwork on the machine to go on, but Erin assumed you were probably a sheriff shooting outlaws. Or Indians if it was from a less politically correct time. But she put her own spin on it and told Izzy they were killing zombies when she handed over the plastic gun controller.

"Oh no! Get that guy!"

Erin pointed at the top of the screen and Izzy aimed and fired.

"Yeah! You got him! Right in the penis!"

Izzy giggled as Erin gestured to another area.

"Look out!"

The trigger clicked three times in rapid succession.

Erin wiped an imaginary bead of sweat from her brow.

"That was a close one."

Then she stopped, staring wide-eyed at the screen.

"Is that…? It can't be… my God! It's a zombie horde!"

A quaking finger shook over Izzy's shoulder.

"Shoot, Izzy! Keep shooting, don't stop or we'll be done for!"

She kept up like that for as long as her vocal chords would allow. Finally, Izzy lowered the gun and blew on the end.

"I think I got 'em all."

Erin put a hand on her shoulder.

"Yep, I think so. Good job, kid. Not sure why you had to shoot all of them in the junk, but I ain't complainin'."

She leaned sideways into the machine, and adjusted something in the pocket of her hoodie.

"Holy cow! You must have set the high score or something, check out all these tickets!"

Erin pointed at the length of red cardstock protruding from her pocket like a limp tongue.

"Go on, take it," she said.

Izzy reached out and pulled. Erin gripped the center of the roll of tickets from inside the pocket, so Izzy could unfurl an uninterrupted strip of reward tickets. Izzy laughed as the tickets formed a spiraling mass at their feet.

"Should we scope out the prizes?"

Izzy scooped the tangle of tickets from the ground and took off for the prize depot.

A plethora of dollar store crap awaited: bouncy balls, stuffed animals, glow sticks, candy, plastic radios, finger cuffs.

Erin pulled a giant inflatable hammer down from the rack and bopped Izzy on the head with it.

"Erin, look!"

Izzy pointed to a bin containing a very recognizable brown, white, and red logo.

"Tootsie Rolls!"

They raced to the bin, each grabbing a handful. Izzy stopped.

"You can taste it first. It's your thing."

Erin reached out and ruffled her hair.

"Let's eat them at the same time. Count of three."

The wax paper wrapper rustled as they counted. At three, they each tossed a little brown candy log into their mouth.

The candy was, not surprisingly, stale. Erin's jaw worked double time to chew it.

Izzy smacked on the candy, chewing with her mouth open. She swallowed, then raised her eyebrows at Erin.

"Well?"

"About how I remember them," Erin said.

That night they set up camp near the Ms. Pacman machine. It wasn't much of a camp. Erin wanted to keep things light in anticipation of bringing home a lot of loot from Cabela's. She hadn't packed sleeping bags, but they each had a blanket. And the new down coats they'd nabbed made decent pillows.

Erin made Izzy close her eyes again. When she opened them this time, there was a Swiss Cake Roll with a tea light on top of it. Erin sang her Happy Birthday, and she couldn't get over how eerie it sounded. One lone voice singing in all this quiet.

Plastic crinkled as Izzy ripped open the snack cakes. She handed Erin a roll before shoving the other in her mouth in one bite. Erin was more meticulous about it, peeling off the outer layer of chocolate first.

"So was it a good one?" Erin asked.

Izzy yawned, mouth gaping.

"Yeah."

"Ready to blow out the candle?"

Izzy grinned, pursed her lips, and blew. Darkness wrapped its waiting arms around them.

Baghead

Rural Arkansas
9 years, 127 days after

When the sun rose, no pink orb emerged from the horizon. No orange hues tinted the road and the plants. No bright flash glared from the hood of the car. Instead the black clouds above showed marbled patches of gray where the sun tried to power through, and the rain doused everything in sight.

Blades of grass nodded in fast motion as the raindrops pelted them. Water funneled down over the shoulder where it gushed in a stream running alongside the car. The rain smacked the windshield too fast for the wipers to keep up, and it pounded out a bongo beat on the roof.

Even still, the girl slept in the back. Bags figured she'd been down 14 hours at this point. Maybe longer. Soon he thought he'd wake her to get her to drink some water. She had to be getting dehydrated by now.

He eyeballed the pistol he'd tucked in the little storage compartment under the door handle. The thing made him uneasy.

"This here is Ozark country," Delfino said.

Bags made eye contact with him, nodded. It was true enough.

The landscape had changed in the night, the flat fields of the plains giving way to the hills of Arkansas. Everything seemed to slope up and away from them now, like the road had slowly etched itself deeper and deeper into the earth, all things rising away from it.

They passed buildings now here and there, too. That was new. Of course, most of them were houses or barns with the shingles all scattered away from the roofs, the naked wood sagging or pocked with wet looking holes with sizes ranging from that of a bowling ball to that of a manhole. Today's rain wasn't doing these structures any favors.

"You know what sounds good?" Delfino said. "A ham sandwich."

Bags remembered the taste of lunch meat, so salty, sometimes cured to the point of having an underlying chemical flavor, though not in an unpleasant way. It'd been so long, but if it were here in front of him, he didn't think he would eat it. Too many beings had died already. No need for more unless it was a life and death necessity, the way he saw it.

"A pile of thin shaved ham on some real good sandwich bread, right?" Delfino said. "Lettuce, onion, pickle, tomato. Slather some Grey Poupon on there. And mayo. Extra mayo, man. Not that Miracle Whip shit, either. Mayonnaise. The real thing."

Delfino seemed so lost in thought, Bags noted, that he wasn't actually talking to him anymore so much as imagining this sandwich out loud.

"Some potato chips on the side. I like those thick, kettle cooked kind. And an ice cold Dr. Pepper to drink. Holy fuck."

Baghead could see the beverage in his mind, a glass that tapers at the bottom, Dr. Pepper gurgling within, freshly poured, that head of foam dying back, carbonation bubbles rushing up the sides, forcing the ice cubes to shift a little along the surface.

And then he realized that there was a black car stopped in the road in front of them, and Delfino wasn't braking or swerving out of the way. He panicked. Tried to yell, to explain what was happening to snap Delfino out of it, but managed only:

"Hey!"

He could already feel the impact, could already hear the headlights smashing, the front end of the Delta 88 buckling as it rammed into the bumper of the black car. He put his hands on the dash, bracing for it. Hoping that the girl's seatbelt would do its duty, at least.

But his one word warning was enough. Delfino swerved, missing the car by less than a foot and skidding to a stop some 50 or 80 feet beyond the vehicle.

For a long moment, nobody moved apart from the tremors rattling Baghead's arms and torso. Despite the spasms quivering through him, he stared straight ahead at the dashboard. He heard the breeze kick up outside, swishing blades of grass around, and he heard the tired hum of the idling engine.

Both men snapped their heads around to look at the black car, finding it empty. Abandoned on the toll road with no one in sight, at least as far as Bags could see.

That established, they looked at each other. Bags mouthed "wow," which Delfino couldn't see behind the mask. The driver took a breath, cupping his hand over his eyes and smearing that hand down his face. He locked eyes with

547

Baghead and said:

"Holy shit. I've always thought -- and I say this in all seriousness – I've always thought that I would die doing some heroic shit, like saving kids from a burning building or something. Instead I just about biffed it thinking about sandwiches. For real, man. I just about biffed it."

He shook his head, eyes drifting back to the car.

And still the little girl slept.

Teddy

Moundsville, West Virginia
76 days after

The flame shot up with a whoosh, and he felt something like wind rushing away from him, like all of the air had been sucked out of the room.

The girl screamed. Her face, though anguished, still lacked the depth of expression a human face would convey, but the noises poured out of her all harsh and dry and shrill.

He reveled in the sound, eyes squinted down to slits from the heat and the brightness, so he watched the whole scene in two zombie silhouettes – one flaming, the other not. Yet.

The scream died down into a moan, a sharp, bright sound. Intense, intimate, almost sexual whimpers, he thought, but clearly pained. This was better still. This was what his guests came for.

Her t-shirt melted, shriveling and tightening against her torso, melted wads of polyester falling away in flaming drips like when he held plastic bags over a bonfire as a kid. From there, the fire climbed up onto her neck and face, just blackening her hair on one side, the ear disappearing in the darkened spot.

Her mouth stole the show, though. It lit her head up from the inside like a jack-o'-lantern, cheeks glowing red, that gaping maw housing a fireball.

God, he wished he could keep her. He wished he could

549

burn her and keep her at the same time, but he knew he couldn't. It didn't work that way.

Erin

Erin counted out Tootsie Rolls in her dream, adding them to the food inventory. Someone hummed in the background as she filled a mason jar with the candies and screwed on the lid. She tilted the jar, rotating it in her hands, watching the candy shift.

They'd need more Tootsie Rolls if they were going to make it through the winter.

But that wasn't what was really bothering her. There was something else.

Slowly she became aware that the humming wasn't just in her dream.

And then she was fighting, pushing, urging herself to wake up. It was like lying at the bottom of a lake and struggling to get to the surface. Through the looking glass of the water, the sun and sky and air looked so close. She kicked and kicked, but the dream held her back, not wanting to let her go yet.

Finally she broke through, jumping awake.

She panicked for a few seconds, not remembering where she was, and then there was a new sound that went with the humming. Feet crunching over broken glass. Broken glass from the window she'd broken to sneak into Chuck E.

Cheese.

She crawled around the side of Ms. Pacman and peered out at the front windows. The silhouette of a man stood outlined there. At the sight of him, her breath caught in her throat.

She froze. Her hand went to her pocket, confirmed that the knife was still there. At least there was that.

There was only the one man, so far. A group would have been worse. Or a zombie. She hadn't gotten a great look at him, but she was going to hazard a guess that zombies didn't hum.

But they were still trapped in here, with the man standing right in front of the exit. They could leapfrog around the place, hoping to stay hidden. Maybe hide in the kitchen. But what if he spotted them? And what if he had a gun?

She cursed their luck at not finding their own gun yet. She wasn't sure she'd be able to use it, couldn't imagine just shooting someone like that, but it would be useful in terms of scaring people off, at least.

Her eyes fell on the keys next to the wadded up coat she'd used as a pillow, and a plan began to form.

First, she needed to wake Izzy. She covered Izzy's mouth and gave her a nudge. Izzy stirred, eyes fluttering open. Erin hoped the finger at her lips and the wide-eyed look of alarm she gave was enough to communicate one word: Trouble. The kid seemed to get it, fear crossing her face. Erin almost felt bad about scaring her. But this was the world they lived in now.

Erin gestured that they should pick up their things. She was most worried about the coats — the fabric seemed the type to rustle with any movement. Luckily, it was just a whisper, and the humming guy was still taking his time poking around the front of the place.

Izzy followed Erin toward the back. They used the game machines as cover, scurrying to get behind them as silently as they could manage.

They paused next to a machine called Big Bertha. Through the netting on the sides of the machine, Erin could see the man. He was still up front, wandering through the play area. It was twenty feet from where they were to the prize counter and the locked door that led to the office. She clutched the keys in her fist, the metal radiating her own body heat back at her.

She grabbed Izzy's hand, counted to ten, and scrambled to the prize counter. She paused, holding her breath, listening for a sign that the man had heard or seen them. She kept waiting for him to come barreling straight at them, but he was still ambling around, humming to himself.

Satisfied, she lowered the keychain to the ground so she could flick through the keys without them jangling together. She finally found the one labeled, "Office."

Erin stuck out a hand between them, indicating that Izzy should stay tucked behind the counter. She walked backward in a crouch until her butt bumped into the door. Inserting the key in the lock reminded her of the game Operation. At least this time there wasn't a loud buzzer if she messed it up.

"Hey!"

Every part of her turned to ice at the sound of the man's voice, except her eyes, which rolled back and forth searching for him, bracing herself. Would he come hurtling out from behind one of the machines to tackle her? Or would he just shoot her on sight?

If he didn't have a gun, she'd have to fight him. She still had the knife. Then maybe Izzy would at least have a chance to escape.

Seconds passed before she realized he hadn't spotted her. He hadn't even spoken at all.

He was singing. Something about murder and blood and guts.

Lovely.

She swallowed, glancing over at Izzy, the look of pants-pooping terror on the kid's face was probably a mirror of her own.

Turning back to the key, she twisted but met only resistance. Jiggling right and left didn't matter. It wouldn't budge.

Fuck.

She could feel the scrape of metal on metal more than she could hear it as she extracted the key. She brought the keys closer to her face to get a better look at the labels, and then the unthinkable happened.

She dropped them. They hit the ground with a slap and a clang, like a bag of pennies.

The singing stopped and so did her heart.

Teddy

Moundsville, West Virginia
76 days after

When the older woman got close enough, she flamed up as well. Another flash, another whoosh, that suction tugging at the flesh of his face again.

Her hair vanished immediately. Just gone. The remaining scalp looked shiny, red, almost wet. And brighter, hotter flames seemed to lick from the top of it, reaching higher, higher.

He knew right away that this wasn't good.

The fire engulfed the exposed joists along the ceiling, the wood going a touch darker, wisps of smoke rolling off of it. He could picture the whole thing going up. His dream house engulfed in flames.

The dead thing stumbled about, so far not standing still long enough for any of the wood to catch, but it was going to be close, he knew. Jesus, he was going to burn the house down.

He lurched forward, pushing the zombie, trying to knock it over. He didn't know what he'd do after that, but he had to do something. The thing wouldn't go down, and he burned his hand some, the flaming liquid clinging to his palms until he smothered them against his pants, hands rubbing up and down his thighs.

The fumes and the smoke twirled dizziness in his head

again, the heat around him only adding to his disorientation. The zombies moaned and moaned, all choked gasps and coos and whimpers that he couldn't even enjoy.

Another whoosh behind him. A bigger one.

He turned. The younger one had toppled down onto the landing and both canisters of lighter fluid went up then in bursts. Every four or five seconds a ball of fire shot out of the blaze consuming the bottom half of the steps. Some of the fireballs rained a fiery spray out into the room, lighting up chunks of the floor like mud puddles of fire where the fluid burned atop the concrete.

The heat shimmered all around him now, hazing and blurring everything, smoke scratching at his throat, the stench of burning bodies intertwining with that of the steps going up quickly.

His head swiveled up toward the basement door, which seemed so far away just then. The stairs were a roman candle. Impassable.

He knew now that he was going to die in his perfect basement.

Ray

North of Canton, Texas
2 days before

They walked among the cars, the heat rising up from the asphalt in a shimmer that pressed its sticky torso against his. He'd sweat through his undershirt, shirt, and suit jacket by now, but there was nothing to be done about it for the moment.

Lorraine drifted along beside him, a pink blob moving in the corner of his eye. She was a graceful, long necked woman, much like his wife had been.

Somehow he knew that she was warming to him, at least a little. He knew now that she had heard all of the bad things about him, had been reluctant to go along with him, but that she was seeing that he wasn't some monster. He wasn't a saint, but he wasn't such an awful person, either. Just a good businessman.

He didn't know how he knew all of that, though. Her outward communication hadn't conveyed a word of it, but he knew it anyway. He thought it was like how a dog could read body language and know what its master wanted with very little aptitude for understanding language. He had the ability to read things in people's motions, in their posture, in the smirks and twitches and creases on their faces that were painted and erased within a fraction of a second.

This above all else he attributed his success to. Not smarts.

Not talent. An animal thing he couldn't explain and didn't understand. He knew people. He knew what they wanted, and he knew how to give it to them.

He realized that they'd reached the front of the parking lot without accosting anyone or committing grand theft auto. His fingers stroked at the canister in his pocket, but he didn't draw it.

They stood in front of the door to Gamestop, about ten feet out from the automatic doors which opened and closed as people flowed around them in both directions. He didn't know what else to do, so he just stood there and watched.

A kid walked out. The uneven mustache sprouts on his top lip made it look like he wasn't old enough to drive, but the car keys cupped in his hand said otherwise. Ray tried to imagine jetting pepper spray into the boy's face, watching his eyelids swell up and tears gush out.

"Christ," he said half under his breath. "This is going to be hard as hell."

Baghead

Rural Arkansas
9 years, 127 days after

Baghead reached a hand into the back seat, clutching the girl's blanketed shoulder and giving it a shake. Her head lolled a bit on her limp neck, and then her breathing changed, a slow inhale. Her eyelids fluttered, opened, pupils momentarily going wide as they looked upon the man before her with the canvas bag on his head, and then contracting to something normal.

"You should drink some water," he said, handing her a bottle.

She took it and drank, her eyes drifting closed as she tipped the bottle back.

"It lives," Delfino said, smiling. "I was beginning to wonder. You slept a long time, baby girl."

The girl chugged the water as he spoke, taking three quarters of the bottle down at once, stopping for a wet, heaving breath and then finishing it off. Both men looked upon her. Baghead realized that he had no idea what she might say or do next. No idea.

She set the bottle down on the seat next to her, blinked a few times, eyes screwing up toward the ceiling in thought.

"I have to piss," she said. "Pretty bad."

After a beat of silence, Delfino busted out laughing, slapping Baghead on the shoulder.

"Come with me," Baghead said. "We'll find a place in the weeds for you to go."

He reached underneath the door handle, grabbing the gun and tucking it into his belt.

Delfino tried to say something, but he couldn't pause his laughter long enough to get the words out. His face went splotchy and red, tears shining on his cheeks.

Maybe it was the rain cutting back to a sprinkle and then dying, but Baghead had some heightened sense of time passing in this moment. It'd only been a few minutes since the near car accident so far as he could remember, but it felt much longer.

"This is Delfino," Baghead said, walking back to the car from their piss spot just off the road. "Tell Delfino your name."

"Ruthie," she said.

"That's a pretty good name," Delfino said, leaning against the driver's side door. "Not exactly Anya, but it ain't bad at all."

"Thank you," she said.

"Her parents didn't make it," Bags said.

Didn't make it. Those were the words he'd used when he asked her about them. She had nodded.

"I was thinking we'd wash Ruthie's hair before we move on," Bags said. "Maybe eat something."

"That makes sense," Delfino said. "Might want to check out the car back there first."

"Yeah?"

"Yeah, I've been thinking. It couldn't have been there

long. Not on the toll road. They would have cleared it within a day or two at the most, I figure. I don't know. Just makes me a little paranoid."

"How do you mean?"

"I don't know how to describe it, man. Just feels like the thing doesn't belong."

"Well, let's go take a look."

"Yep. Bring your gun."

Delfino scooped up his shotgun with one hand and reached in his pocket with the other, pulling out that sandwich bag of deer jerky again.

"Here, Ruthie," he said. "Eat this, and wait in the car. We'll be back in a minute."

The baggie crinkled in Ruthie's fingers. She climbed into the back seat and closed the door behind her. Baghead watched her tiny hand reach in for a piece of jerky, and he wondered if he'd ever ask her about what really happened to her parents or if he'd just let it go.

He turned, jogging a couple of steps to catch up with Delfino, and then he followed the driver's gaze to the car up ahead.

It was a black Lincoln Town Car, he thought – or maybe a Continental – from the mid-to-late 1990s. A boxy thing. Not quite as ridiculous as the Delta 88, but not as far off as one might think for them being manufactured 25 or so years apart from each other.

Delfino's gait slowed as they got within a few feet of the Lincoln, and Bags matched his stride. Nothing stirred within the car, each seat empty.

As they got to within arm's length of the driver's side

door, they stopped. Still nothing of interest visible inside.

Bags looked upon his driver, finding his lips tightened, wrinkles etched into his forehead, a web of lines creasing his eyelids. Observing the alarm in Delfino's features surprised him as he felt no real concern here. Seeing the car was a little weird, sure. They'd literally not seen another vehicle on the road thus far. But the idea of seeing a person – a real live human being out here -- seemed so remote.

"Something ain't right," Delfino said, his voice again grating in that range just above a whisper.

Baghead looked back at the black car, thinking perhaps he missed something. Instead he found his reflection in the window, the canvas bag stretched over the misshapen dome he called a head, the one messed up eye that seemed to be attempting to droop over his cheek bone and off of the side of his face.

Others probably thought he wore the mask because people couldn't bear to look at him, but they were wrong. He wore it because he couldn't bear to look at himself.

It always caught him unprepared, the pang of nausea he felt looking at his own face, even the few bits he could see through the eye holes, but then he looked away and let it go. In a fundamental way, having a face was in his past, being human was in his past. That's how he felt about it, and that's how he moved on.

And then something cracked somewhere behind him. Piercing. An explosion too loud for his ears to make sense of entirely, like pieces of metal colliding at impossible velocities. And his reflection shattered and disappeared as the window fell.

Mitch

Bethel Park, Pennsylvania
41 days before

His skin crawled, every hair follicle on his arms and legs perking up one after the other. Hot breath heaved in and out of his nostrils, made them expand and contract, and perspiration slimed his skin, oozing from the flesh on his back and forehead, cascading into the crevices between his nose and cheeks.

The gun trembled against his bottom lip. He tried to steady it, but he couldn't do it. Any attempt to stop it only made the shaking worse, made the muscles jerk harder, rattled the gun against his teeth and the roof of his mouth.

His finger stroked at the trigger, felt the smooth of the metal there moistened with sweat. It should be so easy, shouldn't it? Don't pull the trigger. Squeeze.

His eyelids parted, opening a sliver to reveal the shelf and concrete floor before him, the gun and part of his fist still hovering at the bottom of his field of vision. No words rushed through his head just now. No poetic monologue occurred to him. No voice inside reflected or reacted or reassured him in any way. His consciousness became a series of feelings only: a churn in his gut and a sting in his eyes and the soggy feeling of all of that sweat pouring out of him.

And fear. Fear constricted like a ball of contracted muscle in his belly. Fear like a child's, like a little kid frozen stiff in the dark, blanket pulled up to cover the head, breath subdued to something that barely moved the ribcage. Fear that throbbed in his skull, some electrical current that made everything outside burn too bright, even with his eyes nearly closed.

It should be so easy, but his finger rested on the trigger unable to finalize this process. He couldn't even imagine applying the necessary pressure, couldn't picture the flex of the hand, the curl of the finger.

He felt like an idiot animal gone rigid at the sign of trouble, like a baby rabbit hunching down and going motionless while the dog charges straight for it. Frightened and stupid. Too dumb to do what had become necessary. Too dumb to move at all.

He tasted the grease and the metal in his mouth. Wanted to make them go away.

And the shelf went blurry, a smudge of brown before him lit up by the daylight streaming in from the cracks above and below the shed door. And the tears caught between his eyelids, and the water made it look like the light formed clear shafts, lines that rotated if he adjusted his squint a little. It reminded him of being a baby, crying in the crib, looking up at the ceiling through his tears.

The water spilled in time, hot liquid draining from his eyes to mingle with the sweat on his skin. It didn't feel like he was crying. It felt like something that was happening in the area, happening around him instead of to him, inside of him. It felt like his body was going through the motions, a courtesy gesture of some kind made in reverence to the circumstances, but he was outside of that now.

He closed his eyes, and he felt his pulse jerk in his neck, and he wished that he could lie down in the shadows under a tree somewhere. He could sprawl on the dusty earth, and he could leave his body, and he could disappear. He could crawl into the black and be done.

He pictured this, felt the dirt on his hands as he lowered himself into the dark, felt the cool of the ground press itself into his person as his shoulder blades touched down upon it, and he looked up into the purple light weaving through the branches, the day fading out, fading away. And a great stillness came over him, a silence inside and out.

And his hand flexed, and his finger curled, and he squeezed the trigger in slow motion, the pressure of his flesh upon the metal growing, his eyelids squeezing tighter as he braced for it. He squeezed harder and harder, pushing past the fear, past the anxiety, past the swirl of mixed feelings.

He squished as hard as he could, the gun shaking like mad now, grinding his lip against his bottom teeth, but the trigger wouldn't budge.

His eyes snapped open.

Oh.

He forgot to flip the safety off.

Erin

Pittsburgh, Pennsylvania
53 days after

She didn't have time to think now, it was all auto-pilot. She snatched the keys from the ground, spotting as she did the label that said, "Main Office."

She jammed the key in and turned. This time it obeyed. The door unlocked.

As she wrenched the handle and shoved the door open, she saw him. Next to the claw machine, craning his neck around, trying to figure out where the noise came from.

His eyes locked on hers, and even from that distance, even in the dimness, she could see the confusion on his face. Like it took him a moment to realize what he was looking at. A person. An actual living human being. She tore her eyes away.

She waved at Izzy, who hadn't budged from her hiding spot. For some reason, she didn't want to speak. Like if she didn't say anything out loud, maybe they could just disappear.

Izzy scurried past her, and then she was stepping into the darkness of the office hallway, and the man was yelling, "Hey!" And this time it was real and not just him singing like some kind of creeper Elvis.

The door slammed behind them, and only a beat later, he was there, pounding on the steel. It sounded like the booming of a bass drum the way it echoed in the hallway.

Erin couldn't see Izzy, but she could feel her standing next

566

to her in the darkness, clutching at her sleeve.

"You OK?"

"Yeah. But I'm scared."

Erin took her hand, squeezing it.

"We're going to be fine. Just take a few deep breaths."

Erin released her grip on Izzy's fingers.

"Don't let go! It's too dark in here."

"I need to get the lighter out," she said.

Erin moved Izzy's hand to her shoulder, then bent to unzip the backpack, fumbling with the straps in the blackness. Her hands shook as she unzipped the front pocket on the bag.

She flicked at the lighter a few times, afraid at first that it was out of juice. She imagined fumbling down the hallway, trying to make their way by feel. Trapped in the maze again. But the fourth time she struck the flint wheel, it caught.

The flame illuminated the cinder block walls in a dim yellow glow. There were three doors before them — two on the right and one straight ahead.

"Now what? We just hide in here 'til he gives up and leaves?"

Even though Izzy was whispering, the hallway amplified her words, bouncing the hard consonant sounds around.

Erin chewed at a chapped spot on her lip.

She wasn't sure he would give up. But she didn't want to tell Izzy that. It had also occurred to her for the first time that there may be another set of keys somewhere in the place. Another thing Izzy didn't need to know.

Erin took a step forward to get a closer look at a familiar sign posted on the nearest door. Another Emergency Evacuation Map.

She leaned in, squinting at the dot marking their location. Her brow furrowed. Could that be right?

She held the lighter out toward the door at the end of the hall, straining her eyes. Sure enough, over the door was a sign that read EXIT in red letters that no longer lit up.

Erin shuffled down the hall, dragging Izzy along in her wake. When they reached the door, she jiggled the handle. Locked.

She had Izzy hold the lighter next to the keys, looking for a label that said "exit" or maybe "back door". Flicking through them again gave her a little tingle of panic. How long had it been since they'd entered the hallway? One minute? Or ten? She wasn't sure if it was the excitement or the dark, but her sense of time felt off.

She went through all the keys, not finding a label that fit. She tried the office key she'd used before with no luck. Process of elimination, then.

Her anxiety grew with each fruitless turn of a wrong key. She couldn't stop picturing the door behind them swinging open, the man's silhouette outlined in the doorway.

It felt like she'd tried all of the keys twice when finally the lock turned. When Erin pulled the key loose, she held it close to her face to read the label. It said, simply, "STARES."

The misspelling made her snort, and she pushed through the door into another pitch black chamber. The scraping and soft thud of their feet echoed in the space. Erin took the lighter back, relit the flame. It was a small alcove with only one direction to go, and that was up.

Next to a No Smoking sign, someone had pasted a computer printout that read, "No Smoking means NO

SMOKING!!! That includes the roof! -Management."

Erin made sure the door locked behind them before she led the climb up the stairs. At the roof door, they had to pause to find yet another key.

"They have this place locked up tighter than Fort fucking Knox," Erin said, flipping through the keys.

For once Izzy didn't scold her.

The lighter jittered around as Izzy wiggled her knees.

"Stop moving the light around."

"I have to pee!"

"Your bladder has impeccable timing."

"I can't help it! It's like when you play Hide and Seek. You get the drenaline rush and then you gotta go."

Erin didn't bother telling her it was *a*drenaline. She couldn't focus on Izzy's vocabulary and the singing psycho downstairs.

When she stepped through the door, the brightness practically seared her eyeballs, but she didn't care. The air smelled so fresh it almost seemed sweet. Was there something blooming nearby or was it just the contrast of the fresh air after the stagnant atmosphere of the abandoned building? Another thought she didn't have time for.

She skirted around a vent, trying to keep her footsteps light, not wanting to give away their position. At least the roof was flat, she thought, which was a lot easier to maneuver than if it were pitched.

When she reached the edge, she peered over, trying to gauge the drop. A row of dumpsters lined the wall below, giving them at least something to break their fall.

"We're not going to jump, are we?" The tremble in Izzy's

voice betrayed her fear.

Just as Erin was about to explain that jumping was their only option, her eyes fell on something.

"Of course not," she said, pointing. "We're going to climb down that ladder."

As Erin swung herself onto the top rung, she couldn't help but worry that this would be it. Just when it seemed like they'd escape, the man would round the corner of the building. Or, having found the keys, would follow them to the roof. She imagined him appearing above her now, grabbing Izzy from behind.

She quickened her pace, scooting down the ladder.

"Alright, start climbing down," she told Izzy.

Erin let go with one hand and hopped to the ground, skipping the last few rungs. She kept an eye on the parking lot while Izzy climbed down. Still clear. As soon as Izzy hit the pavement, Erin grasped her hand and headed for the bikes. And then they were pedaling away. Erin still couldn't quite believe it. She glanced behind her, convinced every time she looked back that she'd see him on their tail.

She kept them pedaling for a long while, not entirely satisfied that they'd put enough distance between them and Chuck E. Cheese.

It didn't fully click that they were going to be OK until they saw the "Welcome to Presto" sign. The familiarity of it put her at ease.

Izzy must have felt the same sense of relief, because she broke the silence that had dominated their ride.

"That was scary."

Erin heaved a sigh.

"Yeah."

Even though they'd been pedaling for over an hour, when the driveway came in sight, they both picked up speed. Erin glided up the path standing on one pedal. She dismounted, leaping off the bike and letting it roll forward on its own for several yards before it tipped and crashed to the ground.

She stretched both arms toward the sky and screamed in victory, forcing all the tension out.

"Woo!"

She'd always thought all the yelling and chest-slapping in sports was kind of silly, but now she got it. Sometimes crowing like a rooster just felt like the right thing to do.

Baghead

Baghead stood there looking at the place where the glass had been, his ears ringing from the gun's blast. Something tugged at his arm. Delfino. The driver's mouth moved, too, teeth bared, spit flying, but Bags couldn't hear him. Couldn't hear anything but that high pitched monotone in his head like some dog's endless whimper.

Another round fired. Another sound too loud for his ears to process, a pop and a crack and a high pitched click all at once, and he realized that the force of it vibrated the ground just a little, made the whole street shimmy a tingle up into his toes, and somehow he knew that everything had gone slow on him, that time itself had decelerated. A second sound came a moment later as though to affirm this thought, a hollow thump as the bullet embedded in the driver's side door.

Delfino screamed at him, though he still couldn't hear him, and the driver yanked his wrist as hard as he could, trying to pull him to the ground, but Baghead twisted and ripped his arm away.

He walked toward the wooded shoulder, toward the place where the gunfire came from. He sensed no fear in himself as he strode forward, taking a jump step over the ditch and moving into the cover of the woods.

It wasn't until he was three paces into the woods that he

looked back through the branches and saw the pool of blood on the asphalt where Delfino had been, the shotgun lying next to it.

Lorraine

North of Canton, Texas
2 days before

"You know, you remind me of my wife in some ways," he said.

They sat on a bench in front of a discount shoe shop. A green and white awning shaded them, though it was still too hot.

"Is that so?"

He nodded and looked out at the lot. She watched him reach into his pocket and feel the unused canister of pepper spray.

"We were married for 27 years, but we've been apart a long while. The death of our son was hard enough, but we made it through. For a while, anyway. After all of the stuff in the media came out about how much money I'd made, and what exactly I'd done to make it, things were different. She didn't see me the same way, I guess."

Lorraine didn't know what to say, so she looked out at the lot, too, and things were quiet for a while.

"I tried to get a hold of her, with everything going on, but she's not answering. Shoot, maybe she's already dead."

This time the quiet lasted longer. They watched the cars jerk into parking spots, watched the people hustle about.

"Why is something about this harder than killing?" he said.

"What do you mean?"

"I mean, I put bullets in those soldiers' heads without a moment's hesitation – just POW, POW -- but this feels different. It's more personal. More cruel. Does it feel that way to you?"

"It does. These people aren't threats to us like the army men might have been. Had we stormed the barricade, the soldiers probably had orders to shoot, don't you think?"

He leaned back, his shoulders touching the bench.

"Could be. Maybe you're right. But still… This is just a little pepper spray. The person will survive."

"Maybe when it's something like this, you can identify with it because it's something small. You can imagine getting pepper sprayed, right? You can picture yourself in that kind of agony, eyes and sinuses and throat on fire. But death? Death is too big to comprehend. You can't picture that for yourself. You can know it intellectually, but your imagination can't conjure images for it, can't believe it to really be possible."

He nodded, and then he turned and smiled at her.

"That was… You know, you have a real way with words. That was very well said."

She smiled, felt a little warmth in her cheeks. Her mind riffled through ideas for a new subject.

"Do you think it was hard for the person that clocked you over the head and stole your Jeep?"

His lips pursed for a moment, a stern look etching lines on his face and then softening.

"Maybe so. It took some gumption, I'd say."

"Didn't I hear you talk about this once in a sermon on

TV?" she said.

"What's that?"

"Do unto others what has been done to you, right? I mean, I'm paraphrasing, but still..."

He laughed.

"I thought you were going to say, 'Bludgeon thy neighbor as thyself was bludgeoned.'"

Baghead

Rural Arkansas
9 years, 127 days after

He felt the pistol in his hand, though he didn't recall prying it from his belt. The texture of the grip pressed its pattern into his palm, and the metal advanced toward matching his body temperature.

And he felt the warmth flush his face, the kind of animal heat he hadn't felt in a long time, his heart banging in his chest, the red blood and adrenalin coursing through him. That little tremor quivered in his arms again, muscles tightening and releasing with incredible speed.

Part of him could see all of this happening and discern its meaning, how this was the response of a threatened animal, part of his survival instinct, bred into animal genetics since way before humankind roamed the planet. But another part of him was fully in the heat, fully in the moment, pressing forward, pupils dilated with bad intentions like a tiger's just before it pounces. And that part of him was driving just now, that part exercised unchecked power over all current activities.

He stalked through the grass and between the trees, moving up the sloping hill before him toward higher ground. He didn't think about where to go. He went where the sound came from.

When it felt right, he got low, walking in a crouch, letting the tall grass and bushes shield his position some. He moved mostly without sound, neither hurrying nor delaying.

Again, he knew when to stop, and so he did. He crouched even lower and waited. He watched and listened for a long while, realizing only then that his hearing had faded back in at least some of the way.

Something rustled in the brush up ahead somewhere, twigs snapping, leaves rustling, and a man took shape, stepping out of the foliage into a clear spot some 15 feet beyond Baghead's position. A man holding a rifle.

Thick black stubble climbed up the man's cheeks, reaching almost to that rounded line at the bottom of each of his eye sockets. He was young and scrawny. Sinewy. He turned the other way and back, almost like he knew he was being watched, though Baghead read no fear on the man's face. His features made him seem bratty, in fact – pouty lips and a twisted up brow like that of a toddler in the full-on thrust of nap refusal.

Baghead checked the safety, verifying that it was off. For a split second, the thinking part of him intervened, so in shock that he was seconds away from killing a human being that it short-circuited his instincts, left him frozen with his thumb on the safety.

But the heat swelled in him again, flaring in his chest and crawling up onto his neck and shoulders before finally seething once more, deep in the deformed flesh of his face. It radiated off of him, warming the canvas draped over his head.

He stood, aiming and firing all at once, knowing the shot would connect, and it did. A head shot, a little low to be fatal, though it dropped the man in a heap.

Baghead waited a second, gun still extended before him, but the man didn't stir. He walked over and stood above the fallen figure.

The man's nose was mostly gone, a red mess and an open hole into his sinus cavity left in its place, split down the middle by a remaining fragment of septum. His eyes fluttered, full of blood.

Baghead didn't dally or gloat. He put two in the brain, retrieved the man's rifle, and stepped away, walking back toward the road.

Ray

North of Canton, Texas
2 days before

The wind blew, and it pressed his sweaty shirt to his chest, adhering it there. Slime coated his body like he was sweating a thin gel instead of liquid, or at least it felt that way.

He strode across the lot, his eyes locked on the back of a man's head. His heart slammed in his chest. His eyelids twitched. And the sweat poured and poured and poured.

This was it. This was all. Life or death determined by a can of pepper spray and a PT Cruiser in fair condition. It was so silly, he almost wanted to laugh, but he was too keyed up on adrenalin for anything like that.

He gripped the canister, positioned it to be ready to extract from his pocket without a hitch, readied his index finger on the button, on the trigger. Sweat drained down the sides of his face, and his vision seemed a little pink around the edges. Everything felt hot and wet and blurry like he was walking around in a bad dream.

He zigzagged between cars, working on a diagonal. He tried to walk fast enough that he would beat the man to the destination, but not so fast so as to arouse suspicion. He let his eyes drift to the car. The one they'd finally picked.

They'd watched the man enter the shoe store and looked at each other. Somehow they didn't have to say anything. They just knew it'd be him. Maybe his suit made it seem like he'd pull through something like this better than most. Maybe it was the notion that no one could truly miss a PT Cruiser all that much.

The cars blocked most of his view of the man. From his vantage point, it looked like a disembodied head floating just over the cars in the parking lot. And somehow that would have been easier. He could pepper spray a floating head. No problem. Sounded kind of fun, really.

He tried not to think about what this man might be up to today, but the questions came to him anyway. What kind of day was he interrupting with this? Did he stop here on his lunch break from work?

From what Ray remembered of the man's attire, he looked to be dressed in formal wear – a black suit. That suggested office work, but it could be something else. A funeral, maybe. Not unlikely with all of this death around. Did he bury a family member this morning?

He could see this man at the service, a child-sized casket framed by heaps of flowers in the front of the church. Light poured through the stained glass windows, casting red and blue shapes on the floor. Hushed weeping rested atop the atmosphere like a wet paper towel, somehow made the air feel heavy and damp, like the tears themselves could be felt all around.

Shit. Better to not think about it.

He focused on his breathing. It was getting away from him, short breaths puffing in and out of his nostrils. No. Deep breaths. That's what he needed.

His lips parted, and the cool air rushed into his throat for what felt like a long time, and there was a pang of anxiety at the apex of his inhalation, at that moment when his chest had fully expanded, some childhood fear he'd long forgotten, like maybe he wouldn't stop inhaling somehow, like his diaphragm would push his ribcage past its breaking point, snap it wide as if preparing him for open heart surgery. But then the exhale came upon him and deflated his torso like it always did, and the feeling went away, to be forgotten until the next time.

The floating head walked past an empty parking spot, the body taking shape beneath it, arms and legs swinging along. He was close now, just a few feet away. And he wasn't a head, and this wasn't just acquiring a car. He was a man. A human being.

He pulled the pepper spray out of his pocket, holding it at his side as he strode the last four paces as the target got close enough to touch.

"Excuse me, sir," Ray said, his voice wavering a touch. "Did you drop your wallet?"

The man stopped mid-stride, hesitated for a second, and turned, eyebrows half-scrunched and half-raised at the same time.

Ray brought the pepper spray up and fired. It squirted a misty stream into his jaw, across his neck and onto the shoulder of the man's jacket, and then stopped.

Everything drifted into slow motion. The man turned his head to look down at his shoulder, his face blank. His tongue flicked out to touch his top lip, and then his eyes swiveled to meet Ray's. His mouth opened, and just as he looked poised to speak, his head jerked away from the shoulder. He brought the heels of his hands to his eyes, fingers curled against his forehead.

"Keys," Ray said. "Give me the car keys."

The man peeled his hands away a little, revealing reddened eyes, the eyelids wet and dark and swollen like moist plums, though the shadows may have enhanced that appearance a bit. He didn't speak, and he didn't move to give up the keys. Ray wiggled the pepper spray at him.

"Look, I don't want to use this again. Just give me the damn car keys. Cell phone, too."

The man didn't move, his eyes locked on Ray.

"You should see how bad your eyes are fucked up already. I'm sure you're feeling it. Imagine if I spray this shit directly into them. This is a goddamn emergency, OK? I'm not saying it again. I'll count to three, and then I'll take the keys once you're blind and writhing around on the ground."

The man's shoulder jerked, but otherwise he kept still.

"One."

Ray raised the can to eye level, finger twitching on the button, closing one eye as though sighting a gun.

"Two."

The man raised a hand, palm facing out, like a policeman directing traffic to halt. He fumbled the opposite hand into his pants pocket, and the keys jingled within. He pulled them out and tossed them to Ray underhand.

"No phone," the man said with a shrug. An "s" formed on his lips after a beat, perhaps to add a "sorry," but he stopped himself.

"Good enough. Now walk away."

No hesitation this time. The man strode back toward the store. Ray watched him walk and paw at his eyes for a few seconds before he climbed into the PT Cruiser.

The key entered the ignition, and as he twisted it he thought, "She was right. Do unto others what has been done to you."

Erin

South of Pittsburgh, Pennsylvania
70 days after

The back door was unlocked. A lucky omen.

Erin gave Izzy one of the hand signals they'd worked out,
the one that meant "stay here." They'd gotten their
scavenging trips down to a science. Usually, they could clear a
neighborhood in a day. Which was why they were out here in
the BFE suburbs.

"What's B.F.E.?" Izzy had asked as they rode through the
empty streets south of the city earlier that morning.

"It means we're in the middle of nowhere."

There was a beat, like Izzy was trying to puzzle something
out.

"Then why is it B.F.E.? Shouldn't it be M.O.N.?"

"It's French," Erin said, feeling a touch guilty for lying.

"Oh."

Izzy nodded as if this made perfect sense.

Erin stepped into the haunting silence of the house.
Someday she'd tell her what it really stood for. When there
wasn't a tax for swearing.

She brushed a stray hair from her cheek and was startled
at how cold her fingers were. She hadn't kept track of how
many houses they'd been through now, but it was a lot. Fifty?
A hundred? She should have counted. However many it was,
she still got that burst of adrenaline. She felt jittery, like she'd

just chugged a couple lattes.

She waited for a moment, letting her eyes orient to the low light, listening for any signs of life or un-death, but hearing nothing. As her eyes adjusted, she found she was in a small kitchen.

Across from her, a door stood open, probably the basement judging from the steps she could see descending into the gloom. She preferred to do the basements last when she could. Save the worst for last, that's what she always said.

When she peeled her foot away from the floor, a sticky sound broke the silence. Again with the next step. The soles of her shoes clung to the floor a little with each movement, like someone had spilled something on the linoleum and done a half-assed job cleaning it up.

She was glad to reach the hallway, where the floors transitioned to carpet. She did a quick scan of the living room, then moved farther down the hall. The bathroom and first two bedrooms were empty, but her pulse quickened as soon as she got to the door of the third bedroom.

She stood in front of it for what seemed like a long time, just staring at the smear of dried blood just above the door handle. She didn't want to go in there. But she knew she had to.

Erin closed her eyes, took two long breaths, and pulled the utility knife from her pocket. She wouldn't need it, but it made her feel better to hold it. She counted silently.

On three she opened the door and her eyes at the same time.

Dark, red-brown splotches stained the bedspread and the carpet. More blood spattered the far wall, a big Jackson

586

Pollock-style spray made of little dots. The bed blocked her view from most of the carnage, but from her position in the doorway, she could see four socked feet protruding from the other side of the bed. Small feet. Izzy-sized feet.

Kids.

Her skin prickled, hot and itchy, and she felt acid rising in her throat. She stumbled backward, wanting out of the room.

Back in the hall, she bent forward and put her hands on her knees in case she passed out or barfed. Both seemed equally possible at the moment.

Maybe it was worse, having it left to her imagination like that, but she couldn't bring herself to go back into the room to investigate further. She didn't want to know.

When the queasy, lightheaded feeling finally passed, she pulled the door all the way closed and went back to the kitchen.

She didn't hesitate at the basement door like she usually did. What she'd seen in the bedroom had put things in perspective. She'd take a creepy basement over that kind of gruesome scene any day.

The wood stairs down to the basement creaked and squeaked under her feet, changing pitch with each step. Halfway down, she stopped to get out her lighter. She'd upgraded to a stick lighter so she no longer had to singe off her fingerprints for a little illumination.

The dim glow showed an unfinished concrete floor below. She padded down the last few steps and inspected her surroundings. Pretty standard basement — washer, dryer, water heater, and furnace. A folded up ping pong table and some Rubbermaid storage bins pushed against one wall.

Erin's foot collided with something. Whatever it was went skittering across the cement floor, the metallic rattle echoing in the stillness. She gasped and jumped at the sound, and the movement made her light go out.

The darkness closed in, and she tried not to panic. She got that urge she used to get as a kid — like she knew there was nothing there, it was just her imagination, but she better run up the last few stairs as fast as she could, just in case.

She flailed with the push-button igniter, forgetting to press down on the child safety lock. After several unsuccessful clicks, she got the flame back. She filled her cheeks with air and let out a long sigh.

The offending object, the one she'd kicked across the room, was an empty Red Bull can. Not exactly the stuff of bad dreams. It had come to rest next to two canvas camp chairs and a cooler. Probably whoever had lived here had holed up down here for a while.

She did a quick rotation around the room before she started back up to the kitchen. Four steps from the top, she paused. There was something there, pushed into the far corner of the step.

Erin stretched out the hand holding the lighter, and the polished surface of it reflected the flame back at her. A pistol.

"Yahtzee!"

She stooped to pick it up, then held it in the flat of her hand, just feeling the weight of it. Now that she could see it up close, she noticed some bits of… something… speckling the surface of it. If she had to guess? Dried blood. Crusted brain matter.

A probable sequence of events started to play themselves

in her mind like a movie. She imagined the family sitting in the camp chairs, a lantern on the cooler, thinking they'd just wait out the chaos outside. And then as things got worse — maybe they started to get sick — the parents took matters into their own hands. A quick death. Painless and efficient.

Something about this proposed scenario bothered her, seemed not quite right, but with the excitement coursing through her from finding the gun, she ignored it.

She took one last look at the spatter marring the smooth metal before tucking it into the back of her pants, like she'd seen people do on TV. Beggars can't be choosers.

A manic chuckle shivered out of her. Man, she knew this house was going to be lucky. She could just tell.

She bounded up the remaining stairs and pushed the door mostly shut with her hip. She couldn't wait to show Izzy.

At the back door she found Izzy steaming up the glass with her breath and doodling smiley faces.

Erin stopped a few feet away, then pulled the pistol from her waistband.

"Check this shit out!"

She made gun noises with her mouth and pumped it in the air, cowboy style.

"Erin!"

Erin stopped air-shooting and lowered the gun to her side. She made a clicking sound with her tongue. Such a stickler.

"Fine, check this *poop* out."

"No!"

Izzy grabbed at the gun, gingerly taking it away from her. She flicked a little switch on the side.

"The safety was off!"

"Oh," Erin said, taking the gun back and looking at it. "Well then, I guess it's a good thing I didn't shoot my own ass off."

Izzy didn't laugh. Not even a smirk. The combination of her seriousness and the adrenaline from finally finding a gun squeezed another half-crazy-sounding giggle from her, even though she tried to fight it.

Izzy's nostrils flared, still not amused, and that just made Erin laugh harder.

"I'll poke around the living room while you check the food sitch. I'm hoping we find a stash of bullets."

Izzy closed the door and followed her inside.

"What's with the giant clock?"

Erin turned, following Izzy's gaze to the grandfather clock in the hall.

"It's a grandfather clock. You've never seen one before?"

"In cartoons and stuff. But I thought it was just supposed to be funny."

Izzy opened the door on the front, her sticky kid fingers leaving smudges on the glass.

"Why is it so huge? I could fit in it!"

She swiveled around and planted her butt inside the cavity.

"Here, let me help you with that."

Erin grabbed Izzy by the ankles and pushed so her legs folded up to her belly. Then she pretended she was going to close the door.

Now Izzy laughed.

"Don't squish me!"

Erin released her, and Izzy wriggled out of the clock.
She turned and stared at the pendulum.

"Too bad there's no power."

"It doesn't need power."

"Then why doesn't it work?"

"You have to wind them up every few days or they stop," Erin said. "Watch."

Erin reached in and grabbed one of the chains. She'd never actually done it herself, only watched her grandmother do it. But what the hell? It wasn't like she had to answer to anyone if she fucked up their clock.

She grasped one of the chains and pulled, watching the weight rise. She repeated this for the other chains until all the weights were at the top, then gave the pendulum a little push to get it going.

"Man, it's loud," Izzy said once the ticking started.

"Just wait until the big bastard chimes."

"Language."

Izzy hopped onto the kitchen counter to better reach the upper cabinets while Erin sifted through a bookshelf. It was mostly paperbacks and a few DVDs, plus a smattering of knickknacks brought back from traditional suburban vacations: sand art from the Florida Keys, a lighthouse figurine from Maine, and a Niagara Falls snow globe.

Not finding anything worthwhile on the bookshelf, she moved to the entertainment center. A black MDF model she recognized from IKEA, because they'd had the same one back home. Her real home. It was probably called something like ARKELSTORP or SANDHAUG or EXPEDIT.

She squatted in front of it, shifting a stack of video game

cases to see if anything was tucked behind. If she had owned a gun, where would she hide the ammo?

Erin heard a thumping noise from the vicinity of the kitchen. Izzy slamming a cupboard door or setting some cans on the counter top.

"Find anything good?" Erin asked.

"Not yet."

There was a bump and a scrape. It wasn't even that it was loud... it was just out of the norm.

She'd never thought about it before, but it struck Erin that they were usually both very quiet when they went through a house — when they spoke it was often in a whisper and doors were closed with care. She thought maybe it was that the stillness of the empty homes was infectious. Or maybe they felt a bit like trespassers, and making as little sound as possible felt like the respectful thing to do.

The drumming continued, and Erin wondered if Izzy was upset about something.

"Everything OK out there?" she called.

There was a pause.

"Yeah."

Did the pause mean something? Was there a touch of attitude in Izzy's tone? Erin abandoned her exploration under the couch cushions. If Izzy was mad — probably about her waving the gun around with the safety off — better to deal with it now.

Erin jumped up on the cushions, the springs squeaking in protest, then vaulted over the back of the couch.

From her position in the hallway, she heard the telltale creaking of the basement stairs. It was curious that Izzy would decide to go down there by herself, but maybe the kitchen had been a bust. Still, Izzy hated the basements even more than she did.

"Hey, if you're done with the kitchen and you're going to start looking around the rest of the house, skip the back bedroom. It's…"

Erin tried to think of an appropriate word. One that didn't use the words *bloody* or *massacre* or *horrorshow*.

"Just don't go in there."

When she reached the archway that looked in on the dining area, she found it empty. There came a high-pitched squeal from the basement door, hinges groaning as it swung open. Slowly. Dramatically. Like a scene in a horror movie. And suddenly Erin understood.

"If you're trying to scare me by jumping out from behind that door, just know this. You are opening a dangerous can of worms, kid."

Instead of bursting open quickly, like she'd been expecting, the door continued to inch open. At the same moment, Izzy rose from where she'd been tucked behind the kitchen counter, out of sight.

Erin's breath caught in her throat, but it took her brain a few moments to process what her pounding heart had already figured out.

It wasn't Izzy on the basement steps.

Mitch

Bethel Park, Pennsylvania
41 days before

Slobber glazed the barrel of the gun, and that empty feeling occupied his mouth again. He left his jaw open for a second, obeying some impulse to keep still, to focus on the emptiness. He blinked a few times, and the muscles in his face contracted, bringing his bottom teeth up toward his top teeth. The motion felt odd and stiff and mechanical with a little hitch at the end that made his jaw jerk and his teeth clack together.

The gun still hovered before him, the muzzle angled away from him on a diagonal, pointed at the ceiling. He looked at it for a long moment, all wet and shiny. He didn't quite know what to do with it. It reminded him of carrying a dirty diaper or a wadded up paper towel full of cat puke. He wanted to find some place to put it without touching anything else. He didn't know if this was because of the saliva slime or growing discomfort with handling the firearm, having thought too hard about its purpose here.

But he knew one thing. He needed water, and his jar was empty.

He stood, ankles creaking, knees popping one after the other, calves and thighs tightening up into knots that slowly let go as he rested his weight on them for a moment. He arched his back, feeling the muscles there squeeze and release with the extension of his spine.

He closed his eyes, standing in the shed, breath flowing in and out of him. He felt the weight of his head resting on his neck, felt the puff of the dried out tongue scraping against the roof of his mouth, the tired sting in his eyes, the dull pain that remained of his headache. He smelled the shed smells, grease and dust and dried out flecks of cut grass, heard the sprinkling rain tap at the roof. Even with his mind blank, he was conscious of all of these things and more, billions of pieces of stimulus if he was remembering right. How could he let that go? How could he let consciousness go? It was all he knew, all he'd ever known. The idea of pulling a trigger and vanquishing it? Of shutting off his brain? Of black nothing forever? Fucking terrifying.

But the fear felt distant in some sense, some massive black cloud looming above that he could only catch glimpses of if he squinted his eyes just right. It was almost too big to feel, he thought. He couldn't quite make it seem real, no matter how dire the intellectual part of him understood things to be.

His eyes opened, and he set the gun down on the shelf before him. It felt good, felt right, to release its heft from his fingers, to feel a lightness take its place. He hesitated a moment, looking down on the firearm there. Part of him wanted to scoop it up and do it, almost catch himself unaware by not planning or contemplating or thinking much at all.

But no. Water.

He stooped and gathered the jar, shuffled over the cement. Again he hesitated at the shed door. Crossing this line seemed to carry some significance. Some gravity. Opening this door, passing through the opening into the

595

light, leaving the shed with his only job here unfinished, putting his boys at risk once more? For what? For a glass of water?

He rubbed at his eyes, the skin greasy and swollen and sore. Shit. Why couldn't he just close his eyes and disappear? Why couldn't he just pay someone to take care of this? Why did it have to be so grim and violent and scary?

He was a pussy, he knew. A coward. Oh, he'd told himself that the fear felt distant, that he needed a moment to build up the nerve, that he would do it any minute now, but he wouldn't. He knew he wouldn't. He promised. He promised himself he would, but what good was a coward's word? He'd promised himself all kinds of things in his life, planned all kinds of things, dreamed all kinds of things that never came to be, so many things that he never even tried.

Even so, he was too tired to feel the full force of the self-loathing. He just shuffled through the motions, slouching toward the end. Maybe that was what he did all along.

He crossed the shed again, plucked the gun from the shelf and tucked it into his belt. He'd go get the water, but he would bring the gun along.

Just in case.

Baghead

Rural Arkansas
9 years, 127 days after

He walked slower on the trek back to the car, trying to find a way for his feelings to sink in before he was around people. It surprised him to find that he didn't feel that much beyond a heightened level of stimulation. Neither ecstasy of victory nor pang of regret for taking a life filled him. Just empty excitement. A vague sense of pointlessness.

Dead on the inside. Maybe he wasn't much of a human anymore, inside or out.

No lightning lit the sky here, but he felt like he did when he walked through the dead cities in that recurring black dream. When he wondered what fire burned inside of the animals still walking the Earth. When he wondered why we clashed against one another, clawing and maiming and killing each other for eternity. When he wondered why this violence aroused us, entertained us. When he wondered how anyone could look up into the stars and find a meaning to any of this.

Lorraine

South of Sulphur Springs, Texas
2 days before

The road opened up before them again, a path she could stare down. The trees grew sparser here, reduced to clusters among barren fields and the occasional trailer park. All of the grass looked half dead. Beige everywhere.

Maybe it was the lack of captivating scenery, maybe it was something else, but she found she preferred to stare down the empty road, to look on the place where the asphalt disappeared into a shimmer on the horizon. With the land so flat and the traffic so non-existent, it seemed like she could see a long, long way. She had no idea what the actual distance might be, but it felt like miles.

Her eyes flicked toward the driver's seat. Ray rolled his neck from shoulder to shoulder, one hand gripping the bottom of the wheel. The tension seemed to have drained from his shoulders, and she was glad for that. Typically driving around in a stolen car would have kicked up new anxieties, but Ray assured her that the police were too busy with other matters. She believed him.

The man had surprised her. He'd done much to ensure their survival already, and he'd shown a level of vulnerability along the way that she hadn't anticipated. He proved to be less of a lizard person than she thought. More like a good dog. She was happy to see him relieved.

And she could understand the feeling. It felt good to be hurtling forward again, to feel the momentum of the car carry them on at top speed, to hear the tires thrum against the asphalt. It felt like home. A new home.

She stared down at that twinkling spot in the distance and let her mind go blank aside from that image. It seemed a comfort for a while.

And then it occurred to her that this was as far as she could see into her future, this visible stretch of road they rocketed down. Houston would be gone. They couldn't go backward. Just forward down an empty road. Anything could happen after they passed through that glimmer down there.

"Where do you think we'll go?" she said.

The sound of her voice seemed to break some silent spell that had fallen over the car, shaking them from some half-dream state that had settled upon each of them.

Ray grunted.

"Don't know," he said. "Away from here is all."

"Shouldn't we make plans?"

"Maybe. I mean, we should get some sleep at some point. I was hoping to get farther on from Dallas before we did that."

He scratched his stubbled chin against his knuckles, his voice trailing away as he finished his thought.

"Don't know how far is far enough."

He fished a hand into the paper bag between them, a crinkling noise erupting as he dug around, and then he pulled a Twinkie free, using his teeth to help rip the cellophane package open with one hand. He leaned forward and spit the plastic flap onto the floor, which was already cluttered with other people's balled up fast food wrappers.

Twinkies. That's what she got when she let him do the shopping at the gas station while she filled the tank. Two boxes of Twinkies, a variety of colas, a plastic jar of peanuts and all of the bottled water he could carry. Most of it got packed in ice in a stryofoam cooler, both of which he also bought. At least they had enough cold water for a couple of days.

He unsheathed the Twinkie, licking his lips as he slid the rounded tip out of the sleeve. After a beat he stuck the yellow tube in his mouth. Something about all of this looked equal parts gluttonous and homoerotic.

She looked away, gazing out the window at the endless fields of dead grass. It crisped in the sun like chow mein noodles. A picture formed in her head of setting foot on it, hearing the crunch of each distinct blade as her heel and toe descended. She remembered reading something about a drought up this way. Apparently, it hadn't been as bad as you moved toward the coast.

Something about that image, the dead grass as they moved away from their homes, didn't bode so well for their journey, she thought.

Teddy

Moundsville, West Virginia
76 days after

Smoke filled the room now, an opaque cloud that hung almost motionless above him, just faintly drifting in most of the room, only really roiling over the landing where the fire raged. The younger zombie lay still in the midst of the flames, her body and clothing now colorless, black, a crisped husk shriveling into the ash of the bottom steps. She no longer groaned, holding silent and still.

The older zombie wandered into his field of vision, wobbling to his right. Her face was blackened now like burnt chicken skin, her features erased into a matte black finish, but the flames on her had died down to almost nothing, glowing red patches of clothing, tiny little flickers around the edges. Her mouth still produced noises, but it sounded tattered and small. Raspy. Perhaps her vocal cords had gotten fried somewhere in there.

Teddy knew what to do now, but he didn't know how.

He thought about taking off his shirt, using it to protect his hands as he grabbed the older zombie. Then he pictured the t-shirt melting, the dripping fiery fabric sinking into his skin, searing all the way to the bone and melding with the flesh there in his fingers, his palms. It made him shudder.

He'd have to bare hand it. It was going to hurt.

He juked around a fiery mud puddle and rushed the

wobbling creature, hands latching on each of its upper arms, fingers sinking just a bit into that burned outer layer, and he flung the thing down like a nose tackle dispatching a running back in the backfield. She toppled over, falling in a heap on the landing atop the other zombie.

It wasn't until the moment after he released her that he felt the scream of the sting in his hands. He didn't look. He didn't have time, but he pictured the heels of his hands and the tips of his fingers and that webbed spot between the thumb and palm all blistered up, bubbled sacs of skin full of yellow fluid.

He ran then, planting one foot and then the other into the back of the freshly fallen zombie, feet landing right between the shoulder blades and pushing off. From there he launched himself up the stairs, jumping clear of the fire and scrabbling up the steps on hands and knees.

He didn't feel safe until he passed through the doorway and belly flopped on the linoleum in the kitchen. His forehead sank to the floor and rested there, the cool of it comforting him. That was close. Too close.

He knew he couldn't relax long, that there was still a good chance the fire from the steps would get to the joists and floorboards above them and the whole place would go. With the way the lighter fluid cans continued to give off whooshing fireballs every few seconds, he thought it likely. This place would be a total loss. Still, he had the opportunity to rest for the moment, so he did.

After a time, he lifted his head and looked down the steps to see the older zombie still squirming there, arms scrabbling in flame and ash, unable to get a grip on anything. It slowed, and soon it would stop. Even still, he wished he could keep it.

Baghead

Rural Arkansas
9 years, 127 days after

Delfino squatted by the Delta 88, a handkerchief pressed to the wound in his deltoid. The shotgun lay across his lap. He stood when Baghead stepped out of the woods, gathering up the gun and pinning it under his good arm.

"Jesus," he said. "Are you OK?"

Baghead nodded.

"You?"

"Well, I got shot, so that blows."

Baghead puffed a laugh from his nostrils.

"Just a graze, though. That fuck didn't have the balls to do any real damage. I heard the sound of your gun. Three shots. You kill 'im?"

Baghead nodded again.

"Damn, dude. I didn't take you for the psycho type, just marching right out there to do something like that."

They just stood for a moment. Not talking. Not making eye contact.

"Is she OK?"

"She's fine. She ate all of the jerky. Kind of acted like she thought she'd be in trouble for it. Figured we'd eat if- when you got back."

Baghead nodded again. He opened the door to the back seat.

"You hungry?" he said to the girl.

"Well, yeah," she said.

Delfino wound around the back of the car to dig in the cooler on the opposite side.

"Shoot. Father's going to have to send a legit assassin if he wants to take out the Baghead," he said. "I guess he's got four more cracks at it, eh?"

Teddy

Moundsville, West Virginia
77 days after

He lay in bed, his old bed, staring up into the darkness, knowing the bare light bulb was up there along with the joists and the wires snaking around them. He fumbled a hand into the black beside him, finding the curve of the top of the two liter and bringing it to his lips. Sweet nectar.

Warm Mountain Dew didn't kill the pain that clawed inside of him, though. He felt small and weak like when the kids called him names in school. Humiliated. Defeated.

He'd watched the house go from across the street, the flicker of the fire raging in the windows, and the roof finally collapsing. It was fast once the fire made that transition from the basement steps to the floorboards above. Even still he could feel the heat on his face like a sunburn. He pictured what he might look like on the bed, his cheeks approaching the red shade of a lobster.

His plan had failed. He couldn't keep them. He couldn't even burn them in his own home, in his kingdom, his domain. What hope did that leave him going forward? A life without a plan quickly becomes meaningless. He'd heard that somewhere as a kid and always remembered it. Now he had none. No plan at all. Nothing to work toward, to look forward to.

His thoughts jerked back and forth, ideas that circled back

on themselves, never resolving, like when one remembers song lyrics incorrectly and gets stuck in a loop without end.

First of all, why couldn't he kill them and keep them at the same time? It's all he wanted. Dumb that it didn't work that way.

He drank again, the citric sweetness exploding on his palate, the acid tingling on his tongue and the inside of his cheeks.

Maybe it didn't matter about the zombies, though. They just weren't that fun. They weren't what he really wanted. Even burning them every day, hearing those ghastly sounds they made, would bring him no satisfaction in the long run, wouldn't soothe the restlessness inside of him.

When he was honest with himself, he wanted a girl. A real girl. To touch. But he knew that the way he wanted to touch girls was wrong. It was bad. It was worse, even, than throwing the cats and dogs in the back of the truck. You couldn't watch videos of it on TV or on the computer. You couldn't talk about it at school.

He guzzled more Mountain Dew, spilling a little on his chin.

Why did everything have to be so confusing? Just like the difference between cats and dogs and meat. It made no sense when you really thought about it. Made no sense at all.

His eyebrows wrinkled then. He sat up, hand resting on the curve of the two liter again, but he didn't lift it. He walked himself through the thought once more and smiled.

Teddy thought he understood. When it was an animal, people cared about it. But after that, after it was dead, it was meat. Nobody cared about meat. And that made it OK to eat and everything.

It would be wrong to touch a girl the way he wanted when she was a girl. But it wouldn't be wrong when she was meat. It'd be no different than hacking up those zombies.

That was all there was to it. He would find a girl. A real girl. He could make her meat, and after that, he could touch her however he wanted.

He lay back and closed his eyes. He tried to stop smiling, but he couldn't.

Mitch

Bethel Park, Pennsylvania
41 days before

The sunlight made it so he could only keep his eyes open for a few seconds at a time. It wasn't particularly bright out, he thought, the sky retaining a bit of an overcast from the rain, but after all the time closed up in the shed, his eyes couldn't take it. He fought it, forced them open, held them as long as he could, the soft flesh all around them quivering, but after a fraction of a second, the eyeballs rolled back, and the lids wove his eyelashes back together.

A vision contrasting white vinyl siding against green grass snapped shut to blackness over and over, but he pressed forward. He knew the way well enough.

Half-blind and stumbling, he kicked through the grass, wetness clinging to his shoes. The yard gave under his feet, squishing like a plush carpet, much softer than the concrete slab he'd grown used to, and the open air all around brushed its cool against his cheeks, the sky above full of it, stretching out forever.

A tingle came over him as he mounted the steps of the back porch. It started when his fingers wrapped around the metal rail, like a spark, an electrical current, passing from the wrought iron into his hand and traveling up his arm, up his neck, behind his face and through his head until every follicle on his scalp pricked up. Even with all that was going wrong, his life disintegrating all around him, he thought it felt goddamn amazing to be alive. To inhale, to feel the air rush into his lungs, pulling his chest taut, to feel the blood thrumming all through him, to feel this crazy tingle bristle across the top of his head for no good reason.

He stopped short of the back door, and the tension in his shoulders released just a little. God, he wanted to push through this door, grab a beer out of the fridge and plop down in his recliner to watch some TV. There was probably a baseball game on. He could heat up some Hot Pockets or something between innings.

But no. No more.

He opened the door and advanced into the kitchen. He stopped in the middle of the room, blinking a few times, letting the feeling of being home wash over him one last time, trying to savor it. He walked to the sink, let the water run over his fingers until it was nice and cold and then filled his jar, that ascending pitch ringing out as the water level rose. All of these tiny details, all of these experiences that filled his life, they'd all be gone so soon, and it was hard to fathom.

He drank, a single droplet of water spilling out of the corner of his mouth and running down his chin. The rest rolled through his mouth and down his throat, cooling him all the way down.

He heard video games in the next room, and he knew that the power had come back on. Damn. The desire to watch TV, to gaze upon that flicker of images, was like an itch behind his eyeballs. Un-scratchable.

He tipped his head back to down the last of the water, mopping the back of his wrist over his lips. When he returned his head to its normal upright position, a dizziness came over him, a weakness in his neck that wanted to let his chin sink all the way to his sternum.

He fought it, tried to keep his head up, tried to keep his eyes open, his vision steady. He felt like a captain fighting to right a listing boat at sea.

And then things went black. Full black. Flipped off like a switch.

His consciousness faded in, and he lay face down on the tile floor in the kitchen. His head hurt like hell and swirls swam along the edges of his vision. He lifted his head, which took considerable effort, and blinked his eyes hard a few times, tried to clear his vision, but everything still flickered and blurred around him.

This was it. This was the end.

Christ, he was lucky to have not already turned. He didn't know how much time had passed while he was out, but he heard baseball on TV in the next room instead of video games now.

He pushed himself up on hands and knees, prying the gun from his belt, and crawled toward the basement door. Not fast, but the best he could muster. Things went gray again right away, and he stopped, taking deep breaths. He just needed to make it to the basement steps. Not all the way down. Just to the other side of that door. That was all.

Color blushed back into things, and he crawled again, hands shuffling forward and legs dragging along behind. He put his head down and pressed forward, no longer even looking where he was going.

He heard a beer commercial on TV in the next room. A

zany one about a guy who built his entire house out of cans of Bud Light, much to his wife's chagrin. It reminded him to drink responsibly, and then the top of his head hit wood.

The door. He'd made it.

He reached up for knob and pulled it open, falling over on his side to get out of its path. Now he slid forward on his belly, his crawl almost more of a slither as he eased himself down a couple of steps. A change came over him as he crossed that threshold, a relief that he could die apart from them, if only separated by this door, and he found new strength in his arms.

He pushed himself up and turned back, reaching out, fingers gripping the bottom of the basement door and swinging it his way. More relief as the door closed and the latch clicked, leaving him in the dark. Breath heaved in and out of him, and he settled back, his head and the top half of his back now resting against the door.

The gun quivered in his hand, and his arm shook pretty bad as he lifted it.

No bullshit now. Just do it.

He brought the gun to his temple and pulled the trigger.

Erin

South of Pittsburgh, Pennsylvania
70 days after

Terror took hold, and for a moment Erin couldn't speak. Eventually she forced out a hiss.

"Run!"

They both bolted toward the back door, but it was too late. The basement door was flung wide and the thing roared, an inhuman noise that made the hair on the back of her neck stand up.

It looked like a man, but not. Something was wrong with it — something that went beyond the fact that it was covered in blood. There was a gaping wound on one side of the head, the eye on that side crusted shut. But even with just the one eye open, Erin could tell the thing was dim. Like a... she didn't want to think it, but it was too late: like a zombie.

The thing swayed there at the top of the stairs, blocking their exit, and the lone eye wandered, never seeming to focus on any one thing. Erin wasn't sure why it hadn't come at them yet. Could it not see them if they held still?

And then it lurched toward Izzy, and without thinking Erin jumped forward.

"Hey you!"

She pulled her phone from her pocket and threw it at the zombie-thing.

It rounded on her, and she fumbled at her belt for the

gun. She lifted, pointed, squeezed the trigger.

Nothing happened.

She squeezed again, and Izzy yelled, "Shoot it! Shoot it!"

And then the zombie launched himself teeth-first at her.

His bulk knocked her to the ground, pinning her there. Up close the smell was nauseating — the stench of rotting flesh and dried blood and unbrushed zombie teeth.

She had a handful of his matted hair in her fist, which was the only thing keeping him from taking a big juicy bite out of her neck. Her other hand still held the gun. She pressed it to his skull and pulled the trigger again, but it wouldn't fire.

Over the snarling beast on top of her, she heard Izzy's voice.

"The safety! You have to turn the safety off!"

The gun was gummed up with zombie goo now, and Erin's hand slid down the grip. She clenched her fingers around it, refusing to let go, and somehow she managed to flick the little switch with her thumb. This time she pulled and it fired and there was an eardrum bursting blast and a wet chunky spray hit her face. The zombie went limp on top of her.

She wriggled out from under it part of the way, but the dead weight pinned her down.

Izzy ran over and threw herself down next to Erin, clutching her shoulder and half-screaming, half-crying. When the ringing in her ears faded a little, she realized Izzy was asking if she was OK.

"Did it get you?"

Erin tried to push the thing off her, but she was all shaky. Her muscles felt like Jell-o.

"I'm fine."

Izzy let out a sob of relief, then started babbling again.

"I told you! I told you there were fucking zombies!"

"Dude, language!" Erin said.

They were quiet for a second, and then they both laughed.

"Now get this thing off of me."

Izzy helped her roll the body to the side. Erin scooted away from it and tried to find a dry patch of her shirt to wipe her face with.

"Here," Izzy said and handed her a roll of paper towel.

"Thanks."

Erin looked over at the zombie. They both did for a long moment, silent.

It seemed different now than it had moments before. Smaller. The expression on its face more pained than aggressive. It wore a blue and purple tie-dye shirt with some iron-on letters that spelled out "MITCH" across the chest.

"What's with the shirt?" Izzy asked.

The tie-dye looked like a do-it-yourself project, and the letters were all a little cock-eyed.

"I bet it was a gift. From-"

Erin pictured the little socked feet in the bedroom then.

"Never mind."

How stupid was she? Finding the gun, coming up with her Jonestown scenario in which the whole family offed themselves, but never wondering where the bodies of the adults were? Dumb.

"How sad is that?" Izzy said.

"What?"

Izzy's eyes were still locked on the swirling tie-dye of the shirt.

"That he ate his own family."

"How did you-"

"You said not to go in the back bedroom. Like I don't know what that means. Kids."

Erin poked Izzy's belly button.

"Stop being so smart, will you?"

A gong sounded, and for a second Erin thought it was some kind of warning, some harbinger of more bad shit to come. They both went rigid and held their breath, bracing themselves for it. And then Erin recognized the melody. It was the grandfather clock, striking noon.

Erin slapped a hand over her chest and let her body slump back into the counter.

"I just peed in my pants a little bit," Izzy whispered.

Erin sighed.

"Me too."

Ray

North of Mt. Pleasant, Texas
2 days before

He brought another Twinkie wrapper to his mouth, ripped it open like a soldier pulling the pin out of a grenade with his teeth, and ate it. He didn't know why. He felt nauseous from eating the first four, and they didn't taste very good. He guessed that he must have liked them when he was a kid, and the desire for them lingered even after the affection for their flavor had faded.

The PT Cruiser hurtled down the road. As they moved, that quiver of anxiety in his chest finally let go. From what little he knew about nuclear weapons, they would now surely be far enough outside of Dallas to survive the initial blast and radiation no matter how big of a bomb got dropped. The long term fallout aspect was trickier, but not getting disintegrated was a nice first step.

His eyes stung, and when he caught glimpses of them in the rearview mirror, he couldn't believe how bloodshot they were, little bursts of red like fireworks everywhere around each of the irises. He was tired as hell, but that was one thing the Twinkies helped with, at least. The sugar seemed to wake him up a bit.

Lorraine slept in the passenger seat. She smiled just faintly in her slumber. He always thought you could tell a lot about a person by their facial expression as they slept. Meek types

617

frowned. Hostile people scowled. And the nice people all wore the slightest of smiles.

He pulled the cell phone out of his pocket and dialed the number again, listened to it ring. He knew she wouldn't answer, and she didn't. He put the phone away, and just as he looked back to the road, she spoke.

"Who have you been trying to call?"

He flinched. She'd startled him pretty good.

"What?"

"Every time you think I'm asleep, you make a call that no one seems to answer. You don't have to tell me. Just curious."

Ray didn't say anything for a moment. His tongue flicked out to lick his lips a couple of times.

"My ex-wife. I'd still like to get a hold of her. Thing is, I can never really know if she is in trouble, or if she's fine and just doesn't want to talk to me. She's not the biggest Ray Dalton fan out there. So I just keep calling whenever I get a moment alone."

"Why so gung-ho to conceal that from me?"

Ray licked his lips a couple more times.

"I don't know. Maybe I just didn't want some lady I just met to know how cut up and bleeding I am about my ex-wife who I've been apart from for nine years."

They were quiet for a while, watching the road signs and the dead grass flit by on the sides of the road.

And then a flash filled the sky, a burst of light that pulsed and seemed to hang there in the air for too long. Ray watched it shimmer in the rearview mirror, hearing a gasp and only realizing it was his own after the fact.

He pulled over to the side of the road as the flash gave way to a billowing cloud of smoke. They got out and stood on the shoulder, watching smoke fill the sky. The sound came upon them after a moment, a sizzling rush more than the thunderous rumble he'd anticipated.

"Airburst," he said.

"What?"

"They burst it in the air to minimize the fallout. That's why we can see it. If the fireball doesn't touch the ground, the radiation will dissipate in the air over the coming days. The power of the blast itself is still enough to wipe out Dallas, even burst way up in the sky."

"Wow."

Her voice fluttered when she spoke. He realized she was shaking, her fingers rising to her lips and trembling there. He reached out for it, took her hand in his, and together they watched the mushroom cloud rise into the sky.

THE SCATTERED AND THE DEAD

For information on the next installment of The Scattered
and the Dead, please visit http://LTVargus.com

SPREAD THE WORD

Thank you for reading! We'd be very grateful if you could take a few minutes to review it on Amazon.com.

How grateful? Eternally. Even when we are old and dead and have turned into ghosts, we will be thinking fondly of you and your kind words. The most powerful way to bring our books to the attention of other people is through the honest reviews from readers like you.

COME PARTY WITH US

We're loners. Rebels. But much to our surprise, the most kickass part of writing has been connecting with our readers. From time to time, we send out newsletters with giveaways, special offers, and juicy details on new releases.

Sign up for our mailing list at:
http://ltvargus.com/mailing-list/

ABOUT THE AUTHORS

Tim McBain writes because life is short, and he wants to make something awesome before he dies. Additionally, he likes to move it, move it.

You can connect with Tim on Twitter at @realtimmcbain or via email at tim@timmcbain.com.

L.T. Vargus grew up in Hell, Michigan, which is a lot smaller, quieter, and less fiery than one might imagine. When not click-clacking away at the keyboard, she can be found sewing, fantasizing about food, and rotting her brain in front of the TV.

If you want to wax poetic about pizza or cats, you can contact L.T. (the L is for Lex) at ltvargus9@gmail.com or on Twitter @ltvargus.

TimMcBain.com
LTVargus.com